KISSED BREATHLESS

"I've been wondering all day what it would be like to kiss you," Jake said. "It's about time I found out, wouldn't you say?"

Her eyes widened. Nervous, she licked her lips, then dearly wished she hadn't.

"Come closer," he whispered. She could feel the heat of his chest through her dress.

"Mr. Chandler, if I came any closer to you we'd melt into each other."

"That's the idea, princess. A man likes a woman to melt right into him when he's kissing her breathless. That's how he knows she likes it."

Jake's mouth closed over hers. A shiver bolted through her. Her fingers curled around fistfuls of his silky hair.

In a foggy recess of her mind, Amanda realized she was closer to this man now — physically — than she'd ever been to any man she had ever known.

And it felt wonderful.

ROMANCE REIGNS
WITH ZEBRA BOOKS!

SILVER ROSE (2275, $3.95)
by Penelope Neri

Fleeing her lecherous boss, Silver Dupres disguised herself as a boy and joined an expedition to chart the wild Colorado River. But with one glance at Jesse Wilder, the explorers' rugged, towering scout, Silver knew she'd have to abandon her protective masquerade or else be consumed by her raging unfulfilled desire!

STARLIT ECSTASY (2134, $3.95)
by Phoebe Conn

Cold-hearted heiress Alicia Caldwell swore that Rafael Ramirez, San Francisco's most successful attorney, would never win her money . . . or her love. But before she could refuse him, she was shamelessly clasped against Rafael's muscular chest and hungrily matching his relentless ardor!

LOVING LIES (2034, $3.95)
by Penelope Neri

When she agreed to wed Joel McCaleb, Seraphina wanted nothing more than to gain her best friend's inheritance. But then she saw the virile stranger . . . and the green-eyed beauty knew she'd never be able to escape the rapture of his kiss and the sweet agony of his caress.

EMERALD FIRE (3193, $4.50)
by Phoebe Conn

When his brother died for loving gorgeous Bianca Antonelli, Evan Sinclair swore to find the killer by seducing the tempress who lured him to his death. But once the blond witch willingly surrendered all he sought, Evan's lust for revenge gave way to the desire for unrestrained rapture.

SEA JEWEL (3013, $4.50)
by Penelope Neri

Hot-tempered Alaric had long planned the humiliation of Freya, the daughter of the most hated foe. He'd make the wench from across the ocean his lowly bedchamber slave — but he never suspected she would become the mistress of his heart, his treasured SEA JEWEL.

Available wherever paperbacks are sold, or order direct from the Publisher. Send cover price plus 50¢ per copy for mailing and handling to Zebra Books, Dept. 3617, 475 Park Avenue South, New York, N.Y. 10016. Residents of New York, New Jersey and Pennsylvania must include sales tax. DO NOT SEND CASH.

REBECCA SINCLAIR
MONTANA WILDFIRE

ZEBRA BOOKS
KENSINGTON PUBLISHING CORP.

To Cathy Beyer, for all her help . . .
and
To Courtney and Adam, who brighten up my life.

ZEBRA BOOKS

are published by

Kensington Publishing Corp.
475 Park Avenue South
New York, NY 10016

First printing: December, 1991

Printed in the United States of America

My children, my children. In days behind I called you to travel the hunting trail or to follow the war trail. Now those trails are choked with sand; they are covered with grass, the young men cannot find them. Today I call upon you to travel a new trail, the only trail now open — the White Man's Road.

Wovoka, Paiute Chief

Chapter One

Montana Territory, 1878

Amanda Lennox sucked in a deep, steadying breath, gnashed her teeth, and glared at the infuriating little brat who sat on the riverbank.

The cuffs of the boy's too-large pant legs were rolled in sloppy bunches to his knees. The wet, pale expanse of his calves and ankles disappeared beneath the river's surface. He made splashing circles with his bare feet, circles that, all too often, rained water over Amanda's already-wet face and hair. With another child she might have thought her periodic dousings accidental. But not with this boy. Oh, no, with *this boy* she knew the splashes were intentional — in the same way she knew *he* knew there wasn't a thing she could do to stop him.

Her gaze lifted, sharpened. Lemony sunlight peeked through a ceiling of rustling leaves. The golden rays sifted over the boy, making the blond hair that clung damply to his scalp resemble a shimmering halo. Tight curls framed his brow, emphasizing the hint of baby-roundness still evident in his ten-year-old cheeks. Though his gaze was down, fixed on the pile of rocks stacked beside his hip, Amanda knew when he looked up she would see eyes bluer than a summer sky, wide and round, ringed with ridiculously long, ridiculously thick lashes.

It wasn't the boy's golden curls so much as his big blue

eyes that gave him a cherubic appearance. Unfortunately for her, in his case appearance was only skin-deep. Amanda knew better than anyone the sly, pampered little brat lurking beneath that sweet exterior. Plain and simple, the boy was a holy terror.

As though to prove it, he picked up one of the fist-sized rocks from his pile and tested the weight of it in his palm. His gaze lifted, focusing on Amanda's forehead. His grin didn't hide the nasty turn of his thoughts.

And why should he hide them? Who was there — besides Amanda, of course — to see? They were alone out here in the wilderness. The bitter cold water swirling around her numb thighs reminded her that she was in no position to climb up the sandy bank and administer the spanking the brat so justly deserved.

With fingers water-wrinkled and shaking from the cold, Amanda swiped the wet, golden blonde bangs from her brow, then tugged her water-heavy skirt out of the way. She gave her right leg a good yank . . . and winced. Pain shimmied up her leg, immediate and sharp enough to convince her not to try twice.

She was stuck. On what, she didn't know, nor was she clear on how she'd managed to get herself stuck in such a way. One minute she'd been wading into the river, coffee pot in hand, past the bank to where the water wasn't so muddy. The next thing she knew she'd felt something solid and rough on the river's bottom, something with a hole carved in it that was the perfect shape to swallow her foot up to the ankle. The second she'd moved, that was exactly what it had done.

While her foot had sunk into the hole easily enough, getting it out was another matter. An impossible one, in her estimation. Her initial pulling and twisting had made her ankle swell, but it hadn't won her her freedom. Now instead of the cold roughness down there merely encircling her leg, it bit into her throbbing, swollen flesh.

The only thing saving her from any *real* pain was the water's frigid temperature. Her feet were numb. She'd

8

long since lost feeling in her toes. The sharpest pain was in her legs, just below the water-line, but even that was dulling rapidly.

Only a fool would think this situation was not serious, and Amanda Lennox was no fool. No sooner had the thought crossed her mind than she felt a sharp sting in her left shoulder. Her gaze snapped up in time to see Roger Thornton Bannister III's malicious grin. His hand was glaringly empty of the rock.

Amanda decided then and there that she must be a bigger fool than she thought. Hadn't she willingly taken charge of this little monster? That should say something about her intelligence . . . or lack thereof.

"I hope you aren't planning to stay in there all day, Miss Lennox," the brat said in his haughty, annoying whine that went up Amanda's spine like chips of broken glass. "I'm getting hungry, and I'd like my breakfast now."

"Go fix it yourself. I'm stuck, remember?" She saw his chin inch up an imperious notch, and her green eyes narrowed. The first time she'd met Roger, Amanda had been reminded of a story her father had told her when she was little. Something about a wolf in sheep's clothing . . .

"I don't see why you can't just get yourself *unstuck*," he countered snobbishly.

Amanda's hands clenched into fists. "I could, if you'd help me a bit."

Roger's eyes widened, his gaze skipping over the water that swirled around her thighs. He shook his head hard enough make the curls clinging to his scalp bounce. "Surely you don't expect *me* to put my hands down in all that," his freckle-dusted nose wrinkled, *"mud."*

Amanda met his horrified glare with a furious one of her own. "You will if you want your breakfast anytime soon."

Shaking his head with even more force, he picked up another rock. As he'd done before, he bounced it in his

9

palm. "I'm not *that* hungry. Take your time getting out of there, Miss Lennox, but see if you can't get free before lunch. Father won't be pleased when I tell him you made me skip meals. He isn't paying you good money to starve me, you know."

He isn't paying me to thrash you to within an inch of your miserable life, either, she thought harshly, glaring at him, *but I'm considering doing that, too. Your father be damned!*

The boy's eyes looked too round, his brow too smooth for her liking. Her palm itched to slap him. Odd, that. She wasn't a violent person. Quite the opposite, in fact. And she loved children: but *other* children, not this one. The little monster perched on the riverbank brought out the worst in her.

The brat should thank his lucky stars she was stuck, Amanda thought, because she was dangerously close to losing what little patience she'd ever had with him. He'd been pushing her hard for the past two months, and she'd just about reached her limit with him. She knew that if he came close enough to reach she wouldn't hesitate to grab him by the collar and yank him down into the cold water and mud with her. Lord knows, he deserved all that and more! A good spanking would *not* be out of order.

The rock clinked atop the pile when Roger set it aside. Balancing his elbows atop his thighs, he leaned forward but, true to form, was careful not to get too close to her. He was a monster, yes, but he was a *smart* monster. Roger knew when he'd pushed a body too far, and the angry glint in Amanda Lennox's pretty green eyes said he'd pushed her too far weeks ago. However, since she was admittedly stuck—and he was obviously free to run—he didn't fear retribution. Not right away at least, and Roger never worried about any punishment that wasn't immediate.

A spark of mischief shimmered in his clear blue eyes as he lifted his feet out of the water. He lowered them fast and hard, making a resounding splash.

Amanda saw his aggravating grin—a split second before she could see nothing at all. Frigid water pelted her face and eyes, blurring her vision. Roger's splash plastered her damp hair coldly to her scalp. Spitting water from her mouth, and sputtering angrily, she swiped the wet hair back from her face. Her glare was cold enough to make Roger's feet freeze, poised in the act of a repeat performance.

Shivering, she hugged her arms around her middle for warmth. Gooseflesh puckered the skin on her forearms. A chill iced down her spine. Her right leg, she noticed worriedly, no longer hurt as much as it had. That in itself was a major concern.

"Go ahead," she snapped through chattering teeth. "Splash me again. Just remember, brat, I won't be stuck here forever. And when I get free . . ." She let the threat hang between them, knowing it was more frightening because it hadn't been finished.

To the best of Roger's recollection, this was the first time *anyone* had ever called him a brat to his face. Added to that was the fact that this was the first time Miss Lennox had threatened him. Worse — much worse — she looked as though she meant it.

Roger swallowed hard. Shock that the woman — an *employee!* — had dared so much gave her words an extra sting. He dipped his feet into the water slowly, with nary a ripple.

Amanda eyed the boy cautiously. To her surprise, he looked genuinely concerned. She swallowed back a grin, deciding to press her advantage while she still had it. Lord knows, she'd never gotten this much of his attention, this quickly, before.

Forcing her teeth not to chatter, she fixed him with a stern glare. "Very good, Roger. Now I want you to get out of the water and put your shoes and stockings back on. Then, you are going to go out there," she jabbed a shivering, water-wrinkled index finger at the pine trees that formed a natural wall to the clearing behind him, "and find someone who can help get me out of here." The tip of her rigid index finger swerved, pointing now at his

11

narrow chest. "I swear to God, Roger, if you even *think* about coming back here alone, your eleventh birthday will be nothing but a wishful dream. Did you hear me?" she demanded when he just sat there, staring at her in open-mouthed astonishment. Warily, he nodded. "Good. Well, what are you waiting for? Don't just sit there . . . *do it!*"

She arched one golden brow as he scrambled to his feet in record time. Good God, the child was actually *obeying* her! This was a pleasant first, she thought, and made a mental note to threaten him with bodily harm hourly from this moment on.

The apprehension hadn't faded from Roger's eyes when, two minutes later, he stood on the sandy bank shifting from foot to expensively shod foot. "There's — um — no one to get, ma'am," he said, his voice unnaturally high, unnaturally nervous.

"And whose fault is that? *I* wasn't the one who scared off the guard your father hired to escort us. You did that all by yourself, young man, and because it's *your* fault our guard isn't here to offer assistance, I think it only fair *you* take on the responsibility of finding someone else who can." Her gaze narrowed, and she was pleased to see he had the decency to flush and look guiltily away. Although he didn't, she noticed, look *too* guilty. "I mean it, Roger. I don't want you to come back here unless you've found someone who can help me."

"And if I c-can't find anyone?"

"Then don't come back," she snapped through gritted teeth. Amanda meant every word. At least, she meant them when she said them. It took a good fifteen minutes for her anger to cool, and for regret to sink in.

Dear God, what had she done? What if Roger couldn't find help? It was more than possible. They hadn't passed a soul in days; the chance of him finding someone today — someone strong enough to get her out of here — wasn't promising. And what would he do if he couldn't find anyone? Would he take her at her word and not come back? Worse, what would *she* do if that happened—besides rejoice in never having to see the brat again, of course.

Aside from the obvious, there was a distinct disadvantage to not being able to move. It gave a body far too much time to think. While Amanda's thoughts were distracting—they kept her from dwelling on how cold and wet and pained she was—they were also more than a little disturbing.

Dammit! She shouldn't have let Roger get her so angry. Now if he didn't return, it was no one's fault but her own. It went without saying that if Roger didn't return, Amanda was in a great deal of trouble. Edward Bannister hadn't hired her to lose his son in what could very well be hostile Indian Territory.

To Amanda's way of thinking, that only went to prove the man couldn't know Roger very well. But that wasn't the point. If she turned up in Pony without Roger, it would be to face the brunt of Edward Bannister's wrath. The thought was more hideous than spending time alone with the man's son. Amanda didn't know much about her employer, but she'd heard rumors. She knew enough. Losing Edward Bannister's son could prove hazardous to her health—especially since she was the sole person responsible for the safety and well-being of the heir to Edward Bannister's recently-acquired fortune.

That fact would have been laughable, were it not so true.

Amanda closed her eyes and groaned when she remembered the stories she'd read in the newspaper last year about Chief Joseph and his turbulent trek toward Canada. How did she know that, at this very moment, there weren't blood-thirsty savages out there slicing off Roger's scalp? Her stomach churned at the mental picture *that* thought conjured up! The thought that she was the one who'd sent the poor boy out to such a fate was unbearable. She didn't like Roger, but still . . .

There were two ways to look at this situation; Amanda, having more than enough time and a desperate need to occupy her mind, looked at it from both angles. The good news was, there was a chance — a small one, but a chance all the same — that the land they were on was as safe as what they'd left behind. The bad news was, the safety of the region had yet to be determined. She would need to know exactly where they were in order establish how hostile the territory was . . . and they'd been lost for weeks.

Again, Amanda wondered how she'd gotten herself into this mess. Again, the only answer that sprang to mind was, blind stupidity. When the need was great, people resorted to desperate measures. She would have preferred to think herself above all that, but the unpleasant memory of Roger Thornton Bannister III's hateful little smirk proved she was not.

Not for the first time, she cursed the ad she'd seen three months ago in the *Boston Times*. The job had seemed like a godsend. She had needed to return to Seattle and the small horse ranch her father had left to her after his death, but she'd had no money for the trip. The ad had seemed like an answer to her prayers. To her way of thinking, the only thing better than immediate money was *easy* money. And how difficult could it be to escort a ten-year-old boy from Boston to Montana?

It had sounded so simple. Truly, she should have known better.

Being hired for the job had been part luck and part ingenuity. She'd fudged her qualifications. A wilderness expert? *Her?* Not likely! Of course, she hadn't said that. She'd told the lawyer who, with obvious misgivings, had hired her, that she had vast experience foraging through the woods for months at a time. It wasn't a complete lie, although only by severely stretching one's imagination could the extensive gardens behind Miss Henry's Academy for Young Ladies be considered "woods." As for the "months at a time" part . . . well she'd exaggerated. But she'd been desperate.

The lawyer, whose name she couldn't recall, hadn't believed a word. That hadn't stopped him from hiring her on the spot. Apparently, the man had been as desperate to find someone to take Roger off his hands as Amanda had been to get the job and put the finishing school and city she abhorred behind her. Of course, once she'd been introduced to Roger, she knew why the lawyer bit back his reluctance and hired her despite her obvious lack of skill. The salary was more than generous . . . but a fortune wouldn't have made an otherwise sane person consider spending time with Roger Thornton Bannister III.

The trip had been delayed four days while the lawyer found a man as insane as Amanda to act as their guard.

Yes, she thought now, getting the job had been a blessing. Keeping it, however, had proved to be a curse that now weighed heavily on her cold, wet, shivering shoulders.

Ten more minutes passed, during which time Amanda convinced herself Roger would not be back. Ever. A worrier at heart, she decided that if savages didn't get to the boy, a wild animal would. Roger possessed no more wilderness skills than she did. It was nothing short of a miracle that they'd come as far as they had; their guard had deserted them shortly after they'd disembarked from the stage in Virginia City.

Scowling, Amanda glanced around and wondered if they had come as far as she'd thought. Without Roger to distract and annoy her, the river that kept sucking at her legs began to look familiar. The thick stand of pine trees; the way the gurgling water cut a twisting path around them; the ankle high, swaying grass and fragrant wildflowers dotting the steep but not too steep bank . . .

"I really wish you'd stop calling me a liar. She is out there. Right past those trees. Go ahead, see for yourself."

The voice, Roger's, was so unexpected that Amanda almost tumbled backward from the shock of hearing it. He wasn't dead? Indians hadn't scalped him? Bears hadn't mauled him? And he'd come back, which meant . . .

Her relief was short lived; it faded at the sound of

15

Roger's laughter. As always, the boy's nasally, high-pitched sneer skáted down Amanda's spine like fingernails raking slate. All the kind thoughts she'd wasted on him when she'd been sure he was dead evaporated, replaced by the memories of all the nasty things Roger did and said on an hourly basis.

It wouldn't surprise Amanda if Roger was out there talking to himself right now . . . just to make her *think* he'd found help. She would be furious when no real help was forthcoming, and her frustration would no doubt feed the little monster's perverse sense of humor.

Leaves crunched, a twig snapped.

Amanda scowled, her gaze narrowing on the trees where the sounds originated. Though she hated to admit it, when Roger set his mind to do something, he usually accomplished it. Since what he usually accomplished was mass destruction, it wasn't an extremely *endearing* trait. In Virginia City, when they'd set out on the last leg of their trip, Roger had loosened her saddle cinch . . . then laughed himself sick when she'd almost tumbled to her death. Oh, yes, she'd learned the hard way to be leery of any "help" the brat offered.

She balled her hands into tight fists, her gaze focusing on the trees. As she watched, one shadow thickened and separated from a particularly wide pine tree trunk.

"I swear to God, kid, if you've dragged me all the way out here for nothing, I'll . . ."

Amanda startled. *That* voice was not Roger's. The timbre was too deep, the drawl too thick and too steeped in adult masculinity for it to belong to a ten-year-old. In case she had any lingering doubts, the man who swaggered into the clearing as though he owned it abolished them in one virile sweep.

Her first instinct was to scream.

Her second, to faint.

Her third—the strongest of all—was to strangle Roger Thornton Bannister III the first chance she got. The little brat! Here she'd been worrying herself sick, thinking the poor child had been scalped by a band of

16

renegade Indians, and what did Roger do? *He brought one back with him!* Even as the thought shot through her mind, another, stronger one overrode it. The man was not entirely Indian. Oh, his cheeks and nose, both high and well defined, suggested a strong native heritage. So did the rich copper tone of his skin, and the sweep of black hair that fell in a sleek line to well past his shoulder blades. His height was the only thing average about him; she judged him to be about 5 foot ten or eleven, only a few inches taller than herself. He had solid shoulders and narrow hips. His form was panther-lean and powerful.

His jaw was hard and square, suggesting a trace of good English breeding somewhere back in his not-too-distant ancestry. As for his eyes . . .

Ah, his eyes. Now they *definitely* didn't belong to any Indian tribe Amanda had ever heard of! She almost — *almost* — felt relieved. Then their gazes meshed. And he spoke. And the relief scattered.

"Well, well well," the man drawled as he thumbed the wide-brimmed, black felt hat back on the crown of his equally black head. A large black-and-white eagle feather had been tucked into the braided leather hatband. Amanda noticed it, just before her gaze dipped.

He'd hooked his thumbs through the belt loops of indecently snug denim pants. As she watched, he rolled his weight back on his heels. His steel-grey gaze never left her, though it was clear his next words were aimed at Roger. "Looks like you weren't lying after all. Is she really stuck?"

The boy shrugged, his gaze volleying between Amanda's pale cheeks and the acute interest he saw darkening the stranger's eyes. "She says she is," Roger answered warily.

"Then it must be true. The lady don't look to be the lying type."

A shiver of heat splashed through Amanda when the stranger's gaze raked the partially dried hair scattered around her face and shoulders. His attention dipped,

17

lazily taking in the water-darkened bodice of her cream-colored shirtwaist and the dark rose skirt that clung to her hips like a clammy second skin.

She'd heard rumors of men who could strip a woman bare with one smoldering glance, but she'd never met one who would dare. Until now. As the man's attention poured over her, Amanda had the unpleasant feeling he could see right through the saturated barrier of cloth. A warm, tight sensation curled in the pit of her stomach: unfamiliar, alarming.

She tipped her chin up defensively. Crossing her arms over her chest, she cut his lewd investigation short.

His gaze took its sweet time lifting to hers. His grey eyes shimmered in the mid-morning sunlight, telling her it was far too late for modesty. His appreciative expression said something else again; that he'd already decided what "type" of lady she was . . . and that he could tolerate her sort with little trouble.

"I suppose you'll be wanting my help now, ma'am?" The way his tongue wrapped around the word "ma'am" sent an odd, warm-cold tremor down Amanda's spine. Somehow, he made it sound less like a title and more like a sensual endearment.

"If it wouldn't be too much trouble," she replied stiffly, and thought, why not? Her left leg throbbed from supporting her idle weight for so long. She was wet and chilled to the bone. She knew if she didn't allow this man to help her, she might never get out of this frigid water.

He nodded and turned his attention to Roger. "Go find some sticks and get a fire started. Don't skimp; I want it blazing. The lady's going to need all the heat she can get once she's out of there. And get some blankets, too. All you can spare. There's a couple rolled and tied on my horse. Use them."

Roger's golden brows slashed high, disappearing beneath the curls that kissed his forehead. He glanced up at the stranger as though the man had lost all grip on reality. "You want *me* to do *what?*"

"Get a fire started," the man gritted impatiently, even

18

as he sank to the ground and began yanking off his knee-high moccasins. "What the hell are you waiting for, kid? I want that fire started, and I want it started *now!*"

It must have been the ring of authority in the man's voice, Amanda decided. Either that, or the veiled threat glistening in his eyes. Whatever the reason, Roger spun on his heel and sprinted into the woods with unheard-of speed.

"Looks like it's just you and me, princess," the man said as, lithely pushing to his feet, he took a step toward the river. His attention rose from the spot where the water lapped at her hips. His gaze ascended — slowly, hotly — over her breasts, her shoulders, her chin, and lips. Finally, he locked onto her fear-widened eyes.

In that instant, Amanda knew why Roger had run. If her foot wasn't stuck, she would do the same thing. The savage glint in the man's eyes, coupled with his insolent perusal, had a terrifying affect on her.

"You have a name?" His question was instantly followed by a loud splash. He'd just taken his first swaggering stride into the icy river.

"O-of course." Closing her eyes, Amanda stifled a groan in the back of her throat. Not for all the money in the world could she have forced her eyes open at that moment, forced herself to watch as that dangerous-looking man stalked toward her like a hungry wolf hunting down its trapped, defenseless prey.

"You going to tell me what it is?"

His voice was closer. Amanda thought that reason enough not to answer him. That, and the feel of the water being disturbed around her. The icy current lapped at her stomach. She rolled her lips inward and ordered herself not to shiver. It wouldn't do for this man to think her tremors were caused by his nearness and not the water's numbing coldness.

And he was near. She could sense it, *feel* it.

"Okay, princess, let me put it another way. You want to get out of this river any time soon?"

Amanda's eyes snapped open. A split second too late,

19

she realized it for the mistake it was. The stranger *was* standing close. Too close. The span of his shoulders and chest cast a chilly shadow over her, blotting out the warmth of the late morning sun, blotting out *everything.* The water was cold, but it would have needed to be covered with a thick sheet of ice to counterbalance the intense male heat his lean body radiated.

The earthy, leather-and-spice smell of him surrounded her, seeped through her, seeped *into* her. The scent warmed her blood, thawing what Amanda had begun to think would be an everlasting chill. She didn't feel chilled right now. Just the opposite; she'd never felt so hot in her life!

The man angled his head to look down at her, and Amanda saw that he'd removed his hat. His straight black hair scattered flatteringly around his face. The breeze tossed the inky strands around his shoulders. Her gaze picked out a thin, tight braid, no thicker than her pinkie, woven into the underside of his hair, just behind his left ear. She trailed the braid down to a small brown feather, anchored by a leather thong tied to the end of it.

On another man, that braid would have looked more than odd; it would have looked feminine. She wondered why it didn't work that way on him.

"Well, what's it going to be, princess?" he asked, his warm breath puffing over her cheeks. "The way I see it, you've only got two choices. Either you stand there gawking at me all day, or you answer my question so I can dig you out. I'd say it's your call."

Question? she thought dazedly. Had he asked her a question? Maybe. She couldn't remember. It was hard to remember her *name* with him standing so close. Amanda told herself her lengthy stay in the water had warped her mind, but she wasn't convinced. No, more likely it was seeing the man's eyes up close that robbed her of the will to speak . . . as well as a good deal of breath!

His eyes weren't grey, as she'd first thought, but a

rich, smoky silver. The intensity of his gaze was enhanced by a fringe of thick, sooty lashes, and emphasized by his deep copper skin.

"Guess I was wrong. Looks like you don't want out after all," he said as, tearing his gaze from hers, he pivoted and began wading back the way he'd come.

Only after his body heat — the smell of him, the *confusion* of him — had been removed, did Amanda shake herself to her senses. By that time he was climbing lithely onto the grassy riverbank. "Wait, Mr. . . . !"

He didn't turn around. "Un-uh. That was *my* question, princess. And until you answer it, you're staying put."

Amanda blinked hard. That was it? All he wanted was for her to tell him her name and then he'd help her out? That seemed reasonable enough. No, it wasn't *reasonable* at all! A gentleman would never leave a lady stranded in the middle of frigid water merely because she hadn't supplied her name the second he'd snapped his fingers and demanded it. Then again . . .

Her gaze narrowed on his back, on the way the tough denim pants clung wetly to his heavily muscled thighs and calves. She reassessed. This was definitely no gentleman. Her deduction had nothing to do with his native heritage. It had *everything* to do with the way he dressed — truly, those pants were indecent! — and the way he walked — make that swaggered. His every move screamed arrogance and authority. Which would have been fine, were it an unintentional, spontaneous thing. It wasn't. Amanda had a gut-feeling this man knew exactly what kind of cocky, insolent impression he made on people, and that he played it to the hilt.

When he turned his head and regarded her from over one shoulder, Amanda knew she was right. She also had an uneasy feeling that *he* knew what she was thinking.

"Change your mind yet?" As he spoke, he sat down in the grass and reached for his moccasins, although he made no move to tug them on. Yet.

The enormity of what he was doing hit Amanda like a

slap. She glared at him. "You aren't really going to leave me here, are you? Just because *I wouldn't tell you my name?*"

He tipped his head to one side. A lock of black hair fell forward on his brow when he shrugged. "What do you think?"

"I don't think you'd dare."

"Then you don't know me very well."

Her chin tipped haughtily. "I don't know you at all."

"We could do something about that."

Was it possible for a grin to be devastating yet emotionless at the same time? Amanda wouldn't have thought so—until she saw the proof of it with her own eyes. Her heart flipped over in her chest, its tempo hammering in her ears. Her trembling fingers closed around the water near her hips in empty fists.

"That wasn't very nice," she snapped, and stifled a groan when his grin only broadened. The smile, she noted, didn't reach his eyes. They remained narrow and frosty.

"I'm not a very nice person," he said. "Ask anyone, they'll tell you." As though to prove it, he started tugging on his moccasins. When he was done, he pushed to his feet. In the same fluid movement he swiped up his hat and settled it atop his head. He pinched the low-riding brim between his index finger and thumb, nodded to her in mock politeness, then turned and walked toward the trees.

Amanda blinked hard. Dear God, the man really was going to desert her. *The rotten bastard!*

She didn't realize she'd said the words aloud until she saw him stop. His shoulders squared. His back stiffened. Even from this distance, she could see tension pull the muscles in his back, shoulders, and arms taut.

"Come again, princess?"

Since it was too late to deny it—the damage was already done—Amanda sucked in a deep breath and repeated herself, loudly, and clearly enough so he would have no doubt as to what she'd just called him.

"Goddamn. That's what I thought you said." He sucked in a sigh and released it in a slow hiss. Then he shook his head—regretfully? she doubted it—and plucked off the hat. With a flick of his wrist, he sent it hurling to the grass. "Guess I'm going have to fetch you out of there after all."

There was something in his tone—too calm, too leashed—that sent a shiver down her spine. Amanda couldn't pinpoint the underlying emotion he'd stressed, and, as she watched him again tug off the deerskin moccasins, she stopped trying. Before she knew it, he was trudging through the water toward her. Forcing herself not to shiver in dread took all her concentration.

Wondering what had made him change his mind, she glanced up.

He glanced down.

Silver and green warred, and in that instant Amanda knew exactly why he'd decided to free her. His eyes were narrowed to steely slits. His jaw was bunched hard, and a muscle ticked beneath the high copper plane of his cheekbone. As she watched, his lips thinned into a tight, uncompromising line.

Calling him a bastard had hit a sore spot with him. The man was quietly furious. Worse—much, much worse—all that tightly leashed anger was directed at her. The knowledge seemed a good enough reason for Amanda to flinch when he stopped so close his chest threatened to graze the very tips of her breasts.

"I-I'll tell you my name," she offered, and winced when her voice squeaked.

"Don't bother. Where are you stuck?"

Swallowing hard, she fixed her gaze on one of the flat metal buttons trailing down his shirt. As for the tight bands of muscle rippling beneath the dark blue cloth . . . well, she refused to notice them at all. "Amanda Lennox. That's my name."

"That's dandy. I repeat: Where are you stuck?" His hand came out of nowhere. His index finger hooked under her chin, dragging her gaze up. His warm, sweet

23

breath blasted over her face when he said, "Better give some thought to answering me this time, princess. You've got exactly ten seconds to tell me what's going on under this water. After that, my hands start doing some exploring of their own."

"My right leg," she whispered hoarsely, trying to ignore the way his calloused thumb was stroking the very tip of her chin — as well as the way her skin smoldered in response. "Actually it's my foot. It's stuck in . . . something. I don't know what."

"What does it feel like?" His hand turned inward, slipping lower. His thumb nestled the base of her throat, pushing against the pulse that leapt wildly in the creamy hollow. The rest of his fingers hooked behind her neck. He exerted no pressure.

"A hole," she said, her voice so shaky and soft now it was almost nonexistent. "It feels like a hole."

"What kind of hole?"

"A — oh!"

A change in the current pulled their bodies together, then just as quickly pulled them apart.

She gasped.

He tensed.

A strained moment passed. Time was marked by the cold water lapping at their bodies.

His hand dropped away. Amanda almost cried with relief . . . until she felt those same strong fingers hauling her water-heavy skirt and petticoat up to her waist. Her knees buckled.

"Goda'mighty, lady, stand up, open your eyes, and pay some attention to what we're doing here. That's better. Now, hold this damn thing out of my way."

The "damn thing" in question was her skirt. He coaxed her cold, water-logged fingers around fistfuls of the saturated cloth. Amanda wasn't sure which was worse; holding her skirt up so a complete stranger could have free access to her naked legs, or watching the man's head dip as he hunkered down in the water and pressed his cheek against her stomach. His breaths seeped through the damp cloth in rhythmic waves, searing the sensitive flesh beneath like a white-hot brand.

He shifted, pressing closer. Amanda almost toppled over. Only the sinewy arm he coiled around her waist kept her upright. The feel of his warm, slippery fingers skimming beneath the hem of her skirt did not fortify her liquidy knees.

His fingers caressed her naked thigh as he adjusted her weight, moving her until her abdomen ground against his shoulder. Against her will, her gaze dipped. The water lapped at a spot below his shoulder blades, soaking the tips of his hair and making the fringe ride the twisting currents. He didn't seem to notice that. She, on the other hand, noticed everything; like the way his hand strayed very slowly over the outer curve of her hip and down her thigh, the way his fingers tickled past the back of her knee, then slid unhurriedly down her calf.

When he reached her ankle, Amanda noticed something else. Pain, and a lot of it. She winced and put her hands on his shoulders for balance. Her fingers curled inward, making deep grooves in his hard, unyielding flesh. She didn't cry out until she felt his fingertips probe her tender, swollen ankle.

"That hurt?" he asked.

"God, yes!"

He sighed.

She shivered, but this time entirely from pain.

"All right. I'll try and be gentle, but . . . Jesus, lady, how the hell'd you get your foot stuck in a tree?"

His voice was muffled from where his mouth pressed into the side of her waist. Amanda felt every movement of his lips. Oddly enough, that overrode the pain stabbing up her leg, as well as the disgust that was evident in his tone.

She glanced down, intending to glare him into silence. The thought wilted when she saw the way they were entwined. The water licked at their bodies like a lover's caress. His arms were around her, pinning her intimately close. She could feel each breath rush from his chest. The way she was forced to either arch her hips into him or risk tumbling backward was . . . well, it was indecent. It was also shockingly nice.

The tightening of his body said she wasn't the only one to think so. "I can't pull your ankle out—it's too swollen," he said gruffly. "I'll have to cut the bark away. Think you can hold still long enough?"

"Do I have a choice?"

He pulled back only far enough to glance up at her. "You want to get out any time soon?" She nodded. "Then no, you don't have a choice. Hold still. It'd be a damn shame if I cut into all that sweet white skin of yours instead of bark."

He shifted, and she caught a glimpse of what he planned to use for the job. The blade of the knife was shaped like a long, thick triangle, the metal shiny and razor sharp. In length, the blade alone rivaled the span of his forearm, and his forearm was not short. The sight of water dripping off deadly metal convinced her not to move a muscle—even when she felt his palm stroke hot paths up and down the back of her calf. His other hand, she noticed dazedly, was trying to work her free. He seemed to be in no great hurry.

"I've got the fire started," Roger called from the bank, causing Amanda to start and glance up sharply.

The man stiffened. "You get the blankets ready?"

"No."

"Christ, that kid's useless," he grumbled so only Amanda could hear. She fought a grin as, louder, he yelled, "What the hell you waiting for? Go get them. Come back when you're done."

Amanda recognized the indignant lift to Roger's chin. She braced herself for the argument to come, knowing the stranger wasn't as familiar with the boy's obstinacy as she was.

"And what, pray tell, will you be doing while I'm fetching blankets?" Roger called out.

"I'll be tanning your backside if you don't get a move

26

on, brat. If you want to sit down anytime in the next month, you'll do as you're told. *Now!*" The man shifted, glancing over his shoulder at the boy who stood, fists straddling hips, on the bank. While Amanda couldn't see the stranger's eyes at this angle, Roger's suddenly pale cheeks spoke volumes. For an unprecedented third time that day, Roger scurried away.

The man bent back to his task. Beneath the churning water Amanda felt gentle tugs on her numb, swollen ankle . . . and a peculiar, scraping sensation when his free hand rose. Without permission or apology, he boldly skimmed the inside of her left thigh. His strokes were smooth, sure, and indecently high. The breath she had been inhaling clogged in her lungs. It pushed free in a rush when he released her and abruptly stood.

"All set," he announced as, without warning, he bent at the waist and hoisted her into his arms.

"Good heavens, what are you doing?" she demanded, even as her arms slipped around the thick trunk of his neck. She hadn't given her hands permission to do that. Then again, she hadn't given her body permission to snuggle into his hard male warmth, but she was doing that, too. And it felt rather nice, now that she thought about it. Amanda tried *not* to think about it.

"What am I doing? Isn't it obvious?"

"Well . . . yes." And, of course, it was. He was carrying her, plain and simple. Yet, there wasn't a plain thing about the firm, wet chest plastered tightly against her. Nor was there anything at all simple in the way her body automatically, *willingly,* reacted by curling trustingly into his.

Amanda drew in a shaky breath. His earthy smell and furnacelike heat engulfed her, flooding her whirling senses. Her protests weakened under the sharp male onslaught. "Please, Mr. . . . will you put me down? I can walk."

"Not on that ankle, you can't," he said, and continued to splash through the water, carrying her as though she weighed no more than a wet kitten.

He reached the bank and scaled the incline without upsetting his balance. Their waterlogged clothes seemed no hindrance to his innate agility. The grass made nary a crunch beneath his bare feet as he carried her to the miserly fire Roger had built. Then he knelt and lowered her effortlessly to the sun-warmed grass.

His chin lifted, his penetrating silver gaze scanning the trees. His sigh of disgust felt hot as it rushed over her face and neck. "Where the hell is that good-for-nothing kid? He should be back by now."

Her reply came from between chattering teeth. "You don't know . . . Roger too well. We'll be lucky if he ever comes back. And you . . . can forget the blankets. He won't bring them."

His gaze sliced back to her, his expression one of slightly veiled surprise. And then he noticed the way she shivered, the cold eating at her from the inside out. His gaze narrowed. His oaths were vivid, long, and graphic.

"I'll get the blankets," he growled, thrusting to his feet.

Amanda watched him swagger away and again was reminded of a wolf on the hunt. She shivered, but even when she looked away, her mind was filled with his lean, wet back and the way his saturated hair swayed with each step.

In all her life, she'd never known a man who dared to wear his hair so long. Funny, but, like the braid, on him she found the style oddly appealing. Flagrantly unconventional, wild and untamed . . . like the man himself.

When he returned a short few minutes later, she was huddled into a tight ball on the ground, as close as she could get to the fire without being burned. The heat was insufficient. She was cold to the bone, and, to make an already bad situation worse, the numbness in her legs was gone. Not only did her ankle throb, but the rush of returning circulation made it sting unbearably.

She was vaguely aware of something warm and heavy being tossed over her. She snuggled into the covering greedily, barely noticing when the blanket was tucked around her. A corner of her mind knew without looking that the hands slipping over her body would be big and strong and coppery.

He didn't stop there. Amanda gasped when she felt his arms slip beneath her. He lifted her easily, shifted, then settled her atop the solid cushion of his lap. She stiffened, but his palm, cradling the back of her neck, coaxed her cheek to the firm pillow of his chest. His arms wrapped around her like steel bands, locking her into place against him.

Amanda knew she should protest the way he was holding her — even if he was only doing it to share warmth. And she would have, had it not been for the way his virile heat burned away her chill. His inviting warmth made pushing him away just a brief, passing thought. One she barely considered, and didn't act upon.

It took forever for her trembling to pass, but it was the most wonderful forever Amanda had ever spent.

She felt a warm cheek graze the crown of her head when she nuzzled her head into the hollow beneath his shoulder. His heartbeat was a strong, steady tempo in her ears. That, combined with the draining excitement of the morning and this man's comforting warmth, lulled her into a deep state of relaxation.

"Oh, no you don't. Don't you dare fall asleep on me now, Amanda Lennox," he grumbled hotly against her scalp. "We've still got some name-calling to talk out between us."

The words were like a splash of cold water. Amanda went rigid in his arms.

Chapter Two

"I'm going to let you in on a little secret here, princess. Not three hours ago I knocked a man's teeth down his throat for calling me a bastard. The guy apologized. So will you."

"I will not, so you might as well get that thought right out of your head," Amanda replied, her haughty Bostonian accent now locked firmly in place. "I've done nothing to apologize for."

Tension crackled in the air between them. Rather, it crackled in what little air managed to worm its way between them. He was holding her dreadfully close.

His fingers tightened on her arms. While his grip was not painful, it threatened to become so soon. "You sure about that?"

"Positive."

"In other words, you don't think calling a man a bastard is something you need to apologize for?"

Amanda pursed her lips. If she'd felt any fear, it was gone; replaced by a nice, warm surge of resentment. "Not if the man in question is acting like a bastard, no. And you *were* acting like one." *You still are,* she thought, but wisely didn't say. "No, I can't apologize to you."

"Wrong, princess. You can, and you *will*. Nobody — and I mean *nobody* — calls Jacob Blackhawk Chandler a bastard and walks away intact. Not even a prissy little white snob who, I might add, could use a good lesson in manners."

30

His voice had taken on a calm, deadly edge; the words were slowly and precisely drawled. Not spoken, *drawled*. Her resentment drained away as though she'd never felt it. Amanda couldn't have felt more intimidated had the man grabbed her, shook her until her teeth rattled, and yelled the threat in her face. Her cheeks drained of color. Rolling her lips inward, she bit back the cowardly apology that sprang to mind.

The wall of muscles beneath her cheek flexed. She stifled a groan. Good heavens, the man was hard as a rock — every inch of him coiled muscle and strength. His grip tightened. She winced, though she knew he wasn't applying all that much pressure. Surely not as much as his whip-cord-lean body said he was capable of. Her newfound courage floundered.

"I'm waiting." His hand shifted, his grip loosening enough for his thick, calloused thumb to stroke invisible circles over the sensitive inner curve of her upper arm. "Don't rush on my account. Can't say I'd mind holding you like this a while longer."

"No? Well, *I'd* mind," she snapped, then instantly wished she hadn't. His laughter was short and merciless. The deep, husky sound rumbled in the chest beneath her ear and vibrated through her body like a bolt of heat lightning.

The muscles beneath her cheek bunched and released, suggesting a careless shrug. "If my company offends you, feel free to get up and leave."

Amanda fisted the damp blankets beneath her chin. She flexed her foot, and winced at the stab of pain. Circulation had returned with force; waves of it ripped up her leg. Without the icy water to dull it, the pounding in her ankle was excruciating.

"You know I can't," she grumbled miserably.

"That's right, I do."

One thing she *could do*, however, was to give pushing him away a good try. Snuggling against his chest the way she was doing, drinking in his body heat and scent, was not appropriate. It suggested that his arms offered a se-

31

curity and trust that only a complete idiot would be feeling right now.

Amanda wedged her fists between their bodies and shoved. Hard. The muscles in her arms screamed with the force she pooled into the action. She felt him ease back half an inch, no more. It was enough space to let the cool autumn breeze sneak between their chests.

The warmth he radiated was intense. She didn't realize *how* intense until it was gone. Amanda shivered, scowled, and took a swift mental inventory of all the spots on her body where the chill originated. It was as she'd feared. The cold was most pronounced in the places where *he* had warmed her.

That settled matters in Amanda's mind. Getting away from the confusing feel of Jake Chandler was now a necessity; one that seemed infinitely more important than her strong Lennox pride. Perhaps if she offered a compromise? As much as it went against her grain to do so, she reasoned that gaining her freedom *had* to be worth relinquishing a small amount of dignity.

Could she do it? Could she say she was sorry when she knew deep down that she had nothing to be sorry for? Amanda didn't know, but she was willing to try it and find out. If it could make this man unhand her, it would be worth the effort.

Her chin rose loftily, and her gaze clashed with piercing silver. "I have a proposal," she said. Her expression hardened when a flash of lewd suggestion flickered in his eyes. "Don't even *think* it! What I propose, Mr. Chandler, is that I thank you for freeing me from the river, and we can call the rest a draw."

It was the "don't even *think* it" that aggravated the hell out of Jake. He saw the contempt shimmering in her eyes. While her expression remained cautious, her mood was easily read by a man who knew what to look for. Jake knew what to look for, and what he saw in Amanda Lennox's eyes, he didn't like at all.

Scorn. Ridicule. Disgust. *Those* were the emotions he thought he saw swimming in her big green eyes. Jesus, she looked like she was afraid his dirty, half-breed hands would somehow contaminate her precious white skin. Oh, how that grated!

"I don't want your thanks, princess," he sneered, "as you damn well know. And as for the draw . . . ?" He shook his head, his grip on her arms squeezing painfully tight. "Hell, no. What I want is my apology."

"You want me to lie, in other words." Though her tone was smooth, it was laced heavily with pretention.

"Yeah, if you have to. That'd be fine by me."

Amanda rarely got angry. It just wasn't in her nature. Few people had the power to arouse her slow-burning fury. Roger was one. Jake Chandler, for whatever reason, was another — and he seemed to know exactly how to use that power for optimum effect. His innate stubbornness stimulated her ire quicker and easier than anyone she'd ever known.

"Fine?" she snapped. "With you, maybe. *Not* with me. Threaten me all you want, Mr. Chandler, but I won't lie and tell you I didn't mean what I said. I meant it." Her tone lowered until it was hard, icy, unfamiliar even to her own ears. "You, sir, are unquestionably a bastard."

That did it! Jake had taken about as much of this woman's lip as he was going to.

Lightning fast, he shifted. His fingers bit into her arms as he hauled her up hard against his chest. He angled his head until their noses touched. "I think it's about time you learned some manners, princess. For a white lady — an *Eastern* white lady — yours are atrocious."

One pale brow slanted high in accusation. Her eyes narrowed, the green depths firing as they flung the insult right back in his arrogant face. "Is that so? Well I see some white in you too, buster, but I've yet to see anything in *your* manners to write home about."

Uh-oh, she'd hit another sore spot. She could tell by the way the muscle in his cheek jerked and by the deadly glint in his eyes. If she hadn't been so mad, Amanda would have been concerned about that.

Inky lashes hooded a gaze that narrowed to furious silver slits. His eyebrows were dark slashes in the rich copper of his forehead. They rode naturally low over his eyes to begin with. As she watched, they pinched into a frown that only emphasized the weathered creases between them — the ones that suggested a man who scowled hard and often.

"You're getting on my nerves, Amanda Lennox," he growled, his lips barely moving over the words. His tone was menacing; it trickled down Amanda's spine like drops of melting snow. "Are you sure you want to do that?"

Now that he mentioned it, no. She wasn't at all sure that was what she wanted to do. She *was* sure that angering him more than he already was might not be in her best interests. His seething gaze said it was already far too late.

Unfortunately, it was also too late to back down, and Amanda knew it. She gave a toss of her head, her eyes sparkling with dark green challenge. "Are you going to deny you're part white, Mr. Chandler?"

"Are you going to apologize, *Miss Lennox?*"

"Are *you* going to let me go?"

His heartbeat slammed beneath the heel of her palms, the rhythm fast and furious, beating out a tempo to match the wild glint in his eyes. Amanda's own heartbeat sounded just as frantic as it thundered in her ears. His fingers dug into her tender flesh. The thin cotton sleeves offered no barrier. She flinched but refused to beg for mercy. She had a feeling that, even if she'd asked, there wasn't an ounce of mercy in this man.

"Looks like we've reached an impasse," he said, his voice tight and strained, giving unneeded evidence to his barely leashed temper. "I want my apology; you won't give it. Problem is, you see, I don't intend to leave until you do."

"*What?*" Amanda glared at him, positive she'd heard wrong. She must have! "That's ridiculous. Of course you're leaving."

His condescending grin didn't come close to reaching

his eyes. They remained hard, shimmering like chips of ice. "Am I?"

"Yes!"

"You're sure?"

"Yes!"

"Guess again." He shook his head, and his damp hair flicked her cheek. Amanda pulled back as if she'd been slapped. "I've got nowhere else to go right now." A tension-riddled pause was followed by, "One thing you should keep in mind, though . . . I get bored easily. And when I get bored with *you,* Miss Lennox, I intend to drag that apology out of you in any way that leaps to mind. Willing or not, I'll hear you say it."

In a way that was meant to convince her he fully intended to wait her out, Jake moved, redistributing her weight atop the solid cushion of his lap.

The movement shifted the air around Amanda's face. She drew in a shaky breath, and found herself inundated with an aroma that was strong and sharp and flagrantly male. Her nostrils stung with the earth-sharp scent of Jacob Blackhawk Chandler.

Courage. Had she ever had any? If so, it evaporated like steam the instant she let out that breath and drew in another. The meaning of bravery was suddenly foreign to her. The fear she'd only touched on before was strong, yet minor compared to the white-hot tingle of awareness that rippled through her now. Her breath clogged in her throat. Her heart clamored against her ribs, pumping hot surges of adrenaline into her bloodstream.

She huddled deeply beneath the blanket, deciding belatedly that she would have been better off keeping her mouth shut; as always, it was getting her into trouble. Since talking reason to this man was like trying to converse with a stone, she decided instead to bide her time, wait him out. Surely he would tire of the game shortly. When he did, he would go. Wouldn't he? Of course. He must have better things to do with his day . . . like finishing whatever he'd been about before Roger had found him.

A half hour ticked by. Except for occasionally shifting his weight, Jake didn't move. He made no signs of leaving.

Amanda sighed. The sun was at its zenith, telling her she'd already missed half a day's travel. Great! At this rate she'd be lucky to get Roger home by Christmas.

Fifteen minutes ago she'd decided she really had only one choice left. She was going to have to give this arrogant beast his apology. Only then would she be allowed to scramble off his lap. Only then would he leave her in peace.

It was the lap in question that gave birth to the decision. As time passed, Amanda had become more acutely aware of it. Now, half an hour later, she found herself much too intimately acquainted with the corded bands of muscle beneath her — not to mention the peculiar, tingly sensations all that raw warmth and strength sparked deep inside of her.

Why, oh why, had she ever called him a bastard? Because he was acting like one. He still was. But that no longer mattered. Getting off his lap *did*.

Amanda swallowed her pride; it tasted sour in her throat. As she lifted her cheek from the cushion of his warm, damp chest, she reminded herself that she really didn't have a choice. She glanced up at him. Her lips parted as their gazes met and held.

She never knew if she would have been able to push the distasteful words off her tongue. A distant scream robbed her of the chance to find out.

The high, ear-piercing wail sliced through the air; the sound more alarming because it was so easily recognizable.

Roger! Oh, dear God . . .

Jake Chandler had heard it too. She felt him tense, even as his grip on her loosened. "The kid?" he asked, his mouth suddenly very close to her ear.

"I think so." She turned her head, focusing her gaze on the thick line of trees. "Roger?" she called out, and the single word felt as if it were torn from her throat. *"Roger!"*

36

Silence was her only answer.

Amanda twisted out of Jake's hands. When she was free, she tried to struggle from the thick, wet wrapping of blankets. Spasms of pain shot up her injured leg the second she put weight on it. She gasped and went still. Dammit! Even if she *could* free herself and stand up, she'd never get to Roger in time.

Jake Chandler's curses cut through Amanda as he lifted her from his lap and settled her roughly on the hard, lumpy ground. The instant her pinning weight was removed, he sprang lithely to his feet, towering over her. Reaching behind his back, he slipped something from beneath his belt. Amanda's heart skipped when a ray of sunlight glinted off the long, familiar blade. Her gaze snapped up and met cold, commanding grey.

"Stay here," he growled. "And I mean *stay*, dammit. So help me God, lady, you move a muscle, you make me go looking for you, and I swear I'll . . . ah, hell, *you* figure it out."

He spun on his heel and stalked off.

Like Amanda's recent threat to Roger, Jake's was the more ominous for being left to her imagination. She had quite an imagination. There were several unsavory ways to end a sentence like that, coming from a dangerous man like him. She thought of them all, one by one, as she sat where Jake Chandler had left her, awaiting his return. When she'd run out of gruesome prospects, she turned her thoughts to Roger — and what had caused him to give that blood-curdling scream.

In ten minutes, she'd whipped herself into a frenzy.

Time crept by. Still, Amanda sat shivering beneath the blankets, letting her imagination run riot. More than once she considered disobeying Jake. Only the throbbing in her ankle — which told her she wouldn't get far — kept her sitting atop the sun-warmed grass. It didn't, however, keep her from thinking about dark, mysterious strangers who shouldn't, by any rights, be trusted.

Who was to say Jake Chandler hadn't gotten on his horse and ridden off, never having looked for Roger at all? It would make sense. He didn't know the boy and had no reason to be concerned for Roger's safety. Why bother trying to find Roger when it would be oh, so much easier to just leave?

Maybe she should go looking herself?

Maybe . . . in a bit.

For all her earlier bravado, Amanda had never considered herself brave. Jake's unfinished threat kept her nailed to the spot where he'd left her. If he really was out there looking for Roger, and he came back to find her gone . . . well, the man's disposition was savage. Lord knows what he'd do once he found her. And he *would* find her. Amanda had no doubt of that.

Huddled beneath the blanket, she marked the minutes by keeping a close eye on the sun. Ten more, she decided, compromising integrity for fear. When she estimated ten minutes had passed, she would assume Jake wasn't coming back. Only then would she get up and start looking for Roger herself.

It was the longest ten minutes of her life. When it was over, she was convinced that not only was Roger lying dead somewhere, but that Jacob Blackhawk Chandler was as well.

Disentangling herself from the blanket, Amanda pushed to her feet. Her knees shook beneath the still-damp folds of her skirt. The grass crunched beneath her awkward, limping steps. Walking proved a new experience in pain. She tried to concentrate more on what she had to do and less on the throbbing in her leg that threatened to keep her from doing it.

By the time she reached the first tree trunk, her almost dry body was bathed in sweat. Her breathing came in hard, labored gasps. The pain in her ankle was intense. She leaned heavily against the scratchy bark, and, to occupy her churning mind, cursed all things wild and savage and less cowardly than herself.

"Thought I told you to stay put."

The familiar drawl cut through Amanda like a knife. Clumsily, she pivoted. When she saw Jake Chandler standing only a few short feet away, she leaned weakly back against the tree trunk and sighed her relief. Then her gaze scanned the area around him, and her heart sank. Roger was nowhere in sight. So much for relief!

"He's gone," Jake said. And that, Amanda quickly realized, was all the explanation he was going to offer.

"Gone?" she cried. "What do you mean he's gone? Gone where?"

"How the hell should I know?" He tucked the knife into the sheath attached to his belt, then raked his fingers through his sleek black hair. To Amanda's jaundiced eye, his shrug looked entirely too unconcerned. "Look, I wouldn't worry about the brat too much if I were you. If whoever's got him was going to kill him, they probably would have done it by — Hey, you all right?"

"No," she groaned, her knees buckling, her back sliding down the tree trunk, "I don't think I am." Her bottom made a jarring collision with the ground. It felt hard and cold beneath her — but not as hard and cold as the despair icing through her veins. No, no, *no!* Roger couldn't be gone. He just *couldn't!* But Jake Chandler said he was, and Jake Chandler had no reason to lie.

She rested her head against the rough bark and forced herself to swallow — twice, dryly — before asking, "How do you know someone has him? I mean . . . he could have wandered off, couldn't he?"

"Doubt it. I mean, hell, it's *possible*. Anything's possible. But, since I couldn't find a trace of him, and we both heard him scream . . ." He frowned. "You sure you're all right? You don't look so good. You aren't going to faint, are you?"

"Not just yet." Amanda's lashes swooped down. Fainting would have been a possibility, had her mind not been so busy spinning out of control. Now what was she going to do? She didn't like Roger, but still . . .

And what about Edward Bannister? How would he react when she arrived at their destination without his son? He wouldn't pay her — that went without saying — but would he seek retribution? Of course! Roger was a monster, but monster or not he was still the man's son. Edward Bannister was paying her good money—damn good money—to see to Roger's safety. And what did she do? She lost the brat, *that's* what. Oh, God.

Her eyes snapped open, and she pulled Jake Chandler into focus. He looked uncomfortable, as though he was wondering how he'd managed to get himself into such a mess. Amanda's thoughts traveled the same depressing path. Only she *knew* how she'd gotten into it. Blind stupidity and more gall than she usually gave herself credit for having. That, and a craving to get to Washington and finally put her life back in order.

"Did you see any tracks?" she asked hopefully. "Anything that would suggest who took Roger and why?"

"Didn't look."

"You didn't—? Wait a minute. Where do you think you're going? Mr. Chandler, don't you *dare!*"

Jake dared. He kept on walking, his swaggering steps never faltering. "I'm going home," he said over his shoulder.

"Home?" she cried and thought, *What is it with this man?* First, when she'd wanted him to leave, he wouldn't. Now, when she needed his help, he wouldn't stay. Would the man please make up his mind? She tried again. "Please, Mr. Chandler, you can't leave now. We have a problem here."

"You do," he conceded gruffly, and continued to walk.

Gritting her teeth, and using the tree for leverage, Amanda pushed to her feet. The bark nipped at her palms, making her wince. Though she had to shift her weight to accommodate her wounded ankle, she hoped her stance looked stiff and commanding.

Sucking in a deep breath, she shouted in her best prim and proper voice, *"You no-good, filthy rotten bastard! How dare you walk away from me at a time like this?"*

As she'd planned, the words stopped him cold.

He turned to face her slowly. Sunlight snuck beneath the brim of his hat, and Amanda caught a glimpse of exactly how hard his expression could be. A drop of fear trickled down her spine. She pushed it aside, and somehow managed to return his wintry glare with a level one of her own.

"That's no way for a lady to talk, Miss Lennox," he drawled, his voice flat and hard. Only the muscle jerking in his cheek hinted at the quiet fury simmering inside of him.

For Roger's sake, as well as her own, Amanda refused to let his anger affect her. For once in her life she was going to be brave and stand up to someone—even if that someone was the rudest, most arrogant, most dangerous man she'd ever met.

Her chin tipped haughtily. "You'll have to excuse me," she said with exaggerated politeness. "Given the circumstances, I'm not feeling like much of a lady at the moment."

"Understandable, seeing how your kid's just been—"

"Roger is *not* my son. Good heavens, no!"

"Didn't think he was." Jake angled his head to the side, his steely gaze drilling into her.

"No? Then why did you . . . ?" She shook her head and released an aggravated sigh. "It doesn't matter." Her gaze swept over the skirt that fell in damp, limp folds around her legs. "Mr. Chandler, please. It kills me to say it, but I need your help. For obvious reasons, I can't go after the boy alone."

"Why's that, princess? Your ankle's bruised, not broken. You can ride." Her inquisitively raised brows made him add, with a sly wink, "I checked you out while we were in the water."

A blush heated her cheeks. The memory of his fingers—thick and calloused and warm, caressing her naked thigh and calf—blasted through Amanda's mind. Oh, yes, he'd "checked her out" all right. Most thoroughly! "That isn't the point," she snapped, angry at her thoughts, angry at the man who'd made her think them—*now* of all times.

"Isn't it?"

"No!"

41

A skeptical grin tugged one corner of Jake's lips, and her palm itched to slap it off. This wasn't funny, dammit! Roger was out there, somewhere, and God only knew what had happened to the poor child by now! Amanda brought herself up short. Poor child? Oh no, she was thinking nice things about the little monster again. That wasn't a good sign. It proved she was more distressed than she'd thought.

When Jake didn't say anything, instead just stood there grinning at her, she said, "Roger and I . . . well, to be perfectly blunt, we've been lost out here for a while now."

"Lost? Lady, you can't get lost out here."

"Maybe *you* couldn't, but I assure you, *I* can. I could get lost in my own backyard with little difficulty."

"Then you have no right being out here in the first place."

Amanda ignored that, and continued with what she'd planned to say next. She wouldn't let him distract her from her purpose. "What I'm trying to say is that even without my bruised ankle I would never be able to find Roger by myself."

Jake's lips pursed. He knew exactly how much that admission cost her in the way of dignity. He also enjoyed watching her pay the price. "And you want my help, in other words?"

Amanda fumed. He wasn't making this easy for her. Couldn't he see that she wasn't used to begging people for help? Couldn't he see that they were *wasting time?* If they hurried, there was a chance they could catch up with whoever had taken Roger today. They might even get the boy back by sunset. *If* they hurried. She nodded impatiently. "If you'd be so kind as to give it, then yes, I want your help."

Jake sucked in a slow breath, his expression thoughtful. Just when she thought he was about to agree, he shook his head. "Uh-uh. People like me learn early on not to poke their nose into other people's business. This problem is your business, princess, not mine."

People like him? And what, pray tell, did he mean by *that*? Amanda didn't have a clue, nor did she have time to waste trying to figure it out. Crossing her arms over her chest — to stifle the urge to strangle him on the spot — she said coldly, "I see. And how much will it cost me to *make* it your business?" Her fingers curled inward, her nails digging past her sleeves and into her skin. "I'll pay you generously for your time. State your price, and I guarantee I'll meet it."

A flash of something — outrage, skepticism? — lit his eyes. Whatever it was, the emotion was gone before Amanda had time to decipher it. His features relaxed as he rolled his weight back on his heels and pretended to contemplate her offer. With a nasty grin, he stated an outrageous sum.

"Good heavens, you can't be serious," she gasped.

His expression said he was; dead serious. "I rarely joke, princess . . . and when I do, it's never about money."

Amanda scowled, and did a quick mental calculation. How much money would be left for her if she agreed? Not much. Jake Chandler's asking price was a full three-quarters of the salary she would get upon delivering Roger to his father — with the boy's scalp, and the rest of him, intact.

On the other hand, she'd get nothing if Roger wasn't found.

Her mind reeled. Facts were facts, and unfortunately the facts of this matter were indisputable. She couldn't find Roger on her own. She was hurt, and her sense of direction wasn't just poor, it was nonexistent. Her supplies were running low, and she had no idea where the next town was so that she could buy more. When it came right down to it, she didn't just *need* this despicable man's help; her very survival depended upon it.

"All right," she agreed finally, "I'll meet your price. *Provided* you do the work you were hired for. You'll find Roger, Mr. Chandler, or you won't get a cent."

Surprise registered in his silver eyes, a split second be-

43

fore one inky brow cocked high. "Do I look like a welsher to you, lady? When I say I'm going to do a job, I *do* it." He laced his arms over his chest and speared her with a dubious glare. "And before I decide to take on *this* job, I want some answers."

Amanda leaned heavily against the tree trunk. She blinked slowly to cover the inner workings of her mind, screening emotions she knew this man would detect in an instant. "What kind of answers?"

He counted each one off on the tip of a coppery finger. "I want to know what the hell you're doing out here, for starters. Then you can tell me who the brat is, and where the two of you are heading, and why."

Instinct told her that lying to this man would not be wise. If he ever found out . . .

But what choice did she have? She couldn't tell him the truth and risk it getting back to her employer. Also, Jake had established in her mind, if not blatant greed, then a definite *need* for money. Look at the outrageous amount he was demanding for his services! Since Amanda was in a similar situation — in need of fast money — she could understand that. However, being in the same position also made her aware of how little Jake could be trusted. If *she* was desperate enough to lie to *him,* who was to say he wasn't desperate enough to lie right back at her?

There was one other consideration: telling Jake who the brat was. Amanda couldn't do that. If she told him Roger was Edward Bannister's son, what would prevent Jake from recovering Roger, then holding the boy for ransom? God, she'd never get *any* of her hard-earned salary that way!

Amanda made the conscious decision to lie. She also decided she'd best make her lies believable, and she'd best tell them right the *first* time. She doubted Jake would give her two chances to answer his questions. He'd already made it clear he'd just as soon turn his back and walk away from all this. And she couldn't, under any circumstances, let that happen.

"Too many questions too fast, princess?" Jake drawled,

44

the cocky grin still in place. He could see her mind working and knew she was about to concoct some hair-brained story. For the sheer pleasure of watching her squirm, he decided to let her do exactly that. It wouldn't matter; whatever she said, he wouldn't help her. But at least his curiosity would be satisfied. "Tell you what. I'll make it easy for you. How about if I ask them one at a time? Will that help?"

"Why, yes, I think it would," Amanda answered sweetly, through only slightly clenched teeth.

"Who's the brat?"

"Roger Lennox, my cousin."

Jake nodded. "Where are you going and why?"

"To Pony, Montana. Roger's father lives there, and we're paying him a visit." Ah, now *that* was the truth. It soothed her conscience to be honest with him at least once. She commended herself on doing better than she'd thought she would. And then Amanda saw his eyes widen at her answer, and she wondered if perhaps she wasn't doing poorly after all.

"Pony?" he nearly choked on the word. *"Pony?* Jesus, lady, do you know you're in *Idaho?"*

Her shoulders squared, her back drew up in a rigid line that would have made Miss Henry beam. "Of course I know. Roger wanted to see the scenery." *Idaho!* Amanda thought. *Good God, how did we get there?* "As I recall, Mr. Chandler, that wasn't one of your original questions."

"I said 'for starters.' Last question. Where are you from that you talk so prissy? And why the hell aren't you on a stage right now, the way any woman with a lick of sense would be?"

"That's two questions." The glare he shot her told her not to argue, just to answer. "I'm from . . . Boston." It wasn't really a lie, she told herself. She'd come from Boston, just not originally. Originally, she was from Washington. She saw no need to elaborate about that. It was none of his business.

"Boston?" He shook his head. "That figures."

The way he said the word made it sound more like the

vilest of curses instead of the prospering city it was, but she ignored the outburst. "Roger and I *did* take the stage to Virginia City, Mr. Chandler. Before that we were on a cramped, smelly, dusty, dirty railroad car. And before *that—"*

"The stage runs right through Pony. You know that, right?"

"I was informed of such."

"Yeah? So why aren't you on it, Miss Lennox?"

Amanda shrugged, as though the reason wasn't important. But it was. Even now, she fumed over the incident that had happened almost two weeks before.

"Well?" Jake pressed impatiently.

"Roger hid the tickets."

Jake grumbled something under his breath. Since his tone was gruff, she presumed it was one of the graphic swears he seemed so fond of muttering. "Now, lady. Why aren't you on a stage *now?"*

She scowled. "I just told you. Roger hid the tickets. We missed the stage. Since I knew Pony wasn't too far away, and since the next stage wouldn't come through until the next morning, I rented two horses and . . . well, you know the rest."

She didn't add that she'd made the decision impulsively, and only because the thought of being shackled to Roger Thornton Bannister III for twenty-four hours longer than was necessary was more repellant to her than eating live worms. She'd wanted to unload the little monster on his father as soon as possible and be rid of him. She hadn't counted on getting lost in the thick, mountainous woods of Montana. No, she corrected herself with a mental shiver . . . *Idaho.*

"You rented horses?" Jake asked, and he rubbed a palm down his jaw as though he couldn't quite comprehend her reasoning.

"Oh, yes." She grinned brightly. "It seemed fitting, since Roger hates to ride. Do you have any more questions before we leave?" He *had* decided to help her, hadn't he? She eyed him closely. His chiseled copper face was as

46

readable as a stone, his steely gaze narrow and guarded. There was no deciphering him. He could be thinking almost anything.

"You rented horses," he muttered again, telling Amanda he hadn't gotten past that point in her story. "Jesus! I've never heard of anyone doing anything so pompous—not to mention hairbrained *stupid!*—in my life. Not knowing where you were going, or how to get there, you and the brat just put your noses in the air and rode right out of town. Then promptly got lost."

"We did *not* 'promptly get lost!' " Amanda wished her ankle didn't hurt so badly. She would have loved to show this man in deed, not words, how much his statement grated . . . because what he accused her of was exactly what had happened. Except for the 'promptly' part. It had taken two good hours after they'd left Virginia City for her to figure out they were hopelessly lost.

"How long have you been wandering around out here?"

"Three days," she lied. It was closer to two weeks. A technicality he didn't need to know about, she decided.

"Three days?" Jake gave a derisive snort and shook his head. There was no way she could have come so far in so short a time; which meant he'd just caught her in her first lie. "Yeah, I'd say you're lost all right. In good weather it's less than a day's ride between The Virgin and Pony."

"All right, so we got sidetracked," she admitted grudgingly, then promptly changed the subject. "I've answered your questions. Now, are you going to help me find Roger or aren't you? And if whoever took him left tracks, shouldn't we be out there following them before they get cold, or blow over, or do whatever it is hoof-prints do?"

We. Amanda thought it was the "we" that brought that sudden tension to his chiseled face and steely eyes. Her poor choice of words implied she assumed he would help. His tight expression said that Jacob Blackhawk Chandler didn't appreciate *anyone* assuming *anything* about him.

In the time it took Jake to make up his mind, Amanda, born with a gift for worrying had thought of countless thousands of hideous fates that might have befallen poor Roger. Each was more gruesome than the last. She didn't dare mention any of them to her stone-faced companion, since most involved bloodthirsty savages, razor-sharp knives, and unattached scalps . . .

Her gaze dropped to the sheathed knife cradled against his taut hip. She remembered the long blade, the metal as cold and as sharp as Jake Chandler's eyes. She thought of the way he'd expertly wielded the weapon, as though it was an extension of himself; something deadly, but precious all the same.

Didn't *real* Indian's carry knives like that one — and use them with the same degree of lethal accuracy? Yes, they did. And why hadn't she thought about that *before?* But Amanda knew why. Everything about him — his clothes, his speech, his attitude — had blinded her to his heritage. Until now. But facts were facts. This man was part Indian, part savage. He'd already proven his disposition to be more wild and dangerous than most, his temper easily leashed, but just as easily aroused.

Amanda called herself all sorts of a fool for offering the man money to help her. Obviously, the situation had clouded her judgment. But she was thinking clearly now . . . and what she was thinking was that spending time alone in this man's company might not be wise. Or healthy.

"I'm leaving," she said suddenly, and pushed awkwardly away from the tree. She hadn't thought it possible for her ankle to throb more than it already did. The second she put weight on it, she knew she was wrong. God, that hurt! Pain edged her voice, making her tone sharp. "With or without your help, Mr. Chandler, I am going to find my cousin."

All of her training at Miss Henry's Academy for Young Ladies was called upon to walk with dignity out of that clearing. Her ankle throbbed mightily, her temples ached from gritting her teeth. She was wet and chilly, and her damp skirt kept twisting around her legs, trying to trip her. A lady did not let such obstacles overcome her. A

48

lady was proud and dignified. A lady did not, even when provoked, say the words Amanda wanted so badly to say as soon as she was out of Jake's range of hearing.

What a lady thought, however, was her own business. Inwardly Amanda cursed him with a vengeance.

She hadn't convinced Jake to help her. She couldn't say she was surprised. From the first, he hadn't struck her as the type whose services could be bought — at any price, for any reason unless it was his own. Now that she thought about it, she'd probably offended him by offering the money in the first place.

Amanda was now left in the unpleasant position of having to find Roger herself. She would have laughed, had she seen anything to laugh about. There was nothing.

After taking a dry skirt and blouse from her saddle bag, she quickly changed, then scrambled atop the chestnut mare. Climbing into the saddle proved even easier than she'd hoped it would be. Following the tracks of whoever had taken Roger was going to be infinitely more difficult.

It was as she was studying the ground from her perch in the saddle, trying to decide what looked like hoofprints and what did not, that Amanda had the unsettling feeling of being watched. Closely. A tingle of . . . *something* raced up her spine and pricked the golden wisps at the nape of her neck. She stiffened, and her gaze snapped over her shoulder.

Jake Chandler was sitting astride a striking white palomino horse that, on closer inspection, had a handwoven blanket thrown over its back, but not the appropriate saddle. Despite the lack, his seat was straight and perfect.

Their gazes met and held. Green silently asked a question of granite-hard silver. Silver answered, reluctantly.

Amanda sat back in shock. Her head still reeling with surprise, she saw Jake reach up and — could it be? — politely tip his hat to her. So, she'd convinced him to help after all. Now why didn't she feel relieved?

"I'll warn you now, I'm no great tracker," he said as he leaned back and studied her. "You should know that up front."

"That's all right," she replied cautiously, "neither am I."

"And I'll want my money as soon as the brat's been found."

She nodded, still unable to believe she'd convinced him to help her; still not sure whether she should be glad she had. "Yes, of course."

"Once my job's over, once you have your cousin back, I ride out. No questions asked."

"All right."

He sighed, and crossed his hands over the white's sleek neck. "You'll do as I tell you, *when* I tell you to do it?"

"I . . ." Oh, why not? It was too late to stop lying now. "Yes."

"You won't argue or complain?"

"Rarely." Well, she thought it only fair to warn him about that. While she might be a coward, she wasn't meek and mild. When her hackles were raised, people knew it. Now that she thought about it, that was one of the reasons Miss Henry had politely asked her to leave the Academy — before the last term was over.

Jake nodded. "Good enough. Well, don't just sit there, princess. Come on. The tracks lead this way."

"But I thought you said you didn't . . . ?" Her mouth snapped shut. It was too late. Jake was already guiding his horse through the woods. If he'd heard her, he gave no sign.

Amanda reined in the mare, and, with a gentle flick of her wrist, began threading her way past the trees, following in Jake Chandler's wake.

Try as she might, she couldn't shake the feeling that she'd just made the biggest mistake of her life.

Chapter Three

It was an hour past dusk when Jake gave the signal to stop.

Amanda glanced at his upraised arm. Her cynical gaze snagged on the way he inclined his head and nodded to the small, moonswept, oval-shaped clearing bordered by pine trees, which their horses had just stepped into.

Apparently this was where he'd decided they would make camp for the night. Of course, she was just guessing about that. The only way to know for sure would be if he'd stopped to consult her about where *she* thought they should stop, and when. He hadn't. Jake had decided the matter for himself. And that annoyed her.

Her gaze narrowed as she glared at the back of that large copper hand. In one sweeping glance she assessed the arrogant set of his shoulders and the casual way his body swayed atop the glistening white horse he was reining in.

He pulled his mount to a stop, then slid lithely to the ground. Not once did he look and see if she was doing the same. In fact, he seemed to have forgotten her presence entirely as he led the white over to a low-hanging branch, looped the reins around it, then swaggered — not walked, *swaggered* — into the thick, rustling coat of underbrush.

Amanda glared at his back. She watched him saunter out of sight; if looks could wound, Jacob Blackhawk Chandler would have landed on his knees. Exactly where he belonged. The man's self-assured attitude said he never doubted she would obey him. His confidence irked her, and for a split second she entertained the idea of continuing on without him, just to defy him.

What would his reaction be when he came back to the clearing and found her gone? Would he be angry or, as seemed more likely, relieved to be rid of her? She wasn't sure. Nor was it likely she'd find out. The urge to spite him was overridden by another, stronger demand: the need for sleep.

She was exhausted. Worrying about what had happened to poor Roger—dear Lord, she was thinking nice thoughts about the little hellion again; she *must* be tired!—had given her a headache. Concern for the boy's safety, as well as her own should his father find out what happened, had tapped more of her energy than she would ever admit to the man who'd just rudely deserted her.

Shifting her weight in the saddle, she was quick to discover that her head wasn't the only thing that hurt. *Everything* hurt. Muscles she didn't know she possessed were sore from spending so many hours in the saddle. With Roger, she'd stopped often to rest. Jake Chandler didn't allow stops—they ate in their saddle. At least, *she* did; he didn't have a saddle. And he never seemed to tire.

Her ankle throbbed from the jostling of the chestnut mare beneath her. Waves of pain radiated up her leg, sliced through her hip and rippled higher. The ache was dulled only by the weariness through which she perceived it.

As much as she wanted to continue searching—the sooner she found Roger, the sooner she could deposit him on his father's doorstep and collect her fee—Amanda knew how pointless it would be to continue looking tonight. The tracks were vague in daylight; they would be impossible to see in the muted light of a quarter moon. Though it was embarrassing to admit, she knew that had they ridden on for even half a mile further, she would have fallen asleep in the saddle. Even now her eyelids felt weighted and scratchy as she forced herself to blink.

Stifling a yawn, she gave a tug on the reins and guided the mare close to Jake's palomino. The two horses, while not really at ease with each other, were at least familiar with each other's scent. Their protests at being forced into close proximity were weak and mostly for show. The soft whickers and stomping hooves halted soon enough.

Good. That was one less problem to deal with. Trying to dismount and still retain some dignity . . . now *that* was going to be a lesson in coordination! Her wounded ankle screamed a protest when Amanda lifted her right leg over the saddle horn and got ready to dismount. Just the idea of putting weight on that leg made her cringe.

Rotten bastard, she thought, and she glared at the shadowy spot where Jake had disappeared. Damn the man! He knew she was hurt. Would it be asking too much for him to stay long enough to help her dismount? Apparently so. He'd probably left the way he had for the sole purpose of forcing her to swallow her pride and call him back. In her sour disposition, she didn't put such underhanded treatment of a woman past a man like that.

Amanda's chin tipped defiantly. Well, if that *had* been his plan, he'd have a long wait. No matter what he thought, *she* knew she wasn't some elite "princess" who couldn't slide off a horse's back — wounded ankle or no wounded ankle. She would get down herself. Then, when Jake returned, she would gloat about her triumph — if she hadn't swooned from the pain by then, of course.

The idea of holding something over the man's black head to gloat about lifted Amanda's spirits somewhat. Now all that remained was trying to figure out how to get down. Her choices were limited. Actually, her choices were nonexistent. There was only one way to get off of a horse without assistance: slip off of the saddle and onto the ground.

Her seat was precarious. All the mare needed to do was sidestep and Amanda would tumble to the ground. That in mind, she tightened her fingers around the saddle horn. Her left hand curled around the grooved leather edge of the seat.

Pursing her lips, Amanda took a second to bolster herself for the collision of her feet hitting hard-packed earth. If she thought her ankle hurt badly now, it was nothing compared to how it would feel when she put weight on that leg.

"Do it." The shaky sound of her voice was less than comforting. "Just do it and get it over with." Amanda glanced down as she spoke. And instantly wished she hadn't. The pain must be distorting her perception, because the ground looked unnaturally far off. It also looked hard and cold. Unwelcoming.

The horses must have sensed her tension. The white's nose came up, the wide nostrils flaring as the stallion snorted, then sniffed the air. She felt the mare tense, a split second before it also snorted . . . and took a panicky step away from the white.

The world tilted.

The saddle melted out from under her. Amanda wasn't quick enough to stop herself from sliding. With a strangled cry, she flung her hands outward, ready to break the inevitable fall.

There was a racket to her left, but she had no time to look to see what it was. The ground was closing in fast.

Rescue came in the form of familiar copper hands. Strong arms encircled her thighs, tightening possessively. Before she could draw a breath, she felt the front of her hips being crushed against Jake Chandler's unyielding chest.

Their position was awkward. He'd been quick to catch her; perhaps a mite too quick. She'd barely left the saddle before he'd hauled her up against him.

She could feel the shelf of his shoulder cutting into her stomach. The hand she'd thrown out to steady herself was now trapped between his shoulder and her hipbone. The heel of her right fist ground into his other shoulder. Muscles bunched beneath his shirt as he took on her weight easily, realigning her body and molding her into the firm planes of his.

The sound of crickets chirping receded to the chaotic beat of Amanda's heart slamming against her ribs. She sucked in a gasp. The pain in her ankle dulled until it felt like nothing so much as a harmless mosquito bite. It took an extraordinary amount of concentration, but she forced her breathing to regulate. Instead of deep, ragged gulps, she sucked in shallow, rapid ones. Her heart continued to race, pounding an erratic beat in her ears.

Distance. She needed distance, and a lot of it! Arching her back, Amanda put enough space between them to glance down at the top of Jake's head. She thought it was a good thing he was holding her right then, because otherwise she might have collapsed. Her knees went weak and watery.

His hair, only a few tantalizing inches away, was cast an appealing shade of silvery-black by the moonlight. There was no part, she noticed. The strands fell where they might; and the tousled way they did it was quite eye-catching.

Her fingers curled inward. She bunched his cottony shirt in her fists, fighting the urge to pry her fingers loose so she could bury them in that luxuriously dark mane. Would his hair feel as soft and sleek as it looked? And how would that defiant braid feel when she traced it with her fingertips? Amanda decided she must be more exhausted than she'd thought, because she was warring with an unreasonably strong urge to find out. Lord, what was wrong with her?

Jake stiffened. Invisible currents charged what little air separated them. The night crackled like static. A bolt of awareness jolted through him wherever their bodies met — and their bodies met *everywhere!* The contact made his skin smolder.

He felt Amanda tremble. With confusion? With fear? He didn't know. Nor did wondering about it stop him from tightening his hold on her or from absorbing her minuscule tremors with his body.

She was still afraid of him, he knew. She should be. Jesus, he'd given her every reason to be terrified. But this was different. Experience said that what Amanda Lennox was feeling right now had nothing to do with stewing about how explosive his temper would be when it finally erupted and was turned on her. Nor did it stem from her natural wariness of his half-breed origins. Oh no, the uneasiness shivering through her was rooted solely in sexual awareness. The awakening of dormant, innocent senses. Jake was sure of it.

A slow, humorless grin tugged at one corner of his mouth. He would have bet his horse that Amanda Lennox didn't have a clue as to what was making her shake so violently.

Jake tipped his head back. He opened his mouth to ask her exactly that. His mouth snapped shut. The words scattered on his tongue like so much dust when he realized how precarious their position really was.

He held her to him, but above. The back of her thighs were firm and round beneath his palms, her stomach soft and tight as it pressed into his right shoulder. That didn't bother him. Oh, no. What bothered him was that, holding her this way, craning his neck to look up at her, put his mouth mere inches from . . .

Jake closed his eyes and prayed his mind would instantly shut down, that he would stop feeling anything, anything at all. It would be better, safer for both of them if he did. But his mind had other ideas. His mind was busy entertaining naughty thoughts, while his body continued to feel every delectable inch of Amanda Lennox's softness . . . whether he wanted to or not.

When he'd caught her to him, the rounded swell of her breasts had cushioned his cheek like a soft, voluptuous pillow — no doubt the reason she'd arched away from him. His eyes opened, his gaze darkened, and his lips burned when his attention fixed on the very tips of her breasts. They heaved with each of her choppy breaths, only a scant fraction of an inch away from his mouth. He had only to incline his head forward to . . .

Clamping his teeth together, he jerked his head back on his neck so hard he felt it crick. There was *no* jerking away from the delicious, petal-sweet smell of her; her scent surrounded him, engulfed him, ignited a desire in his gut the likes of which he'd never felt before and dearly wished he'd never, *ever* feel again; it was that strong.

His sudden movement made the sweep of his hair tickle the back of Amanda's knuckles. Dazed, she thought that, yes, his hair felt every bit as silky as it appeared. She'd wondered, now she knew. Wonderful. That was how his hair felt as it dragged over her hot, sensitive flesh.

An involuntary shudder rippled through her. It was answered by a tightening in the arms clamped around her thighs.

Their gazes met.

"Y-you can put me down now," she stammered. It was embarrassing to be the first to look away, but it couldn't be helped. The way Jake was looking at her — his steely gaze deep and probing, as though he was seeing her for the very first time, and liked what he saw very much — made Amanda's stomach feel all warm and . . . well, fluttery. The sensation was deep, disturbing only in that it wasn't disturbing enough. In fact, it was dreadfully pleasant. "Really. I'm quite all right."

"What about your ankle?"

It was on the tip of her tongue to point out that he hadn't given a fig five minutes ago, when he'd wandered off and left her to her own devices, how her ankle was faring. A stroke of wisdom made her bite the words back. Amanda didn't doubt such a comment would rile his anger and instigate another argument. Truly, she was too tired, too jittery, and far too confused to fight with him right now.

Her gaze swept over Jake. His expression was hard and impassive. The muscle in his cheek had begun to twitch. Amanda wondered why, then decided she'd be better off not knowing. She said simply, "I think I can walk."

"You're sure?" he asked, and shifted to redistribute her

57

weight. He almost smiled when he heard her soft, airy groan. "Your knees aren't feeling watery, are they, princess? They won't buckle the second your feet hit the ground?"

"Probab—*definitely* not," she insisted, and wondered how he could read her so easily. Weak and watery was exactly the way her knees felt. The way her *entire body* felt. That, and very warm, very aware of the hard male contours pressing against her.

Amanda pushed *that* observation aside, and tried to pull her abruptly scattered thoughts into logical order. It wasn't possible. The only thing her mind was capable of thinking about right now was the subtle change in the way Jake Chandler was holding her. Now only one of his arms was coiled around her thighs, while his free hand had blazed a path upward. The palm of that hand was cupping the small of her back. No, she amended swiftly, not the small of her back . . . his hand had settled on the upper swell of her bottom! Even through her skirt and the layers of linen beneath, she could feel the hot, branding imprint of his hand searing her flesh. It was sensation comparable to none. The hot flood of awareness that surged through her sent Amanda's proper Bostonian senses into a tailspin.

"Unhand me, Mr. Chandler," she demanded, her voice husky and sharp with the panic bubbling up inside of her. "I told you I could walk, now *let me down.*"

"Not yet."

"Why not?!"

His pause was long and fraught with a tension that gnawed at Amanda from the inside out. Her fingers tightened, clutching his shirt until her knuckles hurt from the pressure of her grip.

He didn't speak for so long that she'd convinced herself he wasn't going to. His voice, when it came, was so close his hot breath rustled the curls lying softly against her cheek. She started.

"I don't know about you, princess, but right now I'm just enjoying the view." His tone was as lazy and insolent as the silver gaze scanning her anger-reddened face. One corner of his mouth kicked up in a half-grin. His gaze dipped, searing first her lips, then the long, elegant taper of her creamy white throat. His attention settled on the swell of her breasts.

The look in his eyes was sheer fire. Amanda was surprised the cloth separating her skin from his hungry gaze didn't burn away. Lord knows, the flesh beneath her bodice felt as though *it* was smoldering!

Her breath hitched. Her eyes widened. Jake's finely carved face hovered a mere inch from the ultrasensitive tips of her breasts. She closed her eyes, trying to will back just a sliver of sanity. It was a mistake, she realized too late. Shutting her eyes honed her other senses to a finer pitch. She could actually *feel* each hot wash of his breath sluicing over her—seeping through her bodice, seeping through her skin!

Her skin tingled and burned. So did her cheeks when, to her mortification, she felt her nipples pearl against the confining chemise. Was it her imagination, or did her breasts feel fuller and heavier, her nipples stiff and sensitive? No, that wasn't her imagination. Her imagination wasn't *that* good! She felt the rosy crests straining against the linen and cotton as though seeking on their own the hot, moist promise of his mouth.

Her eyes snapped open, and her gaze fixed on the sensuous line of Jake Chandler's lips. The tip of his tongue darted out to wet just the lower one. It was a provocative gesture in itself, made more provocative by the way his attention never strayed from her breasts. His gaze was intent. His eyes burned out of his copper face, out of the shadows of the night. His expression said that similar thoughts had lodged in his own mind.

Amanda felt as if a herd of butterflies had gathered in her belly, clamoring to break free. And that was exactly what she should be doing, she decided instantly. Yes, freedom was what she needed. Perhaps without her body absorbing this man's body heat, without his scent enticing her nostrils, without his steely muscles pressing against her, she'd be able to put a logical thought together. Maybe then sanity would return.

On impulse, she piled her fists atop his shoulders and shoved, hard, arching her back until her spine ached. Either she'd taken him by surprise, or he'd also decided they could use some distance. Whatever the reason, his arms shifted.

Supporting her weight with his elbows and forearms, his fingers coiled around her upper arms. Holding her gaze ensnared, he slowly, *slowly* slid her down the hard length of his body.

Amanda felt her thighs drag against his hips. Her pelvis was acutely aware of every hard band of muscle in his thighs. The tips of her breasts hardened still more when a rock-solid chest rubbed intimately against her.

She turned her head, trying to hide her confusion, but not before she felt the copper velvet of his cheek graze her lips. The feel was like a bolt of lightning coursing through her. Raw sensation shot through her blood, and her toes curled inside her shoes.

The second her feet touched the ground, Amanda winced and rationed her weight onto her left foot. Jake hadn't released her arms, and she was unnaturally grateful for that. His grip was the only thing that kept her upright.

"You okay?"

"Ummm-hmmm, fine," she lied. Somehow, she managed to force a note of confidence into her voice. Odd, she didn't feel very confident right now. In fact, she felt . . . well, damn peculiar, *that's* how she felt! Her gaze fixed on the feather interwoven at the tip of his braid. It lay against his chest, lifting and falling with his every ragged breath.

"Then you won't mind if I let you go?" he asked. Was it her imagination, or was his drawl not so casual anymore?

"Not at all, Mr. Chandler. In fact, I insist upon it."

"Ever the lady, ain't ya, princess?"

"I try to be. Will you please unhand me now?"

"Sure, since you asked so nicely and all . . ." One by

one, his fingers unpeeled from her arms. When he'd broken the grip, he let his hands fall limply to his sides. He didn't step away. His body was still close enough for her to feel, and react to, his searing heat.

They stood that way for one tense moment. Jake let her remain wrapped in her thoughts, mostly because he couldn't shake himself from his own long enough to distract her. What the hell had just happened here? Nothing extraordinary, he assured himself. Something *very* extraordinary, another part of himself argued. No, not really, he insisted.

Dammit, what *had* happened? He'd saved her from falling. It was that simple. He'd noticed the nice way her body was put together. Not so simple — not by half! — but normal for any healthy, red-blooded male. Then she'd moved, pressing herself so close he could feel her heart skipping. And out of nowhere . . . *bam!* Jesus, he'd never felt attraction that quick and strong in his life!

Jake sighed, and dragged a palm down his jaw. He had to get his thoughts back on track. The best way to do that would be to get away from the woman who was causing them to stray. "You hungry?"

Amanda forced a shrug, and eyed him closely. Judging from his expression — granite hard and stoic, as always — she was the only one who'd felt that sizzle of awareness when they'd touched. If Jake had felt it at all, it didn't show. He appeared oh, so calm. Oh so casual. Well, she decided, if *he* could act as if nothing had happened, surely she could do the same. Her gaze strayed back to his flat metal buttons. This time she forced it to stay there. "Yes, a bit. You?"

"Famished."

He wasn't talking about food. Amanda knew it. The information shivered through her, even as her attention snapped up. Their gazes met and held. Absolutely no emotion could be read in either his eyes or his expression, and that annoyed her.

"I have some jerky and beans in my saddlebag," she said tightly, and she limped back a step. A chilly breeze

61

whisked over her. Though the night was cool, the air felt unnaturally brisk. She wrapped her arms around her waist, trying to hold in some of her body heat. "I think I have enough coffee left for one more pot. You're welcome to share it."

His shrug was negligent, as though he really didn't care. "Fine by me. So long as you're not the one making it."

Amanda took offense. "I brew a decent pot of coffee, Mr. Chandler," she argued. The way he continually ordered her about was beginning to grate on her nerves.

"Yeah, princess, I'm sure you do. I was just thinking of what happened the last time you waded into a river for water." His grin was slow and wicked. The sight of it made her heart palpitate. "Then again . . ."

His gaze seared her from the top of her head, down to the arms she clasped at her waist. She had a feeling he was thinking more of the way her wet skirt and blouse had clung to her body, and *not* the foot he had freed from the sunken tree trunk.

Amanda swallowed hard. Her reaction was not so much from his gaze — though that was certainly a part of it — a *large* part of it — but from the memory of his calloused fingertips and the way he'd boldly explored the wet, slippery curves of her legs. Her skin still burned from the intimacy of his touch, even though it was nothing more than a disturbing memory now. She had an uneasy feeling that she wouldn't be forgetting the branding feel of his hands on her anytime soon.

"I'll get the food," she said, and turned away from him.

She hobbled over to the horses with as much dignity as a tired, limping woman could. The cinch strap on the mare's saddle had worked itself tight. It took effort to pry it loose. Her trembling fingers made the chore take longer than it should have.

Jake, in the meantime, retrieved his coffee pot from the possessions he'd rolled up in the saddle-blanket strapped to the white. Her own coffee pot had, of course, been lost to the river that morning.

"You start the fire while I'm gone," he said, sparing Amanda only one quick, piercing gaze before he pivoted on his heel and again disappeared into the thick covering of underbrush.

Amanda listened for the rustle of leaves or snap of twigs that would mark his leaving, but wasn't surprised when she didn't hear any. She hadn't heard him approach before he'd caught her falling off the horse either, but that didn't seem to mean anything. The man was quick, agile, and as silent as a cat.

Though the observation was unnerving, it did help soothe her conscience. It proved her decision to hire Jake Chandler had been a good one. If anyone could find Roger, that person was Jake. He was strong, mentally and physically. His judgment was sound, even if his sense of honor was warped. Make that nonexistent; the man *had* no sense of honor that she'd seen. Though he was, by his own admission, not the world's best tracker, he hadn't lost the trail yet, which meant he wasn't bad either.

She hoisted the saddle off the mare and let it thump to the ground near her feet. When she turned, her gaze fixed on a small stack of firewood scattered sloppily in the center of the clearing. She remembered the clatter of noise just before Jake had caught her. One golden brow arched in contemplation.

Amanda studied the twigs and branches as though they were the most amusing thing she'd ever seen. Hadn't she told Jake she was out of matches? If not, she'd certainly meant to.

Arm over arm, Jake's body sliced through the river. The mountain-fed water felt like a sheet of ice lapping at his skin. Bitter cold and invigorating, it was exactly what he needed. Pity it didn't cool off his thoughts a damn bit.

The turn of his mind was red-hot. The object of his attention? The curve of a certain snobby Bostonian princess's breasts . . . and the more than enticing way she'd felt when he'd dragged her soft, slender body down his length.

63

Lowering Amanda Lennox to her feet like that hadn't been the smartest thing Jake had ever done. At the time it had seemed like a good idea. He'd been bitten by the urge to find out what her luscious curves would feel like sliding against his hardness. Now he knew. In retrospect, it was something he could have lived happily without ever having learned. But it was too late now.

Plain and simple, the woman made him hot. And she did it so quickly and thoroughly, so *effortlessly,* that it staggered him. Even after a brisk swim in a river fed by mountain water so cold it numbed and puckered his skin, Jake couldn't stop thinking about her. Fantasizing about her. His blood still boiled, his gut still churned, and his . . .

Jesus, he was hot for her still!

That knowledge hit him like a fist to the gut. It drove him to double the already furious pace of his arms and legs. The frigid water wasn't working the way it was supposed to. It didn't cool either his body or his mind. It sure as hell didn't diminish the throbbing ache in his groin. Tonight, his body had a mind all its own, and swimming in an ice-cold river wasn't what it wanted.

What it — *he* — wanted was Amanda Lennox. He wanted her soft and willing . . . as hot and as hungry for him as he was for her.

In other words, he wanted what he couldn't have.

Ever.

Soft and willing or hard and fighting, it didn't matter. He couldn't have her. Not Amanda Lennox. Not tonight, not any night. The memory of her creamy white skin and the way it glowed like expensive porcelain in the moonlight told him why. The sight of his own copper flesh as he stopped swimming and waded to where the water was only waist-deep confirmed it.

Amanda Lennox was white. Worse, she was a society snob, born and bred. A — shudder — lady to the core, she was off-limits to a filthy half-breed like himself. It didn't matter that he'd been raised white. It didn't matter that his only memories of his mother's tribe — hell, of his *mother,* for that matter — were so vague they were virtually nonexistent. The white man's blood pumping through his veins mingled with the blood of a savage. And *that,* when it came right down to it, was all that mattered to white people. All white people.

Amanda Lennox was no different. And why the hell did that knowledge disturb him so damn much? Why did *she* disturb him? He didn't know, but she did. There was something about her, something illusive and indefinable, that made him hungry. That made him remember things best forgotten.

Jake had never been one to put stock in memories. In his life, there had been few incidents worth reflecting on for more than a passing second or two. Even those fleeting recollections weren't greeted fondly. This time was no exception.

He'd been twelve years old the first time he'd realized he was different. Oh, he'd known it before then, sure, but no one on his father's spread had dared to come right out and say it, so he'd never thought it mattered. His innocence came to an end the night the foreman's son had cornered him out behind the barn.

Stuart Price. The name twisted through Jake's mind, bringing the familiar ugly face, the familiar surge of hatred.

Price had made it clear that it was high time the little red-skinned boy learned his place. Jake's place, he'd found out shortly, was face-down in the rich Montana soil — if not buried six feet beneath it. Price said he'd decided that Jake's weekly visits to their white neighbor's daughter were not proper, and would no longer be tolerated . . . just before the brawny fourteen year old had planted his beefy fist in Jake's face and broken his nose.

Jake had learned a lot of things that night. The first was just how nasty the word "breed" could be snarled. The second was that a white boy was never, *ever* to be trusted. The third, and most important, was that if he was going to survive in this life, he'd better learn to use his fists — because there was a whole world of Stuart

65

Prices out there, and he was damn well going to need to know how to fight.

Jake shook his head and scowled, his palm absently rubbing the back of his still-damp neck. He hadn't been a good fighter back then. Oh hell, who was he kidding? He hadn't been any kind of fighter. His father was a big bear of a man who, because of his size, had never needed to use his fists. Whether by intent or neglect, Yancy Chandler had never taught Jake how to protect himself. After the night Stuart Price had beaten him to a bloody pulp, Jake had learned to fight back. Damn straight, he had! In fact, as with everything else, he'd taught himself.

Prejudice. *That* was the lesson he'd started to learn that moonlit night behind the barn. In the years since, more lessons had followed. Most had the same theme; stay away from white girls. It was a hard lesson for Jake to learn, but learn it he had . . . years after his encounter with Price was only a bitter-tasting memory. He'd learned how to survive the way he learned everything: the hard way. His body and mind still bore the scars of his last, and final lesson. That was the message that had really hammered the point home. It wasn't an experience Jake cared to repeat. Ever.

Therefore, it wasn't surprising that bedding a white lady hadn't entered his mind in years. What *was* surprising—damn surprising—was that it had not only entered his mind tonight, it had planted itself there. Somewhere between setting Amanda Lennox on her feet, and plunging his naked body into the snow-fed river, the idea of touching her—*really* touching her—*everywhere*—had taken root. Neither his head or body seemed willing to shake the notion loose.

Damn that woman, Jake swore inwardly, as he plowed his long wet hair back from his face. *Damn her for making me remember. Damn her for making me want her!*

Muttering a savage curse beneath his breath, he swaggered out of the river. With brisk strokes, he toweled the water off his body with his shirt, then yanked on his pants. His fingers were cold, numb, and water-wrinkled as he worked the wedge of buttons closed.

It was as he bent at the waist, his hand poised on his belt, that he heard the noise. It wasn't much, really; just a faint rustle of leaves and the soft snap of a twig. Had his nerves not already been on edge, he wouldn't have noticed the sound.

But his nerves *were* on edge. And he *did* notice.

Lightning quick, he straightened. By the time his gaze snapped over his shoulder — a scant heartbeat later — the leather sheath had been relieved of its knife. The wooden hilt warmed to his palm as his gaze narrowed, scanning the trees. He held the blade close to his waist, his knees bent slightly to put him in optimum striking position. He studied each thick tree trunk, waiting for a shadow to disengage itself.

When none did, he scowled. Was he hearing things? Jumping at shadows? Was *that* what entertaining dirty thoughts about Amanda Lennox's tempting white body did to him? He'd rather not think so, but it was possible. God knows, the memory of her sweet curves would distract a saint. And nothing was moving out there. Nothing at all.

The hair at his nape prickled, telling him what his sight did not. Someone *was* out there. And whoever was out there was watching him. Closely.

Again, his gaze scanned the area. This time he noticed something he hadn't seen before. Or that hadn't *been* there before. It was just a speck of color, a splash of blue and yellow down by the base of one of the trees. He squinted, barely able to make it out in the muted moonlight filtering down through the leaves. But he saw enough. He knew who the intruder was.

Jake's grip on the knife loosened, and his hand dropped to his side. "You can come out now, princess," he growled impatiently. "The show's over."

Leaves rustled. More twigs snapped. The splash of blue and yellow grew, melting into the shape of a skirt. More of her came into view when she pushed herself away from the tree she'd been hiding behind.

Jake thought her stance looked unnaturally stiff as she limped into the clearing, cradling a small tin pan to her chest like it was a protective shield. The color in her cheeks was high, the flush enhanced by the moonlight. Against his will, he found himself admiring the way she kept her chin tilted proudly, her shoulders squared, her back priggishly straight — as if her spine were molded out of uncompromising iron.

Amanda pursed her lips, and met Jake's amused gaze with a boldness that astonished them both. But not half as much as her words did.

"Pity, Mr. Chandler," she said, her voice cool and composed, dripping with dignity. "It wasn't a very good show."

Chapter Four

While Amanda heard the words, she found it hard to believe she'd actually had the gall to say them. *Not a very good show?* Was she losing her mind? *No* price was too steep to pay for the privilege of watching Jacob Blackhawk Chandler step naked and proud out of that moonlit river.

The man was magnificent. Raw and rugged. Coppery and firm. Wet. The way he'd strolled onto the bank had given a new connotation to the word *swagger.* He hadn't seemed inhibited by his nakedness. If anything, his carriage suggested a man who owned the night and everything in it. His stance was arrow straight, his shoulders squared at a proud angle that only enhanced the smooth wedge of his chest and his lean, firm hips.

The moonlight glinted off his hair, making the long, damp strands gleam an appealing shade of silver-black. The way the muted light sparkled off the beads of water clinging to his skin . . . well, that was indecent. And fascinating beyond reason.

A proper lady would have gasped, blushed, and beat a hasty retreat. Not necessarily in that order. Amanda thought it a pity all three options were, at the moment, unavailable to her. She couldn't gasp — she had no breath for it — and her feet felt as though they were encased in lead, making it impossible for her to leave. Even if she could have coaxed herself to move, there was no guarantee her knees would support her. Try though she did, she couldn't tear her gaze from his lean, half-naked body.

Jake Chandler swimming naked had been the *last* thing Amanda had expected to see when she'd set out to discover why he hadn't returned to camp. In a way that was typically her own, she'd thought to find him lying in the bushes somewhere, his beautiful carcass mauled by wild animals.

His beautiful carcass, she was both pleased and alarmed to see, was perfectly fit. Every inch of him looked robust and healthy. Her concern about what had happened to him had died a quick, painless death when she'd reached the trees bordering the river . . . heard the splashes . . . saw him swimming . . . and noticed he wasn't wearing a stitch beneath all that icy water.

That was when her knees had turned to mush. They still trembled beneath her skirt. Would the sight of him ever fade from her mind? Amanda rather doubted it. More likely, the image was engraved in her memory; she had an uneasy feeling it would linger there until the day she died.

Clearing her throat, Amanda forced her wayward thoughts to take an abrupt turn. Reminding herself that the man was still half-naked wasn't difficult at all, since her mind had never really strayed from that fact.

He was also, she realized abruptly, standing much closer to her. When had he moved? Why hadn't she noticed? Amanda didn't know, and there was no time to figure it out. Right now she was having a devil of a time trying to shift her gaze from the beads of water he hadn't mopped away. The drops glistened like silver crystals against the firm copper of his shoulder. Her fingers curled around the pan. It took effort to resist the urge to reach out and rub those droplets into her tingling fingertips.

"I don't suggest you keep staring at me like that, princess. A man is apt to take that look in your eyes as a challenge to put on a better show. One a properly bred . . . *lady* isn't likely to forget." Jake grinned as, with the crook of his index finger, he snapped her gaping mouth shut. "Correct me if I'm wrong, but I don't think that's what you want." One inky brow slanted high. His hand turned inward, and she shivered when his palm scorched her oddly sensitive chin. "Or is it?"

"What I *want*, Mr. Chandler, is for you to stop touching me."

"Why? Does it bother you?"

Amanda craned her neck, trying to break the contact. She might as well not have bothered. Jake's hand tracked her. His fingertips felt hot and moist, branding her skin as he cupped the base of her neck. His thumb feathered the spot where her pulse hammered.

Clearing her throat, Amanda forced her voice to sound firm and steady; everything her insides were not. "Let's just say it . . . *annoys* me."

Jake angled his head, and a lock of hair skated over his bare shoulder. The sleek black strands absorbed the beads of water clinging to his skin. When he didn't say anything, her gaze lifted. His eyes sparkled in the moonlight. His grin broadened, as though he was satisfied he finally had her full attention. With him standing there half-naked, there was never really a doubt of that!

"Annoys," he drawled, his tone deceptively lazy, "as in the way an itch that needs scratching would annoy you? Or annoys . . . as in rankles the hell out of you but you don't know why?"

His voice was low and husky, a velvet caress tickling her ears. His breath smoldered over her upturned cheeks. Amanda shivered and decided the man was too sexually magnetic for both their good. It took concentration to push the observation aside. Overlooking her disturbing reaction to him was not so easy, but she managed. She couldn't let her mind or body be swayed by his blatant appeal. It wouldn't safe. No, no, not safe at all!

71

"Which is it, Miss Lennox? What is it about me that . . . *annoys* you?"

Amanda feigned an exasperated sigh, and mentally counted to ten. It didn't help. Her annoyance remained hot inside her; it was only a degree cooler than her unexpected fascination with Jake Chandler. It was a fascination that, in her mind, had roots based in insanity. Obviously, she was losing her mind. That was the only way to explain why the sound of his voice and the touch of his hand caused her heart to skip and her blood to simmer. She was going crazy, and that was that.

"Maybe I should answer the question for you . . . since you seem to be having trouble finding your tongue."

The words broke the spell he'd woven around her. Amanda snapped back to her senses. Hugging the pan tightly, she glared at him. Not for the first time was she relieved that their height was comparable, that she wasn't forced to look up at him. "Is this conversation leading somewhere, Mr. Chandler?"

"Could be." His shrug was casual. The way his thumb traced her pulse, still throbbing against his fingertip, was not. The feel of his calloused skin abrading her sensitive flesh sent tiny quivers bolting down Amanda's spine. "Why did you come down here, princess?"

Ah, she'd wondered when he would get around to asking about that. Did the egotistical cad think she'd come to get a glimpse of his naked body? Ha! Nothing could be further from the truth. Seeing him wet and naked had been an unexpected bonus. Of course, she wasn't about to tell *him* that!

This time when she pulled back, Jake let her go. His hand dropped reluctantly to his side.

Amanda took an awkward step back, and as the cool evening air rushed between them, she felt a nice, calming sliver of sanity return. At least with some distance separating them she could think *almost* rationally. Now, if she could convince Jake to put a shirt on, she'd be all set! The sight of his chest—with its complex cords of muscle and touchably smooth copper skin—was a distraction she could have lived without.

"I wanted a bath," she said suddenly. The half-truth sounded pitifully lame.

The way his brows arched said Jake agreed. His gaze dipped to the pan, and a ghost of a grin tugged at his lips. "In that? Think you'll fit?"

"Fit?"

"Yeah, 'fit'. I mean, let's face it." His gaze lifted, lingering on the swell of her breasts. His steely eyes smoldered. "You aren't exactly what I'd call scrawny."

Amanda bristled. "Are you insulting me?"

"Hell, no. That was a compliment. I don't like my women scrawny."

"Your women? *Your* women?" Her eyes widened; the green depths spit fire. "I am *not* your woman, Mr. Chandler. Nor will I ever be. I have better taste than that. Now, if you'll step aside I can get my water and be out of your way."

"You're not in my way."

"Maybe not. But *you* are in *mine!*"

"So go around me," he said, and didn't move.

Amanda gritted her teeth. Her temples throbbed a protest. It took effort not to reach up and massage the ache away. The only thing stopping her was knowing that Jake would take it as a sign of weakness. A normal man wouldn't have; a headache was, after all, a negligible complaint. But this man wasn't anyone's idea of "normal." No doubt the arrogant beast would take pride in thinking he'd riled her enough to make her head pound. Amanda refused to give him that kind of satisfaction.

Go around, he'd told her. Fine. This once, if it meant getting her precious water and getting away from the confusion this man stirred in her, Amanda would do as

73

he requested and do it quickly. Putting weight on her injured ankle wasn't pleasant. She countered the pain by telling herself she would soon be back at camp, warmed by a crackling fire, sponging the dirt and sweat from her body. And soon after *that,* she would be asleep — and for a little while at least, blessedly unaware of Jake Chandler.

Stepping haughtily around him, Amanda limped over to the icy, churning river. She knelt on the sandy bank and dipped the pan into the water. It was a small pan; the amount of water she scooped up was miserly. It was as she was noticing this fact that Jake's previous words burned past her cloud of anger.

Think you'll fit?

He'd meant, of course, would *she* fit into the pan. She knew that now, knew also that he'd been making a joke. Amanda frowned. Jake didn't strike her as the type who made jokes. Hadn't he admitted as much? So why had he? Why, indeed. She had a feeling the observation was important, though she wasn't sure why. Filing the information away — there would be time to consider what it meant later, when she was alone — Amanda pushed awkwardly to her feet, and turned.

Jake was standing behind her. Amanda saw him, in the same instant she collided with the smooth, hard wall of his chest. Water sloshed from the pan when she stumbled backward.

His fingers coiled around her upper arms, his grip firm yet at the same time oddly gentle. She wondered if saving her from a plunge in the frigid river was his only reason for touching her. Something — the look in his eyes, perhaps? — told her it had been a convenient excuse.

"Mr. Chandler, please," she snapped, trying to shrug from his grip. Why oh, *why* couldn't she think straight when this man touched her? Why . . . ? Oh no, her knees were going weak again. And she was beginning to shake — again.

"Please what?" he asked, and she thought his tone sounded frustratingly calm.

"Please unhand me."

He shook his head. Amanda refused to notice the way the small brown feather, buried in a bed of long black hair, grazed his chest. "Not yet. We've got something to settle first, princess. And the sooner we do it, the better."

She scowled. *Now* what was he talking about? And did she really want to stay here long enough to find out? No, she did not. Of course, his grip on her arms said he wasn't giving her a choice. "Couldn't it wait until morning? I'm tired and my ankle is throbbing. All I want is to wash off some of this dirt and get a little sleep."

"I know," he replied dryly. "Problem is, I want this settled now."

Her gaze narrowed and sharpened. "And you always get what you want. Isn't that right, Mr. Chandler?"

"Always. You'd do well to remember that, Miss Lennox." His hands blazed slow, hot paths down her arms. One by one, his fingers curled inward, manacling her wrists.

At five foot six, Amanda wasn't exactly short. At one hundred and fifteen perfectly proportioned pounds, she was slender but doubted anyone would consider her delicate. Herself included. So why, for the first time in her life, was she feeling tiny and frail? Feminine? Vulnerable? She didn't know, and she didn't like it. It was an unsettling feeling. "I won't have to, since you'll no doubt remind me often enough."

"No doubt. Have a seat." He gave a tug on her wrists.

Amanda, planning to refuse, shifted her weight. Her ankle spasmed with pain. A gasp hissed though her teeth at the same time her knees, already watery from his touch, buckled. The ground felt hard when her tender bottom slammed atop it.

"Is such manhandling necessary?" she snapped, and

yanked her skirt hem primly down around her ankles. She couldn't resist chafing away the lingering feel of him on her wrists. Even though he'd let her go, the skin there still burned with the imprint of his fingers.

"Probably not. But what the hell? It works."

Since she'd trained her gaze on the river gurgling in front of her, Amanda felt rather than saw Jake crouch on the ground beside her. *Closely* beside her. The heat of his leg seared her upper arm. Beneath the scant barrier of her sleeve, her flesh sizzled with awareness.

A tense moment ticked past. Amanda concentrated on the sound the river made as it lapped against the sandy bank. She told herself she wasn't aware of the way Jake Chandler's steady breath cut through the chilly night air. Or the feel of it puffing over her too-sensitive cheek and neck. But she was.

She sighed in resignation. "All right, Mr. Chandler," she said slowly, cautiously, "I'm listening. What do you want?" Glancing to the side, she saw a sly grin curl over his lips. His steely gaze darkened with innuendo. Her stomach sank. She sucked in a shaky breath and quickly looked back out over the water. "What I mean is, what do you want to *talk* to me about?"

Jake plucked a long stalk of grass from the ground. He took his time clamping it between his teeth, rolling it from one side of his mouth to the other with his tongue, knowing he was prolonging her agony.

The grass tasted crisp and sweet. His gaze settled on Amanda Lennox's lips, and he wondered if her mouth would taste as good. He knew it would. Her lips would be soft and honey-sweet, her gasps of surrender hot and airy. The inside of her mouth would be warm and moist and tasty; a flavor that was to die for. Jake could already feel a sliver of his soul die with the need to prove the theory.

His voice turned gruff. "Did I say I wanted to talk?"

"Yes, you—" Amanda's mouth snapped closed. No, now that he mentioned it, he'd said he wanted to "settle"

76

something between them. He'd never said he wanted to do it verbally. She'd simply *assumed* . . .

Amanda detoured her thoughts onto a safer path. She concentrated on the ankle that was throbbing mightily, on the pounding in her temples that refused to dull. She was exhausted, every muscle in her body ached. The nearly empty pan she clutched tightly in her fist reminded her of her previous goal: a hot sponge bath and a good night's sleep. She did *not* want to sit here exchanging riddles with this man all night. Perhaps a determined glare would make him explain himself more clearly?

It didn't. Instead, Jake cushioned his elbows atop the shelf of his rock-solid thighs and leaned slightly toward her.

Amanda did *not* notice the way his shoulder muscles flexed with the movement. Nor did she see the stretch of smooth copper skin hugging his chest, arms, and taut, taut belly. It took effort, but she ignored the sinewy thighs on which his upper body weight was balanced. Of course she did. A properly bred young lady like herself would *never* notice such things.

She tore her gaze from him, but her attention wasn't allowed to waver long. The crook of his index finger hooked beneath her chin, and dragged it right back.

Jake turned his head and spit out the stalk of grass. His gaze never left her huge green eyes. "You've got two choices, princess. Either we get this over with, end the suspense here and now, or I'll be gone come morning. Without you."

"Are you threatening me? Might I remind you, sir, that I'm paying you very good money for your—er—services."

"Go ahead. Then *I'll* remind *you* that I don't have any of that 'good money' warming my pocket yet, do I?" He leaned forward. Just another inch. Just enough to put his chest into searing contact with her shoulder. "Know what I think?" She shook her head. "I think there's a

77

reason for that. In fact, I'm starting to think that maybe you don't have any money to pay me with."

"I do!"

His grip on her chin turned inward. His hot palm scorched her neck. His fingers didn't tighten around the base of her throat, but Amanda had the uneasy feeling that was only because he was leashing the impulse.

"Prove it. Show me the money."

"I can't," she snapped, her mind churning. "Don't look at me like that. I wasn't about to carry a bulky saddlebag down to the river with me. I had enough trouble getting here myself as it was. I assure you, Mr. Chandler, the money is safe."

Oh, God, what was she saying? There was money in her saddlebag, but not much. Only enough to get her to Pony. There would be more once Roger was found and returned to his father, of course. A lot more. Mentally she'd already set aside a large chunk of her salary to pay Jake. Unfortunately, if she admitted that to him, she would also have to explain why she didn't have the money she claimed to have in her possession. He would want to know why she was getting money from Edward Bannister, and somewhere in there, she would have to tell him who Roger was.

Amanda was still convinced that was a bad idea. Her earlier assessment of this man stood firm. Jake was arrogant, dangerous, and highly untrustworthy. Until he proved otherwise, lying seemed a lesser risk than telling him the truth.

While that was all well and good, it didn't tell her how to prevent Jake from deserting her. She'd been lost before they'd joined forces. Without him, she'd be lost again come dawn. She was clever, but her skills were domestic, not the sort needed to survive in the wilderness alone. Since she was unable to find Roger without help, and since Jake was the only help available, it stood to reason she couldn't, under any circumstances, let him desert her.

Jake dropped his hand from her neck. He uncoiled his lanky frame and straightened. The restraining hand Amanda wrapped around his wrist stopped him when he would have walked away.

The tendons beneath her fingertips pulled taut. She might have been able to deal with that, had it been all she felt. It wasn't. A jolt of awareness shot up her arm. Her blood seared with the heat of it. "Where are you going?" she asked, her voice unaccountably husky. Had she just felt him shiver?

"To ransack your saddlebag. Where else?"

"But we aren't done here."

Jake glanced down, his expression guarded. "We're not?"

"No. You said there was something you want settled between us. Or were you referring to the money? If so . . ." She paused. "Excuse my bluntness, Mr. Chandler, but exactly how did you plan to settle the question of the money's existence without talking about it?"

Jake's gaze narrowed, dipped, dragged over her lips. His mouth went dry, his throat tight. "I planned to ask you about that after . . ."

"What?" she pressed. "After what?" Amanda wasn't sure she wanted an answer. She'd asked the question only to stall for time, hoping he would forget about the money entirely. The way his gaze darkened, stroking lustily over her mouth, suggested her plan had worked. Perhaps a bit too well.

Jake knew that the smart thing to do right now would be to turn his back and walk away. And to keep walking. To hell with the money. Even if she did have it, he didn't need it *that* badly. What he *did* need — so badly he ached! — was something he could never get from a prissy white lady like Amanda Lennox.

He didn't leave.

Instead, Jake stood rooted to the spot, his gaze caressing her face. He recognized that as a mistake the instant he saw the tip of her tongue dart out to moisten suddenly parched lips. Again, he wondered how she would taste. Smooth and sweet, like whiskey and honey. It was an odd combination to be sure, but an appropriate one. A damn tempting one. His tongue made a frustrated sweep over the back of his teeth. Hell, he could taste her already. His gut kicked. The air rushed from his lungs, and all thoughts of walking anywhere melted clean away.

Dammit! Before he committed himself to stay with her for longer than tonight, they really *did* have something to settle between them. Something that did not involve talking. Something that had been eating at him — and, he suspected, eating at her — all day. Something hot. Something inevitable. Something that damn well couldn't wait.

He glanced down, and saw that her fingers were still wrapped around his wrist. His pulse drummed a savage beat against her thumb. Her hand looked pale, the fingers long and slender as they rested against the native darkness of his arm. That sight — flawless white against dark copper — should have been enough to break the spell. And it might have been, had he not felt a tremor skate through her fingers . . . and a reciprocal vibration shimmy like a bolt of fire up his arm.

It was all the invitation Jake needed; all the invitation he required. He grabbed her wrist, and tugged her to her feet. His arm snaked around her waist, catching her close when she stumbled against him. Her cheeks went ghost-white. Jake heard her gasp, saw her wince. Only then did he remember her injured ankle.

Indulging in sympathy wasn't one of Jake Chandler's virtues. In fact, he didn't recognize or acknowledge the emotion, even when it sluiced through him. Cursing under his breath, he bent at the waist, scooped her up in his arms, and strutted back toward their camp.

The pan dropped from Amanda's abruptly slack fingers. It clinked against the side of a rock, but Jake didn't bother to stop and retrieve it. He'd fetch it later, when he came back for his things. Right now, he had more important matters to attend to.

Chapter Five

"I insist you put me down." Amanda was striving for a tone that sounded neutral but demanding. Rational would have been nice; pity she couldn't manage it. The *last* thing she wanted was for Jake to know how his strong arms cradling her—his warm, bare flesh *touching* her—made her feel.

"Insist all you want, princess. Won't do you any good."

"And if I were to tell you I can walk?"

She felt his shrug. "I'd say that's just dandy. Walk all you want . . . *tomorrow*. Tonight, you stay off that ankle."

Amanda gritted her teeth. Lord, the man was stubborn! How did he think she'd gotten down to the river in the first place? *Hired coach?* "You aren't going to put me down, are you?"

"What do you think?" he asked, and kept right on walking.

And that, Amanda decided, was exactly the problem. She couldn't think when Jake touched her. And when he held her close, as he was doing now . . . well, she didn't *want* to think, she wanted only to *feel*. Strange, new, and exciting sensations spiraled through her. Was it possible to feel hot and cold at the same time? It must be, because that was how she felt. Warm and tingly, insanely alive and yet . . . just as

82

insanely empty. Yes, that was it. She felt empty.

Amanda scowled. Was she, Amanda Louise Van Simmons Lennox, feeling lonely? No, it couldn't be! Or could it? She didn't know, and her confusion served only to confuse her still more.

Sinking into a pensive silence, Amanda tried to ignore how wonderful Jake's arms felt as he cradled her to his chest. She tried to ignore the way his clean, earthy scent lent a sensuous tang to the brisk night air. Tried, and failed. The man wasn't easily ignored. Even harder to ignore was the way mere thoughts of him created that odd, empty ache inside her . . . and the way mere thoughts of him also served to semi-smoothe that ache away.

The walk down to the river hadn't seemed long. The trip back took forever. That might have been because, somewhere between when Jake had picked her up, and when they neared the clearing, Amanda's once rigid body had begun to melt into him. It wasn't a conscious thing. She didn't relax all at once, but rather, muscle by weary muscle, gradually uncoiled and loosened.

By the time she heard the whicker of their tethered horses, she'd relaxed considerably. Her hands were no longer clenched in her lap, but had at some point inched up the smooth, warm expanse of Jake's chest. Her arms were now wrapped around his neck, her fingers tangled in fistfuls of his silky hair. Keeping space between them had proved too taxing an effort; she'd quickly found she had no energy for it. Her cheek was cushioned against his shoulder. The sculpted firmness of him felt good and natural, as if that part of him had been carved just for her. The fit was warm and perfect.

Jake stepped into the moonswept clearing where they'd set up camp. No, make that where he'd *presumed* a camp should be. From the look of things, Amanda Lennox hadn't lifted one perfectly manicured finger the entire time he'd been gone. The wood was still scattered dead center of the small, oval expanse of grass—exactly where he'd left it. No fire had been lit.

The second he made the observation, Jake wondered why he'd bothered. The woman snuggled so nicely in his arms was, after all, a pampered white princess. She wouldn't have the skill to get a fire started, even if she possessed the knowledge to do it. How she'd managed to stay alive out here this long was beyond him. Luck, most likely, and a lot of it.

He bent and deposited her roughly atop the hard-packed earth, his patience frayed. "Thought I told you to light a fire."

"I was out of matches," Amanda sniffed. Ignoring him as best she could, she lifted her skirt to inspect her ankle. The discolored swelling was no worse, nor was it better. The whole area still hurt mightily. She flicked the skirt back into place, and glared up at him. "Don't look at me like that. I *did* try, but it wouldn't catch. I think the wood you collected was damp."

"Like hell." Jake swaggered over to the pile and lifted a knobby stick. Holding it at waist level, he snapped it neatly in two. The sound of wood splintering made Amanda's spine go rigid. She watched as a few brittle chunks of bark rained to the ground, peppering the toes of Jake's bare feet.

"All right, so maybe *that one* was dry," she conceded grudgingly, and glanced away. "But the *rest* were—"

Another stick snapped. Another. The night echoed with the sound of dry wood cracking.

Amanda's eyes narrowed. Slowly, her gaze swept back to Jake. He looked quite pleased with himself, she noticed—and in the same instant thought she would gladly slap that condescending glare right off of his handsome face, were he within easy reach. As luck would have it, he was not.

"Do you want me to try again?" Her tone was as sweet as her smile. Only the way she pushed each word through clenched teeth suggested her irritation with this man.

Jake crossed his arms over his chest. One corner of his mouth quirked up, and a dark brow cocked high. His steely gaze sparkled with a challenging light that was enhanced by the play of moonlight and shadow.

Amanda's heartbeat kicked into double time. The small act of a smile—a genuine one this time—transformed his features from merely attractive to breathtakingly good-looking. Maybe it had something to do with the way his white teeth flashed against the rich copper of his face? Whatever the reason, she was learning to appreciate his rare, fleeting smiles.

Jake's right hand came away from the corded forearm it was pillowed atop. With an open palm, he indicated the wood. "Yeah, I think I would like that. I've always wondered how a society princess lights a fire."

Her lips thinned. "Is that a fact? Funny, *I've* always wondered how an Indian does it."

An angry glint turned the color of his eyes from sliver to midnight grey. The muscle in his cheek throbbed. "All right, Miss Lennox, let me put this in terms you'll understand. I'll use small words . . . it'll be easier for you to follow. I'm cold, I'm hungry, I'm tired." He counted each complaint off on his fingers, his gaze never leaving her. His eyes were bright with the innuendo that threaded his voice with husky promise. "If you don't get off that cute little butt of yours and get a fire started soon, I'm going to be forced to find some other way to keep myself warm tonight. If that happens, I give you my word . . . come morning there'll be one less white lady wondering how *this* Indian does anything."

He was dead serious. Amanda decided it would be in her best interest to give lighting the fire another try. Not wanting to put unnecessary weight on her ankle, she used her hands and good leg to push herself over the few feet of grass separating her from the wood. She kept her shoulders squared and her spine straight and proud, although she had to admit that hauling herself clumsily over the ground the way she was doing made it difficult to appear ladylike.

Her fingers, she was pleased to note, didn't tremble too much when she selected the two sticks she'd used earlier. One piece already had the proper-sized hole gouged in the center; she laid that one flat on the ground. Inserting the tip of the thinner, longer stick into the hole, Amanda flattened her palms on either side of it. Her skin was chafed from her previous attempt to get the fire started. She *had* tried, dammit! She disregarded the sting of bark against her tender flesh — at least she *tried* to disregard it, but it made her movements awkward.

She paused long enough to suck in a steadying breath, then began rubbing the stick back and forth. Her motions were self-conscious and stiff. The stick flipped from her fingers more times than not, but she doggedly snatched it back and tried again. She would get this fire started or she would die trying!

Amanda was vaguely aware of when Jake swaggered to the opposite side of the pile. He hunkered down in the ankle-high grass, and although she could feel his gaze smolder over her, she was too busy — mentally commanding the sticks to combust in a fiery display that would knock a certain conceited half-breed on his ear — to pay him much attention.

Until he laughed.

His rich, deep, oddly pleasant laughter cut through the night and sliced through Amanda like a knife. The sound won her undivided — not to mention furious — attention. Her hands paused in midrub. Her gaze snapped up. The crease furrowing her brow was a good indication of her fury. "You think this is funny?" she demanded.

Jake nodded. It took effort to trap his laughter in

his throat. The amusement in his eyes didn't fade a bit. "Yeah, princess, I think it's hilarious. Don't you?"

Her gaze flared with indignation. "I most certainly do not. For your information, Mr. Chandler, I happen to be trying my best to get this fire started."

"Is that a fact? Well, for *your* information, Miss Lennox, you'll never do it the way you're going about it." His attention plunged to the stick she sandwiched between her stinging palms. "Want some help?"

"If it wouldn't put too much of a strain on you."

"Okay, listen up." His gaze volleyed between her eyes and the stick. "Think of it as . . ."

One golden brow slanted curiously high. Now what, Amanda wondered, had doused his laughter so quickly? And why did his expression suddenly look tight and strained? The muscle in his jaw had stopped ticking. Why? What sordid thought had crossed his mind? Whatever it was, it must have been a good one to have that sobering an effect on a man that *nothing* seemed to bother.

"What, Mr. Chandler? Think of it as . . . what?"

His gaze shifted, grazing the swell of her breasts before lifting. The corners of his mouth kicked up in a wicked grin as their gazes meshed. "Think of it as like . . . making love," he said slowly, suggestively. He heard her gasp, but ignored it. "You've got to rub the stick harder. Faster. Get enough friction going to make a spark. Then you've got to . . . Well, hell, princess, let me show you."

Amanda squirmed. Her heart fluttered when she saw Jake push to his feet. He sauntered around the pile of wood, and only once he'd breached the barrier did she realize it had made a wall between them. She felt his heat seep into her back and hips before she actually felt him — in all the same places. Was it possible to breathe when one found oneself in a situation like this? Apparently not. At least *she* couldn't!

He knelt behind her, vising her hips between his

legs. His pelvis ground against her bottom when he shifted, settling himself in.

Amanda stifled a groan. The contact between her sensitive bottom and his hard-muscled thighs was jarring. A sensation bolted through her; it was like being struck by lightning. Shock that Jake would take such liberties—both verbal and physical—made her shake. At least that was the reason she gave herself for the quivers shooting through her.

She didn't think he noticed her reaction, and she was grateful for that. And then she wondered if maybe his ignorance wasn't due to the way his attention was focused on positioning himself behind her? His hips wiggled and pressed; it seemed to take forever for him to find a comfortable spot!

Starting at the hips, he rolled his weight forward until his bare chest was plastered against her back. A row of buttons trailed down her dress. The tiny nubs bit into her skin from the pressure of his weight grinding into her. The pain was nominal—more an aggravation, really—easily forgotten, among the sensations swirling in her tummy, sensations that seeped rapidly downward.

Jake's head appeared over her shoulder. He was close enough for Amanda to make out every detail of his sculpted profile. Close enough for her to smell the scent of his skin. It was a heady aroma; one that inundated her with each small, rapid breath she labored to draw into her burning lungs.

He angled his head, and their cheeks brushed. His skin felt smooth and warm as it whisked her own. "Pay attention, Miss Lennox. I'll only show you this once. Now, let's see," he muttered, his voice a hot rush of air in her ear. "First, we'll need some of this." His chest rubbed her back when he moved. As she watched, he fluffed a handful of dry grass around the base of the stick.

"That's the bed," he told her, inclining his chin toward the scattered grass. "The bed is, initially, what you want to start the fire on." He paused. "Are you with me so far?"

"Um-hmmm," she squeaked, then gulped and cleared her throat.

"Good. Now this," he nodded to the stick, "is the . . . Jesus, lady, you're going to snap it in two if you keep holding it so tight! Ease up a bit. No need to strangle the damn thing. Uncurl your fingers and . . . that's better. Now balance the stick between your palms. Good. Now this time I want you to make your movements flow. What you need to do is . . . *stimulate* the bottom stick until it smolders. That'll take a nice, easy, back and forth stroke. Steady, but not jerky. You want to get that friction I was telling you about started. Back and forth, back and forth. I can't tell you how important rhythm is. Once you've established the pace, you can't let up or you'll have to start from scratch. Understand?"

Think of it as like . . . making love.

Amanda stifled a moan and nodded.

"Good. Give it a try."

"Like this?" she asked, and realized she'd overcompensated by making her tone too husky and low. To distract Jake from noticing, she began rubbing the stick. Her movements were still awkward and inept, but this time her clumsiness stemmed from a different source. It stemmed from the man behind her, the feel of his hard body planing her back, the unreasonably strong curl of desire his words caused to simmer in the pit of her stomach.

Her fingers quavered. The stick flipped out of her grasp, and landed on the ground beside Jake's knee.

He picked it up and handed it back to her. His sigh of disappointment rustled the golden wisps clinging to her cheeks. Her skin burned from the fan of his breath. "To tell you the truth, princess, that doesn't do much for me. Try it like this."

Her gaze dropped. Amanda knew she should be protesting this sordid lesson, but she didn't have a voice to protest with. It made her pride feel less battered to think she was only allowing this because learning how to build a fire without the use of matches could come in handy in the future. And it would. But that wasn't why she couldn't move or talk, and she knew it.

Amanda gave Jake her full attention—in more ways than one. There was no forgetting or ignoring the intimate way he'd molded himself to her hips and back. His thighs straddled hers from behind, pressing, arching. She couldn't deny her tumultuous reaction to the hard, firm feel of him. The only thing she could do was *pretend* she hadn't noticed it.

She pulled Jake's hands into focus. He paused imperceptibly before blanketing the back of her knuckles with his palms. His skin felt hot and rough, his fingers thick and strong. The back of her wrist was acutely aware of his pulse hammering against it. The tempo was wild and erratic; it matched her own racing heart.

"Ready?" he whispered huskily. His mouth was close enough for her to feel the movement of his lips against her earlobe.

Amanda nodded weakly. "I-I think so."

"Just do exactly what I tell you, and I'll show you how we Indians set a bed on fire."

"You will?" Lord, but it was embarrassing to hear how small and panicky her voice sounded.

"Sure I will, princess. Anything for a lady." His pause was long enough to make her heart skip, yet short enough to stop just shy of blatant torture. "You *did* want to learn how to light a fire this way, didn't you?"

Amanda felt the vibrations of his laughter against her back. She told herself she didn't *really* tremble—of course not!—but she knew that she did. She also knew Jake was very much aware of the way his sinewy body absorbed her minute quivers.

Not waiting for an answer, he started guiding her small white hands back and forth on either side of the stick. His initial pace was slow, his strokes long and smooth. The stick rolled from the tip of her fingers to the heel of her palm, then back again. The process was repeated.

Once she had the rhythm, he accelerated the tempo.

The insides of his arms rubbed against the outside of hers. A thin sleeve separated flesh from flesh; in no time, it seemed to melt clean away. Amanda could feel the play of his muscles with every stroke. His cheek was nestled against her ear. She felt his breath in the chest that moved against her back, in the heat of each controlled exhalation, and the way it seeped through the material covering the upper swell of her breasts.

The stick, Amanda, pay attention to the stick!

She pasted her shattered concentration together and focused her thoughts on her hands and the stick she whirled between her stinging palms. Her gaze shifted to where the sticks met. She frowned. Was it her imagination, or had the powder the friction had created begun to glow? She blinked hard, refocusing. That *wasn't* her imagination. The wood *was* glowing. A curl of smoke wafted into the air. Some of the grass flickered with a spark. It wasn't much, but Amanda could have sworn she felt the inviting heat of it against her fingertips.

"Blow on it," Jake told her. "Very gently."

She did, and giggled when more of the grass caught. Soon, even the two sticks were burning. The sting of charred wood laced the air. Amanda inhaled deeply, and knew she'd never smelled anything so sweet in her life.

She'd started a fire without matches! Oh, what a heady feeling accomplishment was. Her shoulders squared with pride. It wasn't until she noticed that her back was cold and that there was no firm obstruction holding her in place, that she realized Jake was no longer behind her.

"Proud of yourself, ain't ya, princess?"

Her gaze whipped up. Amanda tracked his voice and found Jake lying on the grass to her right, not too far away. He was sprawled on his side, his lean body stretched casually over the ground. His right elbow was bent, the heel of that palm supported his head. A cigarette dangled from one corner of his mouth. The tip was dark, yet his eyes were squinted as though curls of smoke were trailing up from the unlit end.

Her gaze sharpened on his other hand, the fingers of which were poised over his outer thigh. Her jaw hardened. Her green eyes narrowed furiously when she saw his hand flick upward along the coarse side-seam of his denim pants.

The sound of a match flaring to life was grating against its backdrop of taut silence.

Amanda sucked in a quick breath. Her glare was degrees hotter than the flame Jake held to the tip of his cigarette. She was too angry to yell. Hell, she was too angry to *breathe!* She forced her attention back to the crackling fire. Her fingers shook as she fed the struggling flames a few brittle twigs. "You're not much of an Indian, Mr. Chandler," she said tightly.

"Guess that makes us even then, Miss Lennox. Because you ain't much of a lady."

Her fury grew like the fire she'd built. Both were white-hot, hungry. When she felt sufficiently enraged, Amanda shifted her glare to Jake. "You bastard!"

He wedged the cigarette between his index and middle finger. Taking it from his mouth, he used it to point at her. His gaze was frosty. "Now *that's* the only thing you've gotten right all day, lady. I *am* a bastard. In more ways than one. If you've got a brain in that pretty little head of yours, that's one thing you won't

92

keep flinging in my face. I don't like it."

"I'm not a violent person," she said. Her voice wasn't the only thing trembling with anger now. "But I have a very real need to slap you. Quite hard."

"Why's that, princess? Am I . . . *annoying* you again?"

"I've gone past annoyance. Furious would be a better word."

"And you think giving me a good slap will make you feel better?"

"Oh, yes. I'm certain it would."

Jake put the cigarette to his lips and inhaled until the tip glowed red-hot. "Well?" he said on a thick exhalation of smoke. "What are you waiting for? I may be a bastard, but I've never left a lady in need." He grinned; the gesture didn't reach the gaze that continued to burn into her. "If you get my drift."

Amanda's need for violence—which, she realized suddenly, had been coming quite frequently of late—had never been stronger. Her palm itched to smack Jake hard enough to make his shiny white teeth rattle. And why not? The cad deserved no better after the nasty trick he'd just played on her.

Giving in to impulse, Amanda fed the fire a few more sticks, then pushed to her feet. Her ankle hurt. The throbbing pain that shot up her leg only fed her fury. She hobbled over the space that separated them. Balancing the majority of her weight on her good leg, she planted her fists on her hips. Her spine remained rigid as she glared down at him.

If she'd hoped to intimidate him, she missed her mark. Jake didn't look the least concerned as he flicked the barely-smoked cigarette away. It made a fiery arch from his fingers to where it landed to smolder itself out in the night-cooled grass.

It took a second for Jake to realize she wasn't going to squat down and carry out her threat. That was a shame. He had been prepared to swipe her off balance and cushion her fall with his body. It was the "cushioning" part he'd been looking forward to—maybe more than he should have.

His gaze began at her shoes. While he skimmed the full skirt, shifting in dark calico folds around her legs, he paid more attention to the flare of hips outlined beneath. Her waist was a slender temptation to a man's hands. Above were two firm swells that were even more tempting.

The set of her shoulders was hard and uncompromising, yet even they looked soft and feminine to his appreciative eye. Her throat was long and creamy and white; the center slid up and down with a convulsive swallow. Her jaw worked as she clenched and unclenched her teeth. Her lips looked pinched. Even her high, regal cheekbones looked strained and angry. The skin stretched over them was a hot, furious shade of pink. And then there were her eyes . . .

The moonlight made her eyes look like pools of dark, luminescent green, the color of a storm-tossed sea. It was her eyes that Jake focused on now, because, whether she knew it or not, it was her eyes that gave her away every time.

She was furious with him, he knew. Hell, hadn't he goaded her to it? But anger was only one of the emotions he'd stirred inside of her. Behind her outrage he saw something else. Something stronger. Something she was trying oh, so hard to hide and deny, but couldn't. She was far too innocent to know how; he was far too experienced to be fooled.

The prissy white lady had no idea of how much she desired the man she thought to be a wildly reared savage. But Jake knew. And the knowledge made his heart pound and his blood flow hot.

"Remember down by the river?" he said. His voice sounded raspy and thick. His hand came up, handcuffing her wrist. Her pulse drummed against the

94

heel of his palm. "When I said there was something we needed to settle?"

"Y-yes," Amanda answered, and wondered when the sting of fury had left her voice. When he'd touched her—*that* was when she'd weakened. While the urge to slap him wasn't entirely gone, it had faded considerably.

"It's time."

She stiffened warily. "Time?"

"Yup." His expression was as serious as his tone. "*Past* time. We're going to settle this here and now, Miss Lennox."

"Settle what?" But Amanda had a sinking feeling she already knew. Though she tried to prepare herself, it did no good. Hearing the way his silky drawl rasped over the words, watching the way his lips moved as his spoke them . . . well, there *was* no preparing for her reaction to that!

"I've been wondering all day what it would be like to kiss you. It's about time I found out, wouldn't you say?"

The wrist within his grasp trembled. They both felt it.

"I-I really don't think that's a good idea, Mr. Chandler." She tried to pull from his grasp. His fingers tightened. His grip, while not painful, was firm. Determined.

"On the contrary, Miss Lennox. I think that's the best damn idea I've had all day. Come here. Let's get this over with so we can both put it out of our minds for good."

He tugged, but Amanda was ready for him. Though her knees had turned to jelly, threatening to buckle at any moment, she managed to stand her ground. Again, she tried to slip her hand free. Again, he refused to let her go.

Her temper snapped. She lashed out in the only way she knew how—with her razor-sharp tongue.

"Why, you egotistical bastard! For your information, sir, I have more important things on my mind than . . . Surely you don't think I've spent my day thinking about how it would feel to . . . to . ." She groaned. If she couldn't *say* the words, how on earth could she *deny* them?

"Kiss me? Yeah, princess, that's exactly what I think. And you know what else? I think you might as well quit fighting. We both know I'm going to haul you down here sooner or later. And the longer it takes . . ."

Amanda, lulled by the husky pitch of his voice, failed to notice when it trailed off. Her gaze had dipped to his mouth. Watching him form words was an experience unto itself. The way his lips moved was fascinating. Mesmerized by the sight, she wasn't prepared for another, more insistent tug. Without warning, she felt the world being knocked out from under her.

Jake allowed himself a split-second grin before springing to motion. He sat up, his arm coiling tightly around her waist, drawing her toward him when she would have stumbled backward. Momentum was on his side. He had no difficulty turning her in the direction he wanted her to fall.

Amanda landed hard. Her bottom made a solid collision with his lap. Both of them groaned.

His hand had settled on her thigh. Very high up. His thumb and index finger were spread wide; the webbing between coated the groove separating shapely leg from equally shapely hip.

She wasn't sure how that had happened. Nor did she know how her own hands had ended up splaying his belly. His skin felt hot and smooth and hard to the touch. It felt . . . alarmingly nice.

Jake cocked his head. The tip of the small brown feather, the fringe of the rebellious braid, skimmed

Amanda's knuckles. One of them shivered. She wasn't sure who.

She turned her head, and confused green met lusty silver.

No, that's wrong. His eyes aren't silver, they're . . .

From a distance his eyes looked the color of a stormy winter sky; cold and grey and piercing. Up close, they didn't look that way at all. The center of each iris was an intriguing shade of silver-grey. It was the band of solid blue rimming the circumference that really gave those eyes character, and added a spark of warmth. That, and the small, seasoned creases shooting out from each sun-copper corner. The contrast between his inky hair and dark skin, and the penetrating color of his eyes, made his gaze burn.

"That's better. Now, what were you saying, princess? You weren't really going to deny it, were you?"

"M-maybe," she evaded breathlessly, then swallowed hard when his hand left her thigh. It made a lazy, skimming ascent, never pausing, never once leaving her body. His fingers vised her jaw. Like his grip, his expression was insistent.

"Deny it if you can. I'll just call you a liar. And we'll both know I'm right, won't we? Of course, if you'd rather I *proved* it to you . . ."

She shook her head. It was a quick, jerky motion, vague because it was trapped by his hand. "That won't be necessary."

"Good. Now come here."

Her eyes widened. Nervous, she licked her lips, then dearly wished she hadn't. His gaze shadowed the movement, hungrily tracking the path her tongue made. "I *am* here."

"Uh-un. Come closer."

The arm around her waist flexed. She could feel the heat of his chest seeping through her dress. The heat emanating from his lap was even more pronounced.

And was it firmer? "Mr. Chandler, if I came any closer to you we'd melt into each other!"

"That's the idea, princess. A man likes a woman to melt right into him when he's kissing her breathless. That's how he knows she likes it."

"Oh."

He scowled. *"Oh?* Is that what all proper young ladies are trained to say when a man threatens to kiss them? 'Oh?' "

His words made her breath go all rapid and shallow. It did quite the opposite to her heart rate. Amanda strove to compensate for the warm, fluttering sensations in her tummy by lowering her tone and edging her words with a firmness she didn't feel. "I'm sure I wouldn't know, since I've rarely been kissed. However, since you seem to be the expert on ladies, why don't you tell me what I'm supposed to say at a time like this?"

"Please."

She gulped. His lips were so close she could feel the hot wash of his breath against her mouth. His kiss was a constant threat, and her lips tingled with the promise of it, even as she snapped, "Please!"

"All right ma'am. If you insist." His mouth dipped, and his next words were rasped against her lips. "Lady or no lady, I never could resist a woman who begs."

"Begs? Mr. Chandler, I most certainly did *not — !"*

His mouth crashed down on hers, sealing the words in her throat. There was no time to say more. A second later, there was no breath left in her to say anything with.

There was nothing gentle about Jacob Blackhawk Chandler. The man was hard as granite, inside and out. That wasn't speculation, it was fact. Confusion came in the way his mouth ate at hers in a manner that was hot, yet provocatively tender. If Amanda didn't know better, she might have thought Jake wanted her to enjoy this kiss as much as he so obviously did.

And that was the problem. She *did* enjoy it. So much so, in fact, that it didn't take long for her resistance — if she'd ever really had any — to melt. Oh, who was she trying to fool? Her *entire body* melted the second his mouth had claimed hers. She was soft, willing . . . embarrassingly responsive.

He tasted good. Raw, manly tastes. Amanda tipped her head to the side, wanting, *needing* to taste still more of him. She groaned when he took advantage of the offer. A growl rumbled in the back of his throat as he deepened the kiss.

Her toes curled, her fists opened. She clung to his shoulders, tightening her grip until her fingers tunneled into his warm flesh and the tightly bunched muscles beneath. But even that wasn't enough. She wanted to feel more.

His neck passed beneath her hands. She buried her fingers in his silky hair, cupping his scalp in her palms and urging him closer. She arched her back, straining toward him.

Jake's response was immediate. His mouth opened over hers. The warm, moist tip of his tongue skated over her lips, teasing the crease that sealed them innocently together.

Amanda had only been kissed twice before. Neither time was like *this*. She didn't even know a man and a woman *could* kiss like this! Was it proper for a man to use his tongue? Was it proper for a *woman?* Did it matter? Proper or not, she wasn't going to demand he stop. This felt too good!

Her lips parted invitingly. His tongue plunged into her mouth, and the kiss turned savage. His strokes were wet and deep and bold. He circled the tip of her tongue, mating with hers in a wild rhythm that made her head spin and her blood boil.

Her timidity didn't last long. Jake was simply too

persuasive. In no time she'd joined in the seductive game of thrust and parry, explore and retreat. A shiver bolted through her. Nothing in Amanda's life had prepared her for the first, hesitant feel of her tongue sliding against Jake Chandler's.

Her fingers curled around fistfuls of his silky hair. Her knuckles grazed the thin braid she'd been longing to touch. She touched it now, stroked and fondled it as she arched into him. Her nipples beaded, straining, as though trying to breach the barrier of cloth isolating her flesh from his. In a foggy recess of her mind, Amanda realized she was closer to this man now, physically, than she'd ever been to any man she had ever known.

Jake sensed that, too—and it was for that reason alone he eased away from her. Throughout the kiss, his hands had remained exactly where they'd started; one cupping her chin, the other riding her waist. Except for an occasional twitch, he hadn't allowed them to budge an inch. And for damn good reason! If he moved, he would touch her. If he touched her, just once, he would never *stop* touching her.

He had known—from the instant he'd crushed her mouth beneath his, the instant he'd tasted her sweetness and captured her airy little groan of surrender with his mouth—that it would be like this between them. He hadn't expected that. Then again, he hadn't expected a lot of things. He hadn't expected Amanda Lennox to surrender so quickly. He hadn't expected to *want* her to surrender at all. Mostly, what he hadn't expected was that he would want—really *want*—her so damn badly it hurt.

But he did. He'd wanted Amanda even before they'd kissed. Now, he wanted her with a need that rocked him. His blood still pumped hot. His appetite to possess this woman—this *lady*—this *white* lady!—was one of the few emotions that Jake found he couldn't erase from his mind and pretend didn't exist.

His need for her was hot and strong enough to be a weakness. And weakness of any sort — in others as well as himself — didn't please him. Not at all.

Jake waited until his breathing was almost regular before allowing his hands to move. His fingers curled around Amanda's soft upper arms as he pulled back from her, glancing down.

She glanced up. Her green eyes swam with a confusion of desire and self-derision.

In that instant, Jake knew he had to break the thread he'd just woven between them. He wasn't going to be able to put his desire for her out of his mind — or his body — but he saw no reason *she* had to know that. It would give her a weapon to use over him, a power. He'd be damned if he'd do that.

Amanda felt a sliver of air slip between them. The night felt cold, her body fevered and hot. Her breaths were coming in strangled gulps. Her lips were swollen and slightly bruised, but it wasn't the unpleasant feeling she knew it should be. Quite the opposite; if she'd had her way, she would have tossed away her years of schooling and wantonly molded herself into Jake, begging him to kiss her again. It was a humiliating admission, but it was nonetheless true.

The look in his eyes said that wouldn't be prudent. His gaze was frosty and hard again, his expression carefully blank.

"Gotta say, Miss Lennox, you don't kiss like any society lady I've ever met." The grin he flashed her was boyish enough not to be too dirty. The glint in his eyes . . . ah, that was dirty as hell. "I respect that in a woman."

"Really?" she panted, her breathing not close to normal. Following his lead, she kept her tone neutral. "How many society ladies have you kissed, Mr. Chandler? It must have been quite a few for you to have gained such a vast, working knowledge of us."

101

"Nope. Sorry to disappoint you, princess, but you're only the second. And the last."

Her golden brows arched. "You sound very sure of yourself."

"I am," he said. Tightening his grip on her, he removed·her from the throbbing heat of his lap. Odd, but he felt no relief.

The empty feeling inside Amanda came back in force. She noticed it the second her bottom molded itself to the hard, lumpy ground. Was it a coincidence that the observation was made in the same instant Jake's body no longer touched hers?

That she'd just been cast aside was obvious. Amanda knew she should be annoyed. No, she should be downright furious. She wasn't, and that worried her.

She told herself he'd kissed her only to prove a point, to satisfy his own curiosity. He'd already admitted as much. But the truth of the matter was, there were a number of things a woman could do to thwart a man's unwanted attentions. Amanda had learned quite a few of them. So why hadn't she used a single one? Probably for the same reason Jake had initiated the kiss to begin with; curiosity, and the appeasal thereof.

While Amanda could lie to other people with ease, she couldn't lie to herself. She *had* wondered what it would be like to kiss this man. The fantasies she'd entertained for half the day had been enough to drive a sane woman crazy. She hoped now that their curiosities had been appeased, they could do what Jake had suggested earlier: put it out of their minds for good.

She sent him a sidelong glance. In her opinion, it looked like he'd already done so. Ah, now *that* annoyed her!

"Get some sleep," Jake said as he fished the makings for another cigarette out of the saddle bag close to his hip. "We'll be heading out at the crack of dawn. If you aren't awake when I'm ready to ride, I'll leave without you."

"And go where?"

The fingers deftly rolling the tobacco in paper never missed a beat, though his gaze narrowed. "Where I was heading before your cousin detoured me."

"Which is where?" Bending her legs, Amanda rearranged the skirt around her shins and cradled her knees to her chest. They made the perfect shelf to rest her cheek atop. The pain in her ankle wasn't so bad now that her leg wasn't being jostled and now that she had other matters occupying her mind.

Jake's tongue darted out to lick the paper, sealing it.

Amanda shivered, remembering the sharp taste of him on her tongue. Like the man himself, his flavor was unique, something to savor and never forget. She watched him stash the leather pouch holding the tobacco back into his saddlebag. "Which is where?" she repeated as though he hadn't heard her. They both knew he had.

Jake tucked the cigarette into a corner of his mouth and shrugged. "You're a nosy piece of baggage, ain't ya?"

"So I've been told, though never in such . . . flattering terms. Where are you heading, Mr. Chandler?"

"Nowhere in particular," he said, and scraped a match up the seam of his pants.

Amanda's gaze strayed over his features. She was mesmerized by the way the flare of orange light heightened and defined the rugged planes of his face. He really was handsome, she thought, in an arrogant, untamed sort of way. The observation reminded her of another question she'd wanted, but not dared to ask him. "You aren't really an Indian, are you, Mr. Chandler?"

He drew on the cigarette, holding the smoke in his lungs until it burned. It was released in a long, cloudy stream. "Didn't I tell you to get some sleep?"

"Yes. And I will . . . *after* you answer my question. Are you or aren't you an Indian?"

"Half. There's your bedroll." He pointed to the rolled up blanket coiled on the grass . . . on the opposite side of her little fire. Amanda couldn't help noticing he'd positioned it as far away from his as he could get it—yet close enough so they'd both have heat from the fire.

She sighed, and glanced down. Two inches of moonswept grass separated their hips. The span might as well have been a mile.

"Well?" he prodded when she didn't move.

"In a minute." She nuzzled her cheek atop the pillow of her knees. "I may be a woman, Mr. Chandler, but I'm not stupid. I know you're only half Indian. One look at your eyes told me that. What I meant was, you don't *act* like any Indian I've ever read about. You don't dress like one," she remembered his moccasins, the eagle feather tucked into his hatband, the long hair, braid and feather, "for the most part, and you certainly don't talk like one."

Jake clamped the cigarette between his teeth and squinted at her. The glowing tip dangled when he spoke. "But I look like one, and you want to know why. Is that it?"

"Yes."

Whole minutes slipped past, and still Jake didn't answer. Eventually, Amanda gave up waiting. She had a feeling he wasn't going to discuss it.

The tiredness she'd been fighting seeped back. Her stomach grumbled, reminding her of the supper they'd skipped. She was too tired and sore to get up and rummage through her saddlebag. Stifling a yawn in her throat, her lashes fluttered down. She didn't fall asleep immediately, but instead let the heat of Jake warming her side and the sounds of the night temporarily soothe her. Finding Roger seemed like a world away at the moment.

The sound of the campfire crackling brought a smile to her lips. No matter what sort of trickery Jake had used, she *had* lit that fire by herself. Amanda was more proud of that than she'd been upon conquering her first sampler — and that was saying something! Which reminded her . . .

"Mr. Chandler?" she murmured groggily.

"Hmmm?"

"I owe you a good slap for what you did to me with the matches."

His chuckle was light and airy. It tickled its way down her spine. "Yeah, I expect you do. Tell you what. Slap me tomorrow, princess."

"I will." She half sighed, half yawned. "Remind me if I forget, would you?"

She heard Jake chuckle, but if he ever answered her, his reply fell on deaf ears. A few seconds later she was asleep.

Chapter Six

The grass crunched. Even the chirp of birds couldn't mask the sound. Amanda winced, as much from the pain that stabbed up her leg as from the noise, and tried to soften her tread as she crept around the ashy remains of the campfire.

Her gaze swept the clearing, which was touched by the pink fingers of approaching daybreak. A chilly breeze rustled the carpet of grass, the branches of pine trees. Other than that, everything was still. Things were as they should be. Nothing was disturbed. Nothing looked or sounded out of place.

Amanda wasn't fooled. While the shadows were deceiving, the uneasiness that iced down her spine was not. The curls at the nape of her neck prickled — the wispy gold strands felt alive with the current of unseen eyes, eyes that were watching her every move. It was a disturbing feeling.

Goosebumps dotted her arms. She rubbed them away, more sure than ever that she and Jake were not alone. If instinct didn't prove it, the sound of a twig snapping did.

Her fingers grazed the pocket of her skirt, but the bulge of metal tucked inside brought little comfort. She had fished the antique pistol out of her saddlebag when she'd first been jarred awake. It wasn't loaded; she had no bullets. If anyone *was* out there, she'd hoped just the sight of a gun would scare whoever it was away.

Her gaze fixed on Jake. He lay huddled beneath a thin blue blanket on the opposite side of the clearing. A muted sliver of light filtered through the ceiling of leaves. The pinkish ray glinted off the top of his blacker-than-black head. Though she couldn't see his face — the blanket was drawn up too high — the position of his shoulders suggested he was lying on his side, facing away from her.

Another twig snapped.

Amanda quickened her pace, careful to keep her steps as quiet as her limping gait would allow. Fear made the chore difficult. The feeling of being watched not only persisted, it grew. Her heart pounded in her ears. The tempo was so loud she was surprised the racket didn't wake Jake up.

Sighing in relief, she reached his side of the clearing and went down on one knee behind him. The ground felt cold and lumpy beneath her. An icy chill seeped through her skirt, cooling the fear-warmed flesh beneath.

She shivered, and her hand rose. Her fingers trembled, hesitating for one throbbing heartbeat before making contact with Jake's shoulder, which was padded only slightly by the blanket.

As she'd expected, he awoke instantly. What she didn't expect — wasn't prepared for — was the speed with which he reacted.

Jake thrust off the blanket in the same instant he flipped onto his opposite side. His shoulder grazed her bent knee. The contact was brief, but hard enough to send a stunned Amanda off balance.

Amanda gasped, and lurched to the right. Her hand shot out, her palm crushing the grass as she tried to steady herself. From the corner of her eye, she caught the glint of muted light touching deadly steel. Her gaze snapped to the side. She'd barely had a chance to focus on the long, curved steel blade before Jake hurled it.

A golden curl resting against her cheek stirred as the knife whipped past; the throw was that close.

A startled whimper seeped from Amanda's throat, and all the strength drained out of her arm. As she collapsed onto the ground, she heard rather than saw the *thunk* of the blade sinking into a tree trunk on the opposite side of the clearing. Her body went rigid. Her heart stopped, lodging itself in the vicinity of her dry, fear-tightened throat. Sweet Jesus, the man had tried to kill her! Worse, he'd very nearly succeeded!

Panic coiled in her stomach. Wild surges of it rushed in her veins. From the inside out, she began to shake. Her lashes swept down, and she curled her arms around her waist. Air rushed into her lungs in one jagged inhalation. The grass she crushed flat beneath her cheek felt dewy, cold, and as frigid as death.

"What the — ?" Jake blinked hard, and shook his head to clear it. He gouged the sleep from his eyes with the roughened pad of his thumb and index finger, but . . . dammit! When he looked around again, not a thing had changed.

His curses were loud and explicit, slamming off trees and grass. His gaze volleyed between Amanda and the knife, unable to decide which made him angrier, the blade he'd sunk up to the carved mahogany hilt in a pine tree trunk, or the woman who'd curled herself into a fetal ball in the grass near his hip.

A shaky sob drew his attention to Amanda. His hooded gaze settled on her and settled hard. Her normally pale cheeks were ashen, but she didn't look like she was hurt. He didn't see any blood — thank God! — and no cut marred her flawless white skin. She was, he noted absently, shaking from head to toe.

Good. That made two of them! Keeping his fury out of his voice was an effort Jake chose not to make.

"What the hell goes through your head, woman?"

His lethal glare detected her flinch. It wasn't satisfying. After what she'd just done — what she'd almost made *him* do — Jake wanted a hell of a lot more from her than terror. Begging for forgiveness would be a good start! "Look at me, damn you! I want your eyes open when I strangle the life out of you."

Whether she heard him or not was debatable. One thing he knew for certain; she didn't open her eyes. The lower lip she caught between her teeth was pearly pink and moist; it quivered almost as much as the rest of her. His angry shouts had only made her shake more violently. And whimper.

The sound ripped through Jake's gut like a dull knife.

His fingers were still shaking when he plowed them through his sleep-tousled hair. That . . . *annoyed* him enough to spear Amanda with a hot, angry glare. "I hope you had a good reason for what you just did, lady," he growled, his tone low and gritty with an emotion he didn't dare name — let alone acknowledge he felt. "A *damn* good reason. One that's worth dyin' for . . . because, darlin', I don't think you know how close you came to doing exactly that."

Not know? Amanda thought. As if she could ever *forget!* To narrowly miss being stabbed to death by a wild half-breed wasn't an everyday occurrence for the attendants of Miss Henry's Academy For Young Ladies. It was an event to be remembered, if only because Amanda had never come so close to dying in her life!

Still, for all Jake's fury, his words did serve an unintentional purpose. They tickled her memory. The reason she'd come over to his side of the camp shot through her mind. Also, his callous tone — *she* was the one who'd almost died, for heaven's sake! — burned the edges off her fear and sparked a flame of indignation deep inside of her.

Someone was out there. Someone was watching them. The hair at her nape still prickled with awareness. Goosebumps still tingled on her forearms and legs.

She opened her eyes, and pulled the man crouching beside her into focus. Jake's features were hard. The copper flesh between his brows was pinched in a warning scowl, and the muscle in his cheek pulsed erratically as he clenched and unclenched his teeth.

His expression would have intimidated her, had she time to be intimidated. She didn't. She had to warn Jake about whoever was out there, and she had to do it before whoever it was took them by surprise. "I-I heard a noise, Mr. Chandler."

"A noise? That's *it?*" Jake rolled his weight back on his heels. His hands hung limply between his knees. Too limply, Amanda thought. It was as though he was making a conscious effort not to wrap his fingers around her throat and squeeze—the way his eyes said he wanted so badly to do.

His sleep-tousled hair swayed around his shoulders when he shook his head in disgust. "Well, isn't that dandy! You almost get my knife planted in your skull just because you wanted to tell me you heard a noise. Shit, lady, should I even ask what you'd do if you *saw* a bear?" He held up a hand when she opened her mouth to answer. "Forget I asked."

Resentment coiled in Amanda's stomach. She welcomed the distraction. Anger was good, it was healthy . . . and it was much, better, much safer than the terror that had preceded it.

Feeling suddenly small and vulnerable curled up in a shivering ball at his feet, she pushed herself into a sitting position. She had to look up to meet his eyes, but at least she didn't feel so vulnerable, so miserably feminine! Her fingers, she was glad to find, didn't shake *too* much when she tucked a thick, sleep-tangled curl behind her ear.

Her gaze lifted, and meshed with his hard, steely glare. "I *did* hear a noise."

"I'll bet." His tone said he doubted it, as did the sharp glint in his eyes. Amanda bristled. "Know what *else* I'd bet on? I'd bet the noise you *say* you heard was made by a squirrel. Or the wind."

"Are you calling me a liar?" Her chin tipped, her green eyes shimmering a challenge.

110

One black brow slanted a reciprocal dare. His voice remained as cold as the look in his eyes. "No, princess, I'm calling you an alarmist. There's a difference."

"Not much of one! Would I have woken you up if I didn't think it was important?" She sucked in a steadying breath. It didn't help. Her fingers curled around fistfuls of her wrinkled calico skirt. "I'm telling you, *I-heard-a-noise!*"

"And *I'm* telling *you* it was the wind."

"*What* wind?" she demanded. To prove her point, she licked the tip of her index finger. Jake's glare tracked the movement. Amanda tried not to notice the heat that gaze caused to spread up her arm. It was impossible *not* to notice her reciprocal shiver of reaction. Her tone lost its sting as she held her wet finger up in the air. "There's a breeze, I'll grant you that, but no wind. And even if there was — which there isn't, but if there *was* — it still wouldn't explain the twigs I heard snapping."

She paused for affect — of which there was little, except the veiled suspicion she saw shimmering in his eyes. "*Footsteps,* Mr. Chandler. That's what I heard. *Footsteps.*"

"No, Miss Lennox. What you heard was a squirrel. Or a dog. Or . . . hell, I don't know." His shrug was jerky and strained as he pushed to his feet. "If you were from around these parts you'd know that at this time of morning, sound travels. Things seem louder than they are. Noises get distorted, warped. What you say you heard could have been damn near anything, coming from damn near anywhere."

Amanda gritted her teeth with frustration. There was no reasoning with this man, really there wasn't. "I didn't hear just 'anything,' I heard *footsteps*. And they were close by."

He glanced away. "So you say, and so I still don't believe. Now, if you'd *seen* someone that would be different . . ."

Amanda scrambled to her feet. Hoisting the skirt up so it wouldn't trip her, she dogged his footsteps with a

stilted, limping gait of her own. She contained —
barely — the urge to smack him good.

Why wouldn't Jake believe her? she wondered, as she
stared a point midway between his shoulder blades.
He'd shrugged on a shirt on at some point during the
night. The faded, forest green cotton stretched over his
sinewy shoulders, the color an earthy compliment to his
copper skin and jet-black hair. The material left no
doubt as to the powerful muscles bunching beneath.
Her traitorous heart skipped a beat.

Exactly when her resentment began to fade,
Amanda couldn't say. She only knew that it *had* dulled,
and that she didn't like it one little bit. Fury was sensible, safe. This white-hot awareness of all things male —
of all things *Jake Chandler* — well, that wasn't sensible at
all. And nothing about it — about him — about her *reaction* to him — could be misconstrued as safe. Just the opposite; it was hot and dangerous.

She tore her gaze from his back and found herself
staring intently at his hips; lean and firm, provocatively
molded by tough, clinging denim. Her teeth clamped
down on her lower lip. Lord, he was nicely shaped.
And had she really thought looking *there* would be
a safe, sensible thing to do? She was wrong. Dead
wrong. Glancing at his rock-solid thighs wasn't
any better.

Dammit! Wasn't there an inch of his body that was
safe to look at? Was there a sliver of him that didn't
spark some complex, erotic reaction in her? If so,
Amanda couldn't find it.

She raked him head to toe, her gaze momentarily
cool and objective. The man had no obvious flaws. Oh,
hell! the man had no *un*obvious flaws, either. From the
top of his head to the tips of his bare feet, every inch of
him was formed to appeal to the eye — and the soul.
Every single inch!

He was heading for the tree trunk he'd sunken his
knife into. The progress of his swaggering strides made
the air around Amanda shift. Feeling the kiss of it

against her cheeks, she slowed her pace and drew in a curious breath.

She froze. Her fists uncurled. The skirt slipped from her slackened grasp, rustling around her ankles in wrinkled calico folds. She might as well have walked face first into a solid brick wall; the scent of him had that great an affect on her.

The morning smelled abruptly of spicy man and freshly milled soap. It was a fatal combination; a flagrantly male, blatantly seductive one.

Jake felt the heat of her gaze on his back, but most of his attention was trained on his knife. The hilt bit into his palm when his fingers curled around it. The muscles in his shoulder and arm strained as he wrenched the blade free. Chunks of bark rained to the ground, nipping at the tops of his bare feet.

He stared at the blade, scowling darkly. An image of what would have happened had his aim been true—which it usually was—flashed through Jake's mind. The vision was brief, wispy, gone as quickly as it had come. His reaction was disturbing; it lasted a hell of a lot longer!

A shiver iced through him. The sensation started where the cool wooden hilt was warming to his palm. Tremors vibrated up his arm in increasingly chilly waves, and . . .

Dammit! he was shaking again. A cold sweat broke out on his chest and brow. His gut twisted, and his heart felt tight, as though invisible fingers had clamped around it and squeezed it in a death-grip. Unwelcome sensations invaded his body and his mind, humming through the rest of him with alarming speed and accuracy. If Jake didn't know better, he would have sworn he was getting his first real taste of fear.

He took a few needed seconds to compose himself. The grass felt cold and dewy beneath his feet as, tucking the knife into its leather sheath, he turned to look at Amanda.

His heart sank. She wasn't standing where she

should be. In fact, she wasn't standing anywhere at all.
The clearing was empty.

Miss Abigail Henry owned and ran the best finishing school Boston had to offer. The teachers there had diligently taught Amanda how to make excruciatingly small embroidery stitches, how to master the pianoforte and harp, and how to command a battery of household servants. Roland Lennox had paid a small fortune for his daughter to learn everything she needed to know to become a lady. Amanda had learned it all — grudgingly, true, but she *had* learned it.

Only now did she realize her educators had left out life's most important lesson: how a woman managed to convince a stubborn-as-all-hell male to listen to reason!

That Jake didn't believe she'd heard noises was frustrating. That she couldn't *make* him believe her was infuriating. Truly, he'd left her no choice. Either she searched the woods to see who'd made the footsteps that she *had* heard, or they would never know who was out there. Not knowing, always wondering if she was being secretly watched and evaluated, was unendurable.

It had taken Amanda less than a second to decide to search the woods herself. It was the only way to get the job done, since Jake had made it clear *he* wouldn't do it.

Up ahead another twig snapped. Amanda heard a muffled sound that might have been a voice, but might have been something else — it was too distant to be certain.

She molded her back against a thick tree trunk, and her fingers trembled as she slipped the antique pistol from her pocket. As she'd done before, she prayed that the sight of it would be enough to scare whoever was out there away. And if it wasn't . . . well, she hoped Jake Chandler could live with her death on his conscience! If he even had a conscience, that is — he'd given her every reason to believe he didn't.

The branches above shifted. Tiny paws scampered

through the underbrush. The rustle of grass sounded exceptionally loud. Except for that—and one very shrill bird chirping from a branch high above—the woods were quiet. Too quiet, she thought, as, holding her breath, she slowly peeked around the tree.

Only once she'd proved she was still alone did Amanda realize she'd been holding her breath until her lungs burned. She released it in a rush. The fingers clutching the pistol to her chest stopped quivering. Well, all right, maybe they hadn't stopped trembling completely, but her shaking had begun to ease. The coward in her took that as a good sign. Now, if she could get her heart to stop drumming wildly in her ears.

Easing away from the tree, she cautiously picked her way to the next hazy trunk. The process was repeated two more times, until her fingers really did stop shaking.

The muffled noise she'd heard before came again. It sounded closer . . . she thought. Of course, as Jake had sarcastically pointed out, at this time of the morning distance and place was easily distorted.

Damn Jake Chandler, she fumed as she moved to the next tree, molding her back against the scratchy bark. *Damn him to hell and back!* In less than twenty-four hours he'd turned her world upside down. She wasn't sure how he'd accomplished that in such a short amount of time, and so easily. Or was she?

Last night's kiss—and her wanton reaction to it— had haunted her dreams and fueled her confusion. If it was one thing Amanda hated, it was confusion. She could easily learn to hate Jake for making her feel it.

Another twig snapped. It was closer, she was sure. The sound blended with the whisper of dry leaves scattering on the breeze and the bird that continued to shrill loudly overhead.

Amanda's fingers tightened around the pistol. The handle was hot from the heat of her palm. Her index finger twitched on the trigger. She didn't know why; it wasn't as though the thing was loaded. It wasn't as though she had any bullets to load it *with!* Still, having the gun in her clammy hands made her feel better. Safer. Not a lot, but a bit.

Something—footsteps?—sounded in front of the tree she was hiding behind. The noise was soft, fleeting. If she hadn't been listening for it, she wouldn't have heard it.

Whoever was out there was moving closer.

Amanda's hands started to shake again. She sucked in a steadying breath and promised herself that on its release she would muster her courage and stop stalling. When she exhaled, she would jump from behind the tree, brandishing her weapon, and face whatever, *who-*ever, was out there.

The air pushed from her stinging lungs when she'd held it for as long as she could. Before she could command her feet to move, she'd sucked in another. All right, after *this* one . . .

Coward! a tiny voice taunted in her head.

Amanda's brow puckered in a frown. Her spine bristled. Was it her imagination, or was that voice *not* in her head?

Her gaze snapped to the side. Her eyes widened.

If it took her entire life, she would never know how Jake Chandler could be standing so close without her being aware of him. She was aware of him now. She would have to be dead *not* to be! His presence—his body heat and earthy scent—tingled through every nerve in her body.

His grin was slow and taunting. "Didn't think I'd let you face this alone, did ya, princess?"

A movement caught Amanda's attention. She glanced down, and noticed belatedly that Jake was holding his left hand close to his stomach. Something small and fuzzy and brown nuzzled his cupped palm. As she watched, Jake leaned forward and lowered the furry thing to the ground.

The rabbit wasn't fully grown, nor was it a baby. For

a split second the animal looked stunned, as though surprised to suddenly feel earth beneath it's feet. But only for a second. Tipping its head to the side, the rabbit glanced at Jake, then with a shove from its long, powerful back leg, bolted headlong into the woods. It's small feet crunched over dry leaves and twigs.

The noise it made as it ran sounded remarkably like footsteps.

Chapter Seven

Amanda stifled an embarrassed groan as her gaze strayed to Jake. He was standing beside her—close beside her. His right arm was arched above her head, the forearm resting against gritty bark. His left thumb was hooked through a belt loop at his hip. His ankles were crossed, which made his hips jut at a cocky angle. His thigh, she noticed belatedly, rested a mere fraction of an inch from her own.

"Well?" Jake asked, his voice soft, husky. *"Did* you think I'd make you face that mean little bunny by yourself, princess?"

Amanda ignored his heat, his nearness, his sarcasm. At least, she tried to. What she couldn't ignore was the way her heartbeat stuttered and her breathing shallowed. Her gaze shifted, skimming Jake's lips; her heart stopped entirely when she saw the very corners curve up in a wolfish grin.

"Yes," she hissed softly, "that's exactly what I thought, Mr. Chandler. That's exactly what you *wanted* me to think."

"You must've gotten the wrong impression, *Miss Lennox.*"

"I don't think so." Amanda sighed. It was humiliating enough to know she'd come out here with a gun, chasing what she thought were footsteps but what was in reality nothing more than a harmless rabbit. She swallowed

118

hard, and felt a desperate need to change the subject. "What are you doing here?"

"Isn't it obvious?"

"Not to me."

He shrugged, and his shoulder came into sizzling contact with hers. Amanda knew she tensed, she wasn't sure if Jake did or not. Nor, she told herself, should she care.

Jake nodded to the gun she fisted to her breasts. "Loaded?"

"Yes," she lied with surprising ease. Well, it was either that, or tell him the truth and risk his opinion of her — which was already frighteningly low — lowering still more. She wasn't sure why the idea that Jake would think her a fool should bother her so much, it just did.

He extended one coppery hand and wiggled his fingers expectantly. "Good. Hand it over."

"I will not!"

He grinned again.

Amanda's heart stopped . . . *again,* then throbbed to vibrant life. Her knees felt watery. Oh, how she hated that! Embarrassing though it was to admit it, even to herself, the tree trunk grinding into her spine was the only thing keeping her erect.

His eyes narrowed. The muscle in his cheek jerked. "Maybe you didn't hear me right, princess. I said give me the gun."

"There's nothing wrong with my hearing, Mr. Chandler," she snapped, her voice rising to a very loud whisper, "but perhaps there's something wrong with yours. *I* said no."

Jake sucked in an irritated breath and released it very, very slowly. The hand he'd extended curled into a fist, flexed twice, then gradually relaxed. His voice, when it came, sounded strained. "Give me the f—goddamn gun, lady. *Now!*"

Amanda gasped. She felt her cheeks heat, though she refused to acknowledge that she was blushing. Of course not! She'd heard worse — from this man's lips, come to think of it. "There's no need to use that sort of language, Mr. Chandler."

"No? Well, *I* for one think there is. And what you just heard is nothing compared to what you're *going* to hear if you don't hand over that pistol."

Amanda knew she couldn't give him the gun. She'd told Jake it was loaded and it wasn't. If he discovered the truth, he'd be furious with her . . . again. She'd already seen enough of this man's volatile temper for one day, thank you very much. She tipped her chin and met his gaze with a level one of her own.

"Mr. Chandler—" Her breath caught when he slashed his index finger across her lips, halting her words before they'd really begun. She felt the calloused roughness of his skin, the heat as well as the promise of his touch. His eyes darkened. A tremor rippled through his finger, through her. Her shiver of anger dissolved into a shiver of something entirely different, something strong, potent, distracting.

Amanda leaned back against the tree when Jake angled his head, bringing his face near hers. His lips were a hair's breadth away from her ear. She closed her eyes and tried to ignore the warm puffs of his breath on her cheek. She anticipated the contact of his mouth on hers. Anticipated, yet dreaded it.

"Mr. Chandler . . ." she said suddenly, breathlessly, just to hear the sound of her own voice. At that moment, she would have said anything to break the tension that stretched like a taut, heated wire between them. She'd overlooked just one thing: the way her lips would move against Jake Chandler's finger when she spoke. His skin felt pleasantly warm, pleasantly rough. It abraded her tender lips and sparked a slow burn in her blood. "I'm not entirely sure the noise I heard was made by that rabbit."

"Maybe not that rabbit specifically, but something just as harmless."

"But—"

"Sorry, princess," he whispered softly, seductively, as

120

he leaned closer, "but if I'd thought you really heard footsteps, I'd be honest about it and tell you. You see, I never learned to lie to quite the extent you did."

"I don't lie," Amanda lied, very, very weakly. A bolt of awareness shot down her spine when he moved the arm braced above her head. As she'd dreaded, their thighs made contact. As she'd dreaded, the contact was hard and hot and wonderful. The layers of calico, linen, denim seemed to fade, until it felt like no barrier separated them. Amanda hated the odd, liquid sensations that settled deep in her stomach, spiralling quickly lower. Hated them, but savored them, too. Damn Jake Chandler!

His chuckle was a blast of hot air in her ear, smoldering over her cheek and brow. "Lady you lie like a rug. We both know it. And you know what else? You blush something fierce every time. Bet you didn't know that, did you?"

As he spoke, Jake's finger dipped, and the tip traced her lower lip. He felt her moist flesh quiver beneath his touch. Then again, maybe it was his finger that quaked. He wasn't sure, didn't much care. Touching this woman left no room for thought.

"Give me the gun." His fingertip skimmed her chin, her neck. Her skin was so warm and soft and white it stunned him—but not nearly as much as his reaction to the feel of it did. That was like being stabbed through the heart.

His finger dipped beneath the prim, high buttoned collar of her blouse. He didn't tarry there long, just long enough to see a splash of warm pink stain her cheeks. Her eyes widened when his fingertip inched upward, and the lump in her throat slid up and down in a dry swallow. Her pulse drummed a wild rhythm against the back of his knuckle.

Jake thought about stopping, but only briefly. The notion registered only in his mind. His body had other ideas, other demands.

"I could wrestle that gun away from you, you know."

121

His darkened gaze roved over her, then darkened still more. "But I won't use force. I'd rather you gave it to me. I want you to *want* to give it to me, Amanda Lennox."

Amanda frowned. Was he still speaking about the pistol? Somehow, she didn't think so.

Jake gave her no time to wonder about it. Before she knew what was happening he'd shifted, straddling her legs between his knees, his lean, hard body crowding her against the tree. His chest brushed her breasts. The touch was accidental, over quickly — the first time.

There were some things it wasn't within a man's power to resist. Resisting never entered Jake's mind. He simply knew he *had* to do it again. The firm roundness of her burned past his shirt and burned into his skin. He wondered if the imprint of her would be branded into him hours later, when he took off his shirt. It wouldn't surprise him if it was. Nor would it thrill him.

While he stilled his torso, his finger was never still. He stroked a hot path down her throat, over her collar, lower. He traced the dark tubing that arched around the yoke of her bodice, hesitated, then with a flick of his wrist turned his search inward. A groan rumbled in the back of his throat as his touch feathered the generous upper swell of her breast.

Amanda fumbled the gun.

Lightning quick, Jake snatched it out of mid-air.

He caught the old, beat-up-looking pistol with his free hand. His other hand stayed right where it was, poised in a place it had no right to be; on the inviting upper curve of Amanda Lennox's breast. The sweet, tempting-as-all-hell heat of her seeped into him. He was aware of every choppy breath she drew. Her pulse slammed beneath his fingertip; quick and wild, the beat matched his own.

Jake knew he should break the contact and break it now. It would be the smart thing to do. The safe thing to do. Touching this particular woman in this particular way was against the rules. He knew that. So why, he

122

wondered, was the feel of her in his hand so damn good? Why was touching Amanda Lennox, almost but not quite intimately, the most enjoyable — *the most excruciating!* — form of torture he'd ever known?

And why the hell couldn't he stop?

Jake knew why, and he forced himself to confess it. All of it. He didn't want to stop touching her because, deep down, he knew this was the only time he would ever allow himself to touch a woman — a *white* woman — *this* white woman — in such a fashion. He'd learned his lessons long ago; his previous mistakes would not be repeated. But that didn't mean he couldn't satisfy his curiosity, did it? Hell, no. Just so long as he recognized his limits, remembered the boundaries . . .

Oh, yes, and there was one other reason. Jake was a strong man, yes, but . . . hell, he was flesh and blood — even if his flesh was copper, his blood half savage. Only a saint would have the strength to shun temptation when it came in the form of Amanda Lennox's warm, ripe body. Jake Chandler was no saint. Thank God! He doubted saints were lucky enough to feel anything so earthy and good as the curve of this woman's breast gliding beneath his fingertip.

"M-mr. Chandler . . . ?"

"Jake," he growled, his voice low and raspy. "When I'm touching you like this, call me Jake." He angled his head, and discovered that his mouth now had access to her earlobe. His tongue darted out, wetting the small white shell. Was it possible for earlobes to tremble? God, he hoped so. He'd hate to think those tiny quivers came from him!

His touch drifted lower. Just the one finger, just the tip.

To Amanda, that was more erotic than if he'd used his whole hand . . . because it made her ache for him to do exactly that. At some point, her own hands had risen; they rested against the hard, warm wall of his chest. Her fingers curled inward, bunching his shirt in tight, moist fists. His heartbeat slammed beneath her wrist. Like the

123

man, the rhythm was dark and primitive . . . dangerously out of control.

His breath felt hot and misty against her skin. The strokes of his tongue on her earlobe and neck made her burn. So did his slowly searching fingertip. Her breath caught as he crested the center of her breast, then slid down the full undercurve. He circled her, groaned, then began a torturously slow ascent.

Amanda knew she should make Jake stop — *now,* while she still had the presence of mind left to do it. Miss Henry had made it clear what sort of woman allowed a man to play with her body. The term she'd used was not "lady." Of course, if the man was your husband, it was perfectly all right to let him play in any way he saw fit.

Miss Henry's mandates had made perfect sense to Amanda, at the time. They made no sense to her now. How could feelings this good, this warm, this nerve-shatteringly hot and delicious, be wrong? And *why* was it wrong for her to want Jake to continue touching her? For her to want to touch him?

Jake's fingertip slowly circled the center of her breast. Amanda felt her nipple tingle and stiffen beneath the confining layers of linen and calico. Her blood heated. Unbidden, her back arched away from the tree; she arched into the hot magic of Jake Chandler's touch.

In that instant, she stopped thinking, and started *feeling.* Everything. Her fingers loosened from the folds of his shirt. The material felt moist and wrinkled from the tight heat of her grip when she splayed her hands on his chest. He moved — she didn't know why — and she felt his muscles flex into steel bands beneath her fingertips.

The tip of his tongue traced the line of her jaw, boldly sipping his way toward her chin. She craned her neck and arched toward him. Her tongue ran over her lips as she remembered last night's kiss — the heat of it and the satisfaction. She could still taste his strong, compelling flavor. Pulling in an unsteady breath, Amanda realized she wanted to taste Jake again. Now. Badly.

Jake licked the sensitive underside of her chin. If

124

warmth had a taste, this was it. Whiskey and honey. Salty-sweet and tempting. Warmth, he decided, was the taste of forbidden fruit — or, in this case, forbidden white skin. It was a taste to be savored, like fine French brandy. A flavor to be enjoyed to its fullest before it was snatched away. Jake *did* enjoy the taste of her. Very much. More, he was sure, than he should have, more than would be considered safe for either of them.

A thousand times he told himself to stop. A thousand times his body countered the impulse with stronger, undeniable urges. He had reasons to keep his distance from this woman. Good, solid reasons. Yet logic crumbled when he heard her throaty whimper. The sharp edges of reality blurred when he felt her skin glide beneath his tongue . . . felt her fists reclutch his shirt . . . felt her warm, sweet breath wash over his scalp and neck.

His breathing turned ragged. His self-control was shredded. Had he ever needed a woman as badly as he needed this one; right here, right now? No. And any need that strong scared the hell out of Jake.

His finger paused on the upper swell of her breast. This time it was a conscious hesitation, a very strained one. For the first time in his life, Jake didn't trust himself. He didn't dare move, didn't dare *breathe*.

The urge to find out how well this woman would nestle into his hand was strong. The urge to find out how well his hips would nestle between her perfect white legs was stronger. Too damn strong! The thought — sweet and tempting beyond reason — threatened to break him. In the end, it was the urge not to be broken by any white woman that won out. Regaining his self-control was a victory, though a rather unsatisfying one.

Jake lifted his head. He gritted his teeth when he felt his cheek brush hers. Even that innocent contact wasn't so innocent. Nor did it do his floundering composure any good. Touching Amanda Lennox, even accidentally, was a test of his endurance. His control was proving to be not nearly as good he'd once thought it was. Hell, with this woman, he didn't have any!

He pulled back slightly and glanced down at her. The back of her head rested against the tree trunk. Her lashes were down; the thick, dark fringe flickered against her porcelain smooth cheek. Her color was high, her breathing shallow, rapid. Jake knew it shouldn't please him to see he had that great an affect on her, but it did. It pleased him immensely.

"Jake?" Amanda whispered hoarsely. Her hands dragged down his chest. Her fingertips caressed his taut stomach before she let her arms drop, hanging limply at her sides. She wanted to touch more of him. *All* of him. For that reason alone, it would be best not to touch any of him at all.

Jake sighed and, like her, forced his hands away — with two major differences. He touched her shoulders, but no other part of her sweet, sweet body. And, where she'd trembled, Jake was positive he did no such thing. He was proving himself weakened by this woman, but he would never allow himself to become *that* weak. Not with Amanda Lennox, not with *any* white woman.

Amanda found it easier to think without Jake's hand and mouth caressing her. Not much easier — the memory of his hand and mouth was still sharp, still strong — but a little. Now, if she could make herself stop wishing he would kiss her today the way he had last night. . . !

Her lashes snapped up. In the brightening daylight she found herself held prisoner by his stare.

"You tempt me, princess," he drawled, and his husky voice skated warmly down her spine. "Really you do. But . . ."

"But. . . ?"

He opened his mouth, hesitated, then apparently changed his mind. His eyes said that the words he finally settled on were not his first choice. "Don't look at me like that. We . . ." Jake's gaze dropped to where he'd unconsciously laced his fingers around hers. Her hand felt cool and fragile in his. In the glow of ripening sunlight, her skin looked very white, his own very dark and coppery.

". . . can't." Stronger, he repeated, "We can't."

Amanda had never been brazen in her life. Miss Henry wouldn't have allowed or condoned it. Therefore, she was shocked to hear herself say, "All I want is for you to kiss me again, Jake. Like you did last night. Is that so wrong?"

"Hell yes, it's wrong! It's even more wrong that you can't see *why* it's wrong." His eyes narrowed, his glare swept her assessively. "You really don't understand, do you? You really don't see the difference between us. Jesus!" He shook his head and plowed the fingers of his free hand through his hair.

Amanda, in turn, lifted her hand to gently cup his cheek. His skin felt warm and smooth beneath her palm. It felt nice. His lashes swept down. His expression tightened — in pain, or in pleasure? There was no way to tell. "No, Jake; I don't see it. Why don't you explain it to me?"

Jake meant to answer her with one of the curt, seasoned rebuttals he gave to anyone who pried into his personal life. He was never sure where the answer he finally settled on came from. A place buried in a dark, hidden corner of him? Could be.

"Look at this," he growled. He lifted her hand until their entwined fingers were right under her nose. *"Don't you see it?"*

Amanda's breath caught. She blinked hard, and studied his hand. She saw the rich copper skin; the long, thick fingers; the red and calloused roughness that made her burn wherever and whenever it touched her. She saw a hand that could make her forget she was lady, a hand that made her want to be anything but. Was that what he wanted her to see?

"You're bigger than I am," she said finally, cautiously. "And stronger. I see that."

"Yeah, right," he snapped, frustrated now. "Bigger, stronger . . . and redder. Or did you forget about that part?"

"I didn't forget. I just —" she shrugged. "I didn't think it was important."

With jerky motions, Jake disentangled their fingers. Her hand dropped limply to her side. His balled into an iron-hard fist. He needed to hit something. A tree, a rock . . . anything inanimate would do. The urge was countered by a stronger, inexplicable desire not to frighten Amanda. "It's important, princess. Damn important. To *me*."

"I can see that."

"Can you?"

She nodded. "Yes. I just don't understand it."

"No? Well understand *this*."

He tunneled his fingers through his hair, the side with the braid, drawing the long, thick black curtain back and away from his face. He pointed to a place on the back curve of his neck.

Amanda's stomach muscles knotted. She didn't need a mirror to see that her face had paled, she could *feel* the icy drain of color.

The scar he'd pointed to was four inches long, thick, and curved like a half-moon. It narrowed at the tip, and faded from sight beneath his collar. The skin was puckered and pink; the scar obviously was not new. Not the one creasing his flesh, anyway. Who knew how old the scars on his soul were? Or how deeply *they* cut?

Jake let her look her fill. Only when he saw her swallow hard and glance away did he let his hair sift through his fingers, sliding back into place. His voice was gritty and hard. The cold glint in his eyes said there would be no compromise between them. "Listen to me, lady, and listen good. Because I'll only say this once." He held a rigid index finger up close to her face. "In my entire life I've slept with exactly one white lady. *One*. That scar was what I got for my pleasure."

She still wasn't looking at him. Dammit! Jake wanted her to look at him when he drove his point home. To that end, he reached out, hooked her chin with the crook of his index finger, and roughly dragged her gaze back to

128

his. He didn't label the emotion he saw shimmering in her eyes. He didn't dare.

"Ask. Come on, baby, I know you're dying to."

She shook her head. "Well, yes, but—"

Jake cut her off sharply. "I was working a spread in Texas about five years back. The *lady* in question was the boss's daughter," he sneered, and took perverse pleasure in the way Amanda flinched. Good. He needed to hurt her right now. Not physically—he'd never hurt a woman like that, and he'd be damned if he'd start now—but he had to lash out and make her feel just a little of the pain eating away inside of him.

Jake leaned into her, his voice edgy and flat. "Her name was Cynthia. Cynthia Reed. You would've liked her, princess. She was all sweet and ladylike. So damn refined," his chuckle was short and merciless, "and so damn far above the likes of me it was scary. But, hell, I was young and stupid enough to believe her when she said she wanted to marry me. That she loved me. And why not? At the time I was just gullible enough to believe I deserved to be loved just like any other man. I should be grateful to Cynthia for setting me straight, don't you think?"

Amanda sucked in a sharp breath and glanced away. Jake increased the pressure on her jaw, forcing her gaze back to him.

"Oh, no you don't. You're the one who wanted to hear this. Listen up, dammit!"

"No, Jake, I don't want—"

"Shut up and listen!"

Amanda snapped her mouth shut.

So did Jake, but only long enough to draw in two deep breaths. "Cynthia, as you've probably guessed, didn't love me, but she sure as hell loved what I could give her." His nostrils flared and, if possible, his expression hardened. "I'm not just talking about what I gave her between the sheets, baby. She wanted adventure. A taste of the wild and savage. She told me once she wanted to tame me . . . at least, she wanted to *try.*

"I knew the kind of trouble her sort would bring me, so I made it my business to stay clear of her. The problem was, the *lady* didn't take no for an answer. Cynthia was a spoiled white princess, used to getting everything she wanted before she wanted it. What she wanted was me. It was inconceivable to her that I would refuse. Which I did. Often. Hell, she was the boss's daughter. Off limits for that reason . . . and others.

"I wouldn't give her what she wanted, and that made her want it even more. She started to flaunt, to tease. I wish I had a greenback for every button on that girl's blouse that found it's way undone because . . . Lordy I'd be a rich man right now!

"After a few months of hell, I'd heard her silky love-words so many times I started to believe them. I really thought it was *me* who made her hot, not what I was." He sneered, caught up in the memory, and in the pain of betrayal that still sliced through him like a knife. "I took her to bed. I figured, what the hell? It was what she wanted, what she'd been begging for. And by then, it was what I wanted too. So badly I ached."

"You m-made love to her?" Amanda asked weakly, her mind spinning. Why, *why* did the thought of Jake Chandler with another woman hurt so badly?

"No, Amanda, we had sex. There's a difference. One I don't feel like getting into with you right now. Let's just say I gave her what she'd been begging for. Twice over and then some.

"The rumors started before the sheets were cold. It took a couple of months for them to drift back to me. Cynthia liked to brag that she'd bedded a savage and lived through it, scalp intact. Unfortunately, she talked too much, too loudly, to all the wrong people. It didn't take long for her daddy to find out his baby had been making it with a breed. Do you want know what he did? *Do you?!*"

"H-he beat h-her?"

"Nope. His sweet little girl had been taken advantage of by a filthy savage. Wasn't her fault, of course." Jake

130

gritted his teeth, and his breathing turned ragged and hard. "No, he didn't beat her. He beat *me*. Repeatedly. With a shovel . . . until I couldn't see, couldn't walk, couldn't goddamn *think!*"

Jake saw a flash of sympathy flicker in her eyes, and his entire body hardened against it. There was something else in her gaze. A question. He answered her ruthlessly, knowing Amanda didn't ask because she was afraid of the answer. And wasn't that a shame? Because the fact was, she'd started this, and now dammit, *he* was going to finish it. It was vital she know how poisonous this situation could become if things ever got out of hand between them. "Her daddy didn't cut me, Amanda. *She* did."

"What?" Amanda gasped and sagged weakly against the tree.

"I made it back to the bunkhouse somehow, and planned to gather up my things and get the hell out. She was there waiting for me. The cut wasn't meant to wound, lady, it was meant to kill. You see, by that time Cynthia had realized just how big a mistake she'd made. She took it upon herself to rid the world of one more breed, and in the process rid herself of a problem that wasn't going away fast enough."

"But you just said you were going to leave the ranch! Did you tell her that?"

"Yup."

"And she didn't believe you?"

He shrugged tightly. "I don't know if she did or not. If so, she didn't care. She told me she had a reputation to protect, said no one would believe a word of her story if she didn't try to retaliate in some form or another."

"So she tried to *kill you?*"

"Tried being the operative word there. Of course, even if she'd been lucky enough to succeed, it wouldn't have mattered much. She was a good little white girl. I was the dirty breed who'd forced myself on her. She had every right, Amanda. I, on the other hand, had no rights at all."

Her eyes misted with tears—for him, for his pain. Her voice cracked. "I . . . Oh, God, I'm sorry, Jake. I didn't—"

"Don't you dare!" If his shout hadn't clogged the words in her throat, the molten fire in his eyes would have. That, and the way his grip on her jaw turned savagely tight. "Save your pity for someone who gives a damn, because I don't."

When she flinched, he jerked his hand away from her. His voice harshened as he glared down at her. "I learn from my mistakes, lady, and I damn well *don't* repeat them. If you're smart, you won't ask me to again."

Jake shoved away from the tree. He didn't go far, just far enough to put some needed distance between them. His lungs were filled with the flower-soft scent of her, while his mind was filled with the bitter memories this woman had made him dredge up. The duo was potent—it tore clean through him—and his reaction to it was unnerving.

He pulled in a ragged breath and again felt himself being seduced by the clean, womanly smell of her. The way her scent merged with the piny aroma of the woods made for an erotic combination. It was a fragrance that Jake felt a sudden, overpowering need to run from—fast—or risk drowning in. And he couldn't do that. It wasn't allowed.

Jamming his hands in his pockets, he spun on his heel. The uncertainty in Amanda's tone made him hesitate.

"I'm not like her, Jake. I've never asked a man to kiss me before," Amanda said shakily. Until yesterday, men hadn't interested her. Then she'd met Jacob Blackhawk Chandler. His complexity fascinated her—she didn't know why, it just did. So did the passion his touch unleashed in her, the pain his grudging admission kindled deep in her soul. Pity was not the only thing she felt for this man—her respect for him was far stronger—but she didn't dare tell Jake that. She doubted he would listen even if she'd tried. "I . . . I just thought you should know."

His hair curtained his face and shoulders as only his head came around. Though he studied her closely, Jake detected no telltale color in her cheeks. Her green eyes were dark, shimmering with a sincerity he found hard to look at, let alone believe she felt. Was she telling the truth? Jake didn't think she was capable of it — she'd lied to him so many times already — but it was a possibility. One of several.

"Never?" he asked, agitated. She shook her head, and Jake felt his heart skip a beat and a small sliver of his pain fade. There was a part of him that didn't want to know the answer to his next question. There was stronger part of him that demanded he know. "But you asked me to kiss you. Why?"

Admitting all this to Jake's back had been one thing. Admitting it while staring into those probing eyes of his was something else again. Her hands moved backward, and her palms stung when she pressed them hard against the gritty tree bark.

She shrugged and looked away. "Last night, when you kissed me, you said it was to end the suspense, so we could get it off our minds and put it behind us. It — it didn't work. Not for me, it didn't. I — " She rushed on before she lost her nerve. "I can't forget what it feels like to kiss you, Jake. And I can't forget about how badly I want you to kiss me again."

Jake's expression hardened. No, his *entire body* coiled tight, like a complicated knot he couldn't even begin to unravel. "Great," he growled. "Just great. There's one tiny problem, princess . . . one minor detail you seem to have *forgotten*."

Amanda pressed herself harder against the tree trunk. The brooding look in Jake's eyes was frightening, yet it was also oddly intriguing. Mesmerizing. She couldn't tear her gaze away. "I don't think I've forgotten anything."

"Trust me, you have. You've forgotten that I'm a half-

133

breed savage. A bastard who isn't fit to polish your boots . . . let alone look at you. Or touch you."

She couldn't say it. She *had* to say it. Amanda made her lips form the words her mind was begging her to bite back. Words her heart was pleading with her to say. "But you want to." Then, much higher, much softer, she asked, "Don't you?"

Jake didn't answer. He couldn't. If he said the words, he would have to acknowledge the truth in them. And what would be the point in that? Society had laid the ground rules before he'd even been born. Jake just played the game. There couldn't be anything between a man like him and a woman like the one he now turned his back on. He had the scar on his neck to remind him, just in case he ever forgot. Which he never did.

What he wanted didn't matter. What Amanda wanted *couldn't* matter. Jake wouldn't let it.

When he finally forced his feet to start walking, he didn't stop. Nor did he look back.

Amanda's rigid posture sagged. Her eyes stung with tears she refused to shed as watched him turn his back and walk away from her.

She remembered the day her father had told her he was shipping her East, to Miss Henry's school. He'd wanted her to learn to be a lady, like her mother had been. Amanda hadn't wanted to go. Her father had refused to listen. Finally, he'd given her no choice. The day the train pulled out of Seattle, with Amanda on it, she'd felt heartbroken, rejected, betrayed and abandoned. Unloved and unwanted.

She felt that way now, only this time the hurt cut deeper. She didn't think this wound would heal the way the last one eventually had. No, Jake Chandler's rejection would remain raw and open. It would always sting, a scar she could carry on her soul, just as Jake carried his on his neck.

It was going to take extraordinary self-control to not let Jake see how badly he'd hurt her, but she didn't have a choice. As always, she *would* keep her pain to herself.

She would rather die than let Jake get even a glimpse of it.

Smoothing the wrinkles from her skirt, Amanda straightened her shoulders and stepped away from the tree. Her heels crunched loudly over the moss-covered ground as she retraced her way back to their camp. She was careful to keep a good distance between herself and Jake.

Chapter Eight

When Amanda had agreed to compensate Jake Chandler for his services, she'd been sure she was paying an exorbitant amount of money for a minimal amount of work. Her original estimate about how much time it would take to find Roger had been a day if things went well, two if they went badly.

Things were going very badly.

She and Jake rode all day, stopping only when absolutely necessary to rest the horses or answer nature's call. At midafternoon, Jake picked up the pace. Amanda wasn't sure, but she thought she'd heard him mumble something about Roger and his kidnapper being a mere three hours ahead of them.

That was an hour before he'd lost sight of the prints entirely. At least, Amanda assumed that was what had happened. There was, of course, no way she could be positive; Jake rarely spoke to her. Still, the way he noticeably started slowing the pace around four o'clock, stopping often to inspect the ground, said that was a very good possibility.

He didn't spot the prints again until it was almost dusk, and by then it was too late to track them for more than an hour.

Hate though she did to admit it, Amanda found a lot to admire in the way Jake milked every second of sunlight for all it was worth. He didn't give the sign they

136

would be stopping for the night until darkness had completely enveloped them. By that time, her sore bottom was familiar with every inch of the hard-mold saddle beneath her. Her ankle throbbed and her head ached from gritting her teeth and worrying about Roger.

That she was worrying about the little monster again, Amanda did not take as a good sign. Exhaustion would have to explain it. Truly, she'd never felt this sore and tired in her life!

True to form, Jake led them into a tree-sheltered clearing, dismounted, then, without explanation or apology, rudely abandoned her the same way he had the night before. Amanda was again faced with the unsavory prospect of dismounting unaided. The rat!

This time, she slung her leg carefully over the pommel and slipped to the ground very slowly and cautiously. Last night's incident was still fresh in her mind—her heartbeat stuttered with the memory, her blood warmed. After Jake's earlier rejection, she wasn't about to risk a repeat performance.

Amanda frowned and glanced at her surroundings. She considered gathering up branches and sticks and starting a fire, but only briefly. She was still out of matches. While Jake had helped her build a fire last night, Amanda knew she couldn't accomplish the feat on her own. Besides, she was simply too tired and sore tonight to try.

Her body aching, she limped over to a nearby tree. The hard, cold, lumpy ground made an uncomfortable cushion beneath her sore bottom, and the gritty bark nipped at her tender back when she leaned against it. Despite that, she appreciated the fact that nothing was moving, nothing was jostling her and making her cramped muscles and throbbing ankle hurt even more.

Sighing, she closed her eyes and adjusted herself to as comfortable a position as she was likely to find. Of its own accord, her mind drifted down a sensual path lined with wet copper skin, long black hair, and piercing silver eyes.

Amanda's heartbeat accelerated, and her breathing went choppy and shallow. She promised herself that this time, even if Jake never came back, she would *not*, under *any* circumstances, go searching for him!

"Supper." Jake tossed something onto the ground near her feet, then turned and swaggered away.

Amanda blinked hard. Her eyes were burning, and for the past half hour she'd been fighting a losing battle to keep them open. She seized on Jake's single word as a good distraction from her exhaustion. His gritty tone coursed down her spine like a drop of warm honey, awakening her senses, honing them.

That one clipped word was the first real thing he'd said to her all day — except for occasionally cursing under his breath, he hadn't spoken to her directly since that embarrassing incident this morning. Amanda hadn't realized how greedy she was for the sound of his voice . . . until now.

Supper. The first image to flash through her mind was of stringy jerky and tinny-tasting beans. The second was more appealing. Her stomach grumbled when she replaced the image with succulent pheasant smothered in tangy orange sauce. No, make that lobster sautéed in wine and butter, the tender white meat flaking away under the delicate application of a fork.

"Supper," Amanda repeated, her mouth watering. Her stomach growled with unladylike vehemence. "What are we having?"

"Snake."

Her eyes widened, and the extra moisture in her mouth evaporated to shock. It took two full minutes for her thought processes to kick back in. At the end of that time, Amanda had convinced herself she'd heard Jake wrong. She must have. Surely she'd only *thought* he had said . . . "I beg your pardon?"

Jake was kneeling beside his saddlebag, his big hand rummaging through its shadowy leather depths. He seemed to be ignoring her, but he wasn't. Jake was very much aware of the sharp edge of repugnance in Amanda's tone. It took effort to suppress his grin. "No need to beg, princess. All I'm asking is that you cook it."

Was that amusement she heard in his tone? Amanda hoped for his sake that it was not. Her green eyes narrowed, raking his chiseled profile. There were too many shadows to see details, but in the flicker of moonlight she saw enough. Perhaps too much. There wasn't even a hint of a grin on Jake's lips. His expression, half-shielded by the curtain of hair that fell forward over his shoulder, was as unreadable as stone.

Amanda's stomach twisted. Morbid curiosity, she supposed, would explain why her horrified gaze descended, seeking out the object Jake had so casually tossed to the ground in front of her. Unless her memory was faulty—oh, how she hoped it was!—the thing had made an unsavory *thunk* when it hit solid ground.

It was a good thing her heart had lodged in her throat, or she would have screamed. She could feel the shriek building in her throat the way she could feel the grass break off in her fingers when she clamped handfuls of it in tight, trembling fists. Had her cheeks gone white? They felt cold, bloodless, and chalky, so she assumed they had.

Jake straightened, and moved to stand in front of her. Amanda didn't hear his approach, but then, she hadn't expected to. She could feel his nearness, smell his earthy scent on the air. Pity none of that managed to shake her trancelike gaze from the carcass that curled over the grass near her feet.

"Problems, princess? You look a might peaked."

Jake's voice came from a point far above her head. Amanda barely heard him. The pounding in her ears was too loud and furious. "Th-that's a . . . a . . . ?" She sucked in a sharp breath and tried to get hold of herself. Unfortunately, that just wasn't possible. "That's a s-s-s . . ."

"Snake," he said, hunkering down. Reaching out, he

139

picked up the thing that Amanda was regarding with such abhorrence. The snake was about six feet long, thick and heavy. Its body draped over his palm, the head and tail ribboning over the ground like a limp piece of rope. "A diamondback rattlesnake to be precise."

A rattlesnake, Amanda's mind echoed, dazed. Her stomach gurgled its displeasure. Hadn't she read that rattlesnakes were poisonous? Not that it mattered, she supposed, since the thing was dead as a doorknob. Poisonous or not, it wasn't going to be biting anything ever again. Not that she planned on getting close enough to have that theory proved out!

"Don't look so worried, princess. Unless you're a bigger eater than I thought, there should be enough for both of us."

She glanced up, glad for any excuse to stop looking at that . . . that *snake*. She was just in time to see Jake's steely gaze rake her. His eyes were hot, probing, and assessive. Unexpected heat trickled into her bloodstream, and it was just warm enough, just strong enough, to burn off a tiny bit of her repulsion.

"Nah," he said, and tossed the snake back onto the ground. It made that revolting noise again. Amanda grimaced, her stomach rolled. "You're too skinny to eat much. Probably pick at your food like a bird."

The simile was not lost on Amanda—she only *wished* it had been. Her mind filled with a gruesome image of beaks pecking at a dead snake's carcass. Her head felt suddenly light and dizzy. A bitter-tasting lump of nausea wedged in her throat. Swallowing it back took more effort than she'd ever admit to this man.

"I have a healthy appetite for . . . *normal* food, Mr. Chandler," she said finally. Her voice sounded humiliatingly soft and strained. But that was all right; at least now she *had* a voice!

"Nothing abnormal about eating a little snake now and again, *Miss Lennox*. Out here, you can't afford to be picky. Fresh meat is fresh meat."

"And revolting is revolting," she snapped, her gaze

shifting to the snake. A chill iced down her spine, and she immediately averted her attention. Meeting his gaze, she forced her chin to lift an imperious notch. *"That* is disgusting. I won't eat it."

Jake shrugged. "Fine by me. All I ask is that you cook it."

"I will *not!*"

"Wanna bet?"

"All the tea in China, Mr. Chandler. All the tea in China."

Jake scowled. Now what the hell was she talking about? They didn't have any tea — unless she'd brought it, and if she did . . . hell, he didn't care to know about it. Besides, they weren't talking tea here, they were talking nice juicy snake. Supper. Couldn't the woman follow a simple conversation? He decided her swift change of topic must be her ladylike way of relenting. Whatever.

He pushed to his feet and glanced down at her. Her spine looked incredibly rigid, even for her, and her cheeks were ashen. He shrugged, thinking she'd probably just laced her corset too tight. Making a mental note to talk to her about that later, he turned away. Over his shoulder he said, "I'll get the fire started while you skin supper."

He'd taken no more than a step when he heard "Ugh," then felt something large and heavy slam into his lower back.

Years ago, self-preservation had honed Jake's reaction time to lightning speed. In a beat he'd spun on his heel; the knife slipped soundlessly from its sheath, the hilt cradled in his palm, the blade brandished threateningly, before he'd even completed the turn.

Amanda gasped. The grimace wrinkling her nose faded, and the hands she was scouring on her shirt froze. A tremor that she tried to stifle, but couldn't, racked her shoulders. "Oh, no. Not again."

If Jake heard, he gave no sign. His slitted gaze volleyed between her big, frightened green eyes, and the snake—the body of which now curled like a shadowy coil of rope in the grass near his feet. "Jesus, lady, what the hell'd you do that for?"

"You deserved it." The second she saw him sheath the knife, Amanda began to relax. Unfortunately, her trembling wasn't so easily conquered. "Don't think for a minute that I'm going to . . . to *skin* that . . . that . . ."

"Snake," he finished for her, the word hissing from between tightly clenched teeth. "It's a snake, princess."

"I know what it is!"

"Then say it."

"No."

Jake had always prided himself on having an abundance of patience. He found nothing admirable about how close he was to loosing his temper with this woman now. "Fine, don't say it," he growled. His nostrils flared, and the muscle in his cheek jerked. "Hell, I don't care if you *never* say it. Just so long as you skin it."

Her chin was tipped at a haughty angle. Until that moment, Jake didn't realize just how much he hated the way she did that. Her condescending glare now had to travel the full, pert length of her nose to reach him. The glint in her green eyes made him feel low and dirty, like she found him more repulsive than the reptile that would, with any luck, be their supper. He supposed her expression was a natural gesture for her, just as he supposed it was only natural for his reaction to be an itch in his fingers that begged for the chance to throttle some of that regal disdain out of her.

He leashed the urge. Barely. "Well? You going to cook it or not?"

"Not. I refuse to touch that," she grimaced, and shivered delicately, *"thing."*

His grin was cold and ruthless, gone as quickly as it had come. "You just did, princess. Or don't you remember throwing it at me?"

"I remember. And the only reason I touched it then was because I was too upset to think about what I was doing." Amanda was thinking about it now, though.

142

Thinking about how the cold, scaly hide had felt in her palms. About how heavy it was, the way its body had twisted and moved as though it was still alive. She swallowed hard and rubbed her hands down her skirt, trying to scrub away the disgusting feel. It refused to be banished.

Jake studied her long and hard. He had to admit, at first he'd chalked up her reluctance as a childish desire to . . . *annoy* him—her way of getting even for what he'd done to her last night with the fire. Now he wasn't so sure. The woman looked truly horrified at the thought of touching the snake again. And when he'd mentioned eating it . . . well, her pale white cheeks still had that unflattering green undertone.

Jake scowled, at her as much as at himself. All right, so he'd had a momentary slip. He'd temporarily forgotten that properly bred white ladies rarely if ever saw, let alone *dined,* on snakes. So what? He'd been hungry and tired after a long day of riding and tracking. When he'd seen the snake he'd thought it would make a nice, easy-to-cook, hearty supper. He still did. God knows it would be a refreshing change from jerky and beans. He hadn't given a thought to how Little Miss Prissy Britches would react.

He wasn't going to think about it now. He was still tired, still hungry, and he'd already killed the goddamn snake. He wasn't about to go hunt up something else when they had a perfectly good meal waiting to be skinned, gutted, and cooked.

Which brought up another interesting point . . .

"You *do* know how to cook, don't you, princess?"

"I can fillet and broil a swordfish that would drive you to your knees, Mr. Chandler," she sniffed imperiously. His knees, Amanda thought wistfully. Yes, she would definitely like to see Jake there. Soon.

His laughter took her off guard. It was a deep, thoroughly masculine, thoroughly appealing sound. She glanced up, and found herself entranced. The whiteness of his teeth made an intriguing contrast to his rich copper skin. Laugh lines bracketed his mouth, and his eyes shimmered in a way that was mesmerizing, not to mention breathtakingly attractive. Amanda couldn't look away. Worse, she wasn't entirely sure she wanted to.

One inky brow cocked. "Swordfish? Princess, I don't know how to break this to you, but we're nowhere near the ocean. A few trout is the best I could do . . . providing I found a stream before dark. Which I won't, because I'm not going out again."

"Pity. My swordfish is a real treat."

"No doubt," Jake said, then chuckled and shook his head. Broiled swordfish! Jesus, this pampered white woman was chock full of surprises!

Like his laugh, Jake's low, husky chuckle shot down Amanda's spine like a flash of liquid heat. It sizzled in her blood and melted her indignation. Deep down she knew she should still be feeling at least a smidgen of anger. He was laughing at her expense, after all. She had a right to be upset. So why wasn't she? Why couldn't she, no matter how hard she tried, summon up even an ounce of resentment?

She didn't know, she just couldn't. Amanda thought Jake's suddenly good mood had a lot to do with it. His laughter was infectious. She was having trouble trying to keep the corners of her mouth quirked in a stern frown; her lips begged to curl upward, eager to join in his mirth.

"Tell you what I'm gonna do," Jake said, sounding very much like a carnival vendor she'd seen once, many years ago. "Why don't we trade chores? You get the fire started while I skin our friend here." He crouched down and picked up the snake, letting it drag from his hands down to the ground. "Sound fair?"

Oh, yes. It sounded more than fair. Unless one took into account what he wanted in return for such a magnanimous gesture. And he would want something, she knew. Jake Chandler was too shrewd to offer a favor like that out of the goodness of his heart — if he had one, which she rather doubted. No, there had to be something in it for him. Amanda didn't hesitate to ask exactly what that something he would want in return was.

Jake's attention immediately, albeit unconsciously, dipped to her lips. His gaze burned and devoured— more so when he saw her catch and nibble the full pink flesh with her teeth. His jaw clenched, and he curbed an overpowering urge to replace her teeth with his. To nibble, taste, stroke with his tongue . . .

Remember that she's a prissy white woman. Remember what happened this morning. Jake knew that was what he should be thinking about right now. That, and the bitter sting of years of old memories and hard-learned lessons. Surely, between the two, this urge to taste and touch and push the rules would fade. Wouldn't it? Jesus, he hoped so!

Jake hiked the snake over his shoulder and shrugged. "What do I want?" he said, his tone forcefully light. He retreated to sit with his back propped against a tree that was as far away from the sweetly forbidden temptation that was Amanda Lennox as he could get. "Supper, princess. *That's* what I want. *All* I want. I'm starving."

Amanda had been, too, until she watched him whip out his knife, the blade poised close to the snake's head. She was not hungry enough to consider eating a . . . *snake.* No, no. She would *never* be that hungry. Chewy jerky and watery beans were no culinary delight, and, yes, she was heartily sick of the tasteless, repetitive meal at this point, *but at least* her *supper had never bitten anyone!*

She shifted her attention to gathering wood, all the while doing her best to ignore what was happening between Jake and . . . his dinner. It wasn't easy. Some of the noises coming from his direction were quite revolting. As luck would have it, his humming masked a goodly portion of them.

"That's a catchy tune," she murmured a few minutes later, as she knelt and deposited on the ground the small pile of dry twigs and branches she'd gathered. Actually, the melody had a barroom flavor to it. But Amanda didn't mind. She was willing to compromise her integrity if it meant getting him to talk. She had missed the sound of his voice today. Much, much more than Miss Henry would have considered proper. "What is it called?"

After a noteworthy pause, he said, "Don't ask."

"Really, Mr. Chandler, I want to know."

"No, Miss Lennox, you really don't. Trust me."

Trust him? Trust *him?* Amanda rather thought not. How could she trust a man she hardly knew? A man who, by his own admission, was one part savage, no part gentleman? She couldn't, and that was that.

Amanda yanked out and sprinkled a handful of dry grass around her foundation stick, then sat back on her heels. She almost looked at Jake but, remembering what he was doing, decided against it. She knew her limits, knew when she was pushing them, and watching him disembowel a snake fell into the latter category. She flattened her palms on either side of the stick, positioned it, and, as she prepared to whirl, said, conversationally, "I know a lovely tune about a dog and clover. The melody is similar to the one you were humming. I'd be happy to teach it to you, if you'd like. Unless, of course, you already know it."

"Depends," he asked cautiously. "How does your song go?"

Amanda had always had a uniquely off-key voice. Normally it didn't bother her when people referred to her singing as dogs howling at the moon — or were the canine begging for her to stop? She had a feeling that today it was going to bother her immensely if Jake made that same comparison. Still, not wanting to break the mood, she took a deep breath and tried her best. "Roll me oooover, roll me oooover, roll me over in the clover do it again, bom, bom."

Amanda couldn't put her finger on what emotion was riddled in Jake's pause.

"Yeah," he said finally, slowly. It sounded like it took great effort to keep his tone flat. "I know it. But the version I'm thinking of doesn't have a dog. Could be inter-

146

esting if it did, though. Should I ask who taught you that little ditty?"

Amanda smiled and began whirling the stick, nice and easy, just like Jake had taught her. "My father. I was about . . . oh, ten or eleven at the time."

"Now I *know* we aren't talking about the same song. And if we are, we're *definitely* talking about different versions."

"Why do you say that? Because my version has a dog in it?"

"No. Because *my* version is dirty as hell."

The stick came to an abrupt halt. One golden brow arched. Amanda's eyes narrowed, and she pursed her lips, intrigued despite herself. "Define 'dirty.' "

"Let's just say the first verse alone would tighten your corset a few inches. And speaking of corsets . . ."

Just the mention of such a personal piece of apparel made the article in question feel uncomfortably tight, as though it had just shrunk two sizes. All of a sudden, the whalebone stays felt like they were digging into her ribs. That *was* the reason she couldn't breath . . . wasn't it?

"Wh-what about my—" She couldn't. Amanda simply could not bring herself to mention her unmentionables in front a man like Jacob Blackhawk Chandler. Miss Henry would praise her decorum. As for herself, Amanda wasn't feeling very proprietary at the moment; she was too mortified.

"Your corset?" Jake supplied cheerfully. Too cheerfully, she thought . . . until his next words robbed her of the ability to think. "You know it's going to have to come off, don't you?"

"What is?"

"Your corset."

"What?"

"You heard me, princess. I had to ride slow today because you could hardly breathe, and we don't have time for it. Not if you want your cousin back any time soon. Un-uh. That corset's coming off. Tonight."

The stick dropped unnoticed from her suddenly slack fingers. "It most certainly is not!"

"We'll see. And just for the record, you'll never get a fire started that way. Didn't you learn anything last night?"

Think of it as like . . . making love.

Amanda closed her eyes. A groan slipped past her lips before she could catch it. "Oh yes, Mr. Chandler. I learned quite a bit," she said, somewhat breathlessly. *And it would have made a lot more sense to me if I knew what "making love" entails.* Of course, she didn't say that, because a man like Jake would feel it his duty to tell her. Or, worse, *show* her. A queer, fluttery sensation tumbled in her stomach when that particular thought, and the erotic images it provoked, filtered through her mind like hot, dappled sunlight.

Jake's chuckle did nothing to endear him to Amanda. "Want another lesson?"

The color in her cheeks deepened, and her heartbeat throbbed into double time. "That won't be necessary."

"Okay. Just ask if you change your mind. I'm always willing and able . . . for a lady."

Don't say it, Amanda. Don't you dare say it.

She didn't. Instead, her voice dripping sweetness, she said, "Oh, I will, thank you." And as she reached over and snatched up the stick, she swore inwardly that it would be a cold day in Hades before she *ever* voiced such a request. To any man!

Ten minutes later, kneeling in front of a still cold stack of unlit twigs and branches, Amanda came alarmingly close to choking on that vow. Dammit, what was she doing wrong? She was whirling the stick exactly the way Jake had taught her. She had the chaffed palms to prove it. Her strokes were slow and easy, smooth and fluid enough, she'd hoped, to create a friction that would at least provide a satisfying curl of smoke, if not the wished for flame.

It didn't.

For an unprecedented first time in her life, Amanda

pouted. She couldn't help it, she felt a disappointment that was irrational. And besides, she reasoned, it wasn't as though it was a *big* pout. Just a gentle out-thrust of her lower lip. Jake couldn't see it. The light would have to be perfect, and he would need to be looking directly at her . . .

The light on Jake's side of camp was damn good. And he was looking at Amanda. Directly at her. He saw her pout, and his body reacted swiftly and thoroughly, damn her proper little hide! He felt desire throb to life, straining and seeking, reminding him down to the second of how long it had been since he'd had a woman.

In the corner of his mind still able to function, he thought it was a good thing he'd already skinned and gutted the snake. The knife was safely tucked away, otherwise he would have worried about slicing his hand open — something he'd never, *never* done before. Then again, he'd never been distracted in such a way before. The attention he paid to that thrusting lower lip was all-consuming. He couldn't think beyond it, didn't want to.

Sweet. He'd thought last night that Amanda Lennox would taste sweet, just before he'd stupidly proved it. Now he knew . . . he *knew*! The flavor of her lingered on his tongue, tempting and teasing him until his gut knotted. How in the hell was he ever going to keep himself from kissing, tasting, feasting on her, again?

He leaned his head back against the gritty bark and released a long, slow breath through his teeth.

Amanda wasn't the only one hoping for the fire to get lit. Fast. Jake was hoping for it too. In a way he couldn't remember hoping for anything in his life. Because if she couldn't light it without help, if he had to go over there and guide her again and . . . well, twigs weren't the only thing that were going to combust. If that happened, his pride and her proper Bostonian sensibilities were going to get singed. It was inevitable.

Unless he left. Just for a while. Just long enough to get himself under control. Ah, what a wonderful idea.

Jake tossed his supper aside and pushed to his feet.

He glanced at Amanda, and his senses were suddenly filled with the long thick braid trailing down her spine like a ribbon of captured moonlight. He wanted to snatch the frayed ribbon from the end of that plait and work the silky strands free, to bury his hands in the soft golden cloud, to . . .

His jaw clenched as Jake forced himself to acknowledge the problem that was raging inside of him. Control. That was what he was leaving right now to find. The problem was, he had a feeling he could search until dawn, but it wouldn't be out there in the moonlit woods waiting for him. Oh, no. The ugly fact of the matter was, when it came to this woman — this lady — this *white* lady — he didn't have a whole hell of a lot of control to hang on to. And he should. Dammit, he *should!*

"I'll be back," he muttered as, in one fluid, silent motion, he turned his back on her and stalked from the clearing.

Amanda watched him go, confused by his abrupt departure, even more confused by the nagging emptiness that came back with sudden, breath-crushing force. When Jake had been talking to her, looking at her, even when he'd been laughing at her, the vacancy inside her had been filled. It was empty now, hollow and yawning. For him.

Oh, God. She *really* was losing her sanity. She'd known the man less than two days, yet here she sat missing the sight and sound of him. She wished she could believe that Roger's kidnapping had upset her so much that her logic had been tilted off balance. She was, and it had. But Roger's wasn't the cause. Jake Chandler was; his mere presence knocked her off-kilter.

As she positioned the stick, determined to give lighting the fire another try, her mind flashed her an image of Jake as she'd seen him last night. Tight copper skin, hard bands of muscle, long black hair cast blue in the shimmering moonlight, piercing silver eyes. Wet. All of him. Her heartbeat raced and her palms grew suddenly moist, suddenly sensitive and alive when she thought about those few drops of water clinging to his shoulder and how badly she'd wanted to rub them into his copper skin.

It wasn't possible to breathe, and Amanda wondered ironically if perhaps Jake wasn't right about her corset after all. It could use loosening. *She* could use loosening.

Sheltered and structured was how her life had always been, though not by choice. Yet her years at Miss Henry's hadn't sheltered her from the raw male onslaught of Jake Chandler, naked and proud and wet. Nor had her rigid schooling prepared her for the exquisite structure of his body, the tender torment of his kiss, or the unladylike ache he fostered deep inside of her with a glance, a touch, a word. Nothing had prepared her for that.

When a lady thinks of a man, it is his good character and innate sense of honor she reflects upon. Not his body.

Miss Henry's words. Amanda almost laughed when she thought that perhaps Miss Henry didn't know as much about ladies as she professed. It was obvious the old woman had never in her prim-spinster life met a man like Jacob Blackhawk Chandler.

Jake had no "good character" that Amanda had seen, and his "sense of honor" had yet to be found. That left his body. And oh, how Amanda reflected upon it!

She felt the bark of the stick she'd forgotten she held bite into her palm. Prying her eyes open, she saw the slice of wood was being held in a white-knuckled grip that threatened to snap it in two.

Ease up . . . make your movements flow . . . stimulate *the bottom stick . . . steady, but not jerky . . . get that friction started . . . I can't tell you how important rhythm is . . . once you've established the pace, you can't let up or you'll have to start from scratch.*

Jake's "lesson" replayed itself in her mind as she worked the stick. Amanda remembered everything; his words, his husky-rich tone, the way his cheek felt when it grazed hers, the way his sinewy chest and taut hips felt molded to her back and bottom. Everything.

151

Yet even though she followed his instructions to the letter, the stubborn fire refused to light.

Amanda cursed—vividly, aloud—and felt surprisingly better. Jake Chandler, she decided, was having quite a corrupting affect on her.

Sitting back on her heels, she glared at the pile of wood. It glared tauntingly back at her. She thought about how badly she wanted the fire lit, how much she needed to prove, if only to herself, that she wasn't a complete incompetent.

She sighed, her gaze sliding over her surroundings. The clearing was bathed in moonlight and shadows. Jake still wasn't back, and she didn't think he would be for a while yet. She still had time.

Her attention snagged on his saddlebag, and a crafty grin curled over her lips. So what if it was cheating? It would get the job done, wouldn't it? And Jake would never have to know.

Chapter Nine

"So. You ever play poker, princess?"

The spoon paused on the way to Amanda's mouth. Her green eyes lifted, and her gaze meshed with probing silver. "What?"

"Poker," he repeated flatly as he set his empty plate on the grass beside his hip. "*Strip* poker, to be exact. Ever play it?"

"I . . . well, actually —" Amanda snapped her mouth shut. Was it a lucky guess, she wondered, or did Jake know more about her than she'd thought? No, of course not. How could he? Then again . . . The fact remained that it was Amanda's skill with that particular card game that had prompted Miss Henry to ask her to leave school. The night Amanda had impulsively taught her friends at the Academy how to play, however, the only clothes that had come off belonged to cherished dolls. Somehow, she doubted that was what Jake Chandler had in mind.

The thought had no more receded when her spoon slipped from her suddenly slack fingers and clattered to her plate. Amanda scowled and glanced away. What little enthusiasm she'd worked up for the chewy jerky and tinny tasting beans evaporated like mist.

Jake grinned. Damn, but he liked it when she blushed! He liked it a lot. On one hand he could count the number of women he'd ever seen do that. Four had used an inspired flush as an entrapment

153

measure; not even close to being spontaneous. Cynthia had too, but he'd been too blind to see it that way. He'd been so sure she was different, so sure *her* blushes were genuine. Only once he was in too deep had he realized the truth.

Amanda, for some insane reason, was different. Jake thought he must have developed a cruel streak somewhere along the line, because he found he actually *enjoyed* watching the sweet pink color peek up from beneath her collar, spread swiftly up her neck, splash over her regally carved cheeks and seep all the way up to her honey-gold hairline.

Amanda set her meal aside. There was no way the tasteless food was going to find an easy path down her drier-than-dry throat now. It took effort to keep her spoon from clanking against the tin plate—her hands were shaking quite badly—but she managed. She dipped her head, hoping the muted moonlight and firelight weren't bright enough to betray the hot color in her cheeks. "I've . . . heard of the game, Mr. Chandler."

"Have you? Good. Wanna learn how to play it?"

Amanda surprised herself by giving the ludicrous suggestion serious thought. When Jake had returned to the clearing earlier, his mood had been almost hostile. He'd barely spoken to her, and he hadn't looked at her at all. He was talking to her now, and he seemed congenial enough. For reasons she refused to scrutinize, Amanda was desperate to keep things this way.

Still . . . *strip poker?*

In her mind's eye, she saw Miss Henry wagging a long, bony index finger and shaking her snowy head in stern disapproval. "No," Amanda said finally, if a bit stiffly, "not particularly."

"C'mon, princess, unlace those corset strings a bit, would you? It's only a card game. Something to pass the time. And you never know . . . it might be fun."

154

One golden brow arched skeptically high. "Fun? You think taking off our clothes in a card game would be *fun?*"

Jake's grin was wicked and quick. "I said *might* be fun. I take it you don't think so?"

Actually . . .

Amanda brought herself up short. What *was* she thinking? But, of course, she already knew. The thoughts spinning through her head were decidedly *un*ladylike. And highly intriguing. "Why don't we play a game of gin?" she suggested hopefully. "That's a nice, refined game. We can play for . . . oh, I don't know. Money, possessions, whatever. But *not* clothes."

Jake sighed and shook his head. "First off, I'm not feeling 'refined' tonight, princess. Second, the only money I want is what you owe me." His eyes narrowed, darkened, swept her body. "And the only thing you've got that I want is . . . against the rules." Slowly, slowly, his gaze blazed a warm path back to hers. "I like my idea better."

"Spoken like a true man. However—"

"What's the problem, princess? Afraid of losing your shirt? Is that it? Or are you just afraid . . . of me?"

His tone—soft, cajoling, challenging—reminded Amanda of a cut-crystal snifter of brandy. While the liquor looked creamy and smooth *inside* the glass, it was only once it washed over the tastebuds that the bite could be felt.

Jake's grin broadened. He watched the play of her thoughts on her face—she was so damn easy to read— and he liked what he saw. Her prim resolve was starting to crumble. He almost, *almost,* had her where he wanted her.

Well, no, that was a lie. Where he wanted her was beneath him, *surrounding* him, all hot and wet and tight, her long white legs wrapped around his hips, urging him closer, deeper. While Jake knew damn well he wasn't ever going to get *that* close to her—not if he

155

had any brains—at least if he could get her to play cards he could *see* what self-preservation demanded he miss. No doubt it would make the missing it part that much harder . . . but, hell, it was worth it. He wanted, *needed*, to feast his eyes on her silky white skin, her unbound hair. Just once, just for a little while, he wanted to see what the forbidden looked like. He had a feeling it would look like perfection. Like Amanda.

He watched her scowl, knowing how close she was to relenting. She was tempted to accept the dare, and Jake couldn't honestly say he was surprised. From the first he'd sensed in her a passionate inner spirit swaddled beneath layers of prissy formality. It was only a matter time. All he had to do was play on it, turn it to his own best advantage, appeal to the fiery little imp in her, the one buried and too-long ignored.

"You know you want to," he coaxed.

Amanda remembered last night—Jake naked and wet and proud—and thought that, yes, she wanted to all right. Much more than good sense decreed she should. Her chin notched up; she hoped the gesture looked more determined than it felt. "No, Mr. Chandler, I'm afraid I know no such thing."

He shrugged, and Amanda's gaze snagged on the small brown feather resting against his breastbone. The feather shifted with every supple movement of his body. A gust of the cool night breeze tossed his hair back from his face, billowing the strands around Jake's shoulders like a thick, inky curtain. Firelight danced over his face, sculpting, defining, accentuating hollows while softening rigid bone structure. The diffused orange glow stroked his skin, making it glisten a rich shade of bronze. His eyes trapped the firelight and sent it stabbing back at her, stabbing *into* her.

He looked raw, wild and savage, untamable. Oddly enough, Amanda no longer felt frightened or threatened by him. Perhaps that was because he wasn't cur-

156

rently angry with her? Yes, that had to be the reason. His leashed fury was where most of her fear originated. With the fury gone, her fear had dissipated. Well, most of it had, anyway.

Jake sensed correctly that if he gave her too much time to think, she'd make the wrong choice. Leaning to the side, he began rummaging through his saddlebag. "You can shuffle while I explain the rules, okay? Er — you *do* know how to shuffle, don't you, princess?"

Amanda took offense. "Of course."

"Good. Here, catch."

Something landed in her lap. Amanda gasped when her mind flashed her an image of the last thing Jake Chandler had thrown her way. A snake! She grimaced and, after a brief hesitation, mustered the courage to glance downward. A pack of unbound cards were strewn atop the wrinkled calico skirt covering her thighs.

Her hands were still trembling a moment later when she picked up the cards, stacked them evenly, then automatically cut and started shuffling them. It had been a while since she'd played, yet the cards felt good, familiar in her hands. "Gin?"

"Not hardly."

Well, that was going to be a problem, then. Amanda knew she should warn Jake that, win or lose, she was *not* going to take her clothes off, but the idea of playing just a few hands of cards was too tempting a distraction to pass up. After last night, she decided it would be best if they kept themselves occupied. Cards would be a good pastime, so long as she could convince Jake that she wouldn't disrobe after removing a few unrevealing articles. She felt confident she could do that. Deceptively, so.

Jake's steely eyes narrowed. Amanda's fingers were working the cards with fluid familiarity. That was his first sign that he was being had. The woman might not know much about poker — that had yet to be seen — but she damn well knew her way around a deck of cards! Filing that bit of information away — and thanking God he hadn't agreed to play gin! — he said gruffly, "We'll start off with something simple. The game's five card straight. No draws, no wilds, no opens. We'll ante with our," he grinned wickedly when her eyes rounded, "shoes."

"You are planning to explain all those terms, I hope?" she murmured sweetly. She stopped shuffling long enough to unlace and pull off one shoe. A skuffed but fashionable high-laced ankle boot joined one doeskin moccasin on the carpet of grass between them.

"I'll explain as we go," he griped, waving her on. "Just deal."

Amanda dealt. The third of Jake's cards hit his bent knee and landed face up in the grass. It was the jack of spades. She glanced up, asking with her eyes if he wanted a new card or a new deal. He shrugged, tipped the card face down with the tip of his index finger, and winked. Obviously, he wanted her to continue dealing. Strange man, she thought, and did exactly that.

After they'd each been dealt five, Amanda set the rest of the deck aside and picked up her cards. She arranged her hand meticulously, careful to be sure equal space was distributed between cards. It gave her jittery fingers something to do, and made the fan of cards so much easier to hold.

She looked up just as Jake was lifting his cards off the ground. He picked them up in no discernable order, digested them in one unemotional sweep, then set them aside, face down. She had a feeling he wouldn't look at them again.

Strange, *strange* man, her mind echoed as he began explaining how the winning hands were ranked. His voice, she noticed, and not for the first time, was mesmerizing. Too mesmerizing. She found herself not listening to *what* he said so much as *how* he said it. Her ears warmed to the smooth, underlying drawl, and the lazy way he had of rolling words off of his tongue.

". . . think you can remember all that?"

Amanda was holding the cards high in front of her face, pretending to study them. Jake's question made her peek over the jagged top of the fan. The cards hid her grin. "Yes, Mr. Chandler, I think so. If I have questions, I'll let you know."

Was he returning her grin, she wondered, or initiating one of his own? Did it really matter? The end result was the same either way: the bottom fell out of her stomach.

"Sounds good, princess. Oh, and by the way, it's your bet."

"Let's see. I'll bet my . . . hair ribbon." That seemed harmless enough.

It took effort for Jake to bite back his grin. This was working better than he'd hoped. Her hair ribbon was the first thing he wanted to see go. "Okay. I'll see your hair ribbon with my socks, and raise you my . . . shirt."

Amanda swallowed hard. The man didn't waste time, did he? Now, why wasn't she surprised? She saw his bet with one of her stockings, but didn't raise him. A pair of sevens was good, yes, but nothing to bet the farm — or, in this case, the shirt off her back — for.

As it turned out, she'd risked nothing, but had oh, so much to gain. Her sevens beat his ace high.

"Does that mean I win?" She leaned forward and, grinning widely, extended her hand. She wiggled her fingers in much the same way he had this morning when he was trying to get her to surrender her gun. "I believe you owe me one pair of socks and a shirt, Mr. Chandler."

Jake paid his debt, grudgingly. Amanda could have sworn he muttered "Beginner's luck" under his breath as he wadded up the garments and tossed them to her. Of course, she might have been mistaken. It was hard to tell, because right now she was staring at his firm, lean copper chest . . . and even the simplest thought was rapidly turning into a complicated process.

"Same game," Jake growled, picking up the cards scattered over the ground between them. His thick fingers deftly turned them face down. "This time we'll add deuces and one-eyed's, just for variety."

I get bored easily, and when I get bored with you . . .

"All right," Amanda agreed, and smiled indulgently when he explained, in detail, what a wild card was, how one recognized it, and how it figured into a hand of poker. Good heavens, the man really did think she was an idiot, didn't he?

The woman had seen him in less than a pair of flimsy cotton underdrawers. Hell, she'd seen him wearing nothing but a few beads of water and some moonlight! Jake knew he had no reason to feel uncomfortable, but . . . Dammit, he'd feel a whole lot better if *she* had lost something! Anything. Her hair ribbon. Her stockings. Her *corset*—which was the reason he'd originally started playing this fool game of poker to begin with.

Was it any wonder the lady had put up no more than a token resistance when he'd first suggested strip poker? Hell, no. Amanda Lennox was a card shark!

In the last fifteen minutes she hadn't lost a stitch. On the other hand, she'd acquired quite an accumulation of Jake's clothing. He was down to his undershorts, the eagle feather anchored to his braid, and the half-smoked cigarette clamped tightly between his teeth. That wouldn't be so bad, if the night air hadn't turned so damn brisk!

Amanda delicately cleared her throat and passed Jake the cards she'd collected to indicate it was his deal. Ever the lady, he thought sarcastically. His eyes narrowing against the smoke floating up from the tip of his cigarette, he glared at her sharply. She looked far too pleased with herself.

Jake decided it was time to cheat.

"So, princess," he said as he started shuffling, "where the hell'd you learn to play poker?"

Amanda grinned. "My father taught me."

"That figures." Jake shuddered to think what *else* that man had taught his daughter. The veneer of "lady" was chipping away more every minute. Not a good sign. It would be better, safer, if they kept to their original parts; her the indignant society princess, him the untamed savage. The problem was, the more he got to know this woman, the more he thought he might — *might* — have misjudged her.

"My father was an excellent card player, Mr. Chandler," she elaborated, her upper-crust accent now locked firmly in place. "While poker was one of his many specialties, he excelled at bridge. Have you ever played bridge?"

One steely gaze slitted. "*Contact* bridge, Miss Lennox?"

"Yes."

"Not with cards, no." One corner of his mouth kicked up as his attention dipped to the base of her throat. Her pulse was fast and hard. Jake took perverse satisfaction in that. It was nice to know he was getting under her skin. At least he was winning at *something* tonight, even if it wasn't cards. And speaking of cards . . .

He resumed shuffling, then dealt out a hand of five card draw, nothing wild, pair or better to open, jacks or better to win, progressive. A nasty game, one that could take forever to play through, especially with only two people. However, since he was dealing Amanda's cards from the top of the deck, and his own from the bottom, Jake felt confident that a victory wasn't too far off.

He anted with his sparrow feather. She tossed in a

161

hankie she'd dug out of her skirt pocket. The scrap of cloth was made up of crisp white cotton and frothy white lace. It was also monogrammed, he noted; her initial landed topside. The intricately stitched *A* was staring him right in the face, like a challenge itching to be met.

It defied rhyme or reason, it certainly defied logic, but Jake had a sudden, overpowering urge to win that hankie. Instinct said that she was the one who'd labored over those perfect, tiny stitches. In the cloud of smoke shifting around his face, Jake pictured her golden head bent to the task, her brow furrowed in concentration, her hands plying the needle with the same casual skill his brought to wielding a knife. He suspected the embroidery wasn't a labor of love; she didn't seem the type to enjoy such a dreary task. Still, it was hers, it was personal, and . . . dammit, he wanted it! To hell with the corset. The lady could asphyxiate herself trying to ride and breathe tomorrow, with his blessing. Tonight, he wanted that damn hankie.

Amanda leaned forward and frowned. Now what, she wondered, had put that hot silver glint in Jake's eyes? She didn't know, wasn't even sure she wanted to find out. "I *said* one hair ribbon to you, Mr. Chandler."

"Jake," he replied sharply. "When I'm thinking dirty thoughts about you, call me Jake."

Amanda's mouth snapped shut. Her spine went rigid. Well, that certainly put her in her place, now didn't it? Despite her resolve not to, she wondered what dirty thoughts Jake was entertaining. Just as swiftly, she decided she would be better off never finding out.

It didn't take Amanda long to realize that there was something about this hand of poker that made it different from the previous ones. Jake was playing differently. Betting differently. Recklessly. She could feel the determination in him, could almost smell it in the piny, tobacco-scented air.

Until now he hadn't really been trying, she suspected. Now he was playing to win. When he ran out of the clothes he was wearing, he started betting those in his saddlebag. It was against the rules, but she allowed it. At the rate he'd been losing, the man was in for a long, chilly winter.

Amanda glanced at her cards. It was time to draw. She had the option of discarding three out of five equally unpromising cards. She should think about retreating gracefully. In other words, she should fold.

Frowning thoughtfully, she took stock of all she'd bet so far. Her hair ribbon, two stockings, her pantaloons, and her corset covering. All except the corset covering could be removed somewhat inconspicuously. The next thing to go, if she stayed in the game, would be her blouse. Followed by her chemise. Followed by her skirt. Followed by her . . . corset.

Her corset!

That corset's coming off. Tonight.

Jake's words shot though Amanda's mind like a bullet. Her thoughtful frown turned into an irritated scowl. So *that's* what he was up to, why he'd suggested the game of *strip* poker. The rat wanted her corset! Amanda didn't know why she hadn't realized it sooner. It all seemed glaringly obvious to her now. In hindsight, didn't everything?

"Your bet, princess." Jake took one last deep pull off his cigarette, then flicked it away. Neither noticed the fiery red arc it made through the night. "Well?"

"I'm thinking," Amanda evaded, nibbling her lower lip as she studied her cards. Two of hearts, ten of diamonds, six of hearts, ten of clubs, eight of hearts. In other words, a disorganized mess. Too bad twos weren't wild. Still, she did have three fresh cards coming, and there was a chance, just a small one, that this hand would come together for her yet.

163

"What's the problem, princess? Either you've got a pair or you don't."

"I don't."

His pause was just long enough to make her squirm. "Wanna bet?"

Amanda didn't have to look to know where Jake's gaze was lingering. She could feel it smoldering over her breasts like a lover's fingers. Her heartbeat and respiration responded. Instead of commenting on his lewd remark, she let it pass and instead answered his original question. "I'm afraid I can't open, Mr. Chandler."

"Pity, Miss Lennox. I can."

She wasn't surprised. He'd had enough to open for the last three hands, but not the pair of jacks or better required to win. Was it her imagination, or had his poker game undergone a drastic improvement?

Jake bet his saddle blanket. With her heart in her throat, Amanda called him by betting her blouse.

He discarded one, then picked up the deck. His gaze fixed on her expectantly. "What do you want?" he asked, his voice rich with a meaning that sent her imagination soaring.

Amanda felt a warm shiver splash down her spine, washing lower, as she forced her trembling fingers to remove the two tens and set them aside, face down on the grass between them. It was a gamble, yes—all poker hands were—but a possible flush was worth the risk. It was higher than three of a kind, which was the most she could hope for by keeping the tens.

"Two, please," she said. Her voice low and silky, she specified, "Cards, Mr. Chandler. Two *cards*."

"That's it?" One inky brow tipped challengingly high. "Just two? You're sure?"

"Quite sure."

"Positive?"

"Yes," she sighed, and glanced at him. It was a mistake. One she realized too late.

He'd spread his lanky body over the grass, and was laying on his side, his head propped on the palm of one hand, his long black hair curtaining his steely forearm. His other hand was poised near his waist, the fingers ready and waiting to deal Amanda her cards. Her gaze, all on its own, strayed past those cards, past that hand. His thin white underdrawers were a vivid contrast to the darkening night and his tight copper skin. The fabric wasn't as opaque as she thought it should be. Of course, she'd never seen a man's undergarments before. Maybe they were *supposed* to be almost transparent?

Swallowing hard, Amanda glanced away. Her cheeks were flaming, her heart pounding furiously. She'd stopped breathing some time ago. Her palms felt moist, her fingers trembly, and . . . well, there were other symptoms — hot, vivid symptoms — that she thought it best not to explore or to dwell upon.

Fool, fool, fool! Why did you look?!

How could I not?

"It's not too late. You can change your mind and draw three, princess. I won't hold it against you."

A loaded remark, if ever there was one. Her gaze snapped to his. His eyes sparkled wickedly, saying he knew exactly what lascivious thoughts were spinning through her head, corrupting her senses . . . and that he liked being the inspiration for them just fine. "*Two*, please," she repeated firmly.

Jake shrugged tightly and dealt her two cards, himself one.

Amanda knew in a glance she should have folded. While the queen of hearts was an admirable contribution to her flush, the four of clubs was not. Damn! Now she had the unsavory choice of bluffing or folding. She didn't bluff well, never had. Unfortunately, folding meant she would lose her shirt. Quite literally. Amanda now knew what the expression "between a rock and a hard place" meant. Not an elegant phrase by any means, but then, it wasn't an elegant feeling.

Jake bet his empty saddlebag. Amanda bet her skirt. He saw her bet with his knife, and raised her with his horse—all he had left. She called him with her corset; stripping down any more than that in front of a man was out of the question. Since Jake had bet everything he owned—and when Amanda thought everything, she meant *everything*—she didn't dare contemplate what would happen if she *won*.

"Well, Mister Chandler? What do you have?"

"Read 'em and weep." Grinning, Jake laid his cards out on the moonlit grass. He did so slowly, as though to prolong her agony. Or his. "Three kings."

Amanda gulped. "Does an 'almost' flush count?"

"Nope. With a good little white lady like yourself 'almost' *never* counts." His grin broadened, and his eyes shimmered wickedly. "What've you got?"

"You said I didn't have to show you my hand if I lost."

"Lady, if you lost you're going to be showing me a hell of a lot more than your hand." His attention shifted to her hankie—still lying between them like a limp, sacrificial lamb—then rose once more. An inky brow cocked, but he was already aware of the answer to his next question. "Well? Did you lose?"

She shrugged.

"Amanda . . ."

"All right! Yes, Mr. Chandler, as a matter of fact I lost my shirt. Do you want it this second, or could you wait while I go behind those pine trees to take it off?"

At some point, Jake had picked up her hanky. Amanda's gaze snagged on his fingers. Was he conscious of the way he was caressing the white-on-white monogram? *She* certainly was. Very conscious of it.

He pursed his lips and shook his head. "I think you've missed the point of the game, princess."

"And what point is that?"

166

"They don't call it *strip* poker for nothing." His gaze lifted, and burned into hers. "I want to watch."

Amanda was glad she was already sitting, for the way his words drove through her buckled her knees. "How . . . vulgar."

"Yup." Jake laid back, his inky head cradled in his palms. Her hanky made a crisp splash of white atop his dark copper chest. The scrap of cloth was covering his heart. He said lazily, "Strip, Miss Lennox. I want my winnings."

Jake didn't think she would do it. Oh, he hoped she would—hell, yes—but he doubted it. What he *did* expect was for her to try and fast-talk him out of it. That, he was prepared for. He knew exactly what he was going to say when she started crying—the way any properly raised white lady worth her salt would do if found in a similar situation.

Oddly enough, Amanda Lennox didn't look like she was going to cry. Nor did she appear overly intimidated when she pushed to her feet and glared down at him.

What her stance lacked in meekness it made up for in the way of pride. Her chin was tilted in that haughty way of hers that never ceased to . . . *annoy* him. He thought that if her spine got any stiffer it would snap. Her shoulders were squared, her jaw hard, her expression set with quiet fury. Her green eyes snapped with defiance as she lifted her fingers—trembling only slightly—to the top button of her blouse.

It was Jake's turn to be glad he wasn't standing. Christ, she was really going to do it. He'd thought he would be able to go through with this, he really did. But now that the moment was at hand, he couldn't. His restraint was shot; raw and chafed. If she finished unbuttoning that blouse . . .

"Don't." He was on his feet in a heartbeat. His silent steps cleared the space between them. She gasped

167

when he ensnared her slender wrist in his fist, but Jake didn't care. Scaring her right now was the least of his problems. Amanda had managed to work the top three buttons free. The wedge of tempting white flesh she'd revealed was killing him. Another button and he'd be lost. His voice went husky and gruff. "Just give me the damn corset and we'll call it even, okay?"

She kept her gaze trained on the hand he'd coiled about her wrist. Her tone was edged with suspicion. "But I have to take off the shirt to get to it."

"Yeah, you do, don't you? Dammit!" Jake inhaled sharply and glanced around. He scratched the underside of his chin with his free hand, his gaze fixing on the trees she'd mentioned earlier. He nodded briskly toward them. "Go ahead. I promise not to peek." Silently he added, *Hell, I don't trust myself that much. And with damn good reason!*

While Amanda was confused, she certainly wasn't stupid. Jake was offering her a graceful way out of this mess, and she wasn't about to waste time asking questions. Nodding, she slipped her hand from the shackle of his calloused fingers. Clutching her collar together, she limped toward the cover of pine trees before Jake changed his mind. She was halfway there when his voice called out from behind, stopping her cold.

"You realize you could have won, don't you, princess?"

"I could have?" She nibbled her lower lip. "How?"

"I was . . . out of funds. You could have bet your chemise in perfect safety, thereby forcing me out of the game."

"Really?" Her head was spinning, and her knees felt weak and shaky. She could have *won?*

"Yup. I guess the next obvious question is . . . why didn't you?"

It was an honest question. For once, Amanda gave him an honest answer. Glancing over her shoulder, she met Jake's gaze. Even though he was standing mostly in shadow, his eyes were hot and probing, savagely bright. "My father taught me to play games fairly, Mr. Chandler. He didn't believe in cut-throat anything. It's an opinion we shared."

"Strange man, your daddy. I'd like to meet him someday."

"Yes, well . . ." Amanda glanced away, not wanting him to see the pain in her eyes, not wanting to have to explain it. If Jake asked, she'd be forced to lie to him again, and for some insane reason she didn't want to do that.

When he didn't comment, she walked toward the trees, as glad for the distance separating herself from the confusion that was Jacob Blackhawk Chandler as she was for the privacy itself.

Getting out of the corset was simple compared to putting the painful contraption on. She returned to the clearing in no time.

Jake was gone, as was the pile of his clothes she had won.

The knife sank into the tree trunk with a satisfying *thunk*.

Jake watched the hilt waver from the force of the collision. Moonlight caught on what little of the blade wasn't buried in bark. Silently, he retrieved the knife. Gritty bark clung to the long, deadly blade, he wiped it off on his pants leg, but then instead of sheathing it, stared at the bright metal.

The way the light reflected off the steel reminded him of Amanda Lennox's hair. The razorsharp edge, honed to kill, reminded him of her way with words, of how deeply they sliced.

Yes, well . . .

Jake shoved the hankie he was fisting in his left hand into his pocket. He couldn't stand the feel of it right now.

Yes, well . . .

He'd asked to meet her father. He'd been rejected. Stupid. *Stupid!* What had he been thinking of? Decent little white girls didn't bring savages like him home to meet Daddy. Hell, decent little white girls shouldn't know any half-breeds *to* bring home.

But Amanda Lennox did. She knew Jake. And she sure as hell wasn't going to bring him home to meet her father. She'd made that clear. And . . . Jesus, it hurt.

Jake was not pleased. He'd thought himself past the stage where he handed his feelings to white people on a platter, all but begging them to carve his insides to pieces. He shook his head, his hand straying to the scar on his neck, rubbing the puckered flesh, pinching it. He thought of the one white person—white *"lady"*—who'd done exactly that. She'd carved him good. In the process, Cynthia had taught him that all important last lesson he needed so desperately to learn.

Cynthia. Dammit, he had to remember her, remember what she'd done, remember his own past mistakes and misjudgments. He had to cling to them. Only in that way would he be able to get through the next few days with Amanda Lennox. Only in that way would he be able to keep his hands to himself, and keep what was left of his soul intact.

He'd do it. If it killed him, he'd get through it.

Jake gritted his teeth, stepped back, lifted the knife and threw. The blade landed in exactly the same spot; the fit was so perfect there wasn't enough pressure to keep the blade buried in the tree trunk. It quivered, then tumbled to the ground.

If it kills me, he thought as he went to find his knife, had been a poor choice of words. Because he thought it just *might* kill him to be so close to a woman like Amanda Lennox day after day. To sleep near her, night after night and not touch her . . . not kiss her . . . not have her writhing beneath him in the raw,

170

primitive way he hungered for her.

Yup, it was going to kill him, all right. And it was going to be a slow, agonizing death of the spirit, not the quick death of the body. But he *would* do it. Because he couldn't have her. Not *her*. Not *him*. Because he needed the money. And lastly, because he'd made the woman a promise.

Yancey Chandler had raised no slouch. When his bastard son made a promise, he kept it . . . providing that promise was made to someone else. It was the promises Jake made to himself that he had trouble keeping. And none so much as the one concerning Amanda Lennox, the one about not putting his hands on her.

She was tempting. Damn tempting. He wanted her in his bed badly. The itching in the fingers he curled tightly around the knife hilt told him right off that this wasn't going to be an easy promise to keep. That was a problem. A big one. It was Jake's job to see it didn't become an insurmountable one. The only way to do that was for him to remind himself often of who Amanda Lennox was. What she was. What *he* was.

He could never, not for a second, forget the rules of the game. Because this time Jake had a feeling the stakes were too high.

Chapter Ten

Jake was right.

The corset had been taxing Amanda's stamina more than she cared to admit. While her blouse felt a little snug, at least without the corset she could breathe. Riding took on a whole new meaning. Her ribs no longer ached, and no longer did she become short of breathe or have to slow the pace because her sides hurt so badly. It felt heavenly to not have her middle bound up by those stiff, whalebone stays. She felt free, liberated, and depressed.

Her despondency had nothing to do with her new-found ability to breath unencumbered. No, this feeling centered entirely on Jake Chandler.

Three days had slipped slowly past since the night of their poker game. They were the worst three days of Amanda's life. Being cast aside by her father, being shipped East to school, even the tediously regimented days at Miss Henry's . . . all of it paled in comparison to spending countless hours — days . . . nights! — in Jake Chandler's silent, brooding company.

Yesterday, Amanda had reached the conclusion that the man could not be called moody. Oh, no, when Jacob Blackhawk Chandler got in a bad mood, he stayed there. Indefinitely. The only way his mood went was down. His temperament had darkened by the day, and he always seemed grumpier at night. Like gathering storm clouds, the past seventy-two hours had seen the man's disposition go from murky grey to pitch black. And there wasn't a ray of sunshine in sight.

Amanda sighed and brushed back the bangs that wisped over her brow. The mare plodded through the shadowy woods, instinctively following the white.

Her gaze lifted and fixed on Jake's rigid back. He was wearing the grayish-blue shirt she'd first seen him in. The cloth was slightly wrinkled from having been balled up in his saddlebag, but most of the creases had been ironed out by the heat of his body. The cottony fabric was damp with sweat; odd, she thought, since the day was chilly. The material clung to his shoulders, back, and arms, outlining and defining the bands of muscle rippling beneath.

Jake turned his head to the side, his steely gaze inspecting the area. His hair was secured at his nape with a frayed leather thong. A few black strands on both sides weren't quite long enough to be tied back out of the way; they fell forward, framing his prominent cheekbones, softening the hard line of his jaw as much as it could be softened. There was nothing soft about the muscle throbbing in his cheek, or the brooding slash of his brows.

Amanda recognized his expression instantly; she'd seen it enough these last few days to be familiar with it. He was . . . *annoyed* again. She wondered if losing Roger's trail for the third time in as many days was the sole cause of his frustration. Probably not. She knew it wasn't the sole cause for *hers*.

She sent Jake a speculative look when he slowed the white and began scanning the forest floor. "Anything?" she called out.

"No," he snapped. Not sparing her a glance, he tightened his knees around the white's sides, clicked his tongue, and sent them plunging deeper into the woods.

Amanda gritted her teeth and followed. She supposed it had been a foolish hope on her part that his disposition had improved from yesterday's brisk sourness . . . and the day before . . . and the day before *that*. She should have known better.

Silence stretched taut between them as they picked their way through the woods. It took Amanda a full hour to realize they weren't going to stop for lunch. Finally, she pulled a strip of jerky from her saddle bag and gnawed on the chewy, salty meat. Oh, how she longed for a few precious seconds to sit on something other than a saddle that felt like it had been molded of iron . . . something that didn't sway and jostle her . . . something cushiony. Even the cold, lumpy ground would do — if Jake would only stop!

Amanda knew she should be used to the grueling pace Jake set. She wasn't. Her routine at the end of each punishing day varied only slightly. First, she would clamber awkwardly from the saddle, her muscles sore, her body stiff and aching. Some nights she was too tired to do more than gulp down a quick meal, then fall instantly asleep. Most times she skipped the meal. Baths in icy mountain-fed lakes or rivers were confined to the early hours of the morning, when her energy was at a premium.

Jake, on the other hand, appeared not to suffer at all from the endless hours of riding. If he was sore, if his back ached from so much time spent straddling a horse, he didn't show it. If he was tired from scouting the woods well into the night, long after Amanda had fallen asleep, he didn't show that either.

Each night Amanda had studied him critically in the firelight. Her reaction was always the same. Disgust — with herself, with him. She'd yet to see him look as bone-weary as she always felt. Just the opposite; the expended energy brought a healthy flush to his coppery cheeks. The daily exertion seemed to already be filling out muscle tone that, in her jaded opinion, couldn't stand much more improvement. It was frustrating that he could look so good, while she felt like a wrung-out dishcloth.

What had started off as a cool but sunny autumn day soon turned sour. Shortly after noon clouds began rolling across the sky. The dimming light made finding Roger's trail almost impossible. *Almost,* because Jake *did* somehow manage to locate the prints. Amanda was beginning to think he was a better tracker than he'd let on, and that only confirmed her belief that she'd picked the best man to help her locate Roger.

Roger.

Amanda shivered and hugged the cloak she'd tossed over her shoulders. It didn't help. While the thick black wool kept some of the cold afternoon air at bay, it did nothing to soothe the chill inside of her. What, she wondered, was happening with Roger?

Though she'd been struggling to keep her fears to herself—what good would sharing them with Jake do?—they still ate at her. And now that Jake was no longer talking to her, Amanda found herself with endless hours to think, to dwell on the situation, to worry. What had the kidnapper done to Roger so far? What horrible things would he do to the boy in the future? How was he faring? Was he cold? Frightened? Did he think she'd abandoned him? Better yet . . . *who had taken him and why?*

Her mind whirled, yet she came up with no concrete answers.

Ignoring Amanda Lennox as best he could, Jake followed the tracks. He pushed onward even when the storm clouds began to look ominous. It wasn't until a rumble of thunder echoed in the distance that he grudgingly slowed the pace. Though the storm was brewing a good distance off, it *was* coming. He could no longer hope it would blow past them.

The breeze picked up in the late afternoon. The thunderclaps started coming closer together, louder,

175

reverberating over the densely wooded mountains, making the ground tremble.

Sighing with aggravation, Jake reined in the white.

Instinctively, Amanda knew Jake was stopping because of her. A quick glance confirmed the suspicion. His rigid seat said that, had he been alone, he would have continued, impending rain be damned. His uncompromising posture bespoke an aversion to all things weak and feminine—especially those hailing from Boston.

Amanda's jaw ached and her temples pounded from gritting her teeth throughout the day. It was the only way she knew to contain her anger. What was the man's problem now? she wondered crossly. Did he think she would melt if a little rain splattered on her? That she'd drown in tears from a good dousing? Not likely! She was made of stronger stuff than that—at least she *hoped* she was. And *that*, Amanda decided hotly, was a lesson about her that Jake Chandler sorely needed to learn. The sooner the better.

She maneuvered the mare up close to the white. The horses had long since grown used to the smell of each other; neither shied from the enforced proximity, nor did they give the other more than a curious glance. "Why are we stopping?" she demanded.

He shrugged. It was a tense, frustrated gesture. "In case you haven't noticed, princess, it's going to rain."

"Hard as this may be for you to believe, storm clouds and that distinct, acidy aroma are indigenous to all parts of the country before a storm. And thunder sounds the same no matter where you are." Her fingers tightened on the reins, and her chin tipped up a haughty notch. Amanda thought it a pity Jake didn't glance her way and therefore missed her subtle show of defiance. "I know it's going to rain, Mr. Chandler. What I *don't* know, but what I'd like for you to explain to me, is why we are stopping."

176

Jake kept his gaze riveted to the top of the hill they were only minutes from cresting. His voice, when it came, was low and gritty. "There's a cabin at the bottom of this hill. It's small, not what your used to, not by a long shot, but it's warm and dry. If you hurry you can probably reach it before the storm starts."

"Why?"

His gaze narrowed. Cold and piercing, his attention lit on her briefly, then moved quickly away. "Why what?"

"Why are we stopping? If you can keep going, I certainly can. Contrary to popular belief, a little rain won't hurt me."

Jake kept his opinion on that to himself. He figured that swallowing the words back would, in the long run, be less trouble for them both. The last thing he wanted was to argue with this woman . . . again. They didn't have time to fight. The storm was closing in quickly. Experience said that once the rain began it would come down hard and furious and cold. For some insane reason he wanted Amanda Lennox someplace warm and dry before that happened. He didn't want her caught out in a lashing downpour, and he definitely didn't want her caught out in one with him!

Jake told himself his motives were purely selfish. Logical. Intelligent, even. If Amanda got wet, she, a woman with such a delicate constitution, unused to such harsh weather, would catch a chill. If she caught a chill, she would get a fever. A fever was only one of the many things he wanted desperately to avoid.

What in God's name would he do with a prissy little white woman who also happened to be sick? He'd nurse her, of course. He wouldn't have much choice. Unfortunately, nursing Amanda Lennox wasn't something Jake wanted to do. Ever. It would mean having to bathe the heat from her creamy white body. It would mean having to touch her, to soothe her, to . . .

Don't! his mind screamed. *Don't even* think *about it!*
And he didn't. At least, not consciously.

Jake forced his thoughts onto a safer path. If
Amanda took sick, by the time she recovered Roger's
tracks would be long gone. If that happened, Jake
would never find the brat, and his obligation to this
white woman couldn't be fulfilled. That would never
do. He wanted—*needed*—to get this unpleasant chore
over with quickly. That was the only way to be rid of
her. If not for the brewing storm, he might have been
able to do that. The tracks said Roger and his kidnapper were only a few hours ahead of them. Unfortunately, the storm was only an hour away, two at the
most.

Jake had been caught out in enough early winter
storms to not be overly concerned at the prospect of
being caught out in this one. What he damn well *was*
concerned about—damned concerned about—was the
idea of Amanda Lennox being caught out in it with
him. He was concerned for reasons other than the
obvious; reasons he couldn't let himself think about;
reasons he thought about anyway . . . far too frequently and far too hard.

Wet.

The way her rain-soaked blouse would mold to her
luscious white curves was *not* Jake's reason for deciding they'd be a hell of a lot better off if she weathered
the storm somewhere warm and dry, somewhere as
far away from him as he could get. No, no. He made
sure the idea never crossed his mind. The concentration it took to keep his thoughts from wandering in
that direction was staggering. The effort made him
grumpier than usual.

"How friendly are the people back East?" he asked
irritably.

Amanda scowled, and shifted in her saddle. She
shrugged, confused. "As friendly as any, I suppose.

178

Why?"

"I don't know what you folks do in Boston, but around here people take in travelers." He nodded to the crest of the hill. "There's a young couple living that cabin. They'll give you a bed and a hot meal. You don't have to ask for it, just show up on their doorstep and look needy." He turned toward her, one inky brow cocked high. "Think you can manage that?"

Amanda pulled herself up straighter in the saddle, no longer slouching, no longer tired. Exhaustion channeled swiftly into a hotter, more turbulent emotion. Indignation was the closest she'd come to naming the feelings roiling inside her.

Eight years of Miss Henry's diligent tutelage was evident in the lofty tone of her voice and in the way she glared down the pert length of her nose at Jake. "Mr. Chandler, I've never appeared needy in my life!"

"Is that a fact?" His gaze slid hotly over her. "No, I guess you haven't."

Jake studied what he could see of her casual skirt and shirtwaist. The cloak hanging from her shoulders was made of thick, practical wool. Damn, but the outfit looked wrong on her somehow. All wrong. It wasn't the material or cut of the clothes that bothered him so much as the *way* she wore them. On her, cotton passed for taffeta, calico for yards of watered silk, tailored in the latest Parisian fashion. Her regal bearing modified plain wool, turning it into expensive sable, and . . .

Those were the clothes a woman like Amanda Lennox should be wearing. Not practical cottons and ready-made dresses. Hell, no. She deserved better. She deserved finely tailored outfits cut from the most exquisite fabric money could buy. Nothing bright, nothing flashy, just something . . . classy. *That* was the word Jake was looking for. Classy. Like the lady

179

herself. She was born to it.

Amanda shifted uneasily. Why did the heat of Jake's gaze remind her of the way his fingertip had stroked her breast? She didn't know, but it *did* remind her of that morning in the woods. Vividly. Graphically. His gaze traced her stomach, caressed the flair of her hips and the turn of her calf revealed by the hiked up hem of her skirt. Her flesh burned, and a fragile spark of desire pooled in her stomach. Her gaze lowered to his lips. With breathtaking clarity she remembered how it felt to need — really *need* — that mouth covering, devouring her own.

Except for erotic dreams, her desire for Jake Chandler had been suppressed, forced to lay dormant for days and torturously long nights. But, as he'd so effortlessly proved — and her strong, hungry response confirmed — while her passion had been carefully concealed, it hadn't by any stretch of the imagination been abolished. One hot glance from him, one lazily drawled innuendo, and desire flamed to smoldering life.

Jake's lips burned under the caress of her eyes. His gut twisted. Against his better judgment, he did some painful remembering of his own. He came to the abrupt conclusion that bringing up the word "need" with this woman, in any way, shape, or form, was a mistake. It brought too clearly to mind his body's fierce demands.

His attention skimmed the full, ripe breasts he'd yet to forget the tantalizing shape and feel of. His jaw hardened, and his fingers curled into tight fists around the reins. His grip was so tight his fingers actually hurt. That was fine by Jake. He was tempted, so goddamn *tempted* to reach out and touch her, to stroke her, to feel her creamy white skin coasting beneath his hand the way he'd wanted so badly to do these last few days. These last few hellishly long nights.

Amanda's heartbeat skipped, her blood heated. Her skin felt warm and tingly, as though it was his fingers stroking and caressing her, not merely his eyes. She was surprised by how quickly, how effortlessly, this man could spark passion in her. She was shocked to the core by how deep-rooted that new-found passion ran. It warmed her, *consumed* her. Desire—hot and sharp and alive—flamed inside of her, burning away the indignation she could have sworn she'd felt only a few moments ago.

"Can you do it?" Jake repeated, his voice as harsh as his expression.

"Do what?" Amanda asked breathlessly.

"Can you show up on that doorstep and look needy?"

Oh, *that!* Her wayward thoughts had made her lose track of their conversation. Amanda cleared her throat, and tried to make her reply sound haughty. It wasn't easy. The blood surging through her veins, pounding in her ears, inhibited the anger she should have been feeling, but wasn't. "I'm not a total incompetent. I-I think I can manage to look needy."

"Good. Then do it." Forcing his gaze from hers, Jake gave a flick of his wrist that turned the white around. He started back toward the woods, in the direction they'd just come. From over his shoulder he said, "Meet me back here after the storm passes. Tomorrow, probably. The day after at the latest."

Amanda rocked back in the saddle as though he'd just clipped her jaw. Her lips parted in mute shock. She blinked hard, and filled her vision with his proud, swaying back. Where the hell was he going? Hadn't he just told her they would be stopping at the cabin for the night? Yes, he certainly had. So why—?

Her mouth snapped shut. Her lips compressing in a thin, angry line when a thread of realization wound

181

its way down her spine. *Meet me back here* . . .

He was trying to get rid of her. The bastard! Not only did Jake have no intention of accompanying her to the cabin, but she had an uncomfortable feeling that, if she let him ride off now, he wouldn't come back for her. Not in one day's time, not in one *year's* time!

"Damn him," she muttered under her breath, shocking herself. To curse inwardly was one thing, to do it aloud meant she must be extremely upset. And she was . . . with Jake Chandler, the beast who was deserting her. Well, she wouldn't tolerate it, and that was that. Deciding she would not allow him to ditch her so easily, Amanda swung the mare around and hurried after him. It took less than two minutes to catch up to the white.

Jake heard her pursuit. Drawing in a resigned breath, he released it by letting it hiss slowly through his teeth. The muscle in his cheek throbbed, his fingers tightened on the reins. Those were his only outward signs of annoyance.

"Now what?" he growled when she guided the mare up beside him. Too closely beside him, the sudden burn in his left thigh screamed. "Thought I told you to get to that cabin before the storm breaks."

"You did," she snapped, her tone as annoyed as his. "But at the time I agreed to it, I thought you were going with me."

He didn't look at her. He didn't dare. The memory of his fingertip following the lush curve of her breast was still too fresh in his mind. If he looked at her now, and saw in her large, expressive green eyes just how disturbing that same memory was for her . . . worse, if *she* saw how much the memory kept eating at him . . .

Jake drew himself up short. The tantalizing memory wasn't just eating at him, he realized. Hell, no. At some point during the last seventy-two hours his hunger to possess this woman had blossomed into a gut-grinding need. A full-blown obsession.

He felt the heat of her invade the tough denim encasing his leg. Her warmth penetrated his skin, seeped into it, stole into his bloodstream. A cool breeze blew fragile puffs of her sweet, sweet scent his way. Jake damned the brewing storm for that almost as much as he damned the feminine aroma itself. The smell of her flooded him, threatening to drown him, as it lent a seductive undertone to the acidy tang of imminent rain.

He sensed Amanda's agitation, felt her confusion as though it was his own, and it . . . well, dammit, it bothered him. More than it should have. More than was safe. For either of them. Because with the knowledge came the need to reach out and touch, to reassure. He countered the urge, but just barely.

"With you?" he said finally, her words just now penetrating his distracted mind. He scowled, his steely gaze flashing with annoyance. "I never said I was going with you, princess."

"No, but you implied it."

"No, *you* misunderstood."

"But I thought—"

"Wrong. As usual, lady, you thought wrong. I, on the other hand, think you'd better get yourself to that cabin before you get caught in a downpour."

If he'd been looking at her, Jake would have seen the spark of fury in her eyes. Frustration, not entirely due to his irksome stubbornness, was gathering inside Amanda. It had been brewing for days, fueled first by rejection, then by flagrant neglect. It was whipping itself into a frenzy. Amanda gritted her teeth and thought that the storm gathering inside of her promised to be much more violent than anything the overcast sky could lash down on this arrogant man's head.

It was only when she saw Jake make ready to snap

the reins and move away that the fragile thread on her temper snapped. She didn't think about what she was doing, she just did it. Leaning to the side, Amanda grabbed Jake's reins. She didn't waste time questioning her motives, but instead jerked the white to a halt.

Jake hadn't been prepared for that. The strips of leather slipped from his fingers before he could snatch them back. The second time he reached for them, the prissy little witch held them out of reach. His gaze narrowed, spearing into her. The way she held her delicately shaped chin loftily high annoyed the hell out of Jake. The way her huge green eyes met his glare with a level stare of her own infuriated him.

Three days, he thought sourly. For three agonizingly long days—and nights; Jesus, don't forget the *nights!*—he'd kept his distance from this woman, kept his desire firmly leashed. It hadn't been easy. The strain had cost him, but he'd done it. Now, he found himself praying for one more day, one more *hour.* If he could check his anger until Amanda was settled inside the cabin, he knew he'd be all set. *If . . .*

His gaze sharpened on the slender white hand fisting his reins. "What the hell do you think you're doing?!"

"That all depends on where the hell *you* think you're *going!*"

The first drop of rain, heavy and thick from having gathered on an overhead leaf, splattered on top of Jake's head. It felt mildly cold as it soaked into his hair and scalp. It was frigid compared to the emotions cooking inside him.

"Well?" Amanda pressed when he didn't answer, but instead sat there glowering at her hand. "Where are you going, Jake? I want to know."

"And you always get what you want. Is that it,

184

princess?"

"No, not always."

"But *usually.*"

"Sometimes," she agreed, opting for a compromise. The anger in his eyes made Amanda think better of what she was doing. Jake Chandler wasn't the sort of man a sane woman pushed, or backed into a corner. Not if she expected to live out the day. And why hadn't she thought of that *before?*

Of course, it was too late now. She kept her expression determined, her glare hot and irritated. Somehow. "I know why you won't tell me where you're going. It's because you don't want me to know you won't be back for me. That's it, isn't it, Jake? You've been trying every which way to get rid of me for days. Now that you have the chance, you're going to take it."

"I—"

Her green eyes flashed fury. "Don't bother trying to deny it. We both know it's the truth. That's why you've set such a grueling pace for me to follow day after day, isn't it? You were trying to exhaust me, hoping I'd get discouraged and give up. But I didn't. So now you've decided to strand me in the middle of . . ." She scowled. Where were they? Idaho still, or had they entered Montana again? God, she didn't know! Her voice rose a panicky degree. "It doesn't matter where we are. What matters is that you're skipping out on the job I *hired* you to do."

She'd thought to baffle him with her brilliant mode of deduction. And he *did* look baffled, though his confusion didn't look to be stemming from her intelligence. The slight widening of his eyes said he was puzzled by her sheer lack of wit.

The muscle in his cheek jerked spasmodically. His jaw bunched in a harsh, uncompromising line, and his eyes . . . she shivered, refusing to surrender to a

185

sudden burst of uncertainty.

Jake's voice, when it came, was low and edgy. "Where I'm going, you pampered little idiot, is deeper into the woods where it won't be raining quite so hard. What I plan to do once I get there is build a shelter that will keep me relatively warm and dry until the storm passes. And as for *you* . . . ! Lady, if you've got one intelligent bone in that tempting little body of yours—and I'm seriously beginning to doubt it!—you'll give me my damn reins back before I don't have time to do any of that!"

She'd been fisting the reins in question; her fingers went slack around the chilly strips of leather. "You're going to do *what?*"

"*I'm speaking English, aren't I?*" Jake sucked in a deep, calming breath. It didn't help. Neither did plowing the fingers of his free hand so harshly through his hair that his scalp stung. What he *really* wanted to do—what he *couldn't* do—was either strangle Amanda on the spot, or kiss her breathless. Since both urges were equally strong, he surrendered to neither of them. "I said," he repeated through clenched teeth, "I'm going to find a place to weather out the storm."

"But the cabin—"

"Is that-a-way." He jerked his thumb over his shoulder. "I suggest you find it while the ground's still dry enough for me to find a place to build a shelter on. Or," his eyes narrowed dangerously, "before I lose my temper. Whichever comes first."

Amanda's mouth opened and closed twice, but no words came out. A few drops of rain sprinkled the top of her head. A couple more moistened her cheeks and nose. She was too busy thinking to notice. She had been so *sure* he was going to desert her!

Jake leaned forward. Instantly his hand snaked out to grab back the rudely stolen reins.

Her fingers tightened. Reflexively, she held them

186

out of reach. Not the smartest thing she'd ever done, Amanda realized belatedly. Jake was already furious. To not give him back the reins would be pushing his anger. While she knew that, she couldn't bring herself to release them. Oddly enough, she seemed to have lost control of herself.

Why, she wondered, would Jake rather pass the storm in a crudely built shelter when there was a cabin with warm beds and hot food only minutes away? It made no sense. For an otherwise intelligent man, she thought he was acting like a fool. Amanda took it upon herself to make him see that. But how?

Her scowl deepened. "Jake," she began slowly, cautiously, "you said yourself the cabin would be warm and dry. You said the people living there would offer us a hot meal and a warm bed."

"*You,*" he growled. "I said they would offer it to *you.*" The rain was only sprinkling the ground now, but it would be coming down hard soon. The cold sting in the air said it would probably turn to snow. Jake knew that if he didn't get away from this woman in the next few minutes he could kiss all hope of finding a dry spot anywhere goodbye. Damn Amanda Lennox! Damn her pretty face, her creamy white skin, and her stubborn-as-a-mule disposition to hell and back!

"But what about *you?*" she insisted. "Surely if they'd offer it to me, they'd offer you the same thing!"

"Trust me, they won't. Now give me back the—"

"They won't *offer* you hospitality?" Amanda countered, cutting him short when realization dawned. Her spine went rigid. "Or you won't *accept* it? Tell me something. These people in the cabin are white, aren't they? *That's* why you won't accept their hospitality, isn't it? Well? Isn't it?"

"Shut up," he sneered, his anger mounting in direct proportion to the raw nerve she'd just struck inside of him. "You don't know what the hell you're talking about, lady."

"Don't I? That's funny, because I think I do. In fact, I think the only thing that's keeping you from accepting shelter from those people is that stubborn, misplaced pride of yours." She planted her free hand on her hip and, chin high, huffed with disgust. "God forbid the mighty Jacob Blackhawk Chandler accept *anything* from a white man. Or woman."

"I said shut up, Amanda!"

"The truth hurts, doesn't it, Jake?"

His attention, which had been rivetted on her throat, rose. Their gazes locked and warred. She watched his eyes darken to a murderous shade of midnight blue. The skin covering his cheeks was stretched tighter than a drum. There was a ruddy undertone of anger in his coppery skin.

A warning bell went off in her head. Like its predecessor's caution, it was disregarded. Amanda had an unsettling feeling that their conversation went deeper than surface words. She also sensed that now was the time to drive her point home, while she still had his full attention, and not all of his fury . . . yet.

"I'm right, and you know it," she said coldly. "You have a chip on your shoulder that weighs a ton, and you can't see past it, can you?"

"I've seen what decent white folks do to those they consider filthy savages, lady," Jake hissed. "That's all I need to see."

Don't say it, Amanda. You'll be sorry if you push him.

She was too angry to listen to the warning voice inside her head. "Open your eyes, Goddammit! Not everyone looks at the color of your skin. Some of us 'decent white folks' can actually look beyond that and see the man *inside*."

"Shut —"

"But you wouldn't know about that, would you, Jake?"

"— up"

"Oh, no. You have all us 'decent white folks' pigeonholed into a neat little slot labeled Don't Trust. We're all—"

"Amanda . . ." his voice sounded gravelly, and furious as hell.

"—alike to you, aren't we?"

One inky brow quirked high. His lips were pinched in a tight white line. "Aren't you?"

She shook her head. "No. Not that *you'll* ever open your eyes far enough see it! You think we're all prejudiced against you because you look Indian."

He sneered, "Absaroke, Miss Lennox. Or, as your people call us, Crow. I'm half *Crow.*"

"You can *eat* crow as far as I'm concerned, pal! Half Crow, half Apache, half *whatever* . . . the truth of the matter is, *you* are the only one who's prejudiced around here. I think you—"

"I've heard enough, that's what *I* think!"

"—have a real problem, Jake."

The muscle in his jaw stopped ticking. Had Amanda not been so intent on hammering her point home, she would have taken that as a sign that he'd finally lost what little patience he'd had with her.

"You're right," he growled, his tone gritty and low and ominous. "I do have a problem. *You!*"

He leaned toward her. The tip of his index finger scratched over the line of her jaw. His voice took on a cold, cajoling note that sent shivers of alarm—or of something else, something Amanda didn't want to know about—slicing down her spine. Then again, maybe it was the touch alone that made her quake?

"Don't look so worried, princess," he said, and flashed her one of the iciest smiles she'd ever seen. It chilled her to the bone. His fingertip hesitated on the crest of her chin. "It's a problem I can handle."

Amanda tried to lean back, but Jake's reaction time was much too quick. He shifted, and his fingers coiled like unmerciful steel bands around her upper arms.

She gasped—half in surprise, half in fright. Twisting, she tried to yank herself free without losing her seat. He wouldn't let her go. There was no respite from his punishing grip . . . just as there was no respite from the raw, savage fury she'd unleashed in him.

Amanda had wondered what this man's anger would be like once it was unleashed. Now she knew . . . and she wished to God she didn't. Raw. Savage. Wild. *That* was what Jake Chandler was like when angered. Untamed. Dangerous. Frightening.

He jerked her around in the saddle until she was facing him. With a flick of his wrists, he hauled her up hard against his chest. The action was meant to be brutal, and it was. But not only to her. It was hell for Jake, too. He hadn't expected his method of retribution to backfire so severely, although he'd realized it would . . . a split second too late.

Liquid fire bubbled in his blood when he felt her breasts crushed to his chest. Their horses stepped together. Thighs met, grinding against each other; hard copper rubbed smooth white velvet. Even beneath a layer of tough, weathered denim, his skin burned from every goddamn inch of that contact!

His fingers tightened around her arms. His heart slammed double time against his ribs, and his breathing took a ragged, shallow turn. He wished the moisture beading his brow could be attributed to the rain that was coming down in a steady drizzle now. But he knew that wasn't the cause. And . . .

Jesus, *his hands were shaking!* This was *not* the violent reaction he'd intended. No, no, not even close. Because it was *his* reaction. Not hers.

Amanda was having a violent reaction all her own. Leaning weakly against Jake, she absorbed the erratic beat of his heart with her palms. His chest felt warm and firm, his shirt moist and soft. The fight had drained out of her the second their bodies collided, the second rigid male planes molded to soft feminine curves.

She thought about tipping her head back to look at him — she wanted, *needed*, to see his face — but she lacked the courage for it. What if contact between them didn't have the same dizzying affect on him? What if Jake was still furious with her? What if . . . ?

She decided instantly that she'd be better off without answers to those questions. Truly, she didn't want to know if the tremors she felt in the fingers banding her arms were born from anger, or from something more base . . . something wild and primitive and deeply sensual.

Amanda shivered. The rain was coming down a bit harder. Her hair was damp; it was only a matter of time before both she and Jake became soaked. Her mind flashed her an image of wet black hair and bare copper skin . . . and her trembling increased twofold.

"Please, Jake, come to the cabin with me." Amanda swallowed hard when she felt Jake tense. If she could, she would have taken the words back. He didn't want to go. He had his reasons, even if she couldn't understand the logic behind them. It was wrong to push him. Yet, while she knew she was a fool to force the issue . . . God, the thought of Jake weathering the storm out in the open, unprotected and vulnerable, was incomprehensible.

Unprotected? Vulnerable? Amanda almost laughed. Almost. Those were *not* words one usually associated with Jacob Blackhawk Chandler. Had he known the path of her thoughts, she didn't doubt Jake would have laughed in her face.

Jake didn't feel like laughing. Far from it. What he felt like doing was abandoning his first plan — strangling her with his bare hands — and heading straight for his second — kissing her breathless. The plan had merit; it would keep her mouth busy, and shut her up for a while. It also had a bonus; the feel of her lips crushed beneath his, the unique whiskey-sweet taste of her on his tongue . . .

A kiss. *One goddamn kiss.* Surely he could take that much from this white woman! Didn't she owe it to him? Hadn't she kept him out in the rain for so long that he'd never be able to find a dry spot to build a shelter on? Hell, if he was destined to be cold and wet until the storm passed, didn't he deserve the memory of one more hot, forbidden kiss to keep him warm?

Yes, dammit! He could steal a kiss from her. Just one. Long and deep and thorough. He would take what he needed from this white woman to keep the cold, lonely hours ahead at bay.

Jake, unaware until that very second he'd been cushioning his chin atop the pillow of her golden head, pulled back. The hands Amanda had placed on his shoulders tightened. Her fingers tunneled through his damp shirt, biting into the sensitized skin beneath. She seemed puzzled, as though she was disappointed by the scant distance he'd put between them.

"Look at me, princess."

The tone of his voice had changed. Amanda didn't know how, didn't know why, but the change did register with her. Slowly, her chin tipped up. More slowly, her gaze lifted. She focused on the collar of his shirt. The top button was free; the placket gaped open, revealing a small wedge of damp copper skin. It was a tantalizing sight, in that there was only enough exposed to tease, to make her yearn to slide free the remaining buttons, to see more. To feel and taste and . . .

The lump in his throat slid up and down with a thick swallow when Amanda's gaze skimmed over it, then the hard line of his jaw. Her attention settled on his mouth, and stopped. With the tip of her tongue, she moistened her suddenly dry lips. It had been so long since he'd last kissed her . . . and yet she remembered the unique feel and taste of him, the unleashed hunger and urgency, as though no time had passed at all.

Jake's groan melted like a drop of warm honey down Amanda's spine. His lips were close, so temptingly close. She felt the heat of his rapid, shallow breaths burn over her skin. She had only to hike her chin up a notch to have her mouth settle comfortably beneath his. If she dared.

Amanda was not so brave. Alluring though the thought of kissing Jake again was, she couldn't do it. She was afraid to. Initiating that sort of intimacy would leave her vulnerable and open to yet another rejection. What if he refused to kiss her, the way he'd refused that morning in the woods? What if he turned his back on her again?

Yes, Amanda, what then?

Why, she would shrivel up and die on the spot. *That's* what would happen if Jake spurned her again; her feelings were that strong, the situation was that simple. No, she amended, when Jake Chandler was involved nothing was ever simple.

Amanda forced her attention from his lips, and met his gaze. His eyes were still dark, but the murderous light had been doused. Another, stronger emotion flamed in its place.

"Are you coming with me to the cabin?" she asked softly, breathlessly. Her fingers, hooked over his shoulders, relaxed. Without her permission, her hands skated over the width of his shoulders, then sandwiched his neck between her palms. She was acutely aware of the ridged scar beneath her fingertips, and the matching one carved into his soul.

Jake's pulse throbbed against the feel of her hand—the beat rapid and reckless. Amanda's heartbeat thundered in response.

"No, Amanda, I'm not going with you." His grip on her arms loosened, then melted away. He hesitated. In what seemed to be a reluctant gesture, his left hand stole possessively around her waist, pinning her close when the movement of their horses threatened to drag them apart. He fingered her braid, then with smooth, liquid motions, wrapped the thick plait around his fist.

"Why, Jake? Why won't you come to the cabin?"

He shook his head, his gaze dropping to her mouth for just a second before returning to her eyes. "You wouldn't understand."

"Because I'm white," she stated flatly.

"That's part of it," he said, his voice careful, controlled.

"And the other part?"

"Because right now I can only think of one thing I want you to be doing with that perfect little mouth of yours, lady. And talking sure as hell isn't it."

A blast of heat bolted down Amanda's spine. Unconsciously, she leaned closer to the warmth and promise of Jake Chandler. Her chin lifted, and she lessened the distance between their mouths. "Only one, Jake?" she asked huskily.

The barest trace of a grin tugged at his lips. It was, she realized dazedly, one of Jake's few genuine smiles. She had no time to savor the sight, for at that moment her gaze met his, and she saw his eyes flash with carnal suggestion. "I stand corrected. Make that two."

Her hands slipped around his neck, her fingers tangling in the long, rain-damped hair secured at his nape. Each strand felt baby-smooth and fine, like silk as it teased her palms and knuckles. Her body hummed with an urgent need she couldn't even begin to understand. Her spine arched of its own accord, and she pressed more closely to his hot, hard, male firmness.

"Kiss me, Jake," she whispered oh, so softly. "Please." Her lashes started to swoop heavily downward. Jake's next words snapped them back up again.

"Un-uh, princess," he rasped. "*You* kiss *me*."

Prudish Bostonian morals be damned, if this man wanted her to kiss him, if that was the only way Amanda could taste the wild, intoxicating flavor of him again, then so be it. She'd take the initiative gladly, pay any consequences, because she had to taste him again. Right here, right now. She *had* to!

The leather strip gave away as, her gaze locked with passion-darkened silver, she buried her fingers in his damp hair and cupped his head in her open palms. She lifted her chin, slowly, her lips parting. With an airy sigh of surrender, she gently sealed their mouths together.

Their lips had barely touched when the arm around her waist convulsed. Jake clamped her hard against his chest, as though he was afraid now that they were joined, she would become frightened and try to pull away. He wouldn't, *couldn't,* allow that. Not yet.

The hand fisting her braid tugged, angling her head back even as his tipped forward. His mouth opened, his tongue stroked and teased, insisting hers to do the same. When she did, his mouth ravished hers.

Three days of pent-up desire had whet his appetite. Passion flamed instantly. It felt hot and bubbly inside of him, raging at a fevered pitch, humming through his body and tightening like an iron-hard fist in the more integral parts of him.

He was no longer merely kissing her. His severely weakened restraint wouldn't allow tenderness. Instead, he devoured her soft, moist, willing lips. When she opened for him, he plunged his tongue into her mouth and fed off her honeyed taste like a man parched.

The thrust of her breasts against his chest — firm and oh, so temptingly round — was a bittersweet torture. Even as his fingers flexed, he fought the urge to find the buttons concealing her from his needy palms, fought the urge to rip free the flimsy barrier separating flesh from hot, hungry flesh.

He couldn't do that. He couldn't lose that much control over himself, but . . . Dammit! It was hard to show restraint, especially when her tasty little tongue stole into his mouth and began a slow, timid investigation. How could he not touch her when her delicious body was arching into his, begging him to do exactly that? Touch her . . . all over . . . again and again.

Jake wasn't stupid. He'd lain with enough women to know when one wanted him. Yet he couldn't remember a time when any woman had wanted him this badly. Lord knows *he'd* never wanted a woman to the extent he wanted this one. Here. Now. Fast and hard. The need to claim and possess ate at him, consumed him. He wanted Amanda, and *only* Amanda. He wanted to be buried inside of her, to feel her hot and wet and tight around him. He wanted her in a variety of ways that would probably have shocked her to the prim Bostonian core. And he wanted it all so badly he ached!

The more he kissed her, the more passionately she responded, the more real those possibilities became. And the more the sharply drawn line between past and future blurred, the rules of the game grew hazy. Reality, consequences faded to insignificance.

Jake delved his tongue into her mouth. His savage, claiming strokes fed the fire that was burning out of control inside them both. But it wasn't enough. Dear God, it wasn't enough!

She arched into him, he swallowed her groan. He

deepened the kiss, she swallowed his own low, tortured moan.

He could have her now. Amanda was hot and willing in his arms. Exactly the way he wanted her. Exactly the way he'd dreamed she would be. She wouldn't fight, she would surrender. Rain be damned, she would not turn him away. Her sweet lips moving beneath his, giving as good as she got; her tantalizing body moving hungrily against his, pleading without using words; all of it said he could take her now, make her his. He could pull her down from the mare and join her on the hard, moist ground. He could finally, *finally* soothe the empty, hollow ache this woman's mere presence carved inside of him. If he dared, he could find out how it felt to have her forbidden white flesh skim like silk beneath his rough copper palm.

Jake remembered how her nipple had pebbled to hardness for him once before. His fingertips burned with the memory. Oh, hell, who was he kidding? His *entire body* burned with it! With need. For her. He could learn what the lush fullness of her breast *really* felt like now, without the obstruction of cloth, without barriers.

Memories circled in his mind—sharp, biting pictures that haunted—but they were swiftly being banished by all the frustrated fantasies that rushed to the fore. The prospect of taking Amanda Lennox to his bed was impossible to resist. He wanted her. *Her*, dammit! And he wanted her now. He wanted to know what it felt like to have her long white legs wrapped around his hips as he pumped his life into her. He wanted, *needed* to take her, to feel her heal the hurt inside of him in ways that Jake sensed only she could.

He should resist. Should, but couldn't. He *had* to know what it was like to be an integral part of this woman. Just once. Because the three days—the three hellishly long nights—of wondering had nearly driven him insane. The unbearable desire surging through his body said he was only human. A man could only take so much, and he'd already taken his fair share. He simply could not face needing her this badly another second.

From the way she was moving urgently against him, it was what Amanda wanted too. Even if she didn't quite know it yet.

She shifted. Her hands skimmed his shoulders, then dipped beneath the open collar of Jake's shirt.

The decision, if there ever really had been one, was made. The way her choppy, almost confused sounding sigh rang in his ears was an unnecessary confirmation that, while what he was about to do wasn't exactly right, he was going to—*had* to—do it anyway. Consequences be damned. What was going to happen had been a foregone conclusion—an inevitability—since the second he'd slipped his hands beneath that frigid river-water to free her ankle from the tree branch.

He'd wanted her then.

He wanted her more now.

And he was going to have her. Damned if he wasn't!

The male in him was wild with hunger, driven by urges too essential to deny. Primitive needs rushed to the fore. They had no rhyme or reason. They were too strong and consuming to ignore or deny.

He was going to have her, going to make her his. God help him, he was going to possess this lady—this *white* lady—right here, right now.

Chapter Eleven

The sun peeked from behind a water-heavy cloud, warming the cool breeze that puffed over Amanda's skin, warming the drops of rain that sprinkled her cheeks.

Of course, she could have been in a blizzard for all she would have noticed. Jake was kissing her — deeply, hungrily, as though he never intended to *stop* kissing her. His mouth ate at hers, devouring the giving softness of her lips. His hands stroked feverish paths up and down her arms. Her body burned for him to stroke her just as feverishly elsewhere. Everywhere.

If there was anything else in the world besides the two of them, Amanda didn't notice. She'd waited so long for this moment. She wouldn't let herself be distracted.

Jake's fingers, riding her waist, tightened as he deepened the kiss, lightened it, then deepened it yet again. Amanda snuck her hands under the collar of his shirt. The muscles gliding beneath her fingertips bunched and flexed with his every move, proof of his dormant strength. It was odd that she didn't feel frightened or intimidated by that, the way she had been by his fury. Considering the circumstances, she should be scared senseless. And that, she thought, was exactly the problem. When Jake Chandler held her like this, kissed and touched her like this, she simply could not think straight. Nor did she want to.

Their mouths hungrily locked, Jake shifted and lifted Amanda off of the mare. He turned her slightly, and settled her in front of him atop the white. The animal felt strong and solid beneath her, but not as strong and solid as the big hand that settled possessively on her hip. She sucked in a ragged breath when Jake dragged her up against his chest, tightly, as though he was trying to melt her through his clothes, into his warm copper skin. His fingers curled into her bottom as he molded the side of her hip into the wedge of his parted thighs. The firmness of the horse felt as soft as sun-warm clay when compared to the hard strength of Jake's body, pressing against her.

Jake pulled back only far enough for his tongue to stop plundering Amanda's mouth. His appetite momentarily appeased, he seemed content to let the very tip of his tongue skim her kiss-swollen lips. He licked and savored, sipping at the hot sweetness of her mouth without launching a second invasion. Yet.

While one hand hovered near her waist—the fingers flexing and releasing the wrinkled calico, tunneling possessively into the soft white flesh beneath—his other hand slipped behind her back. His palm stroked a path of fire up her spine, then hooked over a slender shoulder. He yanked her so close their frantic heartbeats entwined.

"Remember the kiss?" His hot, moist tongue stroked her lips between each huskily whispered word. "The first kiss, princess. The one we were supposed to put behind us and forget."

Amanda hesitated, then nodded as best she could with her head thrown back, and Jake's breath burning hotly over her chin, along her jaw, down the sensitive taper of her neck. "I . . . yes, Jake, I remember."

"It didn't work for me either. I didn't forget you,

200

Amanda. I tried . . . God, how I tried! But I didn't, *couldn't* forget how sweet you taste. How much I wanted to taste you again."

"I know," she said hoarsely and sucked in a shaky breath when his teeth nibbled a particularly vulnerable spot, the center of her lower lip. A trickle of heat feathered through her blood, a hot surge of desire poured through her veins. Her hands fisted his shirt, even as she arched more closely against his hard male heat. "I-I know you didn't forget, Jake."

His silky hair tickled her throat when he nodded. He tasted the skin on the side of her neck, just below her ear. With a throaty moan, he sucked a patch of it into his mouth.

Damn, she tasted good! All creamy and sweet. Forbidden fruit, forbidden white skin. He hesitated, abandoning himself to the bittersweet flavor of her, the bittersweet feel of her flesh skimming beneath his hungry tongue. He kissed her neck, nuzzled the possessive red mark his suckling mouth had branded into her flesh. He stopped to gulp in a long, shuddering breath.

Jake's head lifted. His passion-darkened gaze seared into Amanda. Her head was thrown back, cradled against his shoulder, her throat eagerly exposed to him. He could see the pulse pounding in the creamy hollow. As tempting as it would be to caress that frantic beat with his tongue, he didn't. Not yet. But the temptation was there, and it was stronger than anything he'd ever felt before.

His gaze lifted. Wispy strands of spun gold had escaped the braid at her nape. The long, rain-dampened tendrils made spirals to frame her cheeks and brow. Her lips were swollen from his kisses. So moist. So tempting. As he watched, her lips parted oh, so softly, as though begging for a fuller exploration.

Jake promised himself she would get exactly that.

Soon. But there was something his mind demanded he say to this woman before his body took control. He waited until her lashes had swooped up. The fear that he was about to stop this sensuous madness shimmered in her eyes; it was tempered by a determined green glint that said she would not *let* him stop. Not now, perhaps not ever.

"I told you I don't repeat my mistakes, Amanda Lennox," he said, his voice strained. He tightened his hold on her when she flinched. Her eyes looked huge and moist in what little light the day offered. Her attention shifted to the side of his neck, which was concealed from view by the thick black curtain of his hair. Their thoughts meshed on the scar creasing his skin.

Pain swam in her eyes, tightened her expression. The same pain knifed through Jake. The intensity of it might have made him stop talking there and then, had he allowed himself to surrender to it. He didn't.

He sandwiched her cheeks in his open palms and held her steady when she would have looked away. Dammit, he didn't want her looking away from him! Not now. He wanted her eyes on him, nowhere else, when he said what needed to be said and said it as quickly as humanly possible. "Kissing you once and hoping it would get you out of my system was a mistake, lady. One I don't intend to repeat."

"Kissing me is a mistake?" she asked weakly. Her voice cracked, but it was nothing compared to the crack his words chiseled in her heart. He was going to reject her again. She could feel it, dreaded it.

"No, princess. God, no! Thinking I could kiss you once, then turn my back on you . . . *that* was my mistake. I've learned my lesson, though. I know better now. Once won't be enough for me. Not with you." He hesitated, willing himself to continue when he'd rather have kissed her again. "Do you understand what I'm saying to you, Amanda?"

She nodded, but it was an unconvincing gesture. Jake's frustration mounted. Somehow, he had to make her understand the rules of this newer, more dangerous game they were playing—rules he wasn't sure he understood himself—and he had to do it quickly, before things went any further between them.

"I'm only a human, lady. I can't . . . not just once . . . not with you . . . Damn!" For the first time in his life, Jake was tongue-tied. Jesus, the depths he'd sunk to! Maybe if he came right out and *said* what was on his mind? To hell with trying to coat the truth in sugary phrases. He'd never been good with words. And the way Amanda was gazing up at him, her lovely green eyes shimmering with sweet confusion, wasn't making this any easier.

His grip on her tightened as he pushed the truth harshly past his lips. "I'm going to have you, Amanda Lennox. There's no stopping now. I'm going to do things to your body that you'd be too embarrassed to dream about. And you're going to do things to mine. We've both wanted this too long and too badly to hold back. The problem is . . . hell, what I'm trying to say is that one time with you isn't going to be enough for me. I'm going to want you in my bed again. And again. And I *will* have you there, again and again, for however many times it takes to work you out of my system. You have to know that up front. You have to go into this with those beautiful green eyes of yours wide open . . . the way I intend to go into you."

Her hands lifted. She blanketed his roughened knuckles with her trembling palms. "What about me, Jake? Don't I have any say in this?"

"No." The way he said it made Amanda think he acknowledged his answer only as he mouthed the word. "I don't think you do. I don't think I can *let* you have a say in it."

"Pity. I'll have my say anyway." She hesitated, rolling her lips inward. Jake swallowed back a groan, knowing she had no idea how provocative the gesture was to him. "Did it never occur to you, that *I* might want *you* again?" Her gaze burned over his lips, her eyelids thickened slumberously. "And again?" Her lips parted oh, so softly, oh, so invitingly. "And again?"

Her words rustled like a sweet summer breeze in his ears. It wasn't the prissy, sensible answer Jake had expected, had prepared himself to hear. His entire body convulsed, as though he'd sustained a crushing blow. His gaze shifted to where his fingers curled over her shoulder. Her neck was a mere fraction away from his fingertips. The contrast in color and texture — satin-soft and sandpaper-rough, burnt-copper and milky-white — was jarring. What he couldn't figure out was why, *why* that wasn't the stumbling block it should have been?

His eyelids hooded but in no way blotted out the intensity of his gaze. "It's wrong," he whispered, and the words felt like they'd been torn from his throat. It cut him up inside to think them, let alone say them aloud. Not that it made a difference. No matter what he said to Amanda now, no matter what she said to him, it wouldn't matter. Words couldn't stop him. He was beyond caring about logic and consequence. The sharp edges of reality had blurred to the white-hot need sluicing through him. "It's wrong for us to be together. You know that, don't you? Jesus, lady, tell me you know that!"

"In your mind, Jake. Not in mine." With the tip of her index finger she ironed out the creases between his brows. His skin felt warm and smooth and wonderful. Would the rest of him feel this good? Amanda suspected it would, and she had a desperate need to prove the theory out. "The way you make me feel is right, Jacob Blackhawk Chandler. Very right. Very good. That's all I know, all I want or *need* to know."

204

His spine went rigid. His jaw jutted up at a proud angle. At that moment, his silver eyes shimmering with restrained passion, his expression tight, Amanda thought he'd never looked more like the proud, untamed savage. The observation frightened her, but in a way it thrilled her, too.

His gaze sliced downward. Steel grey meshed with luminescent green. "I want you," he said simply, harshly, as if those three words were all that mattered to either of them.

They were all that mattered to Amanda. *I want you* were three words no one had ever said to her before. There were three other words she'd never heard, even from her father, but she knew instinctively that this man would not be the one to say them. Jake wanted her physically, the way she wanted and needed him, but that was all he wanted. It would have to be enough. He wouldn't give her more, and her pride demanded she not ask it of him. Because if he refused her, if he rejected her again . . .

"Show me," she demanded huskily, even as she curled her arms around his neck and tugged. He remained stiff, unmoving, but only for a second. His posture loosened, and he bowed over her, around her, as though sheltering her with his body from the drizzling rain. His cheek caressed her temple. His hot breath blasted raggedly in her ear. The heat of it, of *him,* seeped into her skin, warming her flesh to a feverish degree.

His hair fell forward over his shoulders. The damp, dark strands grazed Amanda's jaw as she turned, her mouth searching out his neck. She nuzzled the warm, earthy scented skin with her lips, and whispered huskily against it, "Show me how much you want me, Jake. Please, I need you to show me."

Jake didn't need an invitation to take from this woman what, to his mind, had been his from the first moment he'd laid eyes on her. But now that she'd given her permission, it dawned on him that he wasn't *taking* anything from her. At least nothing that wasn't freely given. It brought a subtle change to his perspective, added a complex aspect to an act that in past had always been very, very simple; an act that had once been driven only by physical necessity.

Amanda Lennox wasn't for sale. What she offered, she offered freely. Damned if that gesture didn't touch Jake deeply.

He slid from the white, still cradling Amanda close. His movements were slower, gentler than they would have been a few passion-fogged minutes ago. He carried her to a spot where two fallen tree trunks crossed, sheltering the earth beneath and keeping it relatively dry.

Amanda sighed, and curled comfortably within the safe harbor of Jake's arms as he kicked prickly twigs and rocks aside. His heart drummed a wild beat beneath her ear. His breaths burned over her hair, seared into her scalp.

Ingrained morals said she should be protesting right now, not surrendering. But Amanda was honest enough with herself to admit there would be no sense to that. She *wanted* this—wanted *Jake*—too badly to give social standing and racial barriers a thought. How could she? Jake's arms were cradling her to his hard chest, pinning her to him gently, as though she was a priceless, fragile piece of art that needed sheltering and protecting. His tenderness, so unexpected, touched her.

When the hard ground came up to meet her back, Amanda knew she'd never in her life felt a bed so wonderful, or a blanket so warm and inviting as the virile body that eased itself atop her.

They met chest to chest, hip to hip, thigh to thigh. Jake's elbows flanked her ribs, supporting the majority of his weight. Amanda's hands were free to test the tautness of his waist, to slip behind and glide up the corded musculature of his back. His shirt moved with her, gliding over his skin, until she could almost feel his sleek, unpadded flesh beneath her fingertips.

He was hard. Not an ounce of fat clung to his lean frame. He was warm — tantalizingly hot, actually. His body felt so good and perfect molded atop hers that it made Amanda's breath catch.

Jake's attention snagged on the choppy little sound. His gaze shifted, spearing into hers. His eyes were hot with the build-up of three hellish days and nights of denied passion. His body remembered vividly every second of denial, and now it was humming for that time to be over.

His attention settled on her lips. Her mouth looked moist and swollen, well-kissed. Her lips parted. Her lower lip trembled, inviting him closer, teasing him to take another taste.

His restraint snapped.

With a groan, Jake's mouth crashed down on hers. Instead of protesting, as he'd half expected her to, Amanda flowered open beneath him. Her fingers curled inward, tunneling through his shirt, digging into the warm skin beneath. She clung to him, arched beneath him, and pressed her body hungrily against his.

There was nothing gentle about this kiss. It was savage and thorough, hard and demanding. Devouring. Give and take manifested into a white-hot need for immediate satisfaction. Their tongues warred and tasted, plundered and claimed. No one led, no one followed. Desire kindled, fanning the flame burning inside them both. Mutual need flared to demanding life.

Jake wanted to go slowly with her this first time. But then Amanda snuck her sweet, distracting little tongue into his mouth, and urged his to join in a primitive mating dance. A surge of heat blasted up his spine when she sucked his tongue into her mouth.

Her hips arched, rubbing against the hard, aching length of him. Did she know what she was doing to him? Did she care?

Jake groaned, and realized that slow was no longer a possibility. Not now, not with this woman, not ever. When it came to Amanda Lennox, the definition of the word restraint was lost on him. Nor did he have the time or patience to relearn it.

He balanced his weight on his left elbow. His fingers trembled as he reached down and fisted calico and linen, dragging her skirt up until it bunched in wrinkled folds high on her slender white thighs. She wore a single chemise, and a dainty pair of pantilets. The pantilets were quickly dispersed. The crisp white linen chemise proved no barrier. Shifting his weight, Jake nudged her legs open with his knee. His leg rose, and his lower thigh wedged itself against moist, beckoning heat.

His hand opened, splaying over her small, tight stomach. He felt the breaths rushing in and out of her, felt the warmth of those breaths scald his cheek as he dragged his lips from hers, lifted, and let his gaze skim down her perfectly curved body.

His hand blanketed almost her entire stomach. His fingers looked big and dark and strong against the lush feminine backdrop. Beneath the calico, he felt minute tremors quaver through her. The tiny shivers of anticipation vibrated up his arm like the clap of thunder that echoed around them. Matching tremors rippled through his blood like waves of molten heat.

His hand lifted, skimming her ribs, settling only a scant inch from where it needed most to be. The undercurve of her breast felt firm and inviting against the sensitive webbing between his thumb and index finger. He nudged her, squeezed gently, testing her firmness and fullness through the cloth.

His hand turned inward. He didn't cover her, the way his palm begged for him to do. That would be too quick, too unsatisfying. He'd rather linger, let the delay feed the fire building within him, within her, before he extinguished it. Only once he'd made the need unbearable for them both would he give her his full touch. Only then.

He began at the very base of her breast. With an upward stroke he slowly, *slowly* swept over her from the tips of his fingers to the heel of his palm. He paused, sucked in sharp breath, rolled his palm back down, then up once more. He felt her nipple pucker beneath the cloth, felt it burn like fire into the center of his palm. He curled his fingers inward.

Amanda's response was immediate and sharp. A bolt of awareness shot like liquid lightning through her blood. Her back arched off the ground. If it wouldn't have been too bold, she would have peeled free the buttons of her blouse and removed the barrier separating flesh from hot, hungry flesh. What Jake was doing felt wonderful, sinfully erotic. No man had ever touched her like that. Now, she wanted to know his touch without the obstruction of calico and linen. She hungered for it, was desperate for it.

Jake fed her desperation. And in so doing, he fed his own. He didn't remove the hindering blouse, the way they both wanted badly for him to do. Instead, he tested the size and shape of her breast in his palm. And marveled at the fit. She was firm and round and perfect. On second thought, "perfect" didn't come close to describing how it felt to touch this particular woman, in this particular way.

Had any woman ever nested into his hand so flawlessly? None that Jake could remember. That might be because, at that moment, he couldn't remember having been with any woman before this one. His entire life stopped and started right here, right now, with her. No one came before Amanda Lennox, no one would come after her. Not like this, not ever. He knew it.

Jake's hand moved to her buttons. Skill had little to do with his ability to slip them free. His fingers were shaking, his movements awkward and school-boy-clumsy. He managed to work each pearly disk from its hole only by focusing the core of his attention on the sweet rewards that would be bared once the chore was done. Warm white skin . . . hard pink nipples . . .

The buttons came undone in record time.

Jake parted the calico placket wide, his gaze drilling into the splash of white linen chemise beneath. The fragile laces closing the front looked impossibly complex to his passion-dazed mind. Desire was riding him hard. In his current state of mind, the thought of wasting time untying those laces was beyond him.

He shifted, reaching down to slip the knife from its sheath at his belt. The blade glinted in the muted sunlight; the steel was wet, rain-slickened. His gaze volleyed between the knife and the woman, then settled on the latter. He scanned Amanda's face. Beads of rain made her skin shine like moist porcelain. Her eyes looked large and round, slightly dazed as her gaze locked on his.

The knife lifted.

Her eyes rounded, she trembled, and for a split second he thought she was going to scream. She didn't. Instead, after a telling hesitation, she surprised them both by arching one brow and tilting her chin up to allow him better access.

The metal glinted wetly in the dim light as it arched toward the chemise, and its intricate crisscross of laces. Jake's fingers had been trembling before. They weren't trembling now. They never did when he held a knife. His strokes as he cut through the obstructive ribbons were clean and precise, fluid. They were also purposefully slow, revealing her inch by tantalizing inch.

The laces severed, he returned the knife to its sheath, and feasted his gaze on her. In color, her skin wasn't too different from the chemise. He could tell at a glance that the two were worlds apart in texture. Linen was cool and smooth . . . forbidden white skin was hot and silky and tempting as all hell.

Something tickled the hollow of Amanda's throat where her pulse throbbed. She shivered when she felt Jake's warm, rough fingertip stroke a burning path downward, pausing when he reached the valley between her breasts. He nuzzled the shadowy cleft, slipping his finger between, stroking the full underside of each until she burned and whimpered.

It wasn't until her breathing went shallow and gaspy, when she strained against him, her body begging intimate attention, that his fiery touch melted away.

Amanda opened her mouth. Jake's lips smothered what she was about to say. He covered her lips in a grinding kiss. While he let her respond to him, that was all he let her do. When she surrendered with a low, husky moan and tried to lift her arms to caress his back, he batted her hands away.

His tongue was like fire, plundering, claiming. Years of suppressed desire flamed to his kiss, to the sharp nips his teeth made at her lips. Amanda's spine arched, and she molded her breasts to his chest, lifted her hips, straining for more.

Jake had always sensed fire in this woman. Even from the start, when it had been concealed beneath a veneer of ice, her passion had always been there, simmering beneath the surface. She'd just needed the right hand to spark the fire. His hand. He wanted to brand her with his touch.

Again, she tried to move her arms, this time to curl them around his neck. Again, he wouldn't allow it. Jake found her wrists and, ensnaring them in one fist, tugged her arms over her head. The method of restraint was double-edged. The position pressed her more fully into his length. The feel of her breasts crushed beneath his chest made his blood boil, his senses reel.

His free hand skimmed the curve of her hip. The indentation of her waist. Higher. Her bodice and chemise parted. The gaping cloth welcomed the fingers he snuck beneath the cloth. So did the warm fullness of her breasts.

Skin to skin. Jesus, the feel of her in his hand was everything he'd imagined it would be, and more. Her breast was full, ripe, her nipple already rigid. He flicked his thumb over the tip, bringing it to an even harder peak.

Jake captured her hot, airy groan with his mouth even as his hand closed over her. His touch was skilled, her reaction strong and uncivilized. She twisted beneath him, at the same time matching the urgency of his kiss with a wild, hungry response of her own.

The fingers manacling her wrist melted away. The second his grip loosened, Amanda slipped her hands free. She stroked his long, sleek, rain-dampened hair. Her fingertips acquainted themselves with the width and strength of his shoulder, the strong, rippling cords of his upper arms, the firm expanse of his back. As pleasurable as it felt, she wanted to feel it all again . . . *without* the obstruction of cloth.

Jake's mouth left hers. He sipped hot, moist kisses over her chin, down the sensitive taper of her throat. "I'll say it again, princess," he groaned against her. "You're no lady. And . . . damn but I have to respect you for that."

Amanda shivered when his tongue teased the pulse pounding hard and fast in her throat. Her voice sounded low, husky, passion-strained, even to her own ears. "I was taught that a lady represses her feelings," she murmured shakily.

"Repress? Jesus, princess, if you're *repressing* now, I think there's a good chance you'll kill me from sheer pleasure when you finally let loose."

"No, Jake, you misunderstood. I said that's what a *lady* does." She felt him tense, and before she knew it he'd risen up and was staring down at her. His silvery eyes were hooded, but none the less bright, none the less hot as his gaze stabbed into her. Raindrops dripped from the ends of his hair. The beads of water felt warm from the heat of his body as they splattered on, and soaked into, her shirt, her skin, her blood. "In case you haven't figured it out yet, I'm not feeling like much of a lady right now."

His response was choked. "No? Then what are you feeling like?"

"Not 'what,' *how*." Her eyelids felt heavy, languid. Was there as much longing in her gaze as there was humming through her body? Amanda hoped so. She wanted Jake to see it. All of it. She wanted him to know how good, how very *un*ladylike he made her feel. "I'm feeling hot, Jake. Very hot. For you."

His jaw bunched hard as he lowered his head until their rain-moistened foreheads touched. His sigh felt misty and warm against her mouth. "Damn, princess, you aren't the only one. Trust me."

And she did. She had to. She wouldn't be letting him do this to her if she didn't, in some essential way, trust this man. Maybe not with information, no, but with her body. He wouldn't hurt her. She didn't know how she knew it, she just did.

There was enough space between his heaving chest and her own for Amanda to sneak her hands between them. Her fingertips hesitated on the second button of his shirt. She felt his hot skin through the cloth. Her fingers shook, which made slipping the buttons free seem like an impossible task; one she didn't do gracefully. By the time Jake's hungry lips had settled on the upper swell of her breast, she'd resorted to

213

ripping most of the buttons free.

He moved, just a slight angling of his head.

It was enough.

His lips closed over her nipple in the same instant Amanda yanked the shirtsleeves down his arms. She was unsure which felt better; what his mouth was doing to her, or the feel of his flesh coasting beneath her open palms. His skin felt hot. The way he made her blood pound through her veins was hotter still. Unbearably hot.

Jake suckled her nipple into his mouth. He rolled it with his tongue, nibbled, tasted and teased. His hand trailed a fiery path down her waist, over her hips, skimming the inside of her thigh. Her skin skimmed warmly beneath his palm as he dragged the skirt higher, bunching it around her waist. His fingers launched an intimate investigation, combing downy gold curls. Jesus, she felt good. So damned good!

Until she tensed.

Jake's sexual expertise was lacking when it came to seducing innocents—especially white ones. He had little experience to draw on, only instinct. Still, he wasn't stupid. He knew virginal shyness when he felt it, and the way her thighs trembled and then closed against his searching hand was certainly that. Didn't she know it was too late to stop?

He frowned. Or was it too late? If she asked, would he stop? *Could* he? Maybe. For her. He prayed to be spared that test. He wasn't at all sure he could pass it to her satisfaction. He wanted her too damn badly.

"Let me," he rasped, his nose nuzzling the soft, flowery scented hollow between her breasts. Heaven. He'd found heaven. His tongue darted out, licking her. They both shivered. She tasted like rainwater and sunshine. An erotic flavor, one to be savored. "Open for me, princess. Let me touch you."

214

"Not there, Jake. Please. I-I can't—"

"You can."

"But I shouldn't."

"A lady shouldn't," he agreed throatily. "But I don't want a lady right now, princess. A lady isn't what I need. I need . . . God, I need to touch you—now, everywhere—so damn badly it hurts. Let me. Please."

It was the please that decided things for her. The word tripped rustily over his tongue, and she did as he asked, albeit timidly.

Her action was a bit martyred, Jake thought. But it wouldn't be for long, he promised them both. Slowly, slowly, his fingers shimmied down. He stroked, inflamed, sought out and probed the moist heat of her. He slipped inside of her, deeply, searching and stretching, preparing her for what was to come.

Amanda stiffened and grew very, very still. Her breathing shallowed until it was almost nonexistent.

He hesitated, waiting until she was used to the invasive feel of a part of him embedded in the most womanly part of her. Then, with an expert flick of his wrist, he began moving. His strokes were slow, long and smooth, oddly gentle. Insistent.

He lifted himself, gazing down into her passion-darkened green eyes. She looked surprised, somewhat dazed, and pleased. Very pleased. Her enjoyment pumped through Jake, and he couldn't help but grin. "Think of it as like . . . making love," he murmured, as his hand increased the pace.

His words fanned the fire in Amanda's blood. Her hips arched into his touch, initiating a swifter rhythm which instead of satisfying the peculiar ache building inside of her, made her want to cry out in frustration. Something was brewing within her, something white-hot and wonderful. Yet every time she got close to finding out what it was, Jake pulled back. His movements slowed, the feeling ebbed briefly . . .

215

until he moved, and it all started to build again. And again. And again.

Steady, but not jerky. You want to get that friction started. Back and forth, back and forth. I can't tell you how important rhythm is. Once you've established the pace, you can't let up or you'll have to start from scratch. Understand?

She hadn't understood at the time. Not really. She was starting to understand now. If only he wouldn't stop. If only he would continue to feed the fire in her until it blazed . . .

The fire in Jake had never died, but her response to what he was doing made the flames glow red-hot. He lowered his mouth to hers, and the taste of her on his tongue made him impatient to taste more of her. All of her. Now. The feel of her nestled in his hand was driving him insane, chipping away his normally staunch patience, chipping away his usually powerful self-restraint.

A minute was too long to wait to be buried inside of this woman. Sixty more seconds of this would kill him, Jake was positive of it.

That was all the time it took for him to ease away from her, to impatiently rid them both of their rain-dampened clothes.

When they were finally naked, he laid Amanda back down on the ground and let his gaze devour her. The way she was spread out before him made her look deceptively slender, almost fragile. Almost. Her skin was moist from the drizzling rain. The way the water shone against her pale white flesh made Jake ache to sip the wetness off of her skin with his tongue and lips.

He didn't, not yet, but soon. Very soon.

He straddled her hips, and his slitted gaze scanned breasts that were heavy and more perfectly formed than days of fantasies had made him dare dream they would be. She was full and round, her nipples puckered and pink and tempting. His gaze skimmed her slender waist, marveling at the way it flared into temptingly curved hips. His attention snagged on the nest of golden curls between her thighs. The urge to possess returned with staggering force; had he been standing, he would have crashed to his knees.

Jake shifted, blanketing Amanda with his body, nudging her legs apart with his knees. She opened for him, and he sandwiched himself between her thighs. The tip of him probed moist, velvety flesh, but he resisted pressing into her. For just a few seconds, he was content to know release was in sight—content to merely look at her flawless face, to watch her lashes flicker against soft white cheeks.

His contentment burned away the second her thick, honey-tipped lashes swooped up. Her green eyes, wide and questioning, held him prisoner.

A thousand words ran through Jake's mind, phrases that would make this first time easier for her. Easier for him. He didn't utter a single one. He couldn't. The anticipation he saw in her eyes clogged any words he might have spoken in his throat.

Her hands lifted, skimming his back before her fingers tangled in his long, dark hair. Her palms cupped his scalp, drawing his lips down to hers for a searing kiss. Only when their lips met did Jake's hips arch forward. Only then did he slowly, slowly enter the tight, warm core of her.

The barrier was broken as delicately as his feeding passion would allow. He felt her tense, and he captured her startled whimper with his mouth. His scalp burned from the pull of her fingers fisting his wet hair, but the pain didn't last long; it only *seemed* like it lasted forever. Soon, she relaxed. Soon, she began moving in the age-old rhythm beneath him.

Jake pushed forward, sliding into her fully. Only once he'd buried himself as far as he could go did he pause. A surge of emotion rocked through him. The strength of it made him shake.

217

The feeling was that of coming home.

Amanda moved restlessly, arching her hips upward, searching. Now that the initial pain was forgotten, she began to burn again. It was like a slow-building fire that sparked in her thighs, insistent and demanding. The warmth spiraled to her abdomen when Jake began moving atop her, moving inside of her.

His thrusts were smooth and unhurried, deep and long—and much too slow, as far as Amanda was concerned. She wanted a tempo to match the one drumming through her blood. She wanted fast and wild. She wanted more. Of Jake. Now.

She wrapped her legs around his hips. Her grip tightened, her hips eagerly met his as he plunged into her. She held him to her, deeply, until he groaned, shifted, almost withdrew, then thrust into her again.

And again.

And again.

The fire in her blood melted into the liquid heat of all-consuming passion. A need stronger than anything she had ever known before throbbed through her. It was aggravated beyond endurance by the way Jake's head dipped and his mouth and tongue suckled her neck. Her chin shot up, her head twisted atop the ground as, following her urgings, he quickened the pace.

"Remember," she murmured, his words coming back to her with breathtaking clarity, "once you've set the pace you can't let up or you'll have to start from scratch."

He laughed—softly, deeply, a sound that rocked Amanda to the core. His hands slipped beneath her back, holding her close. Their moist bodies slid together and apart and together once more. Flesh rubbed against hot, wet flesh.

Amanda's hands skimmed Jake's back in a smooth,

218

downward stroke. She cupped his hips in her palms. Her fingers tunneled into flesh and muscle as she encouraged him to move faster still.

The feelings inside her were melting together — electric, building, just out of reach. No, just *within* reach. Her body arched to meet powerful thrusts and retreats. Each plunge was longer, deeper, fuller than the last. Each rise of her hips was bolder, more daring, more demanding. She felt herself tightening around him, felt minuscule spasms shudder up her spine, building and building. She was on the brink, the very precipice of . . .

What?

Jake had held himself back for as long as he could, but . . . dammit he was losing it. He couldn't wait much longer. She felt too good, too warm and tight and wet. Her body was milking a response out of him that he didn't want to give her, a response he couldn't, no matter how hard he tried, hold back from her.

Think of it as like . . . making love.

He drove into her, his pace reaching a frantic pitch. Each thrust brought their chests into searing contact. He could feel her hardened nipples grazing against him, burning into his skin. He could feel her rapid, ragged breaths burning over him.

He wanted release. He wanted it right now. And, goddammit, he wanted it for *both* of them!

And what Jake Chandler wanted, Jake Chandler got.

The first tiny quivers of her tightening and releasing around him was the sweetest form of torture Jake had ever known. His control came damn close to shattering. White heat shot through him when he felt her arch, clinging to his back as she buried her face in his shoulder and cried out her pleasure.

That was all Jake had been waiting for. His hands searched the ground until he found hers. Their fingers locked, entwined, their grips white-knuckled and strained as his hips arched forward, his thrusts hard and demanding, the rhythm no longer smooth and controlled, just needy.

Amanda wrapped her legs higher around him, tightening, accepting, *demanding* all of him. Her body rippled around him as Jake filled her time and again. She groaned, shuddered, and felt the earth splinter around her.

Jake knew he'd waited too long. His intentions had been to make this first time feel so good she wouldn't think twice about doing it again. And again. And again.

Good intentions flew right out of his mind when he felt her sweet, hot spasms of satisfaction. He would have liked to wait, liked to bring her to that peak again and again, but he couldn't. Not this time. He had needs of his own that had been too long suppressed and refused to be denied a second longer.

Before he could suck in a breath, his body arched and he was speeding after her, a mere second behind. His climax came long and hard, feathering up his spine, bursting behind his tightly closed eyelids in a blinding haze of earth-shattering completion. He felt the culmination of their joining literally rip through his body, and spill into hers in a burst of liquid heat.

When it was over, when they both lay panting and spent, he groaned and slowly lowered himself atop her. Her body was a bed of soft, moist, feminine curves that welcomed his weight.

Jake was too weak to move. Too weak to breathe. In all his life, he'd never felt anything as depleting as what they'd just shared. Nor anything as good and right.

Home, he thought again as, with a weary sigh, he nuzzled his face against her neck. Making love to Amanda Lennox felt like coming home.

Chapter Twelve

"You all right?" Jake asked as, leaning to the side, he helped Amanda onto the white. His large, warm hands spanned her waist, positioning her between the hard wedge of his thighs.

"Yes, fine," she answered, knowing full well she'd just told the biggest lie of her life. Fine? Oh, no, she felt better than that. Much better.

"You're sure?"

"Positive," she said dreamily. "I'm . . . fine." Actually, what she felt came closer to giddy. Relaxed, unfettered, happier than she'd been in months. Make that years. Make that her *entire life!* Right now, she felt like she could conquer the world. Sighing in contentment, she leaned back and snuggled into the hard contours of Jake Chandler's chest. Not for the first time did she admire the way her body fit into his so nicely, so perfectly. The last time she'd found herself in this position, her blood had been hot with anticipation. While her blood was still hot, this time it was with an entirely different emotion. The feeling was contentment. Pure, physical gratification. It burned away every other emotion she'd ever felt before it.

The firm chest pressing into her spine and shoulders, the hard, corded legs flanking her outer hips and thighs, the arm molded around her waist and the palm possessively riding her thigh . . . not a single inch of

Jake Chandler's body held any mystery for her now. Maybe that explained why even his simplest touch was more exciting now than it had been before. Maybe. Although Amanda thought it more likely her excitement stemmed from how . . . *stimulating* she now knew that touch could be.

Perhaps her outlook had changed because the look and feel of Jake was now stamped in her mind, on her palms, on her body. She no longer *wondered* what he felt like, she *knew*, and she couldn't forget! Sleek and warm and appealing—*that* was how Jake Chandler felt. Her desire to have his mouth on hers had been temporarily assuaged. So had other, baser cravings she hadn't known she had—until Jake had awakened them in her. She knew what it felt like to have his hands scouring her body. And she knew . . .

Well, she knew that what Jake looked and felt like was heaven. Even now, with clothing separating them, he felt good. Very good! Good enough to make Amanda's mind swerve, good enough for her thoughts to turn suggestive and hungry once more.

Again and again.

That was what he'd promised her. She clung to those words, replayed them in her mind. Her heart skipped when she thought of the next time with him, and the time after that.

Again and again.

The words sliced through Jake's mind like a warm knife through butter. He angled his head, and the underside of his jaw scraped the top of Amanda's head. Her hair felt damp and cool against his skin. At some point while he'd been busy satisfying his craving for this women the raindrops had begun to mix with snow. Amanda's hair was now dusted with it. So was his. Most of the flakes melted on contact, cooling passion-heated flesh, cooling passion-heated thoughts. Well, almost.

He glanced down, and noticed that Amanda's skirt was hiked up to midthigh so that she could ride astride.

222

Jake's vision filled with shapely, snow-moistened legs. She was only slightly tall for a woman, and most of her height was in her legs. They went on for miles, all long and slender and white. Perfectly shaped, the muscles firm, yet appealingly so.

His gut fisted when he remembered what it felt like to have those legs wrapped around his hips, urging him on, drawing him deeper and deeper into the hot velvet core of her. He gritted his teeth when he remembered how willingly he'd gone there, how willingly he'd picked up and quickened the pace that she had set.

That was a first. Jake had never before let a woman take the initiative during sex. Then again, with Amanda Lennox . . . well, what had happened between them couldn't be called mere sex. In this instance only, the term seemed too cold, too clinical, too dirty for his liking. But the term "making love" didn't fit, either. Or did it? God, he hoped not! "Making love" to a woman meant a certain amount of give and take. It meant a union of more than two bodies, more even than two minds. It meant . . .

Jake shifted uneasily. *Making love.* The phrase ran circles in his mind, hitting a raw nerve inside him. It was a term he rarely thought. Just the words made him uncomfortable, probably because they described an act he'd never participated in. Jake had never "made love" to a woman. Until now. Until Amanda.

Dammit! He could deny it all he wanted, but the fact was, he *had* made love to her. With Amanda Lennox, it wasn't just sex. As good as *that* had been, there was a hell of a lot more to it. He'd be lying if he said otherwise. There was something about her velvet-smooth touch, her petal-soft scent, her feathery kisses, that catapulted him over the need for physical gratification—strong as that need was—and made him crave something more. Something that was his alone. Something he could wrap his arms around and cling to. Something unattainable and forbidden.

That was what Jake wanted, more than he wanted to

draw his next breath. He wanted Amanda Lennox, all of her, and he wanted her so much it hurt—more so now that he'd had her once. He wanted her, to coin a phrase, again and again. In every way imaginable. Yet he also wanted more than to leave his brand on her body. He wanted to burn himself into her soul as well.

The strength of that desire brought to mind the question of his sanity. Was he *crazy?* Yes, Jake thought, that was a good possibility. It would explain why he'd paid dozens of whores for his pleasure in the past and come away only mildly content. It would also explain why he hadn't paid Amanda Lennox a plugged nickel, yet he'd come away from her feeling like he'd gotten more than he'd bargained for. More than he knew how to deal with.

"Jake?" Amanda shifted, turned, nuzzled her cheek against his shoulder. His shirt felt cool and wet. She didn't mind. The skin beneath felt warm and solid, the play of muscles strong and firm. She sucked in a tiny breath and thought he smelled even more wonderful than he felt. His sharp, woodsy scent wafted around her, enveloped her, made her head spin.

"Jake?" she said again when he didn't answer. She glanced up, but at this angle all she could see was the strong, smooth underside of his chin. The urge to reach out and touch him was strong. She didn't bother trying to deny or repress it. Her palm cupped the hard, square line of his jaw. She felt him startle. "Jake?"

His gaze sliced down to her, over her, *into* her, then quickly returned to the snowdusted woods through which they continued to pick their way. "Hmmm?"

"I want to apologize."

One inky brow rose. Those were *not* the words he'd expected a properly bred society snob would say to the man who'd just stolen her virginity. Amanda Lennox should, to his way of thinking, be having a fit right about now. Wasn't that what all well bred young "ladies" did? Begged a man, teased him until they'd brought him to his knees, then cried that he'd forced her afterward? Yes, that was exactly what *ladies* did. He knew.

But not *this* lady. Amanda wasn't reacting at all the way he'd expected her to. In fact, she seemed oddly pleased with the loss of her innocence. Instead of coy or fearful or repentant, she looked . . . well, downright rejuvenated, *that's* how she looked. And, Jake groaned inwardly, she also looked like she wanted to talk.

"Are you going to accept it?" she prodded.

"Accept what?"

Amanda sighed. Whatever he was thinking about was too distracting. She decided it was time to distract his mind back to her. Lifting one of her hands, she toyed with the buttons trailing up his shirt. Actually, she spent more time on the warm, silky flesh her fingers frequently slipped beneath the plackets to stroke.

"My apology, Jake," she said finally. "What else?"

What else? God, he could think of several dozen things he would gladly accept from this woman right now. Hot, hungry, lustful things. An apology wasn't one of them. He forced a shrug. "All depends, princess. What are you apologizing *for?*"

"All the terrible things I said to you back there, before we . . . you know."

"No, I don't know." The barest trace of a grin tugged at his lips as he slanted her a look. His steely gaze was teasingly hot. "Before we what?"

"You know!" she insisted. Her blush deepened. His grin broadened. Amanda huffed and turned so that her back was again cradled by his chest. "I really am sorry, Jake."

"Did you mean what you said?"

She thought about that a second, then nodded. "Yes."

"Then don't apologize."

"But—"

He sighed. "Drop it, Amanda. Please, just let it go."

Amanda strained against him, craning her neck to look into his face. His long, inky hair was dusted with snow, his skin wet from where the flakes had melted to his body heat. His thick, dark lashes were at half-mast, his steely gaze lazy and hooded. Only his expression looked tight and controlled: tense, anxious.

She stiffened warily. "Jake?"

"Hmmm?" Blinking hard, Jake forced his eyes to pull the snow-dusted woods into focus. He scowled when his attention dipped, and his gaze meshed with haunting green. Her eyes were large and round and confused. He shifted uncomfortably, and pretended to tug on the reins that tethered her horse to his.

"Are you . . . ?" Amanda pulled in a steadying breath. Something wasn't right. Her suspicions were confirmed when she saw the muscle in his cheek twitch, and she took note of the way his body had gone rigid against hers. "You aren't sorry we . . . well, about what happened, are you?"

"Oh, yeah," he said, his voice a soft, throaty whisper. "I'm *very* sorry about it. You should be, too."

Amanda's bubble of contentment burst, pricked by the sharp bite in Jake's tone. She winced, feeling as though he'd just reached inside her and ripped out a chunk of her heart. In a way he had. A very large chunk. While she knew the logic behind his words—his reasons undoubtedly stemmed from their last argument—knowledge didn't make her feel better. He was sorry he'd made love to her . . . oh, how that hurt!

She wasn't the only one hurting. Jake was shocked to realize that he was hurting, too. What had happened between him and Amanda was special—*Jesus, was it ever!*—but it was also confusing as all hell. He needed time to sort out his feelings—whatever they were. Time to think. Time to put his unnatural desire for this woman into its proper perspective.

His gaze had settled on the top of her head. His attention shifted, focusing on the woods the white was weaving its way through. They were almost at the top of the hill. Soon they would crest it. In only a few short minutes he would leave Amanda at the cabin that neither of them had dared to mention for quite a while now. Only a few more minutes.

Jake knew there were things he should say to Amanda right now, while he still had the time. Words he didn't want to say, words she probably didn't want to hear, words that needed to be aired all the same. He should have said them a while ago, but he hadn't. Looking back, he realized that immediately afterward, neither of them had talked at all. It was as though they'd both clung to the same desperate need not to say anything that would shatter the contented afterglow. Amanda hadn't cried, hadn't begged him to make false promises that he would live to regret come sundown. Promises he could never hope to keep to a woman like her.

While they'd dressed, their gazes had met and held often. Quick, hungry glances had spoken all that needed to be said at the time.

Again and again, for as long as it lasts. That was what Amanda's eyes had promised, what Jake's urgent gaze had reinforced. That, and nothing else.

Passion had eventually thawed. Reality had returned.

Never, never again was what Jake's gut was telling him now, what the protective shell encasing his heart demanded. One quick, almost awkward encounter with Amanda had made all the women who'd come before her pale into insignificance. Jesus, even now when he closed his eyes and tried to picture a face or body beneath him, the only one he could see was Amanda's. He couldn't remember another's, didn't *want* to. Only hers.

That was not a good sign. No, not good at all. And it sure as hell wasn't safe. In fact, his fascination with all things white and prissy could wind up being lethal for them both.

Maybe Amanda couldn't see the trouble their being together would bring, but Jake knew. Hell, he'd already lived through the experience once. His jaded eyes saw what hers could not. He saw the pain ahead of them with graphic clarity, and he wanted no damn part of it.

"We're going to the cabin, aren't we?" Amanda asked as she snuggled against him. Something, she wasn't sure what, had changed since he'd helped her onto the horse. Then, they'd moved together, in tune to each other, in tune to the white as it jostled them. Now, the tension in his body, the tension in hers, made them move awkwardly apart.

"*You* are," he corrected. Though his drawl was lazy and thick, there was an edge to his words. "Like I told you, I'll meet you back here in a couple of days, once the storm's over."

Her shoulders sagged. Her chin lowered, and her head hung limply on her neck. A defeated little sigh whispered past her lips. "I thought you'd changed your mind. I really thought—"

"Wrong," he grumbled, and shifted so his body was no longer gloving her slender back and temptingly soft bottom. "As usual, you thought wrong." Sighing, Jake plowed the fingers of his free hand through his cool, damp hair and shook his head. He was glad Amanda wasn't looking at him, glad she couldn't see how much his next words cost him. The fingers cushioned atop her thigh tightened, squeezing the tender white flesh beneath the bunched folds of calico. He hesitated, then his touch melted away. "Time you faced facts, princess. What happened between us was inevitable. And I'd be lying if I said it wasn't good." He swallowed hard. "It was. *Real* good. But it doesn't change a damn thing."

"It doesn't change the color of my skin, in other words," she whispered shakily under her breath, more to herself than to him. Amanda thought she should have known better, should have known Jake would hear. She should have learned by now that little snuck past the man.

"I've slept with white women before, princess," he said flatly. "The color of your skin doesn't bother me

228

much. At least it doesn't bother me in the ways you think."

If he'd slapped her, his words couldn't have had a greater impact. Amanda's chin snapped up, and he grunted when the top of her head bumped his jaw. Her spine went rigid. Her heart drummed a painful, erratic beat against her ribs. "You told me you'd only been with *one* white woman. You said—"

"White *lady*," he growled. "I said I'd only been with one white *lady*. And," he sucked in a long, thoughtful breath, "yeah, I'd have to stand by that. I've still only been with one."

Her voice humiliated her by cracking. "You don't count me?"

"Un-uh." Jake paused, then very coldly, very precisely, drawled, "Don't sound so surprised, Amanda. I mean, you're close, I'll give you that. On the outside you're all prissy politeness and manners, but we both know that's only a front. Because on the inside, you're hotter than a burning coal. On the inside, Amanda Lennox, you ain't no lady."

Amanda had spent too many years trying to emulate her mother's memory to appreciate hearing those words. All right, maybe ladies didn't sleep with half-wild savages and enjoy it, not the way she had. In that respect, maybe she wasn't as refined as she hoped. But she was still a lady, Goddammit! And why couldn't Jake see that?

"Want me to tell you why?" Jake asked.

Despite her resolve not to, Amanda nodded.

He leaned forward, molding his chest to her back. He was close enough for his breath to blast hotly in her ear as he drawled, "Ladies don't scream when they come, princess. Not the way you did."

"I didn't!" she gasped, and felt her cheeks heat even as her mind raced. She had *not* screamed . . . had she? Oh Lord, she couldn't remember. All Amanda remembered about that particular moment was the wonder, the breathtaking *feelings*. Her body had exploded in fiery white sparks. Delicious spasms of sensation had consumed all her attention. She was *still* tingling with the aftereffects! If she'd cried out, she hadn't heard it, didn't remember it. But if she *had* cried out the way Jake said she had . . . then he was right. She was no lady.

"I—I didn't," she repeated softly, and hesitated self-consciously. "Did I?"

"Um-hmmm. You don't remember?"

She shook her head.

Jake felt her tremble, and he leaned back quickly. The distance helped, but not much. That might have been because there wasn't a whole lot of distance between them. Certainly not as much as he would have liked. Her hips were wedged between his thighs. He remembered how the body pressing against him felt in his hands, how it felt to be sandwiched between those long, enticing white legs.

"I remember," he said gruffly. What he didn't tell her was that, if he lived to be a thousand, he'd never be able to forget. "You screamed, lady. You cried out my name, and your voice was all low and throaty and raw. Remember yet? It was just before your fingernails tore bloody ribbons down my back."

Her sob ripped through Jake. He tried not to let the soft, plaintive sound affect him. If he was going to stop this madness, he couldn't do it by half-measures. He would fulfill his obligation—he'd find her cousin, he owed her that much—but when it was over, when she had the kid back, he wanted the break between him and this white woman to be immediate and clean and as painless as possible. For them both. The only way to accomplish that was to keep their relationship as simple as possible. And to not, under *any* circumstances, lay with her again!

They crested the hill in silence, their passage marked by the sound of hoofbeats crunching over newly fallen snow. Jake reined in the white. Though he didn't glance down the snow-dusted slope, he knew the cabin was there. Things around these parts, in particular people's attitudes, rarely changed.

He looked at Amanda. Her head was down, the thick gold hairs that had escaped her braid concealed most of her expression from view. All he could see was the moist curve of the lower lip she was nibbling between her teeth. The lip trembled.

"Ready?" he asked, tearing his gaze away. When he felt her nod, he leaned to the side, helped her to the ground, and untied the mare. He held the reins out to her. She wasn't looking at him and didn't see the offer. "Amanda?"

Her gaze lifted, and her cheeks colored. Her breath quickened, as though she'd been surprised to hear his voice.

"Take the reins, princess. Hurry up. The snow's starting to come down harder."

Was it? she wondered. Odd, but she'd barely noticed, hadn't really cared. The weather was the least of her problems. Her gaze dropped to the hand Jake had extended. With concentration, her gaze managed to pull into focus the leather strips draped over his big copper hand. "Thank you," she mumbled, reaching for the reins.

Her trembling fingers grazed his roughened knuckles. The contact, though slight and blessedly brief, was electric.

Amanda snatched her hand back. Curling it into a fist, she hid it in the folds of her skirt. Her determination that Jake not see how deeply even that accidental touch affected her made her tilt her chin up proudly. Her gaze met his.

Jake saw the telltale moisture clinging to her lashes. Not all of the wetness could be attributed to melting snow. If he'd ever seen anything more heart-wrenching than the hurt shimmering in Amanda Lennox's big green eyes, he couldn't remember it. If his heart had ever fisted so painfully in his chest, he couldn't remember that either.

Amanda noticed Jake's wet, clinging clothes, his snow-damp hair and skin. She also saw the proud way he sat atop the white, the determined line that etched his hard jaw. It was on the tip of her tongue to ask where he was going, how he planned to spend his time until the storm passed. She bit the words back. That type of questioning smacked of caring, and instinct said Jake would shy away from that. Instead, she said, "When the storm ends, you *will* meet me back here, won't you?"

"I said I would."

"That isn't an answer, Mr. Chandler."

The muscle in Jake's cheek jerked, and he shifted his gaze to the falling snow. Why was she calling him Mr. Chandler again? It wasn't hard to guess. He'd reverted into a cold-hearted bastard. Why shouldn't Amanda retreat behind the polite facade of his surname?

He didn't know why he should care what she called him, but he did. It was annoying that she no longer felt comfortable enough to call him Jake. He told himself it didn't bother him — distance was, after all, what he wanted, what he'd gotten — but it did. It bothered him a lot.

"Believe it or not, Amanda, I'm a man of my word," he said finally, his voice giving away none of his inner turmoil. "I said I'd be back for you, and I will be. I can't help it if you don't trust me enough to believe me." He nodded to the downward, wooded slope of the hill. "Go."

Amanda went. She really had no choice. Huddling inside the warmth of her cloak, she went to the mare and climbed into the saddle. Having come from Jake's horse, the saddle felt hard and uncomfortable beneath her. There were other reasons for her discomfort, she knew, but none she would let herself dwell on.

She sent Jake one last, confused look, then flicked the reins and started picking her way down the hill.

Jake watched her go and, try though he did to deny it, he felt a part of him winding its way down that hill with her. What was it about that woman that affected him so strongly? What? Though he searched himself for a reasonable answer, he came up dry. Plain and simple, he didn't know.

He watched Amanda rein in the mare next to the door and dismount. She knocked, waited, then eventually the door opened. She shook off the snow and cold before entering the sweet, beckoning heat of the house.

Still Jake didn't leave. The snow swirled around him long after Amanda had been swallowed up by things he'd put in his past long ago — hospitality, shelter, friendship . . . love. They were foreign terms to a man like Jacob Blackhawk Chandler. But they weren't foreign to gently reared ladies like Amanda Lennox.

No matter what he'd told her to drive her away, Amanda was a lady to the core. That was why he'd had to anger her, had to let her go. Watching her pick her way down that hill had been one of the hardest things he'd ever done. But he'd proved to himself he *could* do it. Jesus, how he'd needed to know that!

Jake sat atop the white, which was growing restless from the inclement weather, and stared at the cabin until a flutter of movement caught his attention. He glanced down, and was surprised to see that he'd removed Amanda's handkerchief from his pocket and was now clutching half of it in a white-knuckled fist. The linen flapped in the breeze and slapped at his thigh. It wasn't possible, but he could have sworn he felt that daintily embroidered *A* sear right through his pants leg, right into his skin and bloodstream.

Fifteen minutes later, Jake turned the horse away and rode into the storm.

Chapter Thirteen

Amanda had assumed the couple living in the cabin were settlers from back East, people she would be comfortable staying with. Wasn't that what she'd been led to believe? Either she'd severely misunderstood things, or she'd again misjudged the ever-perplexing Jacob Blackhawk Chandler.

The man who opened the door to Amanda's insistent rapping was not the eager homesteader she expected. Oh, no. This man was a full-blooded Indian. Unlike Jake, he dressed the part.

Amanda had been studying the scuffed toes of her ankle boots. Her gaze shifted to the man's feet. She scanned the red-and-white beaded moccasins he wore, then traced upward over his thigh-high leggings. The weather-softened deerskin left no doubt as to the heavily muscled legs beneath. His britches were made out of the same material, and they were snug. An unadorned, tuniclike shirt, also deerskin, hung from his shoulders. While the garment was loose fitting, the slackness couldn't conceal the solid bands of muscle in his chest and biceps.

Like Jake's, this man's hair was long and straight and pitch-black. Unlike Jake's, his was gathered into two neat plaits that ribboned down over each broad shoulder.

His face was comprised of hard copper planes and

234

angles. The high-bridged nose and wide brow Amanda recognized from Jake. The rest of his features were foreign to her. Weathered creases bracketed his thin mouth and suspicious brown eyes. The creases didn't look like they'd been put there from years of smiling.

Amanda took an instinctive step back, her gaze lifting those final few inches. She swallowed hard, and her hand fluttered at her throat when her attention was captured by a pair of eyes as cold and as shiny as shards of polished ebony.

"Jake Chandler sent me," she said, and it was a fight to make her voice sound calm and rational — not high and panicky, the way she felt.

The man's gaze narrowed. He assessed her in one cold, sweeping glance, then his attention snapped over her shoulders. He looked marginally relieved to see that she was alone.

Amanda forced a smile when his gaze returned to hers. He didn't return the gesture, but stepped aside, opened the door wider, and waved her in. One inky brow slanted high when she shook the snow off her cloak and head and then immediately complied.

Mustering up her courage and filing away what she was sure was — she hoped — an irrational fear born of surprise, Amanda stepped over the threshold. She told herself that Jake wouldn't have suggested she stay with these people if he didn't think they were safe. No, of course he wouldn't.

I can't help it if you don't trust me, he'd said. Well, she was trying to trust him, while at the same time proving to them both that she was *not* a shallow white princess. But . . . well, this was simply too much! The least Jake could have done was to warn her!

Perhaps this was Jake's way of testing her? Did he want to see how the prissy society lady would react to spending a few days alone with people she was supposed to feel were beneath her? Jake didn't seem the type who played such childish games. Then again, he wasn't exactly what she would call predictable. It was a possibility she couldn't dismiss.

Amanda squared her shoulders as she breezed past the man. If Jake was putting her to the test then, by God, she was going to pass it. Perhaps once she'd met this man's wife—Jake *had* said a young couple was living here, hadn't he?—she would feel more at ease. Somehow, Amanda rather doubted it, the same way she doubted she would be able to keep her anxiety a secret from probing brown eyes for very long.

The man who'd greeted her at the door was *not* a reassuring sight. Far from it. Everything about him—his rugged body, his impassive expression, his wary gaze—seemed coiled and tense, like a twisted wire ready to break.

The door slammed shut. The sound was unnaturally loud, magnified all out of proportion by the taut silence.

Amanda shivered. She felt as if she had been thrown into a jail cell, with impenetrable iron bars being slammed into place, caging her in. Though she tried to shake the feeling off, it clung tight.

"Blackhawk sent you?" the man said thoughtfully. His words were slow and precisely spoken.

Amanda turned to face him, just as he moved away from the door. She watched as, with unnaturally quiet steps, he crossed to the center of the room. Lacing his arms over the firm wedge of his chest, he stared at her, stared *through* her.

A small fire crackled in the hearth at his back. The muted light came low to the ground, casting his features in indecipherable orange shadows. But that was all right. Amanda didn't need to see his face to know his suspicions were aroused. She *felt* it. An icy chill rippled over her shoulders.

"Yes, Jake sent me. Is . . . ?" She discreetly scanned her surroundings. The lower floor of the cabin consisted of this one room and a closet carved into the far right wall. An old curtain fell in tattered folds from the top of the doorframe down to the freshly swept dirt floor. Thick, planked stairs edged the timbered wall to her left. Was the man's wife up there? If so, the woman was sitting in the dark; though Amanda squinted, she couldn't detect a shred of light coming from the upstairs room.

Her attention returned to the man, who was studying her as though she was some rare form of bird. "Where is your wife?"

His eyes narrowed cautiously. "Why?"

Amanda shrugged, her fingers playing nervously with the ribbons that secured her cloak beneath her chin. She considered untying them, then decided against it. At this rate, she wouldn't be here long enough to bother getting comfortable. "No reason. I just thought it would be nice to meet her . . . if she's here, that is. She *is* here, isn't she?"

"No, woman, you misunderstand," he said, and he shook his head. The fringed ends of his blacker-than-black braids bobbed against the solid wall of his chest. On this man, what she had thought of as a feminine decoration most assuredly was not. "My question was why Blackhawk sent you here, not why you would want to see my wife. You *will* tell me."

"Of course I'll tell you," Amanda snapped, her gaze shifting to the table on her right. Her legs felt watery, and her knees were shaking beneath her damp skirt. While she wanted nothing more than to sit before she collapsed, something told her a move like that would be interpreted as a sign of weakness. That was not the impression she was striving to convey.

"So, you will tell me," he insisted coldly.

Amanda waved a hand at the window. Her fear, oddly enough, made her bolder than she normally would have been. It loosened her tongue. She would not let this man intimidate her. Dammit, she would *not!* "I don't suppose you've looked outside recently?" she asked in her most proper Bostonian tone. "If you had, you would have noticed that it's storming. That's why Jake sent me here. He didn't want me caught out in it."

"And where is Blackhawk now?"

Amanda feigned an unconcerned shrug. "I imagine he had better things to do." She wouldn't tell this man the real reason Jake wouldn't come to the cabin with her, mostly because now that she'd seen who was living here, she wasn't sure of his reasons herself!

"You imagine?" He sighed impatiently. "In other words, you are only guessing?"

"Of course. If you know Jake Chandler at all, then you also know that *no one* knows what goes on inside that man's head."

Was it her imagination, or did a hint of a grin tug at one corner of his mouth? It could have been a trick of the light—he *was* standing mostly in shadow—but she didn't think so.

"I know Blackhawk," he said finally, flatly.

One golden brow arched. If the man hadn't had her full attention before, he had it now. And not only because of what he'd said. Something about him— she wasn't sure what—seemed more relaxed, less cautious. Why? "You know Jake?"

He nodded. Briskly. Just the once.

"And do you know him well?"

He nodded again, and this time added the barest of shrugs. "Better than most."

"Then maybe you can tell me—"

"No." The braids whipped against his shoulder as he spun on his heel and stalked to the closet she'd spotted earlier. With a flick of his wrist he swept the curtain back and reached inside.

Amanda took an instinctive step back. She didn't know why she expected his big copper hand to come back with a loaded rifle leveled at her chest, she just *did.* She was taken aback when, instead, he tugged out a woman who was cradling to her chest two small, squirming bundles in either arm.

The woman was shorter than Amanda, thinner, though close to her in age. She had a pretty—albeit thin—heart-shaped face, with smooth white skin and kinky, chestnut colored hair that refused to stay in the loosely coiled bun at her nape. Wispy brown strands curled over her cheeks and brow, softening her features and making her eyes look unusually large and very green.

The woman's attention lifted, locking skeptically with the man's dark, brooding gaze. Amanda sensed the unspoken words flying between them. The man bent forward, leaning his dark head close to the woman's, murmuring something in her ear. The woman's eyes widened, sweeping to Amanda, who shifted uneasily under the intense scrutiny of those lovely green eyes.

The woman nodded, then handed the two bundles—one of which, not surprisingly, gurgled with newborn delight—to the man. Smoothing the wrinkles from her faded, yellow muslin skirt, she stiffened and walked with silent, fluid grace over to Amanda.

"I'm Gail Chandler," the woman said, her voice ringing with the twang of a dreadfully familiar drawl. She extended her small hand in a gesture meant to welcome.

How Amanda retained the presence of mind to grasp those cool, work-roughened fingers and pump weakly as her tongue stumbled over her name, she would never know.

Her lips curling into a strained smile, Gail Chandler inclined her head to the man standing behind her. "You've met my husband, Little Bear. And the two bundles he's holding are our sons, Jacob and Kane." She paused long enough for *that* shocking bit of information to sink into an obviously stunned

239

Amanda Lennox's mind. "You look pale, Miss Lennox, not to mention cold. Please, take off that damp cloak and have a seat by the fire. You can warm yourself while I brew a fresh pot of coffee. And then," she paused infinitesimally, "you can explain to me why my brother sent you to us."

"Brother?" Amanda's eyes widened, positive she'd heard the woman wrong. Her heart skipped a beat when she realized that Gail Chandler had indeed called Jake her brother. And, of course, there was the shared last name to confirm it.

Gail had turned to walk over to the counter nailed to the far wall. At Amanda's shocked tone, she pivoted stiffly and leaned back against the chipped but immaculate countertop. Crossing her arms over her chest, and cocking her head to one side, she sent the blonde woman a shrewd glance. "Jake is my brother." The green eyes strayed to her husband, who'd taken a seat on one of the benches flanking the table. She held Little Bear's gaze, though her next words were undoubtedly aimed at Amanda. "Didn't he tell you where he was bringing you? *Who* he was bringing you to?"

"No. I mean, *yes*. I mean . . ." Amanda drew in a shaky breath. Heavens, she was confused! "What he said, exactly, was that he was bringing me here because he didn't want me caught out in the storm. He didn't tell me who lived here."

"He would never tell you that," Little Bear said as he laid one child atop the table and, holding the wiggling infant still with a massive palm, arranged the other baby over his shoulder. "Blackhawk and my wife are not," a stern glance from Gail made him choose the rest of his sentence with care, "close."

"I see," Amanda said, and glanced at the dark-haired woman. Gail's face was pale, her expression strained as she spun back toward the counter and snatched up a dented tin coffee pot. Without a backward glance or word of explanation, the woman grabbed a red-knitted shawl off its peg by the door, then slammed out of the cabin.

"Did I say something wrong?" Amanda asked cautiously.

Little Bear was busy unwrapping the child on the table. "Yes," he said, not glancing up as he tickled the baby's tiny, naked belly with the tips of his fingers.

"Then I should go apologize," she offered anxiously. Of course it would help if she knew *what* she was apologizing for!

"There is no need. My wife will get water for the coffee, and when she returns she will leave her anger outside." Not taking his eyes off the child, he nodded for her to join him at the table. "Come, Amanda Lennox. Sit beside me and take a look at my sons. I will allow you to tell me how handsome they are."

Amanda peeked at the babies: one cuddling on Little Bear's shoulder, the other laying naked and content atop the scarred plank table. She guessed the infants to be about four months old. Both had Little Bear's inky black hair, and their skin was the same rich shade of mahogany as their father's. On the other hand, both had their mother's luminescent green eyes. The baby on the table giggled and cooed when Little Bear's fingers gently feathered over his belly.

Amanda felt herself soften. She didn't want to — God knows it would be safer for everyone if she didn't — but she simply couldn't help it. The babies were adorable, and their father's pride in them was appealingly open and endearing.

"And what will happen if I don't tell you they are the most handsome babies I've ever seen?" Amanda asked as she untied the laces of her cloak and, slipping it off, flung it over one of the benches beside the table.

241

Little Bear's shrug was negligent, his voice flat. "Then, Amanda Lennox, I will have to kill you."

Amanda gasped.

Little Bear's head came around quickly. He assessed the white woman objectively, from head to toe, his gaze missing nothing. She was not the type of woman Blackhawk favored—he could tell that at a glance—but she was the type any red-blooded male would want. Her beauty was so striking it stopped just shy of being an actual flaw. She was tall, slender, perfectly proportioned. Her movements and speech were cultured and refined. A lady, if ever he'd seen one.

Those were strikes against her in Little Bear's mind, yet there were other areas in which she excelled. It was those qualities he thought of now, those qualities that made him decide to like this woman.

While she was strong in physical beauty, she was stronger in the type of spirit that Little Bear knew and respected. She had shown courage in entering his home, thinking he was alone here, not knowing what he would do to her. And she'd shown enormous trust that Blackhawk would know what was best for her. He admired the respect she showed his friend, but he admired her courage more.

Her gaze lifted, locking with his. She didn't look away, though her expression said she dearly wanted to. Oddly enough, she did not look down at him. Nor up at him. Instead, her stare was that of an equal. A rare display coming from a white-eyes.

His attention shifted, scanning her face. Her cheeks, he noted, were as white as a freshly laundered sheet. Instinct told him that her unnatural paleness stemmed less from her obvious confusion over the situation in general—and more from his just now-remembered threat to kill her.

His dark eyes widened. He had been making a joke. Amanda Lennox, he realized abruptly, had taken him seriously. Her green eyes were narrow with alarm, her gaze dark, contemplative, as though she was trying to decide whether he would really carry through on his threat. And if he did, should she try to run?

It was as he watched her attention volley between himself and the door that Little Bear realized something else. Something shocking. He averted his gaze to Kane, having found all the answers he needed to know in Amanda Lennox's eyes.

Blackhawk had sent his woman here for a reason, and Little Bear now knew exactly what that reason was. Somehow, he doubted Blackhawk knew as much.

The snow was coming down hard, the accumulation heavier than Jake had predicted it would be. He'd wasted precious time making a fool out of himself with Amanda Lennox.

No, he thought, not wasted; never that. Only the making a fool out of himself part stayed firm.

He *had* wasted time after he'd left her at the cabin. He'd wanted to locate the brat's tracks, get a general idea of the direction they headed before snow deepened and covered them. He did eventually find the prints. As he'd suspected, they continued to head east, straight toward Pony.

What Jake hadn't expected, and wasn't at all pleased to see, was that there were now *three* sets of prints instead of the two they'd been following. Another rider had recently been added.

A trickle of uneasiness iced down Jake's spine. The observation was unwelcome, unwanted, yet the course the prints were taking couldn't be denied. *Why* the tracks were heading toward Pony was a puzzle he'd yet to solve. Hadn't Amanda said that was where she and her cousin were heading? Yup. So why would whoever had kidnapped Roger be taking him to the same place the brat had originally been heading? Really, why kidnap him at all?

Suspicion tasted bitter on his tongue. He swallowed it back, but it continued to nag at him. Why indeed?

His mood, already bad, turned sour when, a half hour later he still hadn't found a dry spot on which to build a quick shelter. If there was an inch of ground that wasn't blanketed in moist white snow, he'd yet to find it. Even deep in the middle of the woods the flakes managed to filter through the ceiling of leaves and collect on the ground.

Jake shifted atop the white and sighed. His breath fogged the air as he scanned his snowswept surroundings. His grip on the reins was white-knuckled tight. The muscle in his jaw throbbed with aggravation.

His day was getting worse by the minute. If he hadn't made the mistake of his life with Amanda, he would be somewhere warm and dry right now. Instead, he was cold and tired and wet. His attention fixed on the snow-covered ground. Sure, he'd slept on harder, wetter, more uncomfortable beds than this before. And in worse conditions. If he had to, he could do it again.

Unfortunately, the fact of the matter was that he *didn't* have to. As Amanda had annoyingly pointed out earlier, the only thing keeping him from a dry bed and hot meal was his pride. He doubted she knew how right she was about that . . . although chances were, by now she'd probably guessed.

The white's hooves crunched over the snow. Jake let the horse pick its way through the woods. Sighing, he reached up and eased the hat back on his head, and let his thoughts wander. As they seemed to do with frightening regularity, his mind made a beeline to Amanda Lennox.

He wondered what Gail and Little Bear's reception

to Amanda had been. And what had Amanda's reaction been? Dammit! He should have told Amanda who lived in the cabin. In fact, he almost had. The only thing that kept the information back was, quite simply, he didn't think it was any of her business.

Still . . . dammit! He should have told her.

No doubt she was angry as all hell. The worst part was, she had every right to be. Wouldn't he want to know up front what type of situation he was walking into? Damn straight he would! He didn't like being taken by surprise; he would have *demanded* to know the facts beforehand. Looking back, he thought he owed Amanda the same courtesy he would have taken for himself.

Then again, she hadn't asked. Oddly enough, Amanda had trusted him in the end to know what was best for her. It was exactly that reluctantly placed faith in him that was really eating at Jake now. He wasn't thrilled to admit he'd paid back her trust by slapping it right back in her face.

It eased his conscience a bit to think that, after her initial shock had faded, Amanda had no doubt handled herself just fine. She was made of stronger stuff than she thought. She would get through the awkward spots the way she did everything, with dignity and grace.

So would Gail and Little Bear. Jake was sure of it. While he hadn't seen his sister in years, he knew Gail. She wouldn't hold family squabbles over an innocent woman's head for long. Gail would thaw to Amanda quickly because . . . well, Jake of *all* people knew how hard it was to dislike a prissy white princess who could, when the occasion warranted, swear like a trooper and had enough gumption to conquer an army. Hell, hadn't he tried his best not to like her? He had. And he'd failed. Deep down, he knew Gail would fail to dislike Amanda, too.

The white stopped. The unexpected stillness jarred

Jake's attention back to where it ought to have been in the first place — to finding a relatively dry spot to make camp. He wasn't overly surprised to find he'd unconsciously let his mount wind its way back up the hill, or that he'd come to a halt in the exact spot where he'd sat and watched Amanda enter the cabin.

The snow was coming down hard enough now so he could barely make out the small, square structure. He could see the chimney, though, and the wafts of gray smoke curling up from it. The aroma of a hearty stew hung tantalizingly thick in the air.

Though the day had started somewhat warm, the storm had blown in fast. The brisk air turned Jake's breath to steam. He shivered and pulled the blanket he'd tossed over his shoulders closer to his chest. He hadn't brought a coat. He hadn't thought he'd need one, hadn't expected to be at elevations this high, or to be hot on the trail of some brat for the past five days.

He shivered, his gaze shifting to his sister's small, ramshackle old barn. The thing hadn't been used in years. The roof had started to rot over a decade ago. The walls were slowly crumbling in on themselves. Little Bear, having no need for a barn, hadn't wasted time trying to repair it.

Jake eyed the decrepit building carefully. It was probably the warmest, driest place he was likely to find.

Another waft of stew teased him. His stomach grumbled, even as his ungloved, ice-cold fingers flicked the reins. He wouldn't have his sister's hearty stew to fill him, he knew, but he would have an essentially dry place to bed down for the night. For a man accustomed to making sacrifices in the name of pride, it would have to be enough.

"He is in the barn," Little Bear murmured to Gail

in his native tongue. He watched his wife's back stiffen, watched her green eyes fill with three years of unshed tears. If he had the power to take her pain away, he would have done it. But only one man had that power. Blackhawk. And he refused to use it.

Little Bear gave his wife's shoulder an affectionate squeeze. He watched as she swiped a few dark curls from her brow, then set about scrubbing the plates in the wash bucket with a vengeance. "Did you hear me, wife?"

"I know where he is, thank you. I've known for hours," Gail snapped. Her harshly whispered answer came in the guttural tongue her husband had taught her years ago and which now came to her naturally. In truth, she found it more awkward speaking English to their guest. And speaking of their guest . . .

Gail shot a glance over her shoulder. Amanda Lennox had pulled a chair closer to the hearth and now sat rocking Jacob to sleep. Kane cooed from the padded wicker basket on the floor beside the chair. If Amanda Lennox heard their conversation, she gave no sign. Not that a woman like her could have understood the words even if she *had* caught a phrase or two.

Reassured, Gail shifted her attention back to her husband. "All right. What is it you expect me to do?"

"What do you want to do?"

"Nothing."

One inky brow cocked as Little Bear's hand slipped off her shoulder. "Nothing?"

"Nothing. Jake is in our barn. So what? I won't rush out there and greet him warmly, as though nothing ever happened. Don't you dare ask me to forget all those hateful things he said to me, Little Bear, because I won't. I *can't.*"

"I ask nothing of you. But, as I recall, your brother said those things to *me*. If I am not mad after three year's time, you should not be, either. Also, he

247

brought his woman here to us. Perhaps that is his way of making amends."

Gail shook her head. "First of all, I doubt Miss Lennox is his 'woman.' Secondly, my brother doesn't *make* amends. Jake would have to think he is wrong about something, and Jake *never* thinks he's wrong."

"He was wrong about us," Little Bear said softly.

"Yes, but he doesn't see that."

"Yes, but he will. Give him time."

"Time?" she sneered as, snatching up a dirty spoon from the bucket, she began scouring it furiously. "It's been three years, Little Bear. How much more time does he need?"

"As much time as it takes."

Gail scowled and waved the dripping wet spoon under her husband's nose. "Don't you start talking logic to me, Little Bear. You know how much I hate it when you rationalize."

"Only because you know I am right."

"Is that a fact?"

"It is." He grinned the cocky, insolent grin that had made Gail fall in love with him, even as he snatched the spoon away from her and tossed it aside. The spoon clattered atop the counter as his arm snaked out, wrapping around her waist and dragging her hard against his chest. "Come, woman, give your husband a kiss. It has been four long hours at least."

"And it's going to be at least four more if —" Gail squealed when she felt herself being lifted off the floor. "Brute! Put me down this instant. I mean it, Little Bear! We have a guest. What will Miss Lennox think if she sees you carrying me off to the bedroom now, when the boys aren't even asleep yet?"

Little Bear's gaze strayed to Amanda Lennox. Though she was pretending acute interest in the infant cradled in her arms, he saw a tiny grin tug at the corners of her lips. Ah, he knew he liked that woman for a reason!

248

Little Bear pinned his wife to his chest and, giving her tempting rump a swat, told her to behave, adding, "As for our guest . . . I think she has spent enough time in Blackhawk's corruptive company to not be surprised by anything you and I do."

Gail stilled instantly. "You aren't suggesting they . . . ?"

"I know Blackhawk," Little Bear said with a sly wink. Loosening his hold, he let Gail slide down until her feet touched the floor. But he didn't let her go. "That is exactly what I am suggesting."

"But . . . she's a *lady*."

"So were you the first time I met you."

Something in Little Bear's tone caught Amanda's attention. She glanced up in time to see Gail and Little Bear's gazes lock. Like the last time, unspoken words rushed between them. Unlike the last time, their silence spoke volumes.

Amanda averted her gaze to the infant cradled in her arms, and pretended not to notice the sudden tightening in her heart. Their tones of voice suggested Gail and Little Bear had been arguing before, though their words were strange and unfamiliar. Amanda had recognized Jake's name, and her own, but that was all she understood about what they were saying.

She understood more about what their eyes said to each other. The looks they exchanged fascinated Amanda. Even while they'd been arguing, the love Gail and Little Bear felt for each other still burned brightly in their eyes. It rubbed Amanda raw to know she had never — would never — see that look in a man's eyes. That she would never know that kind of all-consuming love.

Unbidden, her mind flashed her an image that had never really been far from her thoughts for days. It was a picture of Jake rising naked and proud and wet from a river. Amanda sucked in a sharp breath and pinched her eyes closed. It didn't work. In the pitch blackness behind her eyelids she could still see tiny beads of moisture clinging to a firm copper shoulder. Her finger's curled inward, lightly fisting the baby's small, pudgy hand. Even now, days later, she still ached to rub those glistening drops of water into his skin.

The chair creaked as she pushed the dirt floor with her foot, unconsciously urging it to rock faster.

Another image sliced through her. In this one Jake was also naked . . . only this time he was arched over her, and a part of him was buried inside the most intimate part of her. For the rest of her life, Amanda knew she would remember the wondrous look on his face when he'd made that first breathtaking thrust, and how her body had flowered open to welcome him. She would never forget how, for just a while, it felt to be loved by a man.

No, she corrected silently, not by just any man, by Jacob Blackhawk Chandler. There was a difference.

"Penny for your thoughts, Amanda Lennox."

"Hmmm?" Amanda's lashes flickered up, her dreamy gaze instantly pulling Little Bear into focus. She didn't realize she'd been smiling until she forced herself to stop. "I—What?"

"Penny for your thoughts," Little Bear repeated as he settled himself in the chair he'd drawn up beside hers. "That was the first white-eyes phrase Gail taught me. I use it often. What were you thinking about?"

"Nothing," she lied. "Nothing at all."

Little Bear sat back in his chair and, crossing one deerskin clad leg over the other, nodded. "Gail has told me it is impolite to call the few guests we have liars, so I will refrain. I will, however, say that the women I know smile in that particular fashion only when they are thinking of a particular man. Were you thinking of a man, Amanda Lennox?" He slanted her a dark, probing glance. "Were you thinking of Blackhawk?"

Amanda glanced guiltily down at the baby. Jacob was sleeping soundly, curled up in her arms. She stroked the tip of her index finger over his thick, dark hair, and said, "Why on earth would I be thinking of Jake? The man deserted me on your doorstep, for heaven's sake. That's a good enough reason not to waste my thoughts on him. As it is, I'm wondering at this point if he plans to come back for me."

"Did he promise you he would?"

"Yes."

"Then he will."

And that, Amanda suspected by the tone of Little Bear's voice, was that. To this man's mind, if Jake had promised to come back for her, he would come back. It was that simple.

It wasn't so simple to Amanda. After all, *she* was the one Jake had said those ugly words to, not Little Bear. *She* was the one he had loved one minute, then cast aside the next. As far as she was concerned, she wouldn't believe Jake was coming back for her until she saw him sitting astride his white in the woods where they'd agreed to meet, and not a second sooner. Until then, she would cling to her doubts; they alone offered protection from the pain that sliced into her heart.

They lapsed into a comfortable silence. The fire crackled and popped in the hearth. Kane, sleeping in the straw basket beside Amanda's chair, cooed sleepily. An icy wind rattled the window panes.

"Where's Gail?" Amanda asked finally, feeling a sudden need for conversation. Though she felt Little Bear's contemplative gaze on her, she didn't look up.

"Our mat. The children tire her." His pause was riddled with speculation. "You are good with children, Amanda Lennox."

Amanda thought of Roger Thornton Bannister III.

Her stomach tightened with equal measures of distaste and concern. "I like most children," she answered evasively.

"My sons like you."

She smiled softly. "They seem to, don't they?"

"And you like them."

"Yes, very much."

"Even though they are only half white?"

Ah, she'd wondered where he was leading this conversation. Now she knew. Amanda chided herself for not expecting Little Bear's bluntness. It was one of the first things she'd learned about this man; he was nothing if not direct. The second was that if he liked you, you knew it. Gail was the same way. However, where Little Bear had offered his friendship almost immediately after their rocky meeting had been put behind them, Jake's sister was still withholding hers.

Amanda's chin came up, and she turned her head and met Little Bear's questioning ebony gaze squarely. "You know," she said, her voice low and edgy, "I'm getting tired of everyone demanding I look at the color of their skin before I decide whether or not to like them. And I'm equally as tired of everyone seeing me as 'white' and *then* deciding whether or not to like *me*. I'm not just white, dammit, I'm a human being. I have feelings and emotions just like everyone else. Why won't any of you see that?"

"I see it," Little Bear answered quietly, apparently not at all upset by her outburst.

Well, maybe he wasn't, but Amanda was upset by it. And ashamed. Ladies did not yell at one's host. She knew that, and yet . . . God, she was confused! She softened her tone. "I know you do, Little Bear. And I thank you for it, really I do."

He reached across their chairs and patted the smooth white hand that rested atop his son's stomach. "Gail will see it, too. In time."

"How *much* time? I won't be here forever, you know."

"No. But you will be here until Blackhawk comes for you."

Amanda chuckled derisively and shook her head. "Then I'll be here forever. I really don't think he's coming back."

"You are wrong."

Amanda pursed her lips; wanting with all her heart to believe it, yet not daring to—because of that same, aching heart. "You sound very sure of yourself, my strange new friend."

"I have reason to be."

"Do you? I don't suppose you'd share that reason with me?"

"I know Blackhawk better than you do," Little Bear said with a dismissive shrug.

Amanda heard his sigh, and she watched as he settled more comfortably in the chair, his gaze on the flames crackling in the hearth. Her eyes narrowed suspiciously. She would have sworn the glow of the fire hadn't put that devilish sparkle in Little Bear's eyes. His next words confirmed it.

"Oh, and there is one other reason I know Blackhawk will return."

She waited for him to continue. It took almost a full minute before she realized he had no intention of doing so. She decided to wait him out, refusing to be baited. Only one arched golden brow spoke of her curiosity. But Little Bear wasn't looking at her, he didn't see it. He said nothing and instead just continued to stare into the flames.

The baby, sensing her anxiety, squirmed in her arms. Amanda crooned and stroked him. When Jacob had settled, and when she didn't think she could stand the suspense a second longer, she speared Little Bear with a sharp glare. "Tell me," she said finally, almost but not quite desperately. "Please. I need to know. How can you be so sure Jake will come back?"

Little Bear's gaze met hers, and he grinned broadly. "Because the wild bird has already flown home. Blackhawk is here, Amanda Lennox. He has been for hours."

Night you can you're and the would the his come the
find and the you that just and he would
her my him the she life has head
your first cannot body may

Chapter Fourteen

Three times Amanda came oh, so close to going outside the cabin and inside the barn. The temptation was there, undeniable and strong. So was the need to see and touch Jake again.

Three times the humiliating words he'd slapped in her face after they'd made love held her back. No, she would not—*could not*—go to him. She refused to humble herself that way.

That didn't mean she didn't want him. She did—physically, mentally, in any way she could have him, for as long as he would stay with her. Amanda wanted that so badly she ached.

Again and again. The memory of those words were the only thing that kept her sane, that made the pain bearable. His promise burned like fire inside of her.

As she lay in front of Little Bear and Gail's stone hearth, wrapped up in three threadbare blankets, Amanda remembered the passion-dark glances Jake had sent her after they'd made love, and she felt her blood flow hot.

She tossed restlessly onto her back. The dirt floor felt hard and lumpy beneath her. She squirmed, trying to find a comfortable spot. There was none. With a frustrated sigh, she flung the back of one hand over her eyes . . . and remembered a time when the ground hadn't felt so hard, when the only lumps pressing into her were made up of corded male flesh.

Wind rattled the window panes, sneaking through the cracks in the casing. A chilly rush of air skimmed the floor and whispered over Amanda. She shivered. The blanket and the crackling fire helped warm her. Of course, there'd been a time when Jake Chandler's body had provided all the covering she needed, all the heat she could possibly stand.

Groaning, Amanda tossed onto her side. The fire warmed her cheeks and brow, caressing the golden curls that rested there. It was a peaceful feeling, warm and lulling. It might even have eased her into sleep, if her mind hadn't picked that moment to wonder if Jake had built his own fire in the barn. Had he dared? Or were his problems with his sister so irreconcilable that he'd rather sleep on the hard ground without a fire to keep him warm—just in case Gail spotted the telltale glow and came to investigate?

Surely he wouldn't be so foolish, so stubborn.

Surely she wasn't concerned *about him!*

Yes, she was. Very concerned. The idea of him curled up and shivering on the hard, cold ground ate at Amanda. It shouldn't have—after all, it was his own mule-headed pride that forbade him from coming to his sister's cabin—but it did.

Amanda tried telling herself that if Jake was cold and hungry, he had no one to blame but himself, as she kicked the blankets off and pushed to her feet. She told herself he was a grown man who was more than capable of taking care of himself, as she crossed the room, grabbed the cloak that hung drying on a peg by the back door, flung it over her shoulders and tied it hastily in place. She told herself that Jake was perfectly capable of lighting his own fire—God knows, he'd proven *that* point quite well!—and that he didn't need her to goad him into it, as she reached out, her fingers poised and trembling on the cold metal door latch.

Finally, she told herself that what she was doing

was wrong, that if she went to him now, she wouldn't respect herself for it come morning. What followed was a stern mental lecture on why self-respect had become so important to her, and why she would be a fool to sacrifice it over a man who clearly didn't want or need her as badly as she wanted and needed him.

Her hand flexed, fisted, then dropped limply to her side. Leaning forward on the balls of her feet, she rested her forehead against the cold, rough door, and sucked in several deep breaths.

Last, Amanda told herself that she would be a fool to fall in love with a man like Jacob Blackhawk Chandler. He had scars etched into his soul that she could never understand; scars that ran deep, that hadn't healed, that might *never* heal enough for him to love her back. Caring for a man like that would only bring her trouble. Not having her feelings returned would give her more heartache than she could endure.

"Ah, Jake," Amanda sighed to the silent, empty room. She pushed wearily away from the door and started to turn, but was brought up short when the silent, empty room responded in a soft, familiar drawl that curled like sun-warm honey down her spine.

"Yes, Amanda?"

Had thoughts of Jake conjured up his voice? Had she wanted to see and hear and touch him so badly that her mind sought to soothe her by making her *imagine* he was standing behind her? And did she want to turn around only to find he wasn't there, his voice a figment of her wishful imagination? God, no!

"Jake?" she asked hesitantly, hopefully.

"Amanda."

The soft, feathery touch on her shoulder was *not* her imagination. Her imagination wasn't that good. No, the feel of his hand was too warm, too vibrant to be anything but real.

Her heart skipped as she turned her head, her

gaze fixing on the masculine fingers hooked over her shoulder. Slowly, she traced his thick wrist to where the smooth copper flesh dipped beneath the cuff of his sleeve. Her gaze ran over the muscled forearm outlined beneath the clinging blue flannel, stopping only once she'd reached his enticingly familiar shoulder and the inky hair resting against it.

Amanda inhaled deeply. Her eyes flickered closed as she savored the warm, earth-spice scent that belonged to Jake Chandler alone. On its release, she said softly, "I was just coming to see you."

"I know."

She hadn't heard him move, though he must have, because she suddenly felt the raw male heat of him seeping through her cloak, her bodice, her chemise. His warmth caressed her skin, and Amanda shivered. Though she couldn't see where he stood, she could *feel* it; if she turned fully around, her gaze would know exactly where to go to seek his out.

"I've been watching you," he said, and his next step put his chest into sizzling contact with her back. "I know what you were doing, what you've been thinking."

"No, you couldn't possibly," she said, and meant it. Jake couldn't know what she was thinking. He fancied her a lady, and ladies did *not* entertain the hot, lustful thoughts that had been churning in Amanda's mind tonight.

His fingers tightened on her shoulder. "Do you doubt me, princess?"

"I—no, I don't. If you say you know my thoughts, I—I believe you."

"But do you believe *in* me, Amanda Lennox? That's the real question.

Amanda swallowed hard, and leaned back against him. Jake's left arm coiled about her waist. He hauled her close, pinning her against his chest. She let his long, solid body hold her upright, because she could no longer do it herself.

Jake was here. She could feel his heart drumming a frantic tempo against her shoulder blades. He'd come to her, come *for* her. What was there not to believe in?

"Yes, Jake, I—"

The words trapped in her throat when, without warning, he spun her around. Her skirt whipped around her ankles, and his hands settled on her shoulders. He held her at arm's length when she would have sagged against him, molded herself into him.

"I told you once I'd know if you lied to me," he said, his tone low, strained. "Do you remember that?"

She nodded weakly.

"Good. Now look me in the eye, Amanda. I need to see your face when you tell me whether or not you believe in me."

She didn't, *couldn't*. One of his hands came away from her shoulder. The warm, calloused crook of his index finger settled beneath her chin, gently tipping her face up.

Her gaze had settled on his throat and the pulse leaping erratically beneath the copper skin there. Her attention slowly lifted, sweeping over his square jaw, his sensuously carved lips, his high-bridged nose. Swallowing hard, she met his gaze.

The firelight cast half of his face in a soft orange glow. The other half was in shadows—chiseled and sharp. The muscle in his cheek was pulsating. Amanda had expected that. What she hadn't expected was the light of desperation she saw sparkling in his smoky silver eyes. That stunned her.

"Tell me," he urged. "Tell me you believe in me, princess . . . more than I believe in myself."

She nodded as, quite simply and softly, she said the words his eyes said he ached to hear. In her heart, she knew she had never spoken truer words in her life. "I do, Jake. I believe in the man you are, in the man I know you can be. I always have."

His lashes flickered down for one moment of mingled pain and pleasure. Then the black fringe swept up, and Amanda was captured by eyes that were dark with a gratitude that tore her up inside . . . and with a desire that set her blood on fire.

Gently, he cupped her face in his palms and pulled her face close to his. Leaning his body into hers, he rested their foreheads together. His breath puffed hotly over her cheeks and chin. His gaze burning into hers, he rasped, "There's something about you, Amanda Lennox. I don't know what it is, but it draws me. I can't stay away. I know I should. I know it would be better for us both if I did. Safer. But . . . ah, God, I can't do it."

"I don't want you to stay away from me, Jake."

His lashes were at half-mast, hooding the smokey gaze that burned over her mouth. His attention locked with hers, as though the deep green velvet of her eyes was his lifeline. "Don't say that. Don't even *think* it. Can't you see? I'm no damn good for you, lady."

"Let me be the judge of that."

His forehead ground against hers when he shook his head. "No. You aren't objective enough to know what's best for you."

Her gaze narrowed. "Oh, I see. And I suppose you are?"

Jake hesitated, then shook his head again. "No. When it comes to you, I'm not objective at all. I'm here now, aren't I? That should prove something to you."

And it did. In fact, it proved a great deal. It proved that whatever had happened between Jake and his sister, it wasn't drastic enough to overshadow what was happening between Jake and herself. It proved that he had swallowed a smidgen of that over-inflated, misplaced pride of his, enough at least to seek her out here, in his sister's house, where he obviously was not welcome. And it proved . . .

Amanda's gaze widened, searching his face. His expression was still tight, still strained, but his features were no longer a mask to her. Had Jake let his guard down on purpose so that she could see and read his expression? Or did she simply know him well enough now to look beyond the mask? It was difficult to say. Nor did she waste time analyzing it. It was enough to see in his eyes that he cared for her. Maybe not a lot, but a bit. It was enough for her to see that his desire for her had not been doused—as she'd feared—but whetted and aroused.

And that, Amanda decided as her own expression softened, was a good start. No one in her life had ever really cared for her. That this man did—even a little, even reluctantly—gave her something to reach for, something to cling to.

The hands she'd pillowed atop his shoulders strayed upward. She sandwiched his neck between her palms, admiring the strength she felt in a portion of his body where one would not ordinarily expect to find strength. Her hands shifted, her fingers tunneling into silky black hair that was still damp from a sprinkling of melted snow. His skin felt smooth and warm and moist beneath her palms. The scar puckering the back of his neck felt distinct when it brushed her sensitive inner wrist.

"I lied to you, princess." Jake's fingers snaked around her wrist, and tugged her hand down, satisfied only when it splayed the center of his chest. His heart throbbed a wild, erratic beat against her open palm.

"How, Jake? How did you lie to me? *Why* did you lie to me?"

"I said you weren't a lady, but you *are*. You're more of a lady than any woman I've ever known. And no, I don't know why I said it."

Their gazes locked and held. His eyes were dark and serious and sincere. Amanda's free hand was cupping his scalp. She moved it slowly to the opposite side of his neck. With the tip of her index finger she traced the jagged scar down to where it dipped beneath his collar.

He let go of her wrist and settled his hand on her shoulder. His other slipped beneath the cloak, circled her waist, and pulled her closer. Not too close, yet, but close enough for the front of their bodies to threaten contact.

"Do you want me, Jake?" Amanda asked softly, breathlessly. It wasn't a question she'd planned to ask, but now that she had, she waited breathlessly for his answer. When it didn't come immediately, she grew impatient. "Please, I need to know."

Jake saw the desperation in her eyes and knew the emotion was mirrored in his own. He knew that admitting to the desire that was clawing him up inside would be a mistake. It would give Amanda Lennox power over him, more power than any woman had ever had. And yet lying seemed an even bigger mistake. There was an odd sort of honesty crackling between them right now. It felt too new and fragile and . . . dammit, it just felt too damn good to tamper with!

"I . . . God, lady, how I want you!" His gaze strayed to her mouth—temptingly full, naturally pink—and his tongue curled in sweet anticipation. "I want you . . ." He scanned her neck quickly, and then his attention settled on the firm swell of her breasts. They were rising and falling quickly, with each of her rapid, ragged breaths. His heart beat faster. "I want you . . ." The fingers gripping her shoulder flexed as he scanned the appealing roundness of her hips, then slowly followed the same tantalizing course back up. He locked their gazes together and whispered huskily, "I want you more than I want to breathe. Does that answer your question?"

"Yes."

"And is 'wanting' enough for you?"

Amanda's gaze lowered with sudden timidity. "It

shouldn't be. A decent woman would want more."

"A decent woman would demand marriage. A decent woman would demand things I can't—*won't*—give. Then again, a decent woman wouldn't be here with me now, would she? Are you a decent woman, Amanda Lennox? Are you going to demand those things from me?"

Amanda frowned, knowing she *should* demand all that and more. She also knew she wouldn't. If she did, Jake would leave her now, and maybe never come back again. While her mind might not be able to tell right from wrong anymore, her body was telling her, and telling her strongly, not to let this man go, to take what he could give and never demand more. At the moment, her body was stronger than her mind and morals.

"I demand two things from you, Jacob Blackhawk Chandler," she said finally, her gaze riveted on the damp toes of his moccasins. "I demand you finish the job I hired you to do. And I . . ." She swallowed hard. "I demand you love me for as long as you feel you can. Is that asking too much?"

"No, princess, it's asking for a hell of a lot less than you deserve." It was also, Jake knew, asking for all a man like him could ever hope to give a woman like her. Loving Amanda Lennox for a time, he could do. Loving her for *all* time . . . well, that wasn't allowed. That was against the rules.

The arm around her waist tightened, and he closed the scant few inches that separated them. Her cheek found a natural pillow against his shoulder. Her soft curves molded eagerly into his hardness, lighting a fire in Jake's blood wherever they touched. The scent clinging to her hair was soft and flowery in his nostrils, the smell fresh and intoxicating. He turned his head, his nose nuzzling the golden strands, breathing her in deeply.

Amanda's arms circled his neck, pulling him closer even as her body strained against him. He couldn't give her much, but he could give her this moment, this one night. If only for a little while, he could fill the yawning emptiness inside of her.

"Love me, Jake," she whispered hoarsely, her lips moving against the soft flannel of his shirt. Her hips arched, and electricity sizzled through her blood when her abdomen ground against the firm evidence of his desire. "Please, just for tonight, love me as though you mean it."

"Ah, God, yes." Holding her close, he maneuvered her back a few steps.

The edge of the table pressed against the back of Amanda's thighs. And then Jake was there, easing her backward, and she went mindlessly.

He leveled his weight on the elbows flanking her ribs, and met her hip to hip, chest to chest. Her feet didn't touch the floor; it was easy to nudge her legs apart, to wedge himself between her long, firm legs. He turned his head, and saw that their lips were mere inches apart. A slight lifting of her head, a slight lowering of his . . .

Jake hesitated making that last advance toward her, knowing that to do so would be to lose himself in something wonderful, something deliciously tempting, something that, by all rights, he should never have tasted once, let alone again.

Amanda had no such qualms. She wanted to experience again the magic of his kisses, the warmth of his caresses. She *needed* both. Maybe proper ladies didn't have needs like these, maybe they didn't enjoy a man the way she enjoyed Jake. But that was beside the point. Because Amanda was acutely aware that whenever Jake Chandler touched her, she ceased to be a lady. With one glance, he stripped away pretense. With one kiss, he peeled away years of training and ignited a flame of passion inside her.

She wanted to feel that reckless surge of passion again. Now. She needed to feel it pumping through her blood. Only once the fire had been lit and tended did she want Jake to douse it in the way that only he could.

To that end, her hands snuck around his back, under his arms. Her fingers fisted his shirt, and her gaze sought out his as she lifted her head up and very slowly, very lightly, fused their mouths together.

"Again and again," she whispered huskily against his mouth. She dragged her tongue over his tightly set lips. He tasted of tobacco and coffee; a strong, delicious male flavor—one to be cherished and savored. "For as long as it lasts, Jake. That's all I want, all I'll ask from you."

"Good. Because that's all I have to give you," he said, and then his tongue darted out and swirled around the wet tip of hers, teasing them both to distraction. She tasted moist and sweet and so damn good. He groaned as, lowering more of his weight atop her, he sealed their lips in a hard, hungry kiss.

He'd dreamed of this, in the few minutes of sleep that thoughts of Amanda had allowed him to snatch. He'd dreamed of her taste, of how her soft white curves felt beneath him. The dreams—wisps of veiled fantasies and suppressed memories—had gotten him hard and hot. That was what had brought him out of the barn and into a house he'd sworn never to step foot in again. That was what had made him swallow his pride and seek her out tonight. He couldn't stay away from her, couldn't deny this unreasonably strong urge to see and touch and lay with her again. He wanted to know if it would be as good with her a second time, or if good had only been in his imagination.

It hadn't been. His imagination could never conjure up the way this woman felt moving hungrily beneath him, or the way her sweet, distracting tongue met his every thrust and parry. Their mouths clung, their tongues initiated a rhythmic dance that their bodies, straining against each other, begged to follow. Her hips rose, strained into his, retreated, then lifted again. The feminine heat of her meshed with his hard male strength, making the core of his need swell.

He'd had this woman once, barely six hours ago. He shouldn't want her again so soon, and he definitely shouldn't want her again so badly. But he did. There was no rhyme or reason to it, no obstacles or barriers. There was no logic in the way he wanted to plant himself inside of Amanda Lennox so badly it was an acute, physical pain inside of him, a deep, festering, intolerable need.

He eased the intimacy of their kiss, but not the intimacy of their embrace. His lips trailed hot, sipping kisses down her chin and the thin white taper of her neck. He shifted them so that he was now the one laying atop the table. Amanda lay sprawled atop him, her bent knees straddling his hips, her hands splayed on the chipped wood that lay to either side of his head. She arched her neck to give his mouth freedom to roam.

Jake's tongue caressed the pulse drumming wildly in the base of her throat. He reached down and tugged her skirt up and out of the way. And then he lifted his own bent knee as high as it would go. He ground his thigh against the warm, moist part of her that his body was urging him to reexplore. A part that — soon, Jake silently promised them both — *would* be reexplored. Thoroughly.

Amanda gasped and her hips arched forward. The feel of Jake's denim-encased thigh rubbing the most sensitive, most intimate part of her was electrifying. White heat flamed through her blood, leaving a tingling wake of fire.

Her body went weak. The energy drained out of her arms, and she lowered herself onto the hard cushion of his chest. Though her lips nuzzled his neck and ear, her hips remained cautiously still. She was afraid to move a muscle, afraid feelings that good could not be contained. And she wanted to contain them. Forever. She wanted the sensations this man was lighting in her to go on and on and on.

Jake had other ideas. He'd lit the fire in her, ignited her fiery passions, now he wanted to drive her wild with it.

His strong hands flanked her hips, his fingers curling inward, tunneling through the bunches of material, tunneling into the soft white flesh beneath. Slowly, slowly, he guided her hips forward, dragging her up his thigh. Her body quivered violently. He absorbed the vibrations with his palms and chest, even as he guided her in the opposite direction. Again. And again.

It was a gentle parody of lovemaking that was, he discovered belatedly, double edged. As much as the erotic sensations were a sensuous torture to her, they were more so to him. Every time she slid forward, the top of her thigh rubbed against the burning heat of him. The rhythmic friction filled him with new, blinding surges of desire.

"God, did I teach you this?" he murmured huskily.

"Oh yes," she answered, just as rawly. Her hips picked up the pace his hands had set. "Don't you remember? You taught me how to light a fire, showed me how to make it burn."

"Damn. I did, didn't I?" he grumbled, and thought that if this sweet, stimulating torture kept up, he wouldn't last. And he intended to last if it killed him.

He thought it might do just that.

Jake didn't know why the urge to roll her onto her back and take her right now, hard and fast, was so damn overpowering—it just was. God, had he ever been this weak with a woman in his life? No. But then, this wasn't just any woman, this was Amanda Lennox. He should have learned by now that he had no self-control when it came to her. He should have learned that, with her, the desire to give pleasure was as strong, if not stronger, than the desire to get it.

She was hot. He knew by the way she writhed

against him, the way her heart pounded a wild, desperate beat against his. He wanted her hotter, burning up; he wanted her body humming with a desperation that surpassed his own.

His fingers tightened around her hips, halting her. Then they strayed up to cup her ribcage as he lowered his leg. His face was buried in her neck. He nuzzled the silky flesh there before carefully levering her up and away from him.

Her eyes had been closed. The thick, honey-tipped lashes flickered up, revealing glassy eyes that struggled to bring him into focus. "Why did you stop?" she asked, her tone raw and passion-slurred.

His grin was wicked and quick, his gaze darkly seductive. "We can't do much with our clothes on, princess."

One golden brow lifted, and the way her huge green eyes shimmered in the flickering firelight told Jake that she was thinking of at least a dozen mutually satisfying things that could be done completely clothed. The pink stain in her cheeks, and the way she rolled her lips inward, said her thoughts were decidedly unladylike.

That was fine by Jake; his own thoughts were dirty as hell.

"I want you naked," he rasped, and pushed her up until she knelt, straddling his hips. His gaze dropped to the swell of her breasts, and his mind flashed an excruciatingly detailed picture of what she looked like without the barrier of clothes separating her creamy white flesh from his devouring gaze. It was a sight he'd give his life to see again. Now. His attention lifted, his gaze meshed with hers. "Undress for me, princess. Slowly. And do it in front of the fire so I can see all of you, inch by beautiful inch."

Her chin dipped, but not before he saw the way her cheeks flamed. "That wouldn't be . . ." she shrugged nervously, and wet her suddenly parched lips, "proper."

"Or ladylike," he agreed flatly.

"Jake, what if Gail or Little Bear comes down-stairs?"

"They won't."

"How do you know?"

"I know." He said it with such conviction that Amanda instinctively believed him.

Though she didn't lift her head, she did peek at him. His hair was wind-tangled, spread out on the table around him. The small brown feather rested against his chest, lifting and falling with his ragged breaths. His features were hard with leashed desire. His steely eyes seemed to burn out of the chiseled copper of his face. His expression said he wanted, *needed,* for her to strip for him, and—propriety be damned—*she* wanted to do it.

"If I . . . do," Amanda said as, pushing against his chest, she rose shakily to her feet and looked down at him uncertainly, "will you return the favor? Slowly. So that, piece by piece, I can see every beautiful inch of you?"

A spark of desire heated his eyes. "Do you want me to?"

"Yes."

"Then I will." He rose up on one elbow and, bending his knees so his feet were flat on the tabletop, nodded to the fire. "Do it. Take off your clothes for me. And only for me."

She nodded and slowly, hesitantly, walked over to the fire. A log split and fell. The hiss of crackling flames sounded loud in the ensuing silence; it masked the swish of her skirt as she turned to face him.

The heat emanating from the hearth was intense. It seeped through Amanda's clothes, warming her back, her bottom, the back of her thighs. The warmth was nothing compared to the heat in Jake's eyes. The way his gaze fired over her front was inde-cent, naughty, and exciting beyond reason.

Her trembling fingers paused on the top button of

her collar. Amanda felt awkward, uncomfortable. She'd never taken off her clothes for another human being in her life. She was doing so now though, willingly, and she had a desperate need to do it right. She prayed her movements would look seductive and enticing, not trembling and schoolgirl clumsy.

With that in mind, she forced herself to stop shaking. She slipped the first button free. Then the second, the third, the fourth. She sent a quick look at the shadowy stairway, but the memory of Jake's words oddly reassured her that they wouldn't be interrupted. She didn't know why she believed him about that, she just did. By concentrating on what she was doing, not why, Amanda managed to work the buttons free down to her waist.

She parted the material wide, then pushed the sleeves down her arms. The bodice bunched around her waist in soft calico folds which she then pushed lower. With an unconsciously provocative swivel of her hips, the dress went shimmying over her thighs and puddled in a heap around her feet.

It was as she stepped out of the circle of material and was in the act of bending to retrieve it, that she heard Jake's throaty moan. A secretive grin turned her lips as she tossed her clothing aside, then let her fingers stray to the laces of her chemise — the ones Jake had severed hours ago.

Jake wasn't looking at the neckline. He was only indirectly looking at the chemise. *Through* it would have been a better description. His gaze was fixed on the long, shapely legs that the rear-light of the fire outlined beneath the thin white linen. This morning he'd wanted this woman so badly he hadn't taken the time to visually appreciate her. He took the time now.

Tossing and turning on the barn's cold, hard ground, he'd thought time and again of what Amanda looked like naked. He hadn't remembered this much perfection; hadn't remembered how full her breasts were until he saw them straining against the confining linen; hadn't remembered how narrow her waist, how long and tempting her legs, until he saw them silhouetted beneath her chemise. He *had* remembered how much he'd wanted her, but his memory paled in comparison to how much he wanted her now.

"Come here," he growled, his voice ragged and sharp. He extended his free hand to her, and his eyes narrowed when Amanda shook her head.

"It's your turn, Jake," she whispered softly. As she spoke, Amanda slid the sleeves of her chemise leisurely down her arms. Clutching the bodice to her breasts, she rolled her shoulders back and forth, one by one working her arms out. Holding Jake's gaze, she let the swathing of linen drop away. The chemise didn't have to be coaxed over her hips. Unlike the dress, the undergarment was fully cut; it slipped down the length of her body with a gentle nudge and an enticingly whispery rustle of cloth.

"Come here, Amanda," Jake ordered again, his tone harsher, more ragged. When he extended his hand to her this time, she saw that his fingers were shaking. "Please."

She stepped out of the circle of wrinkled linen and, her shoulders square, her chin tipped proudly, walked over to him. "It's your turn," she repeated breathlessly. "Undress for me, Jake. And only for me."

He did. Like a sleek cat, he uncoiled himself and climbed off the table. He didn't move to the fire, and Amanda thought better of complaining about that. He removed the knives he kept tucked in the cuff of each moccasin, the long, fat blade and sheath attached to his belt. Each in turn were carefully, almost lovingly set aside.

Slowly, he freed the buttons on his shirt, then slipped the flannel sleeves down his arms. When he was free of it, he tossed it impatiently aside. He unbuckled his belt, unbuttoned his trousers, then

271

worked the coarse denim down his hips, over his heavily muscled thighs. Lower. Removing the moccasins took a more conscious effort.

Amanda's gaze devoured him greedily. She'd glimpsed the perfection of his body before, but it still amazed her. He was all copper skin and muscle. His chest was wide and firm and smooth, tapering down into a tight stomach and lean hips. Jet-black curls arrowed beneath his navel, drawing her gaze downward.

She started to look away, then decided that if she could strip for this man, and he could strip for her, then it stood to reason that looking at him shouldn't bother her. Her gaze strayed to the part of him that she'd been too fearful to look at this morning. Of its own accord, her hand moved. "Jake?" she asked, poised in the act of touching the part of a man's body a lady was taught at an early age she must never think about, let alone touch.

He reached out and coiled his fingers around her wrist, urging her closer, even as his hips thrust out to meet her. "I want you to touch me. I *need* for you to touch me."

"But—"

"Jesus, princess, don't start acting like a lady on me now! Touch me, dammit!"

She touched him. Softly. A hesitant stroke with the back of her knuckles. She marveled at his length and firmness, then touched him more boldly. Her fingers opened, wrapping around him, fisting him tightly, but not *too* tightly.

If he didn't know for a fact this woman had been a virgin when she woke up this morning, he would have sworn she was more experienced than she let on. She knew just how to move, just when to tighten, when to relax. She knew how to stroke and caress him until he burned. She knew when to hesitate until his body convulsed and demanded she continue or he would go insane.

His hands were on her shoulders, his fingers digging into her tender flesh. His control was shot, plain and simple. It was no longer a question of whether or not he would have her—they both knew he would—it was a question of how long he could hold out before he lost all control. It wouldn't be long. The pulse pounding in his ears, throbbing through the rest of him, told Jake he couldn't hold back long.

With more gentleness than he thought himself capable of, he laid her back on the table. Her hand fell away and she gripped the side of the table when his knee nudged her legs apart. She opened to him willingly, and he found the hot, moist place—*his* place—between her thighs. With one insistent thrust, he buried himself inside of her, as deeply as he could go.

The sensation he'd forgotten, that of coming home, hummed through his body, consumed his thoughts, and honed his awareness to an acute pitch. He rocked against her, rocked into her. Her legs lifted, wrapping around his hips as she moved with him.

"Ah, Jake," she sighed raggedly, her hot breath blasting against the side of his neck. "Please, just for tonight, love me like no one else ever has. Like no one else ever will."

"Yes, princess. Oh, God . . . *yes!*"

He plunged into her, withdrew, and plunged again. Deeply. Their position—her on the table, him on the floor—was perfect; it gave him optimum penetration. Her legs tightened around him. He could feel her breasts crushed beneath his chest. Her nipples burned into his skin, branding him, as he felt her body squeezing around him, wringing a quicker response than he wanted to give.

Jake's blood was pounding. His body demanded immediate release. Somehow, he didn't know how, he held back, wanting, needing to carry her up with him. His head turned, his lips sought hers in a grinding kiss. Their mouths ate at each other, demanding and receiving in kind.

273

She met him thrust for thrust, the tightness of her legs urging him on, urging him deeper. The fingers splayed over his back flexed, then tightened, as her nails clawed his skin. He swallowed her groan and felt her delicious, delicate shivers tremble up his length, milking him, snatching him further and further away from reality, while at the same time plunging him head first toward all-consuming pleasure.

It started as a small, undeniable spark in the middle of his gut. His body tightened, fighting it, wanting to prolong the sweet, torturous sensations, yet unable to. Fire burned in his blood, clouding logic, clouding any thought.

Amanda twisted beneath him as his tongue thrust into her mouth, picking up the rhythm his body had already set.

The first spasms tore through Jake's body like a knife. He couldn't fight it, no longer wanted to. The feel of her rippling around him, the sound of her raw, husky cry of satisfaction, loud in his ear, shattered Jake's world. With a low, throaty moan that might have been her name on his lips — or, quite possibly, words he would rather not have spoken — he spilled his hot, liquid fire into her.

He collapsed atop her, panting and spent. His nose nuzzled the warm hollow between her shoulder and throat. A contented sigh whispered past his lips, and his eyes drifted shut.

It wasn't until Amanda squirmed beneath him that Jake realized his weight was crushing her. With a mumbled apology, he reluctantly withdrew from the warmest, tightest place he'd ever known. He left her only long enough to fetch one of the blankets. Then he spread himself against her side and tossed the scratchy feeling covering over them both. His arm automatically slipped beneath, scooping her close.

I want you more than I want to breathe, lady.

The huskily uttered words swirled in Amanda's mind. A slow, satisfied grin tugged at her lips as she snuggled her cheek atop the hard pillow of Jake's chest, her ears attuned to the lulling beat of his heart drumming in her ear. The heat of the fire in the hearth, combined with the lingering heat of passion, warmed her sated flesh.

"Jake?" Amanda murmured, stifling a yawn with her fist.

"Hmmm?"

"How long will this last? How long will you want me the way you wanted me tonight?"

Forever, princess. I'll want to be hot and full inside of you forever. Maybe longer.

The words, boldly honest and sincere, stabbed through Jake like a knife. They paused on the very tip of his tongue, begging to be said, and it took more than a little concentration for him to swallow them back. Thinking up a safer, lighter answer wasn't easy at the moment, considering the position of their bodies, but his sense of self-preservation insisted. "How long do *you* want me to want you, princess?"

"Forever," she answered sleepily, on what sounded like an airy sigh, but might in reality have been another stifled yawn. "I want to feel this good forever."

His arm tightened around her shoulders, which caused her to nestle even more snugly against him. Her breasts pressed into his ribcage, her hips pressed against the side of his. One long white leg wantonly draped his thighs, as though pinning him down in case he might try to leave her.

Jake had no intention of leaving. He would need strength for that, and making love to Amanda had tapped him dry. He felt weak, depleted, drained. Apparently he wasn't the only one. Amanda's breathing had gone soft and shallow, rhythmic. The hand that had been splayed atop his abdomen was now limp, the fingers curled sleepily inward. He felt her breaths on his chest like puffs of the most delightful summer breeze.

Jake turned his head, and his cheek grazed her head. Her golden hair skimmed his sensitized skin. He glanced down, and saw that more springy curls had escaped the thick plait that trailed over his upper arm. The curls framed her face, softening her sleep-relaxed features.

Though his gaze tenderly roved over her face, it returned to her hair. Curious, he eyed the thick, bulky plait. He had a sudden, inexplicable urge to coax it free. Had he ever seen her with those rich gold strands falling around her? No, he realized, and he was surprised at the oversight.

He sought out and slipped free the tattered ribbon holding the fringed end of the braid in place. With fingers that shook, he worked the plait free, fluffing the silky tresses around her bare shoulders.

Her hair, he was surprised to find, was longer than he'd originally thought, and the texture was much softer as it poured between his fingers. When standing, he guessed the wavy ends would fall to well below her delectable bottom. Lord knows, he'd welcome the chance to find out — providing the delectable bottom in question was as naked as a newborn baby's at the time.

A naughty, provocative picture of exactly that burned itself into Jake's mind. A grin tugged at his lips as, with a contented sigh, he took a handful of silky waves and scattered them over his chest and belly. An odd sensation jolted through him at the unique feel of her hair tickling his bare skin. It was, he thought, a feeling comparable to no other.

And so was the other feeling that coursed like liquid fire through his veins. Loosening her braid had loosened more of her flower-soft scent. It floated around him, mingling with the charred aroma of the fire, honing his senses until he felt every warm, curvaceous inch pressed against him.

Jake felt himself tighten in response, and his steely gaze widened slightly. It would appear that *again and again* was coming sooner than he'd thought. Much sooner than he cared for it to.

Amanda was sleeping peacefully. He didn't want to wake her to take her again so soon, but the urgent throbbing in his body was making him reconsider. It didn't matter that he rarely wanted a woman twice, and *never* wanted one again *this* soon. It didn't matter that if he woke her to make love to her now, he would only be proving to them both just how weakened he was by her. What mattered was that he wanted her. Again. Badly.

What matters, you idiot, is that she's tired and she's sleeping, he grumbled to himself as he plowed the fingers of his free hand through his hair. He turned his head so that the gold strands were no longer tickling his cheek. His gaze strayed over the room, seeking out any distraction to occupy his thoughts from waking her up to possess her again.

From his position atop the table—and a provocative position it was!—he could see almost everything. What his gaze hit upon turned out to be more of a distraction than Jake had bargained for. His attention locked onto the saddlebag on the floor in the far corner of the room. It belonged to Amanda—he'd seen it enough times to know—and it was partially opened.

Jake tensed, his eyes narrowed warily. He remembered their first night together . . . the night she'd watched him bathe, the night he'd questioned her about the money. He couldn't remember her exact response, but he did remember her telling him the money was in her saddlebag, perfectly safe.

At the time, he'd sensed she was lying. He'd been on his way to check when—he scowled when this memory assailed him—she'd distracted him from ever getting that far. They'd wound up making a fire, then kissing . . . and even then her soft, sweet mouth had had the power to push rational thought from his mind.

The muscle in his cheek jerked. Amanda wasn't kissing him now, and although her tempting curves were distracting as all hell, he was thinking with marginal clearness. And what he was thinking, what he was *brooding* about, was that he'd never carried through that night. He'd never checked to see if she really did have the money to pay him, or if her offer was just another one of the lies she'd been telling him right from the start.

His fingers, curled around Amanda's upper arm, flexed. She stirred in her sleep, and Jake forced himself to loosen his grip so he didn't wake her. She settled down, curling trustingly into him once more, but he no longer felt the same enjoyment to have her pressing against him. Her warm, naked body was a distraction he couldn't afford to indulge in right now.

His gaze sharpened on her saddlebag.

It wasn't his. He had no right to go through it. Still, if she was playing him for a fool—and he suddenly had a cold, nagging suspicion that she was—well, that sure as hell wasn't right either!

He deserved some answers, didn't he? Damn straight he did! And if Amanda wouldn't give them to him . . .

Chapter Fifteen

"You little bitch!"

Jake enjoyed a second of satisfaction as he watched Amanda's sleep-relaxed features pull taut. Her eyes snapped open, locking with his in a look of stunned disbelief.

"Wha—!"

"Shut up!" He'd hauled her up by her shoulders until she was in almost a sitting position. His fingers dug into her tender flesh as he gave her a firm shake. "So help me God, Miss Lennox, you say anything—just one damn word—and I'm liable to plant my fist down your lying little throat. *Is that clear?*"

She nodded warily, her eyes huge and round. Rich gold hair scattered around her face and shoulders in soft waves, accenting the paleness of her cheeks. Her lower lip was moist and full, trembling slightly as she nibbled it with her teeth. Jake tried not to notice any of that as he hauled her roughly off the table and onto her feet.

How she managed to keep the blanket Jake had tossed over them earlier wrapped around her body, he would never know. He was just damn glad she did. The last thing he needed was to see more of her soft, creamy white skin. The sight might burn away some of his anger, and he wanted to hold onto that. He needed to cling to his fury, hide behind it.

Anger was familiar, it was safe. And it was a hell of a lot more comfortable than the confusion this woman had stirred inside of him with her wild love-making and whisper-soft words.

"Get dressed," he growled. Bending at the waist, he snatched up the wrinkled pile of her clothes and pushed them into her arms. She was rubbing the sleep from her eyes with her fist, so she didn't take them right away.

With an impatient sneer, Jake grabbed her wrist and forced her free arm around the pile. Then he jerked her around and shoved her toward the hearth. The blanket was wrapped beneath her arms. That left her shoulders bare. The sensation that seared through Jake's palms when he felt her soft, tempting flesh beneath his hands was something he didn't dare study too hard.

He kept his gaze impassive when Amanda stumbled a few steps before catching her balance. Never, not even to himself, would he admit that he'd tensed imperceptibly, ready to catch her should she fall. Thank God she *didn't*. That meant he didn't have to make any moves toward her, meant he wouldn't have to touch her again. Not yet. That was more than fine by Jake.

"Did s-something happen that I should know about?" Amanda asked, her voice shaky as she leaned weakly against the wall.

The muscle in his jaw jerked furiously. His eyes were shimmering grey slits. "Thought I told you to shut up."

"But—"

"Then do it! Jesus, lady, just once I'd like to see you do what you're told." Jake guessed by the way Amanda shook her head that she was trying to clear it of the sleep he'd just so rudely jarred her from. If she thought his screaming in her face was rude . . .

280

hell, that was nothing compared to the other ways of waking her that he'd contemplated after going through her saddlebag. It had taken a good hour before he'd trusted himself to touch her and not to hurt her.

Jake spun on his heel and turned his back on her. Over his shoulder he said harshly, "Hurry up. We don't have all night."

Amanda thought better of arguing. Whatever was going on here, she'd know soon enough. Meanwhile, it would be best to do what she was told and do it quickly. Hopefully, by the time she was done dressing his anger would have cooled.

Her hands shook when she dropped the blanket to the floor, then struggled into her clothes. The normally simple chore of working the buttons on her bodice closed proved to be difficult and time-consuming. The laces of her chemise couldn't be salvaged. They dangled down, making the neckline gape open; the severed tips tickled her skin.

Amanda tried not to think about how Jake had sliced them with his knife, but she couldn't *stop* thinking about it. Her cheeks flooded with heat when she thought of how eager his big copper hands had been to get past the linen, as eager as she had been for him to do it. Their joinings had been savage and greedy and wonderful. She'd thought they were equally as wonderful for him.

Again, his reaction surprised her. What surprised Amanda even more was that, for the life of her, she couldn't imagine what had brought about his sudden burst of temper.

Jake's foul mood and burning gaze implied she'd done something very wrong. Something infuriating. Something unforgivable. In the past, he'd always shown her quiet, leashed anger. There was nothing quiet or leashed about the fury he was showing her

281

now. It was wild, untamed, dangerous. Much more frightening than his previous displays of control had ever been.

It was also, to Amanda's mind, totally uncalled for. No matter what had caused Jake's anger, she didn't deserve to be treated this way. Dammit, no woman did!

She smoothed her palm down her skirt and took a second to compose herself. She wanted an explanation, and she would get one, but not by getting angry herself. She knew Jake better now, knew that losing her own tattered control wouldn't get her that information. If anything, it would infuriate him more; and that wasn't something Amanda felt safe doing right now.

"I'm dressed," she said, her gaze straying to Jake. His stance was open-legged and stiff, his spine a rigid line from lean hips to tensely set shoulders. His hands, straddling his hips, were balled into white-knuckled fists. "Are you going to tell me what's wrong?"

"No."

He hunkered down and picked up one of the knives on the floor. Amanda recognized it as one of the knives he kept concealed in the cuff of his moccasin. The weapon, while not small, was dwarfed by his big copper hand. Silently, she watched as, one by one, he retrieved his knives and replaced them in the strategic sheaths hidden by his clothes.

Only once he was done did Jake turn toward her. The naked fury shimmering in his glare made Amanda take a step back. She couldn't be sure, but she thought she saw a flash of satisfaction momentarily relax his features.

"Get your cloak."

"My—?"

"Cloak." He jerked his chin in the direction of the

chair on which her cloak had been draped to dry hours earlier. "Get it, and anything else you brought with you. Then turn around and walk out that door."

Amanda's blood ran cold. Surely she'd heard wrong. "I'm . . . leaving? *Now?*"

"Damn right."

Her face paled. Sometime in the last few minutes she'd stopped shaking. Her tremors now resumed with force. Dear God, was he kicking her out? Abandoning her? She didn't want to know. She *had* to know. "You're not c-coming with me?"

His gaze narrowed. His eyes were sharp with a fury reflected in his biting tone. "Oh, yeah, I'm coming. Or did you forget you hired me to do a job for you? Unfortunately for both of us, I'm a man of my word. I'll see it through. You'll get your cousin back if it kills me, and I'll get . . ."

"What?" she gulped, not liking at all the ominous way his words had drifted off. "What will you get, Jake?"

"My money. Every last cent of it." He nodded toward the door. "Let's go. The sooner we get that brat back, the sooner I can be rid of you."

Be rid of you . . . be rid of you . . . Amanda tried to ignore the way his words cut into her. She couldn't. They echoed in her mind, slicing deeper into her heart each time.

The last few months had been the hardest of her life. She'd suffered hunger, cold, pain and exhaustion at every turn. Deprivation had become a way of life. Not once during all that time had she broken down and cried. She was proud of that. What she wasn't at all proud of was the way her eyes were stinging with unshed tears now.

Why, *why* did Jake's words hurt so much? Why was the admission he wanted to be rid of her akin

283

to having one of his knives thrust into her chest and viciously turned?

Amanda turned her back so Jake wouldn't see her tears. Snatching up her cloak, she whipped it around her shoulders and tied it sloppily beneath her chin. Then she picked up her saddlebag and hugged it close.

She heard Jake moving behind her, but she didn't turn around to see what he was doing. She couldn't. If she looked at him, if he returned her look with more anger, she would lose what little control she'd manage to retain. Pride forbade her to do that. Pride demanded Jacob Blackhawk Chandler never know how easily he could hurt her.

"Ready?" he asked, his hand poised on the door latch.

Amanda nodded, but didn't move. To do so would have brought her closer to Jake than she could stand to be right now. It was bad enough she could smell his earth-sharp scent mingling with the charred aroma of the fire. Bad enough she could smell that same sensuous scent clinging to her skin and hair. That woodsy aroma, interlaced with her own feminine scent, reminded her of things Jake's fury said they would both do well to forget.

A cold wind blasted through the door when he flung it open. The cloak fluttered around her ankles and the brisk air snuck beneath the hem, caressing her ankles.

Amanda shivered and tugged the hood over her head. She noticed her hair had worked free of its usual plait as she tucked the long strands beneath the hood. She wondered about that, but not too much; she had too many other problems to waste time dwelling on something so trivial. She huddled in the warm, soft woolen folds of the cloak and thought that she'd better enjoy what comfort she could now, because the garment wouldn't provide heat for long. Nor, since the snow had lessened but not stopped, would it stay dry.

Wind kicked the snow over the ground, drifting it against the cabins outer walls. The airy white crystals danced down from the sky. Moonlight glinted off the blanket of whiteness, making the night silvery and bright.

"Well?" Jake asked when Amanda had stepped around him and paused for a moment in the doorway. "What are you waiting for?"

The heat of him invaded her cloak and seeped past the layers of clothes beneath. It was no longer a comfortable feeling, because Amanda could no longer be certain whether the warmth was based in mutual attraction or raw anger. "We should tell Gail and Little Bear we're leaving."

"They'll figure it out."

"No, Jake, I won't leave without telling them goodbye, and thanking them. They've been very good to me."

Amanda tensed when she felt a hot spot near her shoulder. She didn't have to look to know Jake had lifted his hand, that his palm was poised a mere inch from her shoulder. She knew the exact second his hand dropped back to his side; it was the same instant a surge of despair iced through her. God, what had she done that he couldn't even touch her anymore?

"Tell you what, I'll pass the word on for you. Let's go."

She stubbornly refused to move forward. "How? How will you pass the word on, Jake? You aren't speaking to them, remember?"

"Like everything else, you've got that wrong. *They* aren't speaking to *me*."

One golden brow arched. Neither Gail nor Little

Bear had said what caused the rift between them and Jake. Amanda was too polite to ask, but that didn't mean she wasn't curious. She was. And that worried her. Because suddenly she had a deep, burning desire to know everything there was to know about Jacob Blackhawk Chandler. And she wanted Jake to tell her. "Why?"

"None of your goddamn business. Now, let's go."

"No, Goddammit! Not extending my thanks to them would be rude in the extreme."

This time, Jake's hand did make contact with her shoulder. But not in the way she'd hoped. His fingers bit through the cloak, dug into her flesh. His fingers were trembling.

"Rude? Do you think I care?" His voice was low and edgy, his grip on her shoulder painfully tight. "I told you once, Miss Lennox, that I'm not a very nice person. You should have listened. If you had, we wouldn't be in this mess."

"Miss Lennox," she sneered, giving in to a sudden burst of temper herself. The surge of anger felt good. Much better than the confusion and pain that had preceded it. "You keep calling me that. An hour ago you called me princess."

"Yeah, well, an hour ago I liked you."

"You did more than 'like' me, Jake. You made love—"

"Move!" he barked, and started to push her forward.

"No." Amanda dropped the saddlebag and dug her feet into the hard dirt floor. Her hands shot out, her fingers curling around the roughly hewn door frame. "I won't leave until I've thanked your sister and Little Bear. I owe them that much."

"I said I'd pass the words on."

"Well, I don't trust you to do it."

His grip on her shoulder flexed, then melted

away. Amanda wasn't sure which was worse: Jake Chandler's fingers biting into her, or Jake Chandler not touching her at all.

"That's the real problem, isn't it, Miss Lennox? Trust. Or, in your case, the complete lack of it." His tone dripped sarcasm.

She didn't need to face him to know his glare was stabbing into her back, she *felt* it. A shiver of foreboding scratched its way down her spine. "Wh-what are you saying, Jake?"

"Same thing I've *been* saying for the last five minutes. It's time to leave. Let go of the door, Miss Lennox."

"Not until you tell me why you're mad at me, *Mr. Chandler.*"

Amanda heard him shift, felt him move into place beside her. His inky head dipped into view when he snatched up her saddlebag and shoved it roughly into her hands.

"You're a smart girl, figure it out," he growled. The second her arms curled around the weather-softened leather, Jake roughly shoved her through the door, and into the snowy night.

The door slammed closed behind them.

"This way. The horses are in what's left of the damn barn." His feet sunk into the four inches of newly fallen snow as he stalked around her and moved to the far corner of the house.

Amanda almost followed him. Why not? There was no point in fighting any longer. He'd proved his will and physical strength were stronger than hers. Only one thing held her back. Her attention had snagged on the upstairs window, and the sight she focused on rooted her feet firmly to the snow-blanketed ground.

Golden light poured through the glass, slicing a distorted rectangle over the ground, silhouetting the

287

figure who stood rigidly framed in the window.

From the size and shape, Amanda knew it was Gail who was silently watching the scene playing out below. She couldn't see the woman's expression, and Amanda thought that was just as well. She remembered too clearly the stricken look on Gail's face the first time Jake's name had been mentioned. It was the same look the woman got every time conversation turned toward her brother.

Amanda turned her head and glanced at Jake.

He was standing exactly where she'd last seen him, only now he was statue-still. Flakes of snow danced around him, melting on contact with his head and shoulders. His sleek black hair was being whipped around his face by the bitter-cold wind.

Though he stood mostly in shadow, Amanda knew exactly where his gaze rested. On the upstairs window. On his sister.

Amanda lifted her skirt and took a few steps toward him, not enough to put them into contact, but enough so she could see his expression. Instantly, she wished she hadn't.

She didn't mean to gasp, she just couldn't help it. Never had she seen such naked torment on a man's face before. She hadn't expected to see it now. Not on Jake.

The skin covering his cheeks was pale and tight, emphasizing the harshly carved bones beneath. The muscle there throbbed. His brow was wrinkled in a brooding scowl, his sooty lashes lowered to hood his gaze in a way that looked almost self-protective.

Amanda didn't realize she was going to reach out and cup his cheek in her palm until she'd already done it. His flesh felt hot and smooth beneath her fingertips. Damp with melted snow. Gentle tremors played in the corded tendons beneath his skin.

Jake's fingers manacled her wrist, thrusting her

touch aside. His gaze was still trained on the window. It was now empty; Gail had moved away. Jake closed his eyes and allowed himself one painful second of regret. Then he forced the emotion aside and let his gaze slide slowly over the woman who had, he realized suddenly, just offered him comfort.

It stunned Jake that Amanda Lennox would do that. No white person had ever offered him such a gift, and he wasn't sure how to turn the gesture away. He only knew that he must. He couldn't accept her sympathy, couldn't open himself up to her compassion. She'd weakened him too much already. If he let himself feel any more for this woman than he already did, he'd never get her out of his blood, never be whole again.

Jake had a sinking feeling it was already too late for that. Everything about Amanda had burrowed deeply inside of him. Even when he was angry with her, there was something about her soft words, her soft body, that touched a chord in him. She wasn't going to be easy to forget. She'd drifted into his life like a petal-soft breeze, and in so doing she'd changed a part of him. He didn't know what part, or how she'd managed to change it when no one before her had, he only knew that she'd done it, that . . .

Damn, but it was frightening to think a woman—a *white* woman—*this* white woman—could hold that much power over him! He shuddered to think of what would happen if she ever guessed how much control she had over his life. Over his heart.

It was something he swore to God she would never know.

"I'm sorry, Jake," Amanda said softly, soothingly. "I know you—"

"No, dammit, you don't," he snapped, cutting her short. He angled his head, bringing their faces so

289

closely together the steam of their breath mingled. His face was tight with anger, but Amanda didn't know if the anger was directed at her or at himself. Maybe a little of both? "Don't kid yourself, Miss Lennox. You don't know me. If you did, you'd know how much I hate a liar."

She shifted guiltily. "I haven't lied to you."

One inky brow slanted menacingly high. "Haven't you?"

"No. Well, only . . ." She sucked in a quick breath, and wished he wasn't staring at her as though he wanted to strangle her on the spot. "Only when it was absolutely necessary."

"White lies, in other words," he growled irritably.

The meaning was double-edged. They both knew it, though neither acknowledged it.

"Jake," Amanda began. Fingers came out of nowhere, coiled threateningly around her throat, and stifled the words on her tongue. His flesh felt ice-cold against her own fear-warmed skin, but that wasn't the reason she shivered so violently.

His grip wasn't tight enough to cut off her air supply, but it was firm enough to threaten it. Her heart raced as their gazes met and warred. Had she ever seen as much anger and hatred as she saw in the steely glare that met hers? God, she didn't think so. And she hoped never to see it in a man's eyes — in *Jake Chandler's* eyes — again.

"Don't say it, Miss Lennox. Do *not* say it. I'm on the edge right now as it is. You open that hot little mouth of yours to lie to me one more time, and I won't be held responsible for what I do to you. Is that understood?"

He didn't wait for her answer, but instead wrenched his hand from her throat as though he couldn't stand the feel of her skin beneath his fingertips a second longer than was necessary.

Jake sent her one searing glare, then spun on his heel. With his normal catlike silence he stalked to the far end of the cabin and disappeared around the corner, leaving it up to her whether or not to follow. Amanda had no doubt that if she didn't follow him to the barn he would go without her. If it weren't for Roger, she would have considered letting him do exactly that.

She hesitated, glancing one last time at the window where Gail Chandler had been standing. The light had been extinguished. The square wooden frame was now as dark and empty as her insides. Amanda sighed, then hoisted her skirt and cloak and hurried after Jake.

Chapter Sixteen

In three days of hard riding they passed through only two towns. By the time they reached the second, Amanda's nerves were raw.

Jake wasn't speaking to her. While he provided dinner—and shelter, when the weather turned harsh—he performed the services in stone-faced silence. He hadn't said a word since they'd left Gail and Little Bear's cabin. The chores he wanted her to execute—like lighting the fire, or gathering wood—were conveyed with his eyes, never his tongue.

He hadn't touched her.

More than once, as they sat at night with a crackling fire blazing like a battlefield between them, Amanda had caught Jake's gaze on her; his eyes were slitted, hooding the emotions playing in their silvery depths.

Nothing hid his expression. With the orange glow of flames on his face it was easy to see and read his contempt. Not so easily seen was who that disgust was aimed at. At times, Amanda thought it was directed at her. At other times, it seemed to be aimed more at himself. Either way, his silent animosity erected an impenetrable wall between them, one Amanda had no idea how to breech.

It had become a habit for them to sleep on opposite sides of the camp, their bedrolls as far away from each other as they could get. Jake seemed to enjoy the distance. Amanda hated it.

Long into the pitch-black nights she lay awake, replaying the times when his strong arms had held her close. The images were so real she could hear his heart drumming in her ear, feel the black silk of his hair sifting through her fingers. As the coldness of the ground seeped through the blankets and into her bones, chilling her to the core, she remembered the heat of Jake's body, of his mouth and hands gliding over her skin.

Humiliating though it was to admit, at those times she broke down and cried. She couldn't help it. Jake was tearing her apart with his silence, his brooding glares, his anger that hadn't faded a bit. Since he refused to tell her what had caused the tension between them, Amanda couldn't hope to repair it.

That didn't mean she could stop dwelling on it. Her mind worked overtime; speculation was driving her crazy. Jake had spoken of lies, but she didn't know *which* lies he'd been referring to. Confessing to one, only to find out he was talking about another, would only make the situation worse—if that was possible.

Amanda had decided early on that it would be better if she kept her mouth shut for once, no matter how much the silence was tearing her up inside. It was one of the most difficult things she had ever done, but she did it.

They reached the outskirts of a town at noon on the third day out. Amanda sat back in the saddle and surveyed her surroundings with a critical eye. By Eastern standards, this wasn't much of a town. Shacks of buildings lined the narrow streets. Dusty planked boardwalks, unconnected, stretched out in front of hastily constructed false-fronted shops. The chilly air was thick with the odor of dirt and manure.

The majority of inhabitants of this nameless mining town appeared to be male—and of the none too savory variety. Judging from their grimy, tattered clothes, most mined the diggin's on the outskirts of town. The men looked ragged, slightly gaunt, and tired. The image was enhanced by the months-long growth of coarse, untrimmed beard they sported.

There were few women, though an occasional "fancy lady" could be glimpsed lounging in the doorway of one of the many saloons or dancehalls. Amanda's cheeks colored when her gaze fixed on one woman in particular. The woman was unlike any Amanda had ever seen. She had flaming orange hair that couldn't be a God-given shade, and was wearing a gaudy crimson, indecently low-cut dress. The full skirt swished provocatively from hip to ankle as the woman sauntered down the shaded boardwalk.

Catcalls and lewd suggestions could be heard long after the "lady" had disappeared inside one of the dilapidated buildings.

Amanda sent Jake a sideways glance. She wondered if he'd noticed the woman. And if he had, was he as shocked by the redhead's appearance as Amanda had been?

The answer to both questions was no. If Jake had seen the woman, he gave no sign as, with a flick of his wrist, he pulled his mount to a stop dead center of the narrow dirt street.

Amanda fidgeted uncomfortably when a few curious stares turned their way. Thankfully, a brooding glare from a certain pair of hard silver eyes was quick to divert attention from them.

"Why are we stopping?" she asked, and she guided the mare alongside his white. She had to raise her voice to be heard over the commotion of a couple of miners who'd broken into a violent fistfight not too far away.

Jake shrugged. Leaning back, he reached beneath his vest and fumbled with something he'd shoved into the inside pocket. When his hand reemerged, he was holding the antique gun he'd wrestled away from Amanda what felt like a lifetime ago.

Her eyes widened. The pistol wasn't really that small, yet in Jake's hand, it looked like a child's toy. Sunlight glinted off the barrel as, wordlessly, he held it out to her.

Caution mixed liberally with dread flickered in Amanda's eyes as she took it. The coldness of the butt seeped into her palms, chilling the blood that pumped through her veins. Her gaze lifted, locking with his. "What am I supposed to do with this?"

"Use it to defend yourself," he said, and looked away. "What else?"

"Defend myself? But . . ." She licked her suddenly dry lips. "I thought that was what I hired you for."

She'd said something wrong. Amanda knew it the second she saw his eyes darken and his expression cloud over. But what? She thought about asking him, but knew it would be a waste of time. He wouldn't tell her. She decided to save her breath. While they weren't exactly getting along, at least Jake was talking to her now. That was a good start. In the last three days she'd come to hunger for the sound of his voice. Now that she had it she was reluctant to give it up.

"Well?" Amanda asked when she realized he hadn't answered her. "Isn't it what I hired you for?"

"No." His gaze was trained on the street, assessing the people who milled on the boardwalks. "You hired me to find your cousin. Protecting you wasn't part of the bargain."

"Maybe not, but it's something you've been doing up until now," she pointed out cautiously.

"You can't always count on me being around to keep an eye on you, Miss Lennox." Though he nodded to the gun, he didn't look at her. "I'll feel better leaving you alone if I know you've got something to defend yourself with. You keep that thing with you, and you keep it loaded, y'hear?"

295

Loaded? she thought. That was a tall order; she didn't have any bullets to load it *with*. Worse, she couldn't tell Jake that. He obviously hadn't checked the chambers, or he would know the gun was empty. Since he was already angry at her for one lie, she was reluctant to confess to this one, her lie about the gun.

Amanda swallowed back a surge of panic. "Where are you going that you'll be leaving me alone?"

He shrugged, and angled the hat back on his head. With the sunlight glinting off his chiseled copper face and the faded red bandanna tied like a headband around his brow, he looked every bit the wild, untamed savage. His expression was harsh, brooding and dark. "Nowhere. Yet. At least not until we've found a hotel and gotten you a room. After that . . ."

"What?"

"I'm going to go out and buy us some supplies. In case you haven't noticed, we're running low."

Amanda had noticed. Actually, they'd run out of everything but coffee two days ago. That hadn't seemed to bother Jake. He'd simply leave their camp shortly after they made it and, an hour or two later, return with fresh game. How he'd managed to do that using only his knives she never knew. And never asked. She was just grateful he never brought back a snake!

"And after that?" she asked tightly.

His jaw hardened, his gaze narrowed. "You're just full of questions all of a sudden, aren't you, Miss Lennox?"

It was on the tip of Amanda's tongue to deny it, but she couldn't. It wasn't that she wanted answers so much as she wanted—needed, *craved*—the sound of his voice.

She craved the feel of his touch, too, though that was one depravation Amanda thought she'd better get used to. Jake had made it clear he wouldn't be touch-

ing her in the near future. Pity. She had a very unladylike urge to feel his hands on her again. And an
even more unladylike urge to put her hands on him.

"I want to know, Jake," she said finally.

"Do you?" His gaze slid back to her, stabbing into
hers. "Do you *really?* You'd better be damn sure, lady.
Because I might not give the answer you want to
hear."

Amanda hesitated, then nodded. "I'll take my
chances. Where are you going after you buy our supplies?"

"To the first saloon I stumble into."

Well, that wasn't *so* bad, Amanda thought. In fact,
it was a perfectly normal thing to do . . . for a man.

"To get a drink?" she asked, wondering why she
hadn't thought of it before. Her father had often
drank when he was angry. Brandy, if she recalled correctly. She almost laughed at the image that popped
into her mind. Somehow, she couldn't see Jake sipping brandy from a cut-glass snifter. Whiskey was
more his style. And she doubted he'd sip it so much
as chug large, numbing quantities straight from the
bottle.

"Yeah, a drink," Jake murmured, and nodded. His
tone was low, edgy. "Among other things."

Amanda's heart fluttered. Her cheeks went pale,
and her fingers tightened around the gun. "What
other things?"

He trained his gaze on the mountainous horizon.
Cruel words formed an acidic lump in his throat;
there was no swallowing them back. Amanda's betrayal still festered inside him, demanding he lash
out. The urge to hurt her the way she had hurt him
had been brewing for three days too long already. It
could no longer be suppressed. "What do you think,
Miss Lennox? What, besides a good stiff drink, can a
man buy in a saloon? Hmmm, I wonder . . . ?"

Amanda didn't. While she may have spent years

locked away in Miss Henry's Academy, she wasn't dead. Even proper young women were aware of what went on in the questionable establishments where men gathered to drink. She'd heard that the "saloons" out here in the untamed west were twice as bad as their more refined, Bostonian counterparts.

Men visited places like that to get drunk and drown their troubles, if only for a little while . . . and to buy the favors of a warm, willing woman. What Amanda didn't know—couldn't begin to understand—was why the idea that Jake would want to do both hurt her so deeply. She felt as though he'd just sliced her heart to ribbons.

It puzzled Jake that hurting this woman didn't feel better than it did. In fact, it felt incredibly lousy. *He* felt lousy. And cold. And cruel.

It didn't matter that he'd purposely struck out at her in the only manner he trusted himself to do it; with words. It didn't matter that, after hurting him so badly, it was only fair she be hurt in return. No, it should have, but none of that made a bit of difference. What *did* matter—and mattered far too much—was the deep, physical ache that twisted in his gut when he saw the disillusionment and pain swimming in her huge green eyes.

Dammit! He'd said those words to hurt her, to prove beyond a doubt that Amanda Lennox had no hold over him. He realized now that it might be a good idea if he carried through on the threat. Maybe another woman, bought and paid to please, was just what he needed to wipe all traces of this one out of his mind.

It was a long shot. If he were a gambler, he wouldn't have bet heavily on it . . . because there was a good chance it wasn't going to work. But, hell, he could at least give it a damn good try. He was desperate enough to do anything, anything at all, if it meant getting Amanda out of his mind, out of his blood, out of his . . . Goddammit, out of his heart, a place she had no right to be. A place he had no right to *let* her be.

"There's a hotel a quarter mile up the road," he said suddenly, harshly. "It's run by a woman named Mulligrew. Think you can find it on your own?"

Amanda stiffened. Was he *that* anxious to get to his saloon, she wondered with a sudden surge of temper. Her mood was reflected in her tone. "I'm not a complete incompetent, Mr. Chandler. I think I can find the place myself." She paused. "I take it you won't be coming with me?"

He shook his head. "I'll get a room in the saloon for the night. We'll ride out at dawn. Make sure you're ready, because if you aren't, I'll leave without you."

Amanda remembered Jake's reluctance to go to the cabin, and her original assumption on why he wouldn't go there with her. The suspicion that had gnawed at her then returned in force. And then she thought of the words themselves. *I'll get a room in the saloon for the night.*

Yes, but would he sleep in that bed *alone?*

"Very well," she said, her voice cracking only slightly. No tears clouded her eyes. Amanda knew, because she had the devil's own time blinking them back.

She was in the process of flicking the reins—she had to get away from him; she would rather die than let Jake see her cry—when his fingers snaked out, looping around her wrist. His grip was light but insistent, his fingers warm, thick, and calloused.

A bolt of sensation shot from where their flesh touched all the way up her arm, and a wave of desire poured through her. Like a hot steel band, passion, longing, and . . . something else, something stronger . . . banded around her heart, squeezing so tightly she could barely breathe.

"Amanda," Jake said, leaning toward her. For once, the sharp edge of anger had been ironed from his voice. She hardly noticed. What she did notice was that this was the first time in three days he'd called her Amanda . . . and that she enjoyed the sound of her name on his tongue immensely. "You do know how to use that thing?"

"What thing?" she asked vaguely, and looked at him. His gaze was lowered, hooded by thick, sooty lashes. The copper skin stretched over his cheeks had an unusual, ruddy undertone.

Amanda didn't have to see his eyes to know what he was looking at. He was staring at the pistol now resting atop her lap. No, she corrected as a warm tingle washed over her, he was staring at her lap, not the gun, and not the trembling fingers fisted around it. His gaze was hot and intent.

"The gun," he elaborated. "Do you know how to use it, or was that another lie?"

"I—" Amanda glanced away. "No, I don't. This is the first gun I've ever held, and I've never fired one. But I think I could bluff my way through it if I had to."

Jake didn't utter a single one of the swears that slammed through his mind. He didn't dare. But he thought them . . . with a vengeance. Was this woman insane? Had she really traveled all this way, with that brat, not even knowing how to use a gun? Why the hell was she carrying the damn thing in the first place if she didn't know how to use it?

Then he remembered the way her delicate white hands had held the gun that morning in the woods, as though she *had* known her way around it. He thought of the hands of poker they'd played, and he knew that, if the situation warranted, Amanda could bluff. Of course she could. She'd bluffed her way with him from the first, and Jake had only recently discovered it. Her affect on a total stranger would be even more dramatic, more believable.

He let go of her hand, ignoring the way his palm smoldered as he placed it atop his thigh. "Let's just hope you don't have to."

"I'm sure I won't. This seems like . . ." A scowl furrowed Amanda's brow as her gaze trained on the fighting miners. Though both were bloody and battered, neither looked ready to admit defeat. Just the opposite, their expressions said they were trying to kill each other with their bare hands. A crowd had gathered around them; all seemed to be enjoying the disgusting spectacle. "This seems like a perfectly lovely," she choked on the word, "town. I'm sure I'll be safe at Mrs. Mulligrew's."

"This is a mining town, princess," Jake corrected harshly. "It's nothing like Boston. Yes, some of the men here came from back East, but you aren't likely to find a gentleman among them. The men here are hard-bitten miners who, nine times out of ten, haven't seen a decent woman in a long, long time. There isn't an inch of Junction City you can consider safe. The sooner you realize that, the safer you'll be."

Amanda almost, *almost* told him that only if he remained at her side would she feel really and truly safe. Protected. But she didn't, because she didn't want him to think her clingy. It was enough he was concerned about her. Reluctantly concerned, true, but concerned nonetheless. She said, "I'll keep it in mind."

"You'd damn well better."

This time when Amanda flicked the reins, Jake let her go. He watched the mare pick its way around the horses and flatbed wagons jostling down the street. He didn't follow her, nor did he move about his business the way his mind told him he should. Instead, he just sat and watched—both Amanda *and* the impact she had on the grizzled-looking males she passed.

More than one bearded mouth gaped open. More than one man's eyes widened appreciatively upon seeing her, blinked hard, then looked again, staring with open amazement.

Her calico dress didn't hide as much as Jake would have liked for it to. It clung to her breasts, nipped at her uncorsetted waist, bunched enticingly at her hips. A small portion of creamy white calves could be glimpsed beneath the hem.

The dress couldn't hide her voluptuous curves, nor could it hide the raw dignity of the woman wearing it.

Jake sighed and plowed his fingers through his hair. Where his next thought came from, he didn't know. And he didn't like it one damn bit. But he thought it anyway.

Amanda Lennox didn't belong in faded calico. Her quiet grace and dignity said she belonged in silks and satins, with swathing of intricate lace. In frilly, fashionable bonnets and thick sable cloaks, not threadbare cotton. She belonged in a richly decorated mansion with a battery of servants and a loving, devoted husband . . . not a cheap hotel room in Junction City with a temperamental half-breed.

Where she belonged, Jake thought miserably, was back in Boston. Not here. Not with him. Not ever.

With those thoughts eating at him, Jake nudged the white into motion, his glare trained on the hand-painted signs announcing each building. His attention fixed on the saloon to his right, and automatically he guided the white toward it.

The supplies, he decided abruptly, could wait. Right now he needed a drink. Badly.

Chapter Seventeen

Amanda's boot-heels clicked atop the scarred, planked floor as she paced from one end of the hotel room to the other. Her arms were crossed over her chest as though to protect her from the chaotic thoughts racing through her mind. Her wrinkled calico skirt rustled with each agitated step. A scowl had been brewing on her brow for the last two hours; it now etched deep crevasses into her smooth white skin.

The first fingers of dusk threaded through the single window on the far wall. Slices of muted light cut pale purple streaks over the floor. Outside, the sounds of Junction City seemed to magnify with the coming night. Horses whickered, wagon wheels creaked and jostled, men cussed, degraded, and goaded each other at incredible volumes. Tinny piano music drifted up through the floorboards under Amanda's feet. Husky male laughter wafted up the stairwell and crept through the crack under the door.

Tired of pacing, yet not nearly tired enough to sleep, she spun on her heel and perched on the edge of the narrow bed. The straw-filled mattress crunched under her weight as her gaze scanned the room. She remembered the sign that hung above the door of the hotel, the one she'd glanced at briefly before entering. Bold, handwritten letters proclaimed

Mulligrew's Hotel as the finest in the territory. One golden brow lifted skeptically, and she thought that if *this* was the finest the Montana Territory had to offer, she'd hate to see the *worst!*

What little furniture there was matched only in that it was all old. A single bed rested against the wall beside the window, and it looked as though the rickety piece of furniture was the only thing holding the wall up. The lumpy bed didn't look big enough to fit one person comfortably. An off-balance table squatted beside the bed. That was it. The chipped crockery pitcher and basin for washing didn't have a table; instead, it had been set off on the floor in a corner near the door. The wallpaper was decorated with big, water-damp brown splotches.

She could be thankful the bedlinen was clean. Faded and dingy, but clean all the same. There was no bedspread. Two blankets had been tossed atop the mattress and sloppily tucked in at the bottom corners. They were threadbare and thin, but also clean. So was the hand-stitched cotton pillow casing. Cleanliness was something to be grateful for, considering the state of the rest of the room.

She slipped her hand into the oversized pocket of her skirt. Her fingertips stroked cold, hard metal. She shivered even as she wrapped her fingers around the carved wooden butt of the pistol.

Slowly, Amanda pulled the gun free, her gaze fixing on it. The weapon wouldn't offer much protection. Not without bullets. And hadn't Jake known when he'd returned it that . . . ?

The scowl etching her brow deepened, and her gaze fixed on the chamber that should hold the bullets—had she any to load it with. A nagging suspicion tugged at her.

Jake Chandler wasn't the type of man who left *anything* to chance. While she may not know the man as well as she would like to, she knew enough. Returning an empty pistol when he thought it might be needed for protection was out of character for him. Quite simply, he wouldn't have done it. At the very least, he would have checked the gun to be sure it was loaded.

Her fingers trembling slightly, Amanda toyed with the bullet chamber. Figuring out how the thing opened took her a few minutes, but in the end her patience was rewarded.

More so than she'd expected.

Her gaze widened. Five shiny bullets now nestled within the chamber. Only the hole the hammer would close on was empty.

Amanda smiled. So, Jake *had* checked! He must have purchased the bullets in the last town they'd stopped at.

Her heart skipped a beat, and her smile faded. The trembling in her fingers spread throughout her body. Dear God, he had checked! That meant he knew she'd lied that morning when she'd told him the gun was loaded.

You don't know me. If you did, you'd know how much I hate a liar.

Was *that* what he'd been talking about the night they'd left his sister's cabin? Was her lie about the gun what had caused the fury that had been festering in him for the past three days?

It didn't seem likely. A lie that small shouldn't prompt *that much* anger. And it wouldn't, Amanda thought, in a normal man. Jacob Blackhawk Chandler wasn't "normal," he was . . . well, he was Jake. Plain and simple, he was unlike any man she'd ever met. He was wild, unpredictable, and in possession of a savage temper with a very short fuse. He was also stubborn and arrogant, and he had a chip on his shoulder a mile wide.

Yes, it *was* possible her lie about the gun was at the root of his fury. Then again, knowing Jake,

305

maybe not. The only way to know for sure would be to ask him. And Amanda couldn't do that. Jake wasn't here.

Carefully, she snapped the chamber of the gun shut, then tucked the pistol back in her pocket. Lacing her hands atop her lap, her gaze shifted to the door, and her mind strayed past the thin wooden panel.

Where was Jake now? More precisely, *who was he with?* Did she really want to know? Good God, no! The thought of Jake Chandler wrapped in the arms of another woman brought a crushing pain to Amanda's chest. Her breath clogged in her throat as the dull ache wrapped around her heart and squeezed tight. With each torturous beat, the pain grew, until it was excruciatingly sharp.

She told herself that despite their one night of love-making, she hardly knew Jake, that it shouldn't hurt so badly to imagine him with another woman. Unfortunately, she couldn't make herself believe a word of it. The image whirlwinding through her mind *did* hurt. Unbearably.

Worse, she knew why.

With a stifled groan, Amanda balanced her elbows atop her thighs and buried her face in her hands. When, she wondered miserably? When exactly had she broken her own staunch rule *and fallen in love with Jacob Blackhawk Chandler?*

Was it that first day, that first instant she'd seen him standing in that sunswept clearing? No, not then. He'd been rude and arrogant and annoying then.

Maybe it had been later that night when she'd glimpsed him walking naked and wet from the river? Maybe. Lord knows, the memory of *that* breathtaking, moonlit image had never been far from her thoughts since! But, as aware of him as she'd been, Amanda was certain that seeing Jake splendidly na-

306

ked wasn't a strong enough reason to fall in love with the man.

Their first kiss. Could she have fallen in love with him that early on? Was it possible? She didn't know. Her heart still fluttered when she remembered the first claiming touch of his mouth on hers, remembered the way his tongue had plunged into her mouth, demanding her response. Even now, if she closed her eyes, it didn't take much imagination to remember the potent taste of that man. The potent *feel*.

Amanda released a shaky sigh and dragged her hands down her cheeks. She supposed it wasn't important *when* she'd fallen in love with Jake, so much as that she had—and she had fallen hard. The range of feelings he aroused in her were incredible, complex, and stunning. He could make her tremble with a glance. One silkily uttered word, one feather-light touch, and she was hot and breathless. No man had ever done that to her before. But Jake did. And he did it so damn easily!

It had to be love. Nothing else explained the confusion roiling inside of her, the feelings that had been there almost from the first, each raised to a higher pitch with every day she'd spent in Jake's company. Why else did he consume her thoughts so completely? Why else did the idea of him being intimate with another woman feel like torture?

Worse, much worse . . . why, why, *why* had she fallen in love with a man who could never love her back? A man who saw not one world separating them, but two?

Amanda curled up atop the hard, lumpy bed and closed her eyes. What should she do now? Should she keep the information to herself? It wouldn't be easy; even now, she bubbled with the need to tell someone—to tell *Jake*. On the other hand, telling him the truth would leave her open to yet another rejection.

Her tolerance for pain had always been low. Until recently, until Jake, Amanda hadn't thought it possible to hurt more than she had the day her father had shipped her East. Now she knew better. She'd dealt with the pain of her father's rejection . . . but that would be nothing compared to another rejection from Jake. Telling him she loved him, only to have him turn his back on her . . .

No, she couldn't do it. She simply could *not* do it! She couldn't risk that much. She couldn't risk losing a part of herself to a man who could never return her love.

In the end, she decided to do as she always did; take the cowardly way out. She would keep this disturbing information to herself, cherish it always, but she would *not* share it.

A tear trickled down her cheek. She sniffled loudly, the sound meshing with the rap of footsteps echoing in the hallway. She barely noticed the footsteps . . . until they hesitated right outside of her door. She tensed, swiping away her tears with her fist, and sat up. Her heart was throbbing by the time her gaze latched onto the door.

Slowly, slowly, the tarnished brass doorknob turned.

Jake Chandler was not a clumsy drunk. Just the opposite, in fact. Even after downing the gut-burning contents of an entire bottle and a half of bourbon he didn't stumble, didn't stagger, didn't slur. The only way to tell he'd consumed too much was by listening to the tread of his feet. When he was drunk, his feet made normal walking sounds. For a man whose gait was normally as silent as a cat's, that was unusual; it was also the only way to measure the true extent of his inebriation.

As he climbed up the shadowy stairwell leading to the second floor of Mulligrew's "The Finest in the

Territory" Hotel, Jake's feet made noise. Not a lot of noise—the thump-thump of his moccasined heels was easily swallowed up by the rowdy laughter and tinny piano music drifting up from the drinking room below—but enough to tell Jake that he was in no condition to be doing what his mind only now registered he *was* doing.

His insides were hot as fire, his head feather-light. He couldn't remember how much bourbon he'd drunk. Had he finished that second bottle or not? Shrugging, he decided it didn't matter. While however much he'd drunk was enough to blur the razor-sharp edges of reality, it wasn't nearly enough to bulldoze his obsession with Amanda Lennox from his mind. In fact, the more intoxicated he'd become, the more desperate he'd found himself for the sight and sound and smell of that woman. He had to see her creamy white skin, had to hear the sound of her voice whispering in his ear, had to drown himself in the flower-soft scent of her just one more time. He *had* to.

Just once more, he thought as he concentrated on putting one foot evenly in front of the other until he reached the top of the stairs. *Yes, I need to be with her just this one more time, and then I'll . . . What? Stop wanting her? Not likely! Then what?* his subconscious demanded. *What will you do after you've had her "just this one more time?"*

I'll want her again! his liquor-fogged mind answered without hesitation. *And again and again and . . .*

Jake brought himself up short. His feet felt as though they'd been cemented to the bare planked floor as he hesitated on the stairlanding. His grip on the railing turned white-knuckled tight. Good thing, too, since his knees felt suddenly weak. His expression couldn't have been more stunned if he'd walked face-first into an invisible brick wall. In a way, he had. Only this brick wall—the one that had sprung up all by itself in his mind—had a name. It was Amanda Lennox.

Jake sighed and shifted his weight until he was leaning back against the sharp corner of the wall. His thoughts swerved to the redhead downstairs, the one who'd spent the last two hours of her life molding her voluptuous bottom to his lap. He remembered each graphic suggestion she'd purred into his ear. He thought of her warm, ripe body. Of her blatant interest. And then he thought of his own surprising lack of it.

It had taken him a full hour, and God knows how much liquor, for Jake to realize he wasn't going to bed the redhead—although he suspected the woman herself had figured it out quite a while before him. It had taken him less than two seconds to realize *why* he wouldn't seek his release with her.

Amanda Lennox.

Right or wrong, she was the *only* woman he wanted, and he wanted her with an urge so strong it almost didn't seem real. It was Amanda's sweet white skin he craved to feel beneath his open palms. Amanda's curves he yearned to have complimenting his own male hardness. Amanda's airy breath he would kill to feel scorching his bare flesh, seeping into his bloodstream.

The redhead wouldn't do. Jake didn't want her. He didn't want what she'd been offering—or, more precisely, selling him. He didn't want a nameless woman, bought and paid for in a nameless saloon. A woman whose body he would forget long before sunrise. A woman whose face he would forget even sooner. He'd had enough encounters like that to last him two dozen lifetimes.

What he wanted, needed, *hungered* for now was Amanda. And *only* Amanda. His desire for her was like nothing he'd ever known. It was a fire in his blood that had sparked the first time he'd seen her; a

310

fire that had kindled to an unendurable flame the first time he'd made love to her.

There was no end in sight. There was no hope of finally putting an end to the desire burning inside of him. At least, not when the very woman who inspired it was tucked inside a room located only a few dozen feet from where he now stood. She was so damn close, so damn accessible!

What would happen if he went to her now? She wouldn't turn him away. Jake knew it, just as he knew that to go to her would have to be the stupidest thing he'd ever done in his life! But he was tempted. Ah, God, was he tempted!

While he didn't slur when he was drunk, liquor always greased his tongue. If he saw Amanda tonight, in this condition, he might inadvertently tell her a variety of things she was better off not knowing—and he was better off not saying. Like why he'd been so angry with her. Like what he had—no, what he *hadn't*—found in her saddlebag three nights ago. He was just drunk enough, just desperate enough, that he might—*might*—listen to any convoluted excuse she gave him, because . . . Jesus, he was so damn hungry to hear one!

At this point, Jake didn't even care if she told him the truth anymore. And that scared the hell out of a man who put more stock in honesty than he did in breathing.

A vague shuffling sound tunneled down the hall to his right, coming from the direction of Amanda's room. While Jake's ears registered the noise, he didn't look in that direction. Why bother? This was a hotel, after all. People came and went regularly; the hour of day or night didn't matter much.

While the noise itself didn't snatch his attention, the voices did. Both were gravelly, thick, and as coarse as their owners—two stooped shadows he had to squint to identify as men.

Jake's hand hovered over the hilt of the knife sheathed on his belt. Even though he didn't touch it, the cold of the steel chilled his palms. Scowling, he concentrated on the voices of the two men. His blood ran cold as their words burned the dull edges of liquor from his mind.

"She's in there, I tell ya," the short, fat one huffed as he released the doorknob.

"And *I'm* tellin' *you* this is the wrong room," the other man, equally as short but thin as a rail, argued.

"It ain't. I saw her go in there with my own two. Ain't *no* woman in these parts ya can confuse with that one, pal."

"Not in Junction," his thin friend agreed, "but that ain't the point, Cal. The point is, if we barge in there and find out it ain't the right room . . ."

"It is," Fat Cal snarled. "I know it is. Trust me, Billy, the breed's woman is in there. I'd swear my soul she is."

Thin Billy stiffened. "Better start swearin' then. Cause if you're wrong . . . well, ain't no man lives in Junction's gonna want to see our grubby faces looming over his bed, Cal. And if there's a miner in there with his gal . . . well, he'll think we come to steal his dust and kill us fer sure."

"Ain't no miner. And ain't no one gonna get killed, just so long as we're quiet."

"Quiet?" Thin Billy huffed. "Yeah, *we* can be quiet all right. *She* won't be. Least, she won't be once she figures out what we've got in mind. And *I'd* swear to *that*."

"Far as I'm concerned, she can make all the noise she wants . . . *after* we's done with her. 'Sides, once she's gagged and tied up, she'll be quiet enough."

"What if she screams before you gag her, Cal? What then?"

"Think of what you're sayin', Billy! Any yellin' she

does is just for show. Hot-damn, the gal's been puttin' it to an Injun. An *Injun!* Prob'ly be a nice change for her to spread those perty white legs for the two of us." Fat Cal chuckled nastily, and jabbed an elbow into his companion's ribs. "After she's had *us,* she ain't gonna welcome no piece of red trash back in her bed. I'd stake my life on it."

"That's exactly what you'll be doing if you open that door, Cal."

The soft, deadly reply didn't come from either of the two men. It seemed to take a second for Fat Cal to realize that.

When realization came, it came all at once—in the form of a steely band wrapped around his paunchy middle, crushing the air from his lungs. A knife materialized out of nowhere; before Fat Cal could blink, the long, thick, deadly blade was resting against his jugular. A sinewy body molded itself into his fatty back. The chest he was suddenly brought up against—and brought up hard—was lean and solid and strong. So was the arm that continued to squeeze the air out of him.

Thin Billy's eyes widened, his shocked attention straying over his friend's beefy shoulders. His gaze met cold steel grey, and held. His gaunt jaw loosened and his mouth gaped open. At the same time, his cheeks drained a chalky shade of white.

If Jake had wondered if the two men would fight for each other, Thin Billy's reaction took care of that. They wouldn't. Not if they were smart. Then again, considering what they'd been about to do . . .

Jake's attention shifted to the door. It was a miracle the wood didn't combust, his gaze was that hot, that furious. He thought of Amanda, of what these two men would have done to her had he not come along when he had. His gut kicked, hard. His heart was pounding fast and furious, each beat pumping more and more fury into his system, wiping away the fog of liquor, wiping away everything except the image of his woman being violated by these two filthy pieces of white scum.

Had he ever wanted to kill a man as badly as he wanted to kill these two? If so, Jake couldn't remember it. No fury he had ever felt before matched what he was feeling now. No *fear* equalled the fear that was eating at him from the inside out.

Good God, *if he hadn't come . . . !*

"H-hey, now just a minute, mister," Fat Cal stammered. It took a conscious effort not to let the lump in his saggily fleshed throat bob too much. Any movement, no matter how slight, could sink that blade right in there. "Listen, f-friend, we wasn't gonna do nothin' to the woman."

"Right," Thin Billy agreed nervously. He shifted from foot to foot, licking his fear-parched lips at regular intervals. "We was just—we was just gonna keep her busy till you got back is all. Ain't no crime in that."

Jake's gaze stabbed through the thin man. "You don't call rape a crime?" he said, his gaze sliding contemptuously from the top of the man's dark, wispy head to the tattered toes of his boots. A cold, satisfied grin curled over his lips when he saw Thin Billy take an instinctive step backward.

"Rape? Wouldn't've been no rape," Fat Cal huffed. "Hell, no." He grunted when the arm around his waist tightened. The air whooshed from his too-full lips. After a full minute of the pressure, his cheeks took on a bluish tinge.

Jake angled his head so his lips were close to the fat man's ear. The stench of Fat Cal's body was strong, but not nearly as strong as Jake's fury. "You don't call rape a crime?" he repeated slowly, precisely.

The arm that threatened to snap the fat man's ribs loosened enough for Fat Cal to swallow a gulp of air. The hallway filled with the sound of the fat man's gasping and wheezing. The raspy noises almost masked the sound of the thin man's steps. From the corner of his eyes, Jake saw Thin Billy easing his way toward the stairs, clinging to the wall, to the shadows. The expression on his gaunt, haggard face said he was praying to get away undetected. Pity it was too late.

Jake's gaze swung to the side, freezing Thin Billy in his tracks. The small man shivered, molding his back against the planked wall. "Come here, Billy."

For a second, Jake expected Thin Billy to make a run for it. And then the little man's gaze shifted to the blade poised against the folds of his fat friend's throat . . . and he saw the big copper hand that looked more than capable of ending two lives in just as many strokes.

Thin Billy sucked in a deep, shaky breath, then cautiously eased closer to Jake.

Had Fat Cal guessed what Jake's intent was, he might have tried to make a run for it. As it was, the hand wielding the knife left his throat for only a fraction of a second—just long enough for a rock-solid copper fist to slam the hilt of the knife into that sensitive place between Thin Billy's shoulder and neck—before it returned in lightning time.

Thin Billy's eyes rolled back in their sockets, and his body slid quickly down the wall as his knees buckled beneath him. He slumped to the floor with a *thud* that sounded hollow, and not nearly satisfying enough to Jake. For now, it would have to do.

Fat Cal still hadn't caught his breath. The air cut through his lungs with choppy, raspy sounds, but his sudden whimper was distinct enough to drag Jake's attention back to him.

"Last chance to answer, Cal. Do you call rape a crime?"

"I-it ain't . . . rape when ya take . . . a woman like that'un," the fat man managed to wheeze.

315

"Any gal who'll . . . give it to a breed'll—"

The too-soft body pressed against Jake's front began to tremble—undoubtedly because the copper hand wielding the knife had increased its pressure. The blade sliced like butter through the top layer of the fat man's skin. Deep enough to draw blood, deep enough to sting like a son of a bitch and to leave a scar . . . but not deep enough to kill. Yet.

Blood trickled down Fat Cal's neck. It was absorbed by his grimy collar.

Jake uncurled his arm from around the fat man's waist and grasped the man's tattered shirt collar in his fist. Before Fat Cal knew what had happened his back had been slammed up against the wall. The back of Fat Cal's balding head collided with the wall hard enough to make the wood vibrate. A strangled gasp rushed past his lips. And then the knife was back at his throat, and Fat Cal thought better of making any sound at all.

Jake had to look down to meet the fat man's gaze. The eyes that stared back at him were narrow, the irises a swamp-water shade of greenish-brown. His flabby cheeks were fear-reddened, and the folds of skin sagging beneath his jaw shook with the violent trembling of his big body.

"Look, mister, we didn't mean no offense. If'n ya want to be paid for the whore's time . . . well, that's fine by me. I got me some money."

Cautiously, Fat Cal's hand inched toward his pants pocket. He made it only halfway before Jake's words stopped him cold.

"The woman's mine. She can't be bought."

The swamp-green eyes widened. "Yours?"

"Mine," Jake growled, angling his head until their noses almost touched. Fat Cal's breaths rushed past his parted lips, blasting over Jake; the feel was hot, the smell stomach-rolling sour. "And make no mistake, I protect what's mine."

316

"I . . . well, yeah, I can see that ya do, b-but—"

Jake found that yanking Fat Cal away from the wall by his collar, then slamming him back against it hard, shut him up fast. "Damn straight I do. Want to know something else, Cal?"

"N-no." If he hadn't been trembling before, the furious glint in the steely eyes glaring at him, and the steady, capable fist curled around that knife, would have set Fat Cal shaking in his boots.

"I swear," Jake said, his tone low and edgy, "I'll kill any man who lays so much as his rancid breath on my woman. You dare touch her, you dare to so much as *look* at her again, and I'll kill you. Very slowly, very painfully. Do you understand me, Cal? *Do you?*"

"Y-yes. Oh, God, yes!"

"Good. Now, get the hell out of here." With a shove, Jake sent Fat Cal stumbling clumsily down the hall. The man's tattered boots collided with his friend's prone body, but that didn't stop the fat man from hurrying toward the stairwell.

Jake plowed his hands through his hair and watched the man's meaty back disappear around the corner. Then he turned, his gaze fixing on the door. Or, more accurately, on the woman who stood framed in it. He was just in time to see Amanda tuck the pistol into the pocket of her skirt.

He'd sensed her presence there for a while now. In fact, Amanda Lennox was the only reason he'd spared Fat Cal's life. He would rather have killed the slimy bastard, but he didn't want Amanda to see him kill a man. He didn't want her to think any worse of him than she already did. And he didn't want to know why that was so.

His gaze slid upward, locking with shock-widened green. Her cheeks were pasty. Her lower lip trembled. So did the arms she'd wrapped tightly around her waist.

"Jake?"

"Don't say it," he sneered, slashing the hand wielding the knife through dead air. "Just . . . Jesus, lady, don't say it."

"But—"

With jerky motions, Jake wiped the blade down his thigh. A thread of blood marred the denim when he returned the knife to its sheath. His gaze was trained on the unconscious Thin Billy. "Pack your gear. We're leaving Junction. Now. Tonight."

He expected a fight, yet he wasn't entirely surprised when Amanda turned and walked back into the room. He heard the shuffling sounds of her doing what he'd ordered her to do.

What Jake hadn't expected, hadn't prepared for, was the after-shock of vibrations now shivering through his body. Fury had burned away all residue of the bourbon. His mind was working now, and it was working overtime. He was capable of thinking only one thought, and he thought it over and over. Like a chant he didn't know how to stop, he thought, *My woman . . . my woman . . . my woman.*

The hell of it was, that was exactly what Amanda Lennox was. His. Jake may have been able to deny it before, but he couldn't deny it any longer. Whether Amanda realized it or not, whether she *wanted* it or not, she was his. Body and soul.

And Jacob Blackhawk Chandler kept what was his, even if he had to pay for it with his life.

Glancing over his shoulder, he saw Amanda bending over her saddlebag, stuffing something inside of it. Yeah, Jake thought, it just might kill him to keep her by his side. But it was a price he was seriously considering paying.

Chapter Eighteen

Jake's words echoed in Amanda's mind as she crammed her belongings into the saddlebag. There wasn't much to pack. If she'd been in the mood to reflect, she would have thought it sad that a woman who'd once had so much, now had so little.

My woman . . .

Amanda drew in a shaky breath as she rolled up her only other dress and shoved it into the saddlebag. Had Jake meant to say that, she wondered, or had they been meaningless words, said to scare off her would-be attackers? Did he even *realize* what he'd called her, or that she'd heard him? Did he know how very much hearing those words on his lips had meant to her? How deeply it had affected her? Even now her reaction was staggering.

She'd placed the gun atop the bed. It wasn't until she reached for it that something else occurred to Amanda. Something every bit as shocking. Something even more alarming.

The butt of the gun felt cool in her hand, hard and deadly. Knowing that there were five fresh bullets inside made her handle it with extra care. She lifted the pistol slowly, letting it lay on her open palm, her gaze rivetted on the blue-cast barrel.

Stunned, her heart racing madly, she thought, *I would have killed for him. If it had come down to it, I wouldn't have hesitated. I would have killed for him!*

Her hand trembled as the impact of that realization hit her. Her fingers curled around the gun before it could tumble onto the bed. She felt Jake's gaze on her, and her spine stiffened. Slowly, her head came around.

He was standing in the doorway, his left shoulder leaning negligently against the frame. His arms were laced over his chest, his ankles were crossed. His lazy stance in no way suggested he was a man who had just come dangerously close to ending two lives.

The orange lamplight danced off his head, making his long, sleek hair glisten a rich shade of blue-black. Shadows played over his face, sculpting the hollows beneath his cheeks, making the already hard line of his jaw look even harder.

Their gazes met and held. Neither spoke, yet volumes of unspoken words hovered in the air between them.

Amanda was the first to glance away. She looked down at the gun. Then, with trembling fingers, she tucked it into her saddlebag.

And that was when it hit her.

Her saddlebag!

It had been lying in the corner of Little Bear and Gail's cabin when she and Jake had made love. When she'd awoke—no, when *Jake* had woken her—it had not been in the corner where she'd left it. Scowling, Amanda forced her mind to pick out frayed memories that were now three days old.

She distinctly remembered picking the saddlebag up off the chair. She remembered thinking at the time that something wasn't quite right about that. But Jake had been so furious with her . . . and all she'd been able to concentrate on was stilling her panic and finding out what had caused his anger.

Now she knew, at least she thought she did, and . . . dear God, she wished she didn't!

You'll get your cousin back if it kills me. And I'll get . . .

What? What will you get, Jake?
My money. Every last cent of it.

Amanda closed her eyes and sucked in a sharp breath. She held it until her lungs burned. She didn't realize she'd fisted handfuls of the saddlebag until she felt the worn leather crinkle in her grip.

The money. He'd found out about the money and . . .

She opened her eyes and glared down at the saddlebag. With trembling fingers, she rummaged through her belongings. Though she searched frantically, it took only a second for her to realize that what she was looking for wasn't there.

"Finally figured it out, did you? Took you long enough." Jake's voice was low and deadly; his ridicule cut into her as sharply as one of his knives.

Her shoulders sagged, and her head lowered until her chin rested atop her collarbone. Her voice, when it came, sounded low and defeated. "Jake, I can explain . . ."

"Save it. I don't want to hear any more of your lies."

Oh, that hurt! But, since she knew she deserved it, Amanda only winced inwardly. "I wasn't going to lie."

"Yeah, I'll just bet you weren't."

"I wasn't! I was going to tell you the truth. All of it."

"Uh-uh. Pity the truth according to Amanda Lennox is never the truth at all. It's just one big pack of lies. Little white lies which, I suppose when told to a stupid half-breed, don't count." His pause was short, riddled with tension. "Pack up, Miss Lennox. Like I said, we're heading out tonight."

"But—"

"Pack!"

"No!" As tempting as it was to back down, to take the coward's way out, Amanda's conscience refused to allow it. For once in her life, she was determined to fight for something important; she was going to fight

321

for Jacob Blackhawk Chandler. Her chin lifted a notch. Even that minute gesture made her feel braver. The difference in attitude was reflected in her tone. "I'm not going anywhere until you've given me a chance to explain why I did what I did. I have reasons, Jake. Good reasons."

When he made no reply, she glanced at him. He'd moved, his tread as silent and graceful as a cat's. He was standing a mere foot away from her. She hadn't heard him ease the door closed, but he must have done so at some point, because it was closed now. He towered over her, his size and fury dwarfing the room — dwarfing *her* — until everything but him faded to insignificance.

Amanda felt cornered, trapped and desperate. That surge of innate cowardice crowded in on her again, but she steadfastly pushed it aside. It was time — past time — that Jake learned the truth. Her back rigid, she clasped her hands tightly in front of her and nodded to the chair next to the window. "Have a seat, Mr. Chandler," she said, her prim Bostonian accent locked firmly in place. "This could take a while."

She expected him to argue. She expected him to spin on his heel and walk out. She expected anything, except what he did.

Jake retrieved the chair and dragged it close to the bed. Turning it backward, he straddled it so that he was sitting facing her. By accident or intent, the back of the chair acted as a shield between them.

His smokey gaze sharpened on her. A thousand times Jake told himself not to listen. A thousand times he told himself to get up and leave, to get on his horse and ride the hell out of Junction — to get as far away from Amanda Lennox as he could. To run and never, *never* look back.

And then his traitorous body flooded with a thousand and one soft, sweet reasons to stay. To listen. To hope that once, just *once*, she would trust him enough to tell him the truth. In the end, it was his body that won out.

When it came to Amanda Lennox, didn't it always?

Gritting his teeth, and calling himself all sorts of a fool, he slanted a dark brow at her. "Say it and say it quick, princess. I want to be out of this hellhole before dawn."

Amanda nodded and, before her knees could embarrass her by buckling, walked over to the side of the bed and perched on the edge of it. Jake was close — close enough to reach out and touch, close enough for her to smell the earthy tang of him in the air, interlaced with the potent fumes of liquor.

Her hand lifted from her lap, her fingertips tingling with the need to make contact with him, to draw from his seemingly bottomless well of strength and control. His gaze darkened and glared her hand back to her lap.

Amanda swallowed hard, her attention straying down to the hands she now clenched tightly in her lap. "Where do I start?"

"The beginning is always a good place." *Leave, Chandler. Get up and leave,* now, *while you still have the chance.* The advice Jake's mind dictated was sound. Pity his body refused to listen. He was glued to that chair, and nothing on heaven or earth was going to budge him until he'd heard Amanda's story. Until he had the truth.

"The beginning," she murmured. "No, in this case I don't think that would be appropriate. Why don't I start with Roger?"

Jake shrugged. "Your story, princess. Start where you want."

His tone was less than encouraging, Amanda noticed, even as she nodded. "He isn't my cousin."

"Nope."

Her chin snapped up, and a flicker of anger sparked in her blood. "There's no need to be sarcastic, Jake. I know you found the letter from Edward Bannister in my saddlebag. I know *you know* who Roger's father is."

Jake had crossed his arms atop the chair's back rest. He now lifted his left hand, and pointed an accusing finger at her. "What I *don't* know—but what you *are* going to tell me—is why the hell you lied to me about that."

"I had to."

"I don't think so."

"Well I do!" In a burst of restless energy, Amanda pushed from the bed and started pacing the room. She needed some space, some fresh air, some . . . No, what she needed was Jake's understanding, *that* was what she needed. Desperately.

The skirt whipped around her ankles as she spun on her heel and stalked a path toward the door. Her heels clicked atop the bare flooring. "What was I supposed to do, Jake? Can you tell me that? Roger and I had been lost in," she cringed, "Idaho? . . . for two weeks before you came along. And then I got stuck in that damn river, and Roger was kidnapped, and I knew the only way I was going to get him back was with your help."

"So you hired me on, even though you didn't trust me as far as you could spit," he growled when she hesitated. "And then you lied to me. Repeatedly. About Roger, about the money you said you'd pay me, even about not knowing anything about who took the kid." Jake gritted his teeth and plowed his fingers through his hair. The fury was building in him again, and the fury said he should have listened earlier and left when he'd had the chance. "Everything, lady. You lied to me about *every goddamn thing!*"

Amanda whirled around to face him. Any fear or alarm she might have felt before fled; replaced by a sharp stab of defensiveness. "What did you expect me to do? You said yourself you aren't a very nice person. And how could I be expected to trust a man who blackmailed me into telling him who I was just to get some help getting out of that river? I couldn't. I simply could not risk telling you who Roger is. How was I supposed to know *you* wouldn't kidnap him and hold him for ransom?"

Jake's eyes narrowed to dangerous silver slits. "Are you serious? Do you really think that little of me?"

Amanda sucked in a steadying breath and tried to control her temper. Her tone matched the leashed, controlled pitch of his. "Not any more. But you have to remember that I didn't know you very well then. At the time, I didn't know what to think of you. You . . . you weren't exactly like any man I'd ever met before."

"Meaning . . . ?"

"Meaning no Bostonian gentleman of my acquaintance would have quoted me such an outrageous price to help me find Roger. The second you did that, I knew you needed money. Since I was in the same situation myself—needing money—I knew how desperate a person could get. That's when I decided it would be better if you thought Roger was my cousin."

"And is he?"

Amanda shook her head and resumed her pacing, her gait only a little slower than before. "I just told you he isn't. Didn't you wonder why I wasn't too concerned over his disappearance?"

"I didn't lose any sleep over it," he shrugged, "but now that you mention it . . . ?"

"I can't stand the boy, Jake. That's not to say I'm not worried about him, because I am, but . . . well, quite frankly, Roger Thornton Bannister III is a spoiled, malicious little brat. He makes it very hard for a person to worry about him. If it weren't for the money—"

"Lie number two," Jake cut in with a sneer. "The money. Rather, the lack of it."

Amanda tripped over the hem of her skirt. "I was going to pay you."

"Were you, princess? With what?"

It was his deceptively lazy drawl that alerted her to his burgeoning anger. Hoisting her skirt out of the way, she went back to the bed and sat down. "You have the letter, right? You know how much Edward Bannister is going to pay me when I deliver his son to Pony. I was going to pay you with my earnings."

"You were going to pay me *three quarters of your salary?*" His grin was quick and cold and fleeting. The sight of it sent a chill down Amanda's spine. "I don't know, princess, but for some reason I find that real hard to swallow. More likely you figured you'd use me to get the kid back, collect your money, then, with any luck, ditch the stupid breed the first chance you got."

Amanda's head snapped back as though she'd been slapped. And she had, only with words instead of a hand, and that made it sting all the more. "The stupid breed," she repeated flatly under her breath. Her tone belied the turmoil within her. It took every ounce of courage she possessed to lift her gaze, and to meet his. "So, we're back to that again, are we? I guess it's my turn to ask. Do *you* really think so little of *me?*"

Jake studied her long and hard. Her green eyes glistened with unshed tears, while at the same time her posture remained rigid and proud. Contrasts, he thought. Amanda Lennox was chock-full of intriguing little contrasts that both excited and *annoyed* him.

It would be easy — so damn easy! — to let himself get lost in this woman. She'd already burrowed under his skin and carved a place for herself so damn close to his heart it was scary.

Did he think badly of her still? God knows he should! But he didn't. He *couldn't.* Dammit! No matter how many lies she'd told him, no matter how little trust she put him, he still wanted her, so badly he ached inside just looking at her. The hell of it was, the need coursing through him wasn't merely physical any more. Oh, yeah, he still wanted her writhing beneath him, still wanted to be buried deeply inside her warm, tight heat . . . but he also wanted more. So damn much more!

What he wanted, as always, was impossible. He wanted Amanda Lennox, the one thing in his life that he knew damn well he couldn't have. Not for long. Not forever. Not a man like him.

"You're silence is condemning," Amanda said, and commended herself for keeping her voice low and even. If he only knew how badly she was shaking on the inside, how much his silence hurt! He could slash her flesh to ribbons with one of his knives, but she doubted it would hurt nearly as much as this did.

Smoothing trembling fingers down her skirt, Amanda stood. She closed the saddlebag, then hoisted it over her shoulder. Her gaze fell on Jake, and something he'd said earlier tickled the back of her mind. She scowled and asked, "What did you mean when you said I'd lied about knowing who took Roger?"

"Exactly what I said." Jake stood and, with a flick of his wrist, sent the chair careening across the room. It slammed into the wall, then clattered to the floor. "The tracks are leading to Pony, Miss Lennox. And what's more . . . there are no longer two sets of prints, there are *three*."

"Pony? *Three?*"

"Yup."

Her scowl deepened. "But that's impossible. Why would they . . . and who—?"

"How the hell should I know? It seems whoever we're after either kidnapped someone else, or enlisted help. It also seems a might peculiar that whoever took the brat, they're taking him exactly where *you* were!"

"Peculiar? It sounds *suspicious*, if you ask me." Her mind whirled in confused, disjointed thoughts. "Are

327

you *sure* they're heading toward Pony? Are you absolutely positive?"

Jake planted his fists on his hips and glared at her. "I'm not the best tracker in the territory, but I can damn well follow a steady set of prints. I know my way around these mountains, and I know where Pony is. Those tracks are heading toward Pony." He took a slow, measured step toward her. "Now, I want to know why. What kind of mess have you gotten me involved in?"

Amanda's heartbeat accelerated when Jake took a step closer. Another. His body heat and earthy scent invaded her from every quarter. It made her knees weak, her head spin—and, as always, his nearness made logical thought impossible.

Jake reached out and cupped her chin, lifting her gaze back to his. Her eyes were large and confused, but he wasn't stupid enough to believe that she didn't know what was going on. She'd lied to him too many times already; his mistrust had a solid foundation to grow on. "Why, Amanda? What's going on that you haven't told me?"

"Nothing. Jake, I've told you everything I know. I have no idea why the prints are heading to Pony. And I don't know why there are three sets now instead of two. I just . . . *I don't know!*" She reached up and curled her fingers around his forearm. Even through the flannel sleeve she felt the thick, tight bunch of his muscles. She felt his heat, his strength, and she drew from it, letting it bolster her floundering courage.

Jake decided he must have lost all grips on reality sometime in the last few weeks because, against his better judgement, he believed her. He *had* to. The idea that she was lying to him yet again was unbearable. "You have no idea who could have taken the kid, or why?"

She shook her head. "None."

"And the new set of prints . . . ?"

Again, she shook her head.

"If you're lying to me again, princess, I'll—"

"I'm not. I swear it."

"Ah, God, I wish I could believe you!"

"You can, Jake. You have to. I'm all out of lies." Amanda lifted a hand and cupped his cheek. His whiskers abraded her palm, but she didn't complain. It felt good. Wonderful. How long had it been since she'd touched him? Three agonizing days too long, her body told her. She felt every second of that absence ripple up her arm in a wave of white heat.

Jake stifled a groan. He was torn between the urge to break the contact, and the equally strong urge to make it more intimate.

The memory of the two men outside her room came back to torture him. He wanted to touch her—everywhere, slowly—wanted to brand her with his possession until she finally realized what he was beginning to think he'd known all along: that she was *his*. Maybe not forever, but for here and now, for as long as he could make it last. *Again and again . . .*

Amanda saw his gaze dip, tracing her lips, devouring their shell-pink softness. His gaze darkened to midnight gray, sparked with undeniable desire. Her fingers trembled. Her blood heated, tingling with sweet promise as it surged through her veins.

She saw the muscle in his cheek jerk and knew that he was fighting the attraction, fighting the overwhelming passion that even the most accidental touch between them caused to burn out of control. She could have told him not to bother, not to waste his time and energy fighting the inevitable. In the end, with them, desire always proved stronger than good sense.

His hair fell forward on his shoulders as he angled his head to the side. His mouth lowered, dipping in a path aimed for complete possession. He stopped midway, his hungry gaze still riveted to her mouth. "I don't want this," he said, his voice low and husky.

Tortured. "I don't *want* to want you. Not this badly. Not at all."

"But you do," she whispered, and closed the distance between his chest and hers. She'd forgotten how hard he was, forgotten how perfectly her soft curves nestled into his rigid planes. "You want me, Jake. You can't deny it."

He sighed raggedly, his liquor-scented breath blasting over her, heating her skin. "I can try."

"You'll fail." She went up on tiptoe, circling her arms around his neck, pulling him closer. Then closer still. Her next words were whispered against his mouth. "Love me, Jake. Just for a little while, just for tonight, love me. Please."

She stretched, and sealed their mouths together.

Jake hesitated for only a heartbeat. And then his arms were around her waist and he was hauling her so close he thought it was a miracle that the soft promise of her body didn't melt right into him. Dammit, she was right. He couldn't fight this. He wasn't strong enough. Her flowery smell made his blood run hot. The touch of her body molding into his sent a bolt of desire sizzling through him. The second her lips touched his he was lost.

He kissed her ravenously, as though he couldn't taste enough of her. His hands scoured her back, her arms, her waist and bottom. That he should be tired of bedding this woman by now, that he should have by all rights worked her out of his system days ago, occurred to him only briefly. He wasn't tired of her. Not by a long shot. If anything, his appetite had been whetted, and now he was starved for her. His palms ached to feel her creamy white flesh. His tongue thirsted to taste parts of her that no man had ever tasted before. And that no man besides him ever would!

His woman. His woman!

Yes, when he held her like this, when she kissed him like this and moved her body so sweetly against him, Jake could almost believe that she was his. In her arms his life started and stopped. In her kisses there were no yesterday, no tomorrow, no pain or regret. There was only here and now. There was only desire — hot and raw and consuming — unlike anything he'd ever known in his life.

"You're mine," he growled against her kiss-swollen lips, as he bent and scooped her into his arms. He crossed to the bed, and laid her out atop the threadbare blankets. His hands shook with a deep longing that was almost incomprehensible as, one by one he peeled her buttons free.

In record time, he had them both naked.

Amanda's white skin glistened in the flickering lamplight. Jake's glowed a deep shade of sun-kissed copper. In his present mood, he thought the colors complimented each other perfectly.

His hands roamed her body, touching, igniting passion, making her groan his name aloud. But it wasn't enough. Touching her was never enough any more. He needed more, needed everything, and he needed it now. Fast and hard.

"Mine," he said as he spread himself out atop her. He buried his face in her neck, and his tongue tasted the sweet cream flavor of her throat, pressed against her thundering pulse. His left hand found her breast. Her nipple was already rigid; he teased it to an even more alert, more sensitive peak.

Then his hand drifted down, and he found the moist, burning heat of her. He fondled and stroked until she begged him to stop, begged him to fill her. Until his own body humbled itself and did a little begging of its own.

"Jake. Ah, Jake . . ." She arched beneath him, straining against him, filling his hand, filling his heart.

She was hot and moist and tight. She was ready for him. It took the very last of Jake's self-control to lift himself above her and not plunge into her the way he wanted so badly to do. He supported his weight on the elbows flanking her sides. His hips found the spot nature had carved just for him between her legs. He cupped her cheeks in his palms while his mouth hungered for another taste of her honey-sweet lips.

Gritting his teeth, and holding himself absolutely still, Jake perched on the very threshold of her. "Mine, Amanda Lennox. You are *mine*."

"Yes," she panted. "I'm yours. Now, Jake. Now."

His control splintered. He growled, thrust, and buried himself deeply inside of her.

He wasn't going to last. The second he felt her warm and tight and hot around him, Jake knew he wasn't going to last. And he didn't care. It had been so long!

Amanda moaned low and deep, and arched to accept him. All of him. She moved in time to his beat, glorying in the violent tremors that came upon her almost instantaneously with his entry.

Fast, fast, the spasms of completion shook her and carried Jake right along in her wake.

"My woman, *my* woman," Jake murmured, the words timed to coincide with each piercing thrust and retreat. He couldn't hold back. She felt too damn good. And then she started to shudder around him, and he was thankful he didn't have to wait, because he couldn't. Not a second longer. "Mine," he gritted as he lost control, and toppled over the edge.

His climax was long and deep, and more intense than anything he'd ever felt before. This time when it came, he poured more than his hot, liquid fire into her; he filled Amanda Lennox with his heart and soul. His very life.

Jake collapsed atop her, sweaty and spent. Deep down he knew that without this woman — *his* woman — he would never be whole again.

The lamp had been extinguished.

Amanda awoke to a room flooded with pale moonlight. She scowled sleepily, her thoughts disoriented as her gaze swept her surroundings. Where was she? And who . . . ?

Junction City. She was in a rented hotel room in a mining town called Junction — wherever that was . . . Idaho, still?

And she was with Jake Chandler. Ah, yes . . . Jake.

His solid weight, not the least bit burdensome, pinned her to the narrow, lumpy mattress. His face was against her neck, and she felt the warmth of his breath puff over her in steady waves. The upper part of his body rested mostly atop the bed, to keep from crushing her, but from the stomach down he blanketed her. His left hand rested loosely atop her right breast, as though even in sleep he was seeking to brand her with his touch.

The outside of his thighs felt warm and appealingly hard where they were nestled between the inside of hers. The muscles in his back quivered beneath the fingertips she only now realized she'd been stroking down his spine. She scanned the breadth of his shoulder with her palm, then tunneled her fingers into his sleek black hair.

Amanda sighed and closed her eyes. Nothing in her life had felt as good as waking up enfolded in Jake Chandler's arms. She was sure nothing would ever feel this good again.

Jake mumbled something in his sleep, and shifted. He nuzzled her neck, while at the same time the part of him that was still buried inside of her quickened.

Amanda tensed at the hot spark of pleasure that shot through her. Her instinctive reaction caressed him, causing him to harden still more.

She knew the exact second Jake woke up, was aware of the instant his eyes flickered open. She felt the bat of his dark lashes against her earlobe. His tongue and teeth played on the sensitive underside of her jaw. The fingers caressing her breasts flexed, then curled possessively inward. His thumbnail flicked her nipple, and she marveled at how, with just one pass, the rosy bead pearled. For him. Only for him did her body react this way. Only for him did her senses spin out of control with one glance, one touch.

She fisted his long, silky hair and guided his head down to where she wanted — needed — to feel the heat of his mouth. Her body was hungry for the feel of him. Like the last time, her need was building, quick and urgent. She wanted to feel his hands on her. His mouth. She wanted him to fill her, wanted him to make her soar again. Now. Before it was too late.

They would reach Pony soon. He hadn't said it, but she knew. In a few days they would find Roger. In a few days Jake would be out of her life. He'd said he wanted to be rid of her, and that time was coming quickly. Soon, the only time she would see his face, feel his body, would be in dreams and in her preciously preserved memories.

It was those memories Amanda intended to carve for herself tonight. With Jake. She wanted something wild, something delicious. She needed for him to give her a memory that would burn inside her heart, something that would help ease her through the lifetime of cold, lonely nights ahead.

Arching her back, she invited him to taste her. She groaned when he suckled her nipple into the warm, moist heat of his mouth. His teeth nipped, his tongue teased and tormented. She shivered and cried out. She wasn't sure, but she thought she felt a reciprocal tremor shudder through him.

Again and again . . .

"I have to," he murmured against her. His hot breath blasted over her even hotter flesh, making her tingle and tremble in turn. "I have to have you again, princess. Now. I . . . ah, God, just one more time."

Jake buried his face in her neck, inhaling deeply of her sweet, sweet scent as his body moved inside her.

She wrapped her legs around his hips, and he matched his beat to the rhythm her body set. Home, Jake thought. The way her body gloved his, warm and moist and welcoming, felt like home.

With the first taking, desperation had ridden him hard. It had been so long since he'd had her that he couldn't have gone slow if he'd wanted to. This time, he promised himself . . . this time will be different. They had all night. This time he would take her slow and easy. He'd set the spark inside of her, then make it burn until she was begging him to douse the flames. He would . . .

It took less than five minutes for all of Jake's promises and good intentions to go straight out the window. He was wrong. Nothing was different this time. She felt just as good. No, she felt *better.*

It shouldn't be like this. He shouldn't want her again; not so quickly, not so badly. But he did. The hard edge of desire may have been smoothed over with one taking, but in seconds the ache inside of him began building anew. The warm, tight heat of her milked his need, honed his desperation to a sharp edge. With every thrust, every acceptance, his hunger for her intensified, until his need for Amanda—and *only* Amanda—felt like it was slicing right into the very core of his soul and cutting him to pieces.

Their lovemaking was fast and hard and urgent. Ragged breath mingled. Racing hearts clattered in time to each other. Tongues mated and warred. Hands roved, the strokes quick and hot and demanding.

Their loving was bittersweet, edged with desperation. With hands and mouths each strove to commit the other's body to memory, desperate to touch and be touched—everywhere, quickly—while there was still time.

In minutes they drove each other over the brink. When the climax came, it was welcomed, celebrated. Fulfillment crashed over them like a tidal wave, dragging them under as one, deeper and deeper into the violent, shuddering undertow.

Their mouths fused together, even as their bodies strained in the last tremors of release. The kiss was long and desperate and deep, their lips sealing the words a dizzying sea of passion would have wrung from their hearts.

"My woman," Jake murmured. Though his passion was momentarily spent, he felt no urge to ease the intimacy of their embrace. It felt comfortable to be a part of her like this. It felt good and right and perfect. For the first time in his life, Jacob Blackhawk Chandler felt contented and complete.

"My woman," he whispered into her soft, flowery-smelling hair. His eyes flickered shut, and he unconsciously timed his breathing to match Amanda's.

Chapter Nineteen

A floorboard creaked as Jake moved from one side of the hotel room to the other. The noise was unaccountably loud and grating. He froze, his attention snapping to the woman huddled beneath the faded blankets. Had he woken her? Jesus, he hoped not.

Amanda was lying on her side, facing away from him. Her shoulders gently rose and fell, her shallow breaths whispered in his ears. At this angle he could see her profile. The whiteness of her skin was enhanced by the early morning light filtering in through the window. Her hair was unbound, scattering over the pillow and sheet. Each thick gold curl glistened like shimmering silk in the muted sunlight. She sighed. Her honey-tipped lashes fluttered a split second before she turned onto her back.

Jake stiffened, his gaze narrowed. A long, tense minute ticked past. Another. A third.

Amanda's eyes remained closed, her face sleep-softened and relaxed, her breathing light and even. As he watched, a smile tugged at her lips. He felt his gut twist, his curiosity perk. Was she dreaming about him? And . . . dammit, did he really want to know if she wasn't? God, no!

She was still asleep, and right now that was all Jake wanted to know. All he *needed* to know. There'd be hell to pay if she woke up now and caught him sneaking out like a thief in the night. To say she would be angry would be an understatement.

If she caught him leaving, Amanda would undoubtedly be furious. She would demand an explanation and, not that Jake wouldn't have given her one—he would have—but he didn't have time to waste pacifying her. Not now. Not until after he'd found Roger Thornton Bannister III.

It was time the kid was found and returned to his father. No, it was *past* time.

The vow Jake had made upon awakening held firm. From here on out, he was following those tracks alone. Whether Amanda liked it or not, he was leaving her behind. For her own good. There was the extra set of prints now, along with the direction they were heading. No, as far as he was concerned, the situation was getting too damn dangerous, and he simply wasn't willing to risk her life anymore. Common sense said that anyone desperate enough to kidnap a kid was capable of anything. Survival instinct made a cornered rat bite . . . and a cornered *man* shoot.

Jake planned on cornering Roger's kidnapper—he'd do whatever it took to get the kid back and uphold his promise to Amanda—but there was no way he was going to let her get caught in the cross fire. No goddamn way!

His gaze scanned Amanda one last time. Then he sighed and hoisted the heavy saddlebag higher on his shoulder. The contents rattled as the worn leather bag slapped against his back. Careful to avoid any creaking floorboards, he crept to the door and quietly let himself out of the room.

Dawn was breaking over the mountainous, snow-capped horizon when, ten minutes later, Jake stepped onto the slatted boardwalk outside the hotel. He barely glanced at the pink-and-purple-streaked sky as he swaggered toward the stables.

His thoughts refused to leave a certain second floor hotel room. He couldn't stop thinking about the

338

lady—the *white* lady—he'd left behind.

He told himself the separation would be short. This time. With any luck, the outcome of what he was about to do would be successful. What he couldn't understand was why, if that was true, he felt an unfamiliar squeeze in the region of his chest—an inexplicable, painful sensation that seemed to increase with each step that carried him away from Amanda Lennox.

Jake didn't analyze the feelings pumping through him—he pushed them aside and buried them. He concentrated on the sound of his denim pants legs brushing together, on the jostle of wagons or the muted voices in doorways. He concentrated on anything to take his mind off wondering why leaving Amanda hurt so badly.

The answer was there—simmering inside of him, just beneath the surface—but it was an emotion he wasn't ready to feel, let alone acknowledge. Not now. Not for a white lady. Not ever . . . if he was smart. That was half the problem. Because Jake had been questioning his intelligence ever since he'd taken his first step into that icy river days ago. Since he didn't like the answers he was coming up with, he wondered instead what Amanda's reaction would be when she woke up and found him gone.

"Gone? What do you mean he's gone?"

"Jesus, lady, don't you understand English?" The rotund, middle-aged clerk who was standing behind the desk didn't glance up from the three-week-old newspaper he was reading as he spoke. The limp paper rattled as he turned the page and, in an annoyed tone of voice, added, "Last time I'm going to say it. Your—er—*friend's* gone. Checked out. *Left-the-hotel.*"

A shiver of alarm coursed down Amanda's spine. As always happened when she was upset, her tone lifted and took on a haughty pitch. "Obviously, there's been some mistake. Jake wouldn't leave without telling me. He—well, he just wouldn't."

One corner of the newspaper sagged. A dark, bushy brow slanted high in the clerk's forehead as his gaze raked her from head to toe. The grin that curled over his lips was condescending and cold. "I hate to be the one to point this out to you, honey, but obviously he did."

"When?"

"How the hell should I know?" The clerk sighed heavily, snapped the paper closed, and slammed it down on the scarred oak desk with his fist. "Early, would be my guess. He was gone by the time I got here, so it would have to have been before eight."

Her eyes widened. Before eight? But that was *three hours ago!* Jake could be miles away by now, heading in who knew what direction. While she might not be trail-smart, Amanda wasn't stupid. She knew the chance of her catching up with Jake were questionable at best—and her chances of finding him decreased with every minute he was gone . . . and she remained in Junction.

If she'd been alarmed before, it was nothing compared to how she felt now. Gripping her saddlebag in trembling fists, she glared at the middle-aged man. No, more correctly she glared at a three-week-old headline, for he'd picked up his paper again and was ignoring her.

Amanda gritted her teeth and cleared her throat. When the man didn't so much as glance at her, she stepped to the side and glared at him. He didn't even blink, the scum. Finally, she said in her loudest, most intimidating voice, *"Excuse me . . . !"*

His lips puckered with annoyance, but he continued to read.

Left with no alternative, Amanda snatched the newspaper from his hands. *That* got his attention! Too much of it, if his quivering jowls, angrily slitted brown eyes, and tightly clenched fists were anything to judge by. She tipped her chin high, and smiled a contemptuous smile that would have made Miss Henry beam. "I don't suppose you could tell me where *Mr. Chandler* went?"

The clerk was unimpressed. "I don't suppose you're going to give me my goddamn paper back?"

He reached for the paper, but Amanda held it out of reach. His growl of annoyance was almost feral. She tried not to cringe. "I'd be happy to . . . *after* you tell me where Mr. Chandler went."

The clerk planted his huge fists on the scarred oak desk and leaned toward her. His expression was hard and threatening. Amanda's resolve weakened, and she took an instinctive step back. His grin made her blood turn to ice.

"I don't know where he went, lady," the clerk said slowly and precisely. His meaty jowls shook with each tightly uttered word. "Nor do I give a rat's a—er . . . nor do I *care*. What I *do* care about is reading my paper. You've got five seconds to give that newspaper back to me. If you don't, then I'm coming around this desk after it."

He wouldn't dare. Would he? Lord, Amanda hoped not. And was it her imagination, or were the man's voluminous cheeks redder than normal? His eyes narrower and brighter? Yes, yes they were. Uh-oh.

Amanda swallowed hard and hugged both her saddlebag and the clerk's newspaper to her chest. Her innate cowardice was telling her belatedly that perhaps pushing this man wasn't in her best interest after all. Of course, the paper she crunched in her quivering fists said it was too late for second thoughts now. Not that she could afford to entertain any. She had to know where Jake went. She *had* to! And this obnoxious clerk was the only person who could tell her. Or so she hoped.

"Three . . . two . . ." He pushed away from the desk. "Better move quick, honey."

"Please, Mister . . ." Amanda hesitated. The man hadn't told her his name and, judging by his hard, tight expression, he wasn't going to. She quickly changed tactics. "It will only take you a minute to tell me where—"

"One. Times up." He moved around the desk. For a big man, she thought his gait unusually agile. His boot-heels made loud thumps atop the plank floor, like reports of gunfire echoing through the small foyer, echoing through Amanda.

He rounded the corner and stalked toward her. She smelled him—the sour, chickeny odor of days-old sweat—long before he drew close. Her gaze dropped to the meaty fists he clenched at his side. Unless she'd horribly misjudged the man, he was at that moment giving strangling her serious consideration.

Amanda's throat constricted. The paper crinkled as she clutched it tighter still. "If *you* don't know where Mr. Chandler went, then perhaps you know of someone else who does?"

"Give me back my newspaper, lady."

"I told you, *after* you—"

"What? Strangle you? Yeah, keep pushing me and I might do exactly that. The paper . . ." He was six steps away. Five.

The saddlebag tumbled from Amanda's suddenly slack fingers. It fell to the floor at her feet with a heavy thump. Any courage she may have felt evaporated like steam when she saw this large, burly man stalking toward her. In her life, she'd never seen a sight so menacing. The hand not clutching the paper lost all its strength, and dropped limply to her side.

And that was when she felt it.

Her heart stuttered, her breath caught. Six months ago, she wouldn't have believed herself capable of contemplating what she was about to do next. She was contemplating it now, though, and contemplating it hard. She was also shaking like a leaf. But that was something she would have to get over in order to find

Jake. And she *had* to find him. Surely this man could tell her where he'd gone, or tell her someone who could—or, at the very least, give her a hint as to what direction Jake had set out in! She was sure he could. That knowledge pumped through her, bolstering her courage. Not much, but a bit.

He was four steps away her now. Three. In a fraction of a second, he would be almost on top of her.

There was no more time to think. As it was, Amanda barely had time to react. Tossing the crumpled newspaper to the floor, she slipped her hand inside the pocket of her skirt. Her fingers wrapped around the butt of the pistol. Her arms felt liquidy as she aimed it—accurately, she hoped—at the man's barrel chest.

The clerk froze. His eyes narrowed until the angry brown depths were barely visible in the meaty folds of his face. Of course, there was no need for Amanda to *see* his eyes to know where his gaze was resting: on the pistol. She could *feel* his attention perk, *feel* the fury rolling off of him in tangible waves.

Though the gun trembled in her hand, her aim never wavered. She was glad the clerk's chest was so big; it gave her more of a target. At this distance, she would have to work to *miss* him. He must have been aware of that fact as well, for he didn't move an inch.

His gaze shifted past her, scanning the small foyer. Though noises sifted out from a room off to the right, the foyer itself was empty. No help would be forthcoming unless he hollered for it, and he didn't want to do that. It would be embarrassing to be caught on the business end of a pistol as it was; it would be downright humiliating to have anyone see that the pistol in question was being held in the hands of a *woman!*

His hands came up, meaty palms out. "Listen, lady, I don't want trouble. Put that thing away."

"After you tell me where Mr. Chandler went."

His tongue darted out to moisten his fleshy lips. "I already told you. I-don't-know."

"And *I'm* telling *you*, I-don't-believe-you." It was true. Amanda hadn't believed him from the first; she believed him even less when she saw the way his cheeks took on a splotchy red hue. He was lying, she was positive of it. Goddamn him! He knew which direction Jake had headed out in. He *knew!* Yet he wasn't telling her. Well, she'd just see about that! A surge of anger tingled through her. It felt nice and warm and soothing as it overrode her fear and fueled her determination.

"Which way did he go?" she asked, surprising even herself at the calm, demanding tone that echoed in her ears. Her voice was low. It didn't shake, didn't waver. It was amazing what a little desperation did to a body. "You saw him leave. I know you did. All I want to know is what direction he was heading in."

The man's hands dropped to his sides, his palms slapping his thick hips as he shrugged. "Why do you care? Christ, lady, the guy's a *breed*. A nice white woman like you shouldn't care—"

Amanda stared at the man, stunned. Good God, she thought, how did Jake put up with this everyday of his life? What gave complete strangers the right to judge him on sight and deem him lacking? It was annoying, frustrating, infuriating. It was so damn *unfair!* The anger pumping through her was reflected in her tone. "You bastard! That . . . *breed*, as you call him, is more man than you'll ever be. And *I* care where he went—enough so that I'll do whatever it takes to find out what direction he rode out in." The click of the hammer being jerked back was loud and ominous.

The lump in the man's throat, almost concealed beneath the layers of sagging flesh that spilled over his collar, rose and fell in a dry swallow. He glanced at the dining room, frowned, then returned his attention to the woman. "I . . . well, yeah, I . . . tell me something, honey. Do you—er—know how to use that thing?" He nodded to the pistol.

Amanda's smile was cold and forced. The gesture didn't reach her eyes, which remained frosty and determined. "No. But I'm a quick study. And I think you'd make a nice, big target to practice on. Don't you agree?"

"Hell, no!"

"Then tell me which way Mr. Chandler went!"

The clerk clamped his teeth together and glanced guiltily away. Grudgingly, he said, "I can't. He paid me not to."

"And I'll pay you with a bullet . . . somewhere, if you don't. It's your decision." Her pause was short and tense. "Just so you know, I doubt I'll be able to kill you with my first shot."

The man's gaze shifted back to her. His lips pursed with indecision, and his attention volleyed between her eyes and the gun—the aim of which was now steady and true. With a sly glance, he measured the distance between himself and the dining room door. The golden brow Amanda arched convinced him that she could squeeze off a shot before he had time to pick up one heavily booted foot.

Three hours, Amanda thought as she watched the fat man wrestle with his decision. Jake was already at least three hours ahead of her. And counting. If this man didn't answer her soon she just might be tempted to put a bullet in him out of spite!

The clerk must have sensed her thoughts, for his expression became guarded. Plowing his fingers through his thinning black hair, he shook his head and muttered, "East. That breed of yours rode out heading East, just after dawn." His eyes shimmered a warning not missed by Amanda. "Now put that gun away and get the hell out of this hotel. *Before* I yell for help. I'll warn you, lady, the guys in Junction don't look kindly on white women who take up with breeds. They won't go as easy on you as I have."

Amanda thought of the two slimy men from last night. She shivered and, nodding, bent to retrieve her saddlebag. The gun stayed in her hand. She didn't uncock it. If Jake had taught her nothing else, he'd taught to be prepared for anything. He had also taught her not to trust anyone but herself; his leaving this morning without a word had driven home that lesson.

Her eye on the clerk, Amanda backed toward the door. The barrel of the pistol stayed trained on the him, though she was careful to conceal it against her side as she passed the door leading into the dining room.

It was awkward balancing the saddlebag and holding the gun while she turned the cold metal doorknob, but she managed it. A blast of cold air wafted over her back, stirring the wispy hair that clung to her neck and cheeks. The clerk, she noticed, hadn't budged an inch, but continued to watch her with a brooding glare.

"East," she said, as much to herself as to him. "Toward Montana?"

He scowled, and looked at her oddly. "Lady, you're *in* Montana. Have been for at least a week if you're on horseback."

"Oh," she murmured, backing over the threshold. "Of course. I knew that. How-er-how far away is Pony? And how do I get there from here?"

He shrugged tightly and in clipped, obviously reluctant words, said, "A day's ride. Two if it snows, which it will. As for getting there, just keep riding East through the valley. In seven or eight hours you'll reach a few small mountains. After that, another valley. Pony's about half a day's ride from where the land gets relatively flat."

Amanda nodded and, mumbling her thanks, slipped out the door. As soon as it had clicked into place, she uncocked the pistol and slipped it into her pocket. Her fingers, she noticed as she hurried toward the stable, had begun shaking again. So had the rest of her. Her heart was slamming against her ribs, and the cold morning air sliced into her lungs with each ragged breath she drew.

She hadn't been nervous while holding the gun on the fat clerk—she'd done what she had to do at the time. Only now that it was over did the shock set in. Had she *really* just held a gun on a man? Yes, incredible as it sounded she had, and twice in less than twenty-four hours! Astonishment—and, yes, a smattering of pride—rushed in to replace her newfound courage.

A month ago she wouldn't have had the nerve to do what she'd done last night and today. Thank God she did now, because a month ago she wouldn't have been able to find out where Jake was heading. A month ago she would have taken the clerk at his word, and would probably have ended up picking her way to Washington with her tail between her legs, feeling lost and defeated.

Amanda wasn't feeling defeated right now. What she was feeling was angry as holy hell. The focus of her fury was aimed at Jake Chandler's sleek black head.

He'd run out on her, the rat! After promising to help her find Roger, he'd run out on her! Oh, how that hurt!

She thought it was a good thing he was heading East. That made it easier, since she was heading East, too. If she had to do it herself, she was going to find Roger Thornton Bannister III and return him to his father. And after she'd collected her hard-earned money . . .

Then she was going to find Jake.

She didn't know how, but somehow she would do it. If it was the last thing she did, she'd see to it that the rotten bastard paid and paid *dearly* for abandoning her the way everyone else in her life had. He may not have died like her mother had, or pushed her away like her father had, but he *had* run out on her. And that made the hurt and disillusionment worse. It made the pain of waking up and finding him gone — no note, no nothing — unbearable.

Oh, yes. He was going to pay for that. Amanda swore it.

"Valley, mountains, valley. Half a day's ride," she mumbled over and over under her breath as she wove her way past the people milling on the boardwalk. The directions sounded identical to the ones she'd gotten in Virginia City . . . shortly before she and Roger had set out and become hopelessly lost!

Chapter Twenty

The snow started falling just after noon. Large flakes danced from the sky, light and airy. Out of the mountains, the ground was warm, so the accumulation wasn't much. Yet.

Despite the weather, Jake made good time. The men he was following did not. He'd picked up their tracks an hour out of Junction. Since one of the horses had a nicked hoof, the prints weren't difficult to identify.

He rode hard, gaining ground. Dusk was painting the cloudy sky when he drew the white to a halt and slipped to the ground. After carefully inspecting the ground as well as leavings from the kidnapper's horse he decided he was only half an hour behind. Good. He'd made better time than he'd hoped.

He didn't set up camp. A fire could be spotted, and cooking food was easily smelled. A mistake like that would alert the kidnapper to his presence, and he didn't want to take that chance. Not when he was so damn close. If all went as planned, the kidnapper wouldn't know he presented a threat until it was too late to do anything about it.

He let the white drink from a nearby creek, then rubbed it down and tethered it to a pine. He settled himself down on the cold, damp ground and rested his back against the tree trunk. An unlit cigarette dangled from the corner of his mouth.

His eyes narrowed and he gazed unseeingly at the

flurries being tossed about on the cool, evening breeze. Every muscle in his body felt itchy and tight, impatient to get this game over with. But he couldn't. Not yet. He had to force himself to give the kidnapper time to think he'd made his camp undetected—and that would take a few hours. Damn!

Jake shifted atop the hard, lumpy ground. He hated waiting. Always had. It gave a body too much time to think about things best forgotten.

His thoughts automatically shifted to a certain prissy Bostonian. He closed his eyes and saw her hair flowing like a curtain of raw gold silk down her back, over her bottom, the ends curling inward at the very top of her thighs. He heard her voice whisper on the breeze, the tone so soft and sweet.

Sucking in a sharp breath, Jake struck a match on the seam of his pants. Squinting, he cupped the flame, holding it to the tip of the cigarette. The burn of smoke in his lungs felt good, familiar, but it didn't come close to taking his mind off Amanda Lennox. Hell, no. A keg of dynamite could have exploded right next to him and it *still* wouldn't have dislodged the memory of her smooth white skin skimming beneath his open palm. He remembered her airy sighs of surrender, and he remembered how . . . ah, God, he remembered how good it felt when she wrapped her legs around his hips, arched up into him, meeting him thrust for hungry thrust.

From the first, there had been nothing proper about their relationship, nothing refined about their lovemaking. Nor was there anything ladylike in her response to either. Her passion, once freed, had been wild and untamed and demanding. For the first time in his life the desire he'd kindled inside a woman had *exceeded* that pumping inside himself. It was the last thing he'd expected from a prissy white woman—white *lady*. But then, Amanda was nothing if not filled to the voluptuous brim with contrasts.

Jake had always prided himself on being able to peg

a woman on sight, but not Amanda Lennox. In fact, his first impression of her had been haughty and frigid. The type of woman who would make love only reluctantly — probably with all her clothes on — in a pitch black room — at *night* — and still not enjoy it.

Proving himself wrong had been both a delight and a curse. The contrast between how she behaved in his arms and how she behaved *out* of them intrigued him more than he cared to admit. Her uninhibited love-making had accomplished the exact opposite of what he'd hoped it would.

Instead of satisfying his thirst for her, each time he had her served to whet it. When she touched him, he forgot for a time who she was — who *he* was — *why* they couldn't be together. Remembering how it felt when her warm breath puffed over his skin made him want her more than he thought it possible to want a woman. *Any* woman. That was so damn dangerous for both of them.

Again and again. That was what he wanted from her. Again and again . . . for a good long time. That was enough reason for him to want to run from her. Far and fast. Soon. Before he lost all sense of himself. Before she became a part of him that he couldn't live without.

Jake's gut twisted, and a strange tightness wrapped around his chest. He had a feeling it was too late to run from his feelings for her, but he *could* run from acknowledging them. The two white men he'd caught outside Amanda's door last night were still vivid in his mind. The incident had proved what he'd known all along. As long as she was with him, what happened last night would happen again. And again. Next time someone might get hurt. Next time, that someone might be Amanda.

Any white woman who took up with a breed was considered trash, fair game for ridicule and worse. Jake would rather die than let Amanda find that out the hard way. He would rather die than let her get hurt because of him, because he was too weak to put a stop to something that should have been stopped before it had even begun.

He took a deep drag off the cigarette, exhaling with a long, slow hiss. His gaze turned hard as he watched the curls of smoke waft on the air. They'd been apart less than a day, and already he missed her. His body hungered for her body, yet his mind demanded so much more! Jesus, if he felt like hell now, he could only imagine how he would feel when the separation was permanent.

With an angry growl, he hurled the half-smoked cigarette into the snow-dusted grass. The tip continued to burn hot and red; just like his thoughts.

Somehow . . . *somehow,* he was going to have to find the strength to walk away from that lady. No matter how much it tore him up inside.

The white gave a toss of its head and whickered. The sound trickled like icewater down Jake's spine. Cursing inwardly for allowing himself to be distracted—for allowing thoughts of *Amanda Lennox* to distract him—he reached for his knife.

A split second too late.

A damp twig snapped. Leaves rustled. No sooner had his fingers grazed the wooden hilt when he felt the cold metal barrel of a gun jab at his temple.

"Go ahead, breed. Try it," a gritty voice drawled in Jake's ear. The tone was low and menacing and rough as stone.

Gritting his teeth, Jake sucked in a deep, steadying breath and almost gagged on the stench of sour breath and rancid sweat that assaulted him. A quick glance from the corner of his eye revealed a large, shadowy form crouched close . . . but not close enough. The glance also confirmed what he had, until now, only suspected: the hand holding the gun was big and causally skilled; the thick index finger curled around the trigger was rock-steady, ready to fire at the least provocation.

The gun nudged Jake's temple. "Well? You gonna pull that knife or what? I don't know about you, but when it's a choice between a bullet or a blade, my money's on the bullet any day. Quicker, more accurate . . . and messy as hell. Especially at this range." A dry, humorless chuckle was followed by an equally dry, equally humorless, "But, hell, I'm game. Always did have a hankerin' to see if your kind bleeds red. Come on, pull that mean lookin' knife and satisfy this ole boy's curiosity."

The words were uttered with cold, hard precision . . . and reinforced by the click of a hammer being cocked. The metallic grind of chambers rolling to place sounded loud and grating. That, combined with the raw yet blasé timbre of the man's voice, convinced Jake to stay his hand. Temporarily.

Flexing his fingers, he cautiously moved his hand out of reach of the knife. Resting his open palm atop his thigh, and thinking of how very glad he was that he'd left Amanda behind, Jake drawled, "Your call, *ole boy*. The knife stays where it is. The question now is, is your bullet going to do the same?"

"Shit. I figured you'd say that, but can't blame a guy for trying, can you?" The man sighed heavily. Jake heard the damp leaves shuffle, and knew the man had shifted his weight. "Tell you what, breed. I'm sportin'. What say I give you one last chance to pull that knife?"

"Nope."

"No?"

"No."

"Well, guess that settles it then."

Jake tensed, readying himself for when the gun wavered. It was a short wait. The second he felt it shift, he pounced.

The intruder had been expecting such a move and his big body reacted faster than Jake had hoped. The man dodged to the side. Jake lunged in pursuit, his aim not completely off. He felt the fatty waist give, and heard a nice, satisfying grunt of surprise.

Unfortunately, the intruder's surprise burned off quickly. Too damn quickly, Jake thought, as he watched the big man pivot and start to fall backward. Jake didn't see the trunklike arm lift, didn't see the gun spin expertly in his hand so the meaty fingers were gripping the barrel instead of the butt . . . until it was too late.

Hand and gun arched down with lightning speed. Jake lifted his arms to deflect the blow, but he wasn't quick enough.

He heard the thump of metal hitting bone a split-second before thunder exploded in the base of his skull. A wave of white pain radiated outward from that core, spreading through his head and slicing down his spine. The earth swam dizzily. Darkness edged his vision, but he blinked it away, fighting desperately to retain consciousness.

A groan—his?—rumbled in his ears. The strength drained from his arms and legs. His eyes rolled back; he seemed to have no control over it. The pounding in his head faded as he felt himself crumple onto the snow-dampened ground.

Everything went black.

"A lady is quietly, elegantly resourceful," Amanda muttered as, for the third time in as many minutes, she leaned to the side and studied the snow-dusted ground from her place in the saddle. She wasn't sure what she was looking for, but she was positive that, whatever it was, she'd know it when she saw it. Of course, there was always the chance that she was wrong.

An icy breeze snuck beneath her hood. Shivering, Amanda pulled the cloak about her and nudged the mare on in what she hoped was still an eastward course. Of course, there was no way to be sure of that, since thick clouds blotted out the sun. She refused to consider the possibility that she'd set out from Junction

354

three hours ago . . . heading in the wrong direction.

Then again, she couldn't not consider it, could she? What if she had? What if she was traveling *away* from Roger instead of *toward* him? What if . . .

"A lady never curses aloud, no matter what the provocation." She thought of Jake's seemingly constant, always imaginative swears. Then she thought of the way he'd left her. Her voice lowered, her jaw tightened. "No matter how badly she might wish to curse a blue streak, she *does not* do it."

The thin layer of snow covering the ground made the land wet and slippery. The jostling of the horse aggravated her aching body. The rhythmic clump of hooves, crunching through the snow, was the only sound to reach her ears.

The sounds going on *inside* her head were something else again. Her thoughts were loud and chaotic, much like the rumble of a brewing thunderstorm. Though it may waver, the focus of her concentration returned again and again to the arrogant half-breed who'd had the gall to desert her when she needed him most.

"A lady never, never, *never* strikes a gentleman." Amanda's lips twitched with a humorless smile. Since Jake had proved—no, *admitted*—to being no gentleman, that particular rule did not apply. Surely under the circumstance even Miss Henry would understand a temporary slip from grace . . .

Because the next time she set eyes on Jake Chandler's hard copper jaw, Amanda intended to slap him hard enough to make her palm sting, and his head reel. With each snowy mile that passed by her, her anger and sense of betrayal grew. Repeated instructions as to the benefits of turning the other cheek faded, overridden by the sharp sting of fury. In this instance only, Amanda was willing to overlook her lessons. Because if ever a man deserved a good hard slap, that man was Jake Chandler. And she fully intended— *needed*—to see that he got it.

But first she would have to find him.

355

And before she could do that, there was the problem of finding Roger Thornton Bannister III.

Her breath misted the air when she sighed and again glanced down and to the left. So sure had she been that she would see nothing out of the ordinary down there, that she almost missed seeing the faint hoof-prints embedded in the newly fallen snow.

With a jerk of surprise, she reined the mare in. The horse tossed its head and snorted, protesting the pressure to its sensitive mouth. Mumbling a quick apology, Amanda dismounted.

Heart racing, she crouched and ran her fingertips lightly over one of the indentations in the snow. Her smile was wide and proud. "Well, I'll be damned." She gulped, but continued to smile broadly. "Ooops."

While Jake hadn't taught her much during their time together, by constantly watching him, she'd inadvertently learned enough to get by. Many nights of watching him taught her how to light a campfire without matches, and watching the way Jake constantly glanced at the sky had taught her a bit about how to use the sun as a gauge for direction. And, by glancing at the ground whenever he did, she'd learned how to recognize clear hoof-prints when she saw them.

While not exactly clear, these were definitely hoof-prints!

Amanda frowned. Yes, they were hoof-prints, all right. No doubt about it. But *whose?* There was no way to tell. Jake might know how to differentiate between one horse's tracks and another's; Amanda had yet to learn that. Nor was she sure how one went about deciding how old the prints were. Unless . . .

She lifted her head and stared thoughtfully at the breeze-tossed snowflakes dancing from the sky. One golden brow slanted as she again glanced down at the ground. She smiled. Could it truly be that simple?

What wouldn't be as simple was following the prints through before they were obliterated by either the snow or the breeze. While it was still only flurrying, the flakes were starting to accumulate. The breeze occasionally gusted into a bitter cold wind. If she didn't hurry, she would lose all sight of the tracks. And once lost, she knew she would never be lucky enough to pick them up again!

A heartbeat later she was back in the saddle. In two, she was moving. Unless she missed her guess—and a guess was really all it was—the kidnapper was still hours ahead of her. Only if her luck held would she find him by nightfall.

With a bit *more* luck, by this time tomorrow she would have Roger Thornton Bannister III back. Amanda thought it a sorry state of events to think the prospect of having to endure that little monster's company again actually excited her.

"Christ, Henry, I swear there are times you're so stupid I start wondering if I'm really related to you." Tom Rafferty glared at his brother. He had to leash in his anger when all Henry did was grin, shrug, and continue securing the rope that held his "prize" to a thick tree trunk. "You listening, Henry? *Henry!*"

The big man glanced up, his brown eyes as narrow and vague as his expression. His thick fingers continued tying complicated knots at the breed's wrist as he drawled, "I heard you fine, Tom. I'm just ignoring you."

"Then you're a fool. What the hell were you thinking to bring him back here? We got enough trouble, yet you gotta bring us *more?*"

"Nope. I wasn't thinking that." Henry rocked back on his heels and shrugged. "I was thinking I'd rather he'd pulled his knife on me, and I was wondering why he didn't. *That's* what I was thinking. Why?"

Tom grunted and dragged his narrow palm down his stubbled jaw. He shook his head, eyeing his brother sadly. "It was a rhetorical question, Henry. Don't you know anything? You don't have to answer a rhetorical question."

357

"Huh?"

"Never mind." Tom jerked his chin at the unconscious man now bound to the tree. "What are you going to do with him?"

"Haven't decided. But don't worry, I'll think of something fun."

"That's what I was afraid of," Tom grumbled. His brown eyes narrowed, and his gaze shifted to the boy who slept soundly, huddled beneath a dirty, threadbare blanket. As far as he was concerned, putting up with the brat day in and day out was about all the "fun" he could handle.

Only the top of the kid's head was exposed, and that was dusted with snow. Beneath the melting flakes, the once shiny blond curls were dark and matted and badly in need of washing. Tom didn't need to look beneath the blanket to know the rest of the kid could use a good scrub, too. There was no help for it. They couldn't let the brat bathe by himself because he might try to escape, and neither Rafferty was willing to do the chore himself. It would be too big a temptation to keep the kid's head under water, if only to shut his arrogant little mouth for a bit. It went without saying that they wouldn't get a plugged nickel for toting a dead body into Pony, tempting though the idea was.

Tom turned his attention back to their second captive. As if they didn't have enough problems, Henry up and brought this breed back to camp with him. God only knows why! And what, Tom wondered, were they supposed to do with the guy now?

Well, there really wasn't much of a choice. They'd have to kill him. If they let the breed go, they'd risk him being able to describe them. Not that anyone was likely to believe a breed, of course, but there was a chance someone might. That was too big a risk to take, especially when they were so damn close to Pony, so damn close to ransoming the brat and getting their money.

Nothing was going to stand in the way of that!

There was only one problem as far as Tom Rafferty could see. Even unconscious and hog-tied to a tree, that breed looked wild and savage and vengeful. Relentless. And that knife Henry had showed him before looked downright dangerous.

Tom fingered the lock of long, scraggly brown hair resting against his shoulder. If given half a chance, that breed would lift their scalps without a second's pause. He shivered, and his hand dropped limply to his side. "Tonight," he told Henry, who was skinning the rabbits he'd caught for supper, and doing it with his normal, unnatural glee. "If you don't take care of that breed tonight, Henry, I will."

Henry didn't glance up. "No rush, Tom. We're still two days ride from Pony. Think of all the fun we could have in two days."

"And *you* think about all the teeth I'm going to knock down your throat if you don't do what you're told. Tonight, Henry. I mean it.

Henry pouted. Eventually, grudgingly, he nodded. "All right, all right. But it won't be as good, I tell you. Won't be *near* as good."

"Maybe. Then again, it'll be worse if he gets loose. He saw you, Henry, and as soon as he wakes up, he's going to see me. He can describe us, for Christ's sake!"

"So what? Who's he going to tell, Tom? And even if he did, who'd believe a breed anyway?"

"Maybe nobody. But it's a chance I won't take." Again, Tom fingered the greasy hair that fringed his shoulder. Again, he suppressed a shudder—but just barely. "Not only that, but . . . shit, Henry, the guy's a *breed*. He'd track us to hell and back."

Henry scowled. "You think he can track that good? I don't. We've been covering our prints all along, and no one's found us yet."

"Yet," Tom agreed. "Then again, who's looking?" Henry opened his mouth to answer, but Tom overrode him. "She don't count. That prissy little thing would get lost following her *own* trail. In fact, I figure she got lost right off, and probably gave up days ago. Trust me, Henry, this fella wouldn't give up so easy, and if he wanted to find us, he would. I don't know how I know it, I just do. Hunting and scalping and tracking are in their blood. Injun's are born with it, like copper skin and savage tempers. Like you said, we're two days out of Pony. We *don't* want to screw things up now."

"All right, all right. I said I'd do it tonight, Tom," Henry said, and turned his attention back to the rabbits he was skinning with the knife he'd taken off the breed. It was a nice, big knife; it felt real good in his big, capable hand. He turned it this way and that, admiring the way the carved hilt warmed to his palm, the way the muted sunlight glinted off the long, thick, razor-sharp blade.

Mesmerized, he wondered if it would cut through copper skin as easily as it cut through the rabbit's hide. Well, he'd know soon enough. Tom said it had to be done tonight, and Henry was starting to think that maybe that wasn't such a bad idea after all. He was curious to see if a breed's blood was red. He'd heard it was so, but he was curious. He wanted to see for himself. Tonight, he would.

Lord, was this exciting! This was *fun*.

Chapter Twenty-one

"I said *tonight*, Henry. Christ, the way you're going at it, it'll take a *week* for you to kill that breed off."

"Will not. And I won't rush. Pa always said if a man's to do a job, he should take his time and do it right. I aim to do this Injun up right."

"Yeah, but . . ."

The voices faded in Amanda's ears, overridden by the loud, erratic slamming of her heart. Her breath sawed in and out, stinging her lungs. The pistol she clutched to her chest felt cold and solid . . . and so damn useless! Her fingers were trembling too badly for her to shoot with any degree of accuracy even if she knew how to, which she didn't.

She had found them. Dear God, she'd done it! She didn't know how, didn't really care. The fact was, she'd done it. That was the good news. The bad news was, there wasn't one kidnapper, there were two. The very bad news was, they had Jake—*what was he doing here?*—and the situation didn't look promising.

Amanda stifled a hysterical hiccup in her throat when she realized her fingers weren't the only things trembling. Her *entire body* was shaking like a leaf! The quivers started on the inside—cold and gnawing in the pit of her stomach—and worked their way out with alarming speed. Each word that passed between the two men chipped at what little courage she'd been able to muster. Now, after less than ten minutes of listening, her bravado was slipping, dominated by her fear for Jake, for herself, and for Roger Thornton Bannister III, whom she'd caught only brief glimpses of so far.

Sweat beaded on her upper lip and brow. Beneath her cloak and dress she felt her linen chemise cling damply to her skin. Her blood surged through her veins like ice water. The feelings were not caused by the chilly breeze that steamed the breath in front of her face. No, no, they were caused by fright — sharp and cutting and more intense than anything she'd felt in her life.

The gritty bark of a thick Ponderosa pine bit into her back as she molded herself up hard against it. Her knees felt watery and weak, and they were threatening to buckle. Sheer force of will kept her erect. That, and knowing that if she collapsed now, there would be no one to save Jake. No one to get Roger away from those two crazy men.

Roger. The surge of guilt came out of nowhere; it hit Amanda like a fist to the jaw. The boy was now tied to a tree on the border of the clearing, where the circle of firelight barely reached. She'd spotted him accidentally, while trying to discern the safest route down the hill, a way to approach the kidnappers' camp unnoticed.

What she'd found instead was an unconscious Roger Thornton Bannister III. The child was barely recognizable; Amanda had had to look twice, closely, to be sure it was him. Even now she remembered how worn and haggard Roger had looked. His small body had looked noticeably thinner as it slumped against the tree he'd been bound to. A gag, as filthy as the child it was tied to, had been secured around his mouth.

Until that moment Amanda hadn't been overly concerned about how Roger had fared with his kidnappers. And then the firelight had touched his dirty, tear-streaked face . . . and the sight had cut her like a knife. In that split second she'd taken a quick, critical look at herself, and she was ashamed with what she'd seen. Dear God, when had she become so cold? So uncaring? When had money begun to mean so much to her?

It was a difficult thing to admit, even to herself, but the salary Edward Bannister was going to pay her was the only reason Amanda had searched for Roger with such a vengeance. Oh, yes, she'd been concerned about the boy's safety—but not *overly* concerned. She'd been more concerned with whether or not Edward Bannister would still pay her in full should she deliver a child who sported a few bruises.

Her indifference toward Roger was totally selfish. It didn't matter that the boy was a monster. It didn't matter that he'd taken pleasure in aggravating her at every turn. He was a *child*, for God's sake! Spoiled and willful and obstinate beyond reason, yes, but a child all the same. There was no excuse for her callousness. Shame was only one of the emotions warring inside of her, but it was the strongest.

Henry Rafferty's voice drifted up to her again. His tone was low, whiny, laced with the beginning of anger. His words cut into Amanda's thoughts like a knife slicing through butter.

"One more piece, Tom. Just another inch or two. Hell, he isn't really even bleeding yet."

"And how much skin do you plan to slice off him before he *really* bleeds, Henry? That's my question."

Though she was too far away to see it, Amanda could *feel* the pout tugging at Henry's lower lip. It took little effort for her to remember the way his brown eyes would go all big and mopey and pleading. In the two months Henry Rafferty had acted as her and Roger's guard—that traitorous bastard!— she'd glimpsed a like expression on Henry's face often. Months ago, that expression had frightened her. Now, the mere thought of it terrified her.

Of the two, Amanda deemed Henry the one to watch out for. Though she'd only glimpsed Tom Rafferty from a distance, it was obvious Henry surpassed his brother in size and strength. As far as intelligence went, it seemed an even split. Of course, she had only Tom's voice to go by, but sometimes that was enough. There was something in the man's timbre and word choice that hinted at a little more than surface intelligence. Henry Rafferty was another matter all together. While he was adept at hiding the internal workings of his mind behind a bland expression, the craziness was there in his eyes if one looked close. More than once in the past Amanda had seen it, and rationalized it away. She was regretting that oversight now.

Down in the clearing, a glint of firelight flashed off steel. "Jake," Amanda whispered, and felt a cold shiver course down her spine. "Oh, God."

The hatred she'd nursed since waking up to find Jake gone evaporated. He hadn't left her, at least not permanently, the way she'd feared. Instead, for his own reasons, he'd set out to find Roger alone. She knew that now, and the knowledge would have delighted Amanda were she not so afraid Henry Rafferty would kill Jake before she had the chance to apologize to him for all the horrible things she'd been thinking since that morning.

And what if Henry does *kill Jake before I can get down there? Or, worse, what if by some miracle of God I do get down there . . . and still fail to save him?*

Yes, Amanda, what then?

Her heart convulsed when she thought of facing a day — an hour, a *minute* — without Jacob Blackhawk Chandler in it. All the things she wanted to say to him but hadn't been able to — would *never* be able to — clogged in her too tight, too dry throat. If Henry killed Jake, she would never have the chance to tell him how much he meant to her, how much she loved him. Her thoughts spiralled. He had to live. He *had* to! She refused to even *think* of the possibility that he wouldn't. It hurt too badly.

Where all else had failed, *that* thought inspired a genuine drop of bravery to trickle through her veins. Amanda fed on it, drew strength from its bolstering warmth. Anger. The fledgling emotion surged through her. It felt good and safe and much more comforting than her original panic. She was going to need every ounce of courage she possessed in order to save Jake and Roger. This time, dammit, she was going to be brave and do what needed to be done. No matter what, she would *not* let her cowardly streak hold her back. She couldn't. Because if she did, if she faltered, Jake would die, and possibly Roger as well. The thought of money never once crossed her mind.

She peeked cautiously around the tree trunk. The Raffertys had set up camp at the bottom of a thickly wooded hill. That was both good and bad. The good part was, the trees would act as a shield, covering her presence as she worked her way down to the camp. The bad part was, the trees hid all but Jake's moccasined feet from view. Damn. Amanda would have given anything at that moment to feast her eyes on Jake. She wanted, *needed,* to see him, if only to prove to herself that he was still alive. The need was strong and hot inside her. It prompted her into action.

Jake hadn't taught her how to walk with pantherlike silence and agility. Instead, Amanda had watched him on more than one occasion and, bored on the days he'd ignored her, she'd practiced while she was alone. Her interest was paying off. By walking lightly on the balls of her feet instead of the heels, by testing the ground before trusting her weight to it, and by avoiding clumps of leaves and broken twigs, she was able to move from one shadowy tree trunk to the next in relative silence.

Although it felt like hours, it really took only two short minutes for her to reach a tree that was only three tree trunks behind Tom Rafferty's lanky back. Her heart was pounding and her breaths were shallow and strained, erratically fogging the air in front of her face. Her trembling had resumed with force. This time Amanda found the strength to fight the surge of cowardice bubbling up inside of her. She *had* to fight it. Jake's life was at stake . . . as was Roger's and her own.

Her gaze fixed on Henry Rafferty. The big man was hunkered down beside Jake's hip, facing his captor. Henry's broad back hid most of Jake from view, but that was all right, Amanda could see enough. In fact, if her churning stomach and suddenly light head were anything to go by, she saw too much.

Jake's left arm was fully extended. Rope was knotted around his left wrist, securing it to a nearby tree trunk. As she watched, Jake's fingers curled around the rope in a white-knuckled grip. She felt him tense. Or maybe she was the one who stiffened. Henry moved, and did something that his body, thankfully, blocked her from seeing. Amanda winced when she heard Jake's muffled grunt of pain.

"Well, I'll be damned."

Twigs snapped as Tom Rafferty moved closer to his brother. Hands on hips, he peered over Henry's shoulder. "What?"

"It *is* red!"

"What the hell color did you think it'd be, Henry?"

"Shit, I don't know. Black maybe. Like his Injun soul." Henry paused and glanced up at his brother. The movement gave Amanda an unobstructed view of Henry's scowl; the sight did nothing to fortify her courage. "You don't suppose it's the white in him that makes it red, do you, Tom? Do you?"

366

Tom mumbled an answer that Amanda's heart, throbbing in her ears, prohibited her from hearing. She leaned weakly against the tree trunk that concealed her and tried her best not to gag or cry; though she wanted badly to do both. They could be talking about only one thing: the color of Jake Chandler's blood. Pain sliced through her; she wondered if the emotional agony she felt was worse than the physical agony Jake must be experiencing.

They'd cut him. *Dear God in heaven, they'd cut Jake!*

Amanda drew in a shaky breath and tried to still her panic. She'd always sensed that Henry was insane. Hadn't she said as much to the lawyer in Boston? The lawyer, desperate to get rid of Roger, hadn't listened to a word, and he'd eventually convinced Amanda that her imagination was playing tricks on her. But now the proof of Henry Rafferty's derangement scared her senseless.

"Time's up, Henry. You've had your fun. Now, get the rest over with and do it quick. Best kill him while the kid's passed-out. Bannister won't pay us squat if we bring him a kid who's raving and carrying on about you skinning a breed."

"Aw, Tom—"

"Shut your damn trap and do it!"

"All right, all right." Henry's whiny, petulant tone said what his words did not—that he would rather have tortured "the breed" for a while longer yet.

Though her hands were shaking badly, and her knees felt weaker than sun-melted butter, Amanda knew that if she was going to act, she had to do it now. Taking a deep, steadying breath, she stepped from behind the tree. Slowly, she extended her arms and locked her elbows. The gun, clenched tightly in her fists, never wavered from Tom Rafferty's lanky back.

In three steps, she was close enough to feel his heat, smell his rancid odor. Another step and she was close enough to shove the barrel of the revolver between his bony shoulder blades.

Tom Rafferty tensed. Amanda grimaced as she watched the grimy fringe of hair scrape his collar as his chin came up. It took effort to keep her hands steady, but she did it. Thoughts of what would happen if she *didn't* made sure of that.

Tom started to turn toward her, but the ominous *click* the revolver made as she yanked the hammer back with her thumb convinced him not to. "I-ahem-I think you'd better hold off a bit after all, Henry," he said, his voice high and oddly nervous.

"But you just said—"

"I know what I said. *Now* I'm saying to wait." The barrel of the pistol grinding into his spine forced Tom to add, "And put the knife down, too."

"Dammit all, I—"

"Just do it, Henry!"

A foul curse and a crunch of leaves said Henry had obeyed. Thank God! Quite honestly, Amanda didn't know what she would have done if he hadn't. Luckily, she was saved having to find out. Swallowing a sigh of relief, she told herself not to get too excited. Not yet. She'd prevented Jake's immediate death, but that was *all* she'd done. The crisis was far from over.

Out of the two Rafferty brothers, she deemed Henry the most dangerous. He was bigger, stronger, more insane. Therefore, it was Henry she addressed when she said calmly, precisely, "I want you sitting down in front of a tree by the time I count to five, Henry Rafferty. No second chances. One . . ."

The additional voice shocked Henry. His spine stiffened, and his head whipped around. His eyes narrowed, squinting into the shadows behind his brother's back. His gaze fixed on Amanda, and his brown eyes shimmered first with shock, then with fury. "And what if I don't?"

In an act of confidence she didn't feel, she tilted

her chin and returned his glare. "I'll shoot your brother. Two . . ."

Henry's laughter was cold, biting. "Honey, I rode with you and that brat for almost two months. As I recall, you don't have the guts to shoot a *rabbit*, never mind a *man*."

The truth of his words hit Amanda like a slap in the face, but she refused to let that deter her. She forced herself to meet Henry's gaze, all the while praying he wouldn't sense her uncertainty. If he did, it was all over.

Lifting her chin, and sending him a haughty glare that would have made Miss Henry beam, Amanda decided not to argue or waste time trying to change Henry Rafferty's opinion of her. If she talked too much, it would sound like she was trying to convince *herself*, instead of them of her newfound courage. A mistake like that could prove fatal.

Amanda flashed Henry a cold, challenging smile that didn't reach her eyes. It was a mock imitation of the many Jake had given her in the past. "Three . . ."

The ploy worked. Henry licked his fleshy lips and ran his big palms down his thighs. He sent his brother a questioning glance. "Tom?"

The cold metal barrel Amanda ground into the back of his skull convinced Tom Rafferty to keep quiet. It was Amanda's voice that answered. "Four . . ."

"Honey, I think you'd best take a second to think about what you're doing," Tom said. He moved his head only a fraction, yet still managed to glare at Amanda from the corner of his eye. "You don't want to shoot me." He wavered slightly. "Do you?"

"What I want doesn't matter. What *does* matter is that if your brother doesn't do what he's told—and do it *now!*—you're going to die, Tom Rafferty. I *will* pull this trigger. Fi—"

"Okay, okay! I'm going!" Henry bellowed. His

brown eyes were wide, and he looked convinced that Amanda Lennox *would* end his brother's life if he didn't do what he was told. His hands, which had lain atop his huge thighs, lifted in defeat.

Faster than a man his size should be capable of moving, Henry was on his feet. Like a disgruntled grizzly, he moved to sit in front of the tree to which Jake's left hand was tied.

"Now what?" Tom growled over his shoulder.

"Now you tie your brother up."

"And then . . . ?"

"Let me worry about that." Amanda nudged Tom with the gun. His shoulders stiffened, and the muscles in the back of his neck pulled taut. "And now, I'm giving you the same amount of time I gave Henry. If he isn't tied *tightly* to that tree by the time I count to five, I *will* kill you."

Tom hesitated. Unlike Henry, who'd given in much too easily, Tom wasn't convinced Amanda Lennox had the guts to spill a man's blood. Hell, hadn't Henry said that the first time he'd skinned a rabbit in front of her, the prissy little thing had scampered into the underbrush and vomited? Surely a woman *that* sensitive couldn't put a bullet through a man's head. Surely!

Or could she?

The hell of it was, Tom wasn't sure. The Amanda Lennox that Henry had described wouldn't have had the guts to sneak up on a man and *aim* a gun at him, let alone threaten to pull the trigger. Yet she'd just done both. Maybe she could kill after all, if the stakes were high enough? Christ, what a gamble!

Tom's gaze shifted to the breed, who was staring at Amanda Lennox with those predatory grey eyes. He saw pain in the breed's gaze, no doubt from where Henry had sliced into him. And he saw fury. But there was something else there; something vague that simmered just beneath the surface. Desperation?

370

Fear? Tom wasn't sure, but whatever it was, it was informative. It told him something about the breed and the woman that, with luck, he could use against them. If he lived that long.

"Three . . ."

"I need rope, honey."

"Then get some, *honey*."

"Can't. No more left. Henry used it all."

Amanda hesitated. "Untie Jake. You can use that rope."

"Jake? Who the hell is 'Jake'?"

She nodded to the breed, and Tom Rafferty shrugged. "Fine by me."

Amanda felt a trickle of unease ripple down her spine. The man had agreed too easily, and she watched him all the closer because of it. The second he took a step toward Jake, she knew what the sneaky rat was up to.

Reaching out, she grabbed the man's bony arm and shoved the pistol hard into the small of his back. "On second thought, *I'll* untie Jake."

She stepped around Tom, and split a cautious glance between the two devious looking Raffertys as she bent and retrieved Jake's knife from where Henry had tossed it to the ground. The hilt felt cold and heavy in her palm. The long blade glinted like silver ice in the firelight.

Her attention trained on the Raffertys, Amanda stepped to Jake's side and squatted beside him. Until now, she'd avoided looking at him, even when she'd felt his gaze on her. Knowing he was alive had been enough to keep her going. She was afraid to look at him, afraid to see what Henry had done. Her grip on courage was tenuous at best. Seeing Jake's familiar copper skin cut and bleeding might have made her slip; it might have been her undoing. It was a risk she hadn't been willing to take.

Until now. Now, she *had* to look at Jake.

371

Amanda restricted her gaze to his face, staunchly resisting the morbid urge to look lower. Her glance was brief, probing — she didn't dare take her eyes off the Raffertys for more than a split second. The tension hanging like a thick cloud in the air said they were waiting for any chance to jump her.

Jake gritted his teeth and forced his gaze and expression to remain neutral; a direct contrast to the emotions burning inside of him. Had he ever in his life been as furious with a woman as he was right here, right now, with Amanda Lennox? Hell, no!

The stupid bitch! Here he'd aimed to keep her safe — keep her *alive!* — by leaving her in Junction, and what did she do? She not only *followed* him — *how* she'd done that, he'd yet to figure out — but she'd also meandered right into the thick of things, at a time when the situation was at its dangerous worst. Did she know those two idiots would just as soon kill her as spit on her? Did she have any idea how much danger she was in?

Or did she know, and not care?

White women, Jake thought with an inward snort of disgust. *Who could figure 'em?* Jesus, it seemed like every time Jake thought he had Amanda Lennox pegged, she up and did something that surprised him. Again. And yet again.

His gaze shifted from the pistol to the knife. He wondered how she planned to cut through his ropes, and at the same time train both her gaze and weapon on *both* Raffertys. A quick glance at her face told him that Amanda was wondering much the same thing.

"Give me the knife," he growled.

Amanda shook her head and frowned, her gaze again fixed on Henry and Tom Rafferty. "I can't. Your hands are tied."

"So what? Give me the goddamn knife!" Jake's words were sharper than he'd intended, but he didn't care. His inner forearm stung like a son of a bitch

372

from where Henry had cut him. And when his body tensed with annoyance—as it usually did when Amanda Lennox was around—the pain was incredible.

After a split second of indecision, Amanda put the knife into the hand not tied to the tree. Jake's fingers curled around the familiar wooden hilt, deftly turning the weapon so the deadly tip pointed downward. He sliced the rope in one smooth stroke, then made short work of the one securing his wrist to the tree.

His relief was instantaneous. The rough hemp had been tied tight enough to make his wrists bleed, but not so tightly that he'd lost all circulation. Of course not. Henry Rafferty hadn't wanted him numb; he'd wanted Jake to *feel* every torturous second of the pain he'd gleefully inflicted.

A soft crunch of leaves snapped Amanda's attention back to the Raffertys. Her gaze speared into Tom Rafferty who, sensing her and Jake's distraction, had seized the chance to move a few steps closer to his brother.

Amanda swallowed a surge of panic, knowing that every step Tom took lessened her chances of hitting him should she be forced to shoot. Her fingers tightened on the pistol, and she leveled the snubby barrel in what she hoped was the direction of his heart. "Take one more step and I swear to God I'll shoot."

"Uh-huh," Tom muttered. His voice no longer wavered, but was tight and controlled. A cool grin curled over his lips as, his brown eyes meeting Amanda's gaze, he took not one step . . . but three. "I'll just bet you will, honey. That doesn't mean you're going to hit anything though. Not at this distance."

"*I* will."

Jake's voice came so closely behind her that Amanda could feel the kiss of his breath on the back of her neck. She hadn't heard him stand, but she knew Jake well enough now to not be surprised by it.

373

She also knew what that flat, cold tone meant; the threat in his voice was unmistakable.

Amanda wasn't the only one to notice. Tom Rafferty stopped dead in his tracks, his brown eyes fixed on a spot just behind Amanda's back. His gaunt cheeks drained to a ghostly shade of white, and his jaw tightened with indecision. "You'll miss," he said suddenly, but his tone lacked conviction. "Henry cut you good. No way you can throw with your arm sliced up and bloody."

"I'd agree," Jake replied dry, "if your brother had cut into my right arm." His pause was short, and pregnant with tension, his grin cold and sinister. "He didn't, he cut my left."

"Don't listen to him, Tom," Henry said as he pushed to his feet and leaned back heavily against the gritty tree trunk. But, despite his words, even he wasn't sure. He could have sworn he remembered the breed reaching for his knife with his left hand—the reason he'd chosen that arm to skin. But, hell, he *could* be wrong. Did he dare take that chance? Did he dare *not* take it?

With more conviction than he felt, Henry repeated, "I'm telling you, Tom, the breed's lying. He throws with his left. I-I'd bet my life on it."

"Glad to hear it, Henry. Because those were exactly the stakes I had in mind." Jake smiled coldly. Pinching the tip of the blade between his index finger and thumb, his right arm lifted.

Chapter Twenty-two

Henry pushed away from the tree and stepped to his brother's side. His gaze volleyed between the breed and the knife. Unlike Tom, he could gauge the weight and balance of a knife on sight. And he'd already held that knife once. The thing was meant for hunting, not throwing. In his estimation, the breed's chances of hitting a Rafferty were sketchy at best.

His gaze shifted to the woman. More precisely, he glared at the pistol Amanda Lennox cradled in her hands. As far as he was concerned, any woman aiming a loaded gun was cause for worry. But what *really* made him nervous was . . . hell, the prissy little thing didn't know squat about *cleaning* a gun, let alone *firing* one! And she was trembling like a leaf. Not a real reassuring sign. Her fear and inexperience were palpable; they made her dangerous.

"Well?" Jake sneered, his gaze locking with Henry's. "What's it going to be? Are the three of us going to ride out of here peacefully, or do I have to kill you and your brother first . . . *then* ride out? Either way, the end result's the same."

"Not quite," Tom Rafferty said. He must have guessed the warped path of Henry's thoughts, for his spine stiffened, and his stubble-coated chin tipped up. His brown eyes shimmered with newborn confidence. "The way I see it, you're going to have to hit us—*both* of us—before you ride anywhere. Can't do that when you're only holding one knife."

Amanda opened her mouth. She was in the process of pointing out how, if the blade did hit a Rafferty, and the remaining brother did try to charge Jake, he'd still have her bullet to contend with. A soft, low groan whispered out from behind her, snatching her attention before she could utter a word. She glanced quickly over her shoulder, her gaze sharpening on Roger. His head bobbed as he struggled to lift his chin.

A gasp lodged in her throat. Big, ugly bruises marred the side of the boy's face; bruises the shadows cloaking him could not conceal. He moaned again, his lashes fluttered. He was only able to pry one dazed blue eye open; the other was swollen shut.

Dear God, what had these two monsters done to the child?

Disgust stabbed at Amanda; disgust aimed at herself for letting Roger be taken in the first place and at the two men who'd done that to the poor boy. A wave of guilt made her stagger back a step. Her blood flowed cold as a wave of shock washed over her. She didn't realize she'd lowered the gun until it was too late.

Neither Rafferty wasted a second.

"Amanda!" Jake shouted when he saw Henry charging her.

Gritting his teeth against a surge of pain, Jake reached for her arm. He'd no more felt her sleeve beneath his fingertips before it was wrenched away. Dammit! A feral growl rumbled in his throat when he saw Henry Rafferty struggling to wrest the gun from her.

Tom Rafferty's shoulder crashed into Jake's gut. The air whooshed from Jake's lungs as he was sent hurdling backward. The world tipped, and he lost sight of Amanda. An unfamiliar wave of panic washed through Jake when he realized that there was no way he could help her. Not until he'd taken care

376

of Tom Rafferty.

Amanda fought bravely, not to mention dirtily. She lashed out with her feet, connecting with Henry's meaty thighs and shins more times than not. He grunted in pain, but the fingers coiled around her upper arm didn't loosen. Though he tried diligently to get the gun, he was forced to use his free hand to ward off the fingernails clawing at his cheeks and eyes.

"Give it up, honey," Henry panted. "I'm bigger than you. Like it or not, I'm going to get that gun. And when I do . . ."

Amanda didn't waste her breath responding. Instead, she redoubled her efforts to fight off both Henry and the panic she felt bubbling inside her. To her right, she heard the sound of a fist hitting flesh. It was followed by a muffled grunt of pain.

Jake's? Tom's? She didn't know. The faster her mind raced, the more her panic grew. Jake was wounded, weak, and he'd lost God knows how much blood. She'd seen Henry remove the knives hidden in Jake's moccasins; Jake now had only one blade to defend himself with. How long could he last before Tom Rafferty wrested the weapon from his hand? How long could *she* hold *Henry* at bay? The answer to both questions were the same. Not long enough.

"You ready to give up yet?" Henry sneered, and gave a tug that threatened to dislocate Amanda's arm from her shoulder. God, how it hurt!

She was struggling to aim the gun at Henry's chest, but he must have known what she was about, because he leaned to the side. Big, strong fingers curled crushingly around her upper arms. Before she could gasp, Amanda felt herself being hauled up against Henry's chest.

A quick glance to the side told her Tom and Jake were wrestling for control of the knife. And Jake did not look to be winning. Dear God, she had to get away from Henry, now, *before* Tom got his hands on the knife. An image of that steely blade being shoved between Jake's ribs flashed through her mind. Her heart squeezed unbearably tight.

Amanda resumed her struggles with a vengeance. And when Henry's beefy upper arm veered close enough, she sank her teeth into it without compunction.

"You little bitch!" Henry yelped. His fingers went slack around her arms, and he pulled instinctively backward. "I'll kill you for that, honey. Damned if I won't."

"And I'll be damned if I'll *let* you!" she yelled right back in his face.

If there was any leash on Henry Rafferty's temper, that remark snapped it neatly in two. He sneered and lunged for her.

Amanda made to side-step him. Her gaze trained on a charging Henry, she didn't see the thick branch curling over the ground. She did, however, feel it slam into her ankle, tipping her off balance. She cried out when she felt herself going down. There was no way to stop the fall, though she shot her free arm out with exactly that intention.

The hard, cold earth crashed into her front just as Henry Rafferty's body slammed onto her back. The air was shoved from her lungs. Amanda reeled from both blows. Her only conscious thought was to keep a tight hold on the gun.

Henry grabbed her roughly by the shoulders. His weight eased only long enough for him to toss her onto her back. Her hips felt like they were being crushed when he settled his weight atop them.

"It's over, honey. Might as well give up." A sinister grin curled over Henry's lips as he lunged for the gun.

Over? Amanda was damned if that was true. She hadn't come this far to give up now. Nor would she until she'd weakened herself so much she no longer had the energy to struggle. She hadn't reached that point yet. Close, but not yet.

Henry's fingers wrapped around her wrist, squeezing tight. She felt her fingers go cold, felt them loosen around the gun.

"No!" With the last of her strength, she shoved at Henry, trying to dislodge him. He didn't budge, but the move did surprise him enough for his grip to loosen. It was only a fleeting weakness, but she took full advantage of it. She yanked the gun up between them and leveled the barrel at Henry's chest. Her fingers felt icy and numb, but she retained enough feeling in them to keep her index finger coiled around the trigger.

"I'm going to enjoy making you suffer for that," Henry snarled. "I'm going to enjoy hearing you beg me to—"

His fingers tightened around her wrist. Her fingers reflexively curled inward. A flex was all it took to slam the trigger home and to halt Henry Rafferty's words forever.

Surprise glinted Henry's eyes, then pain, then nothing at all. The brown orbs glazed over. His big body went limp and fell to the side. He hit the ground with a resounding *thud*.

"*Amanda!*" The shot had barely rung out when the name tore from Jake's throat. Tom Rafferty's hands were wrapped around his wrists, tightly, trying to squeeze Jake's fingers from around the hilt of the knife. With his free hand, Jake delivered a blow to Rafferty's shoulder. The result was double-edged; while Rafferty let go of Jake's wrist, Jake's fingers were too numb to retain hold of the knife. The weapon tumbled to the ground, far enough away to be no threat to either of them.

The air still rang with the repeating echo of the gunshot. Jake's heart constricted, and a stab of pain unlike anything he'd ever felt sliced through him. Dear God, he was shaking. The reaction had nothing to do with his wounded arm, or the exertion of struggling with Tom Rafferty. It had *everything* to do with thinking for one heart-stopping, gut-wrenching minute that Amanda Lennox was dead. And that he, by not getting to her soon enough, had inadvertently killed her.

Amanda heard Jake's voice, but it came from a distance. Her gaze, wide-eyed and horrified, was fixed on Henry Raffertys lifeless body. Blinking hard, she forced her gaze away from the gaping hole in the big man's chest, a hole that continued to pump blood onto his shirtfront and the ground. Suppressing the shivers that racked her body wasn't possible. She didn't try.

"J-Jake?" she whispered hoarsely. Amanda glanced to the side, and winced when she saw Tom Rafferty's fist make solid contact with Jake's already swollen jaw.

Jake grunted as his head snapped to the side. Alarm coursed through Amanda when she saw how weak his struggles were.

Tom Rafferty landed another stinging blow. Then another. Jake tried to deliver a punch of his own, but missed. Rafferty's aim was more accurate.

A fist connected with Jake's temple hard enough to make stars dance behind his eyes. He blinked them away. Only sheer force of will — and raw fear for Amanda Lennox's life — kept him conscious. He was panting, and his brow and upper lip were coated in the same sweat that pasted his hair to his scalp and face. His efforts to dislodge his attacker were becoming slow and clumsy. Gritting his teeth against the pain that tore through his arm, he aimed a punch at Tom Rafferty's temple. And missed again.

Tom waited until the fist whizzed past his face, completing an arc that would have knocked free quite

380

a few of his crooked yellow teeth, had it connected. Chuckling evilly, his hands snaked out. Long, thin fingers wrapped around a thick copper throat. And squeezed. Hard.

"You don't look so dangerous now, do you, breed?"

Jake croaked, but didn't — couldn't — respond. He tried clawing at Tom Rafferty's arms, but the pain in his body, combined with lack of air, made his efforts ineffectual.

Tom laughed harder. "That's right," he sneered, "you go ahead and fight. Won't do you any good. Nothing's going to stop me from strangling the life out of your miserable red hide. Or, better yet, maybe I'll let Henry finish skinning you. He'll like that."

Jake's vision was going black and fuzzy around the edges. His lungs burned, and his head and arm throbbed unbearably. It was only a matter of time before he died — dammit, this was *not* the way he'd intended to go! — but he continued to fight.

His bleary gaze fixed on a spot just behind Tom Rafferty's lanky shoulder. He decided he must be in more dire need of air than he thought, because now he was seeing things. He blinked the sweat from his eyes and squinted, but . . . damned if the image would go away. If he didn't know better, he'd swear he saw Amanda Lennox standing a few short feet away, that blasted pistol of hers aimed at Rafferty's back.

Jake told himself it was an illusion, a product of wishful thinking. But he didn't believe it. A part of him needed to believe Amanda was there, needed to believe that the prissy white princess — *his* prissy white princess, dammit! — was ready and willing to kill for him. It took effort to look past the irony of *that* thought!

"You hear that, Henry?" Tom Rafferty said, and his grin was pure evil. He scowled, his fingers loosening just a bit when his brother made no reply.

"Henry?"

"Henry's d-dead, Mr. Rafferty. I k-killed him."

Tom's head came up. His gaze narrowed, snapping over his shoulder. His eyes widened when he saw Amanda Lennox. *Amanda Lennox?* Now wait just a second! He'd heard a shot, and he'd naturally presumed that Henry had . . . But if *Henry* hadn't . . . His attention shifted to the firelit spot where he'd last seen his brother struggling with the woman. What he saw now snapped his tenuous hold on sanity.

She'd killed him! That bitch had killed Henry!

And now . . . dammit, *now* he was going to kill the only person he figured meant anything to her. He was going to kill the breed. Then he was going to kill her. Slowly. Painfully. Until she begged him to end her life. Just the way Henry would do it. Tom was going to have some fun.

Tom's gaunt cheeks went crimson, and a feral growl issued from somewhere deep in the back of his throat. He bared his teeth like a rabid dog and turned his attention back to the Injun. His fingers squeezed so hard his knuckles hurt.

Amanda was breathing hard and fast through her mouth. She felt dizzy and sick to her stomach. Her knees were shaking so badly it was a wonder she was still standing. She wasn't too far from Tom Rafferty, she could probably hit him . . . but not if she didn't bring some of her trembling under control. And what, she wondered frantically, would happen if she did pull the trigger . . . and missed? What if . . .

God, what if she *hit Jake instead?*

It was a risk she would have to take. Because if she did nothing, Jake was going to die. Amanda squinted until her eyes were almost closed. She planted her feet firmly on the ground, turned her head . . . and pulled the trigger.

The bullet roared from the barrel in a deafening explosion. The repercussions of the shot slammed up

Amanda's fear-weakened arms. Though she wanted nothing more at that moment than to collapse, she forced herself to stay erect. *She had to know who she'd shot!*

Time slowed to a crawl. For a minute, it looked like she hadn't shot anyone. Tom Rafferty continued to straddle Jake's stomach, but neither man moved. Both seemed frozen eerily in place, as though they'd been sculpted from ice.

It wasn't until she yanked the hammer back and prepared to shoot again that she saw Tom waver. His chin went up, and a cry of alarm gurgled in his throat as his spine arched. A wet stain soaked through his shirt; it spread quickly. Firelight and moonlight made his blood glisten a gruesome shade of black.

The gun slipped from Amanda's hands. She barely noticed as she covered her face with trembling palms. Her shaking, which had never really ceased, resumed with a force that rocked her. The tremors started on the inside, working their way to the surface in numbing, ice-cold waves.

Her sobs bordered on hysterical; she couldn't control them. In seconds, her hands were slick. Hot tears dripped paths down her wrists, where they were finally soaked up by her sleeves. She didn't realize she'd fallen to her knees until she felt the collision of hard, lumpy ground beneath her.

"Jesus H. Christ!" Jake wasn't even aware of hissing the blasphemy under his breath as he struggled to roll Tom Rafferty's weight off and to the side. The effort put his wounded arm through a burning sort of hell, but he didn't give up until the chore was done.

Getting to his feet proved a hard-won lesson in agony. Not only did his arm hurt, but the way the blood rushed from his face made the bruises there throb. He sucked in a sharp breath, swayed, and came damn close to falling right back down again. If there was an inch of him that didn't hurt, he couldn't find it. He ached in places he didn't even know he had!

Oddly enough, the pain raging through him was secondary. More important was the gut-wrenching need to get to Amanda, to wrap her in his arms, to somehow ease the anguish he could hear in her heartrending sobs. He realized only now that he'd never heard her cry before. Damn, but he'd had no idea the sound would tear him apart this way.

She was kneeling by the time Jake reached her. Her arms were coiled around her middle, and she was rocking back and forth. Her eyes were scrunched closed. Tears streamed down her paler-than-pale cheeks, running in wet rivulets down her neck, beneath her collar. The way her jaw and lower lip trembled cut Jake up inside.

"Ah, God, I'm sorry, princess. So damn sorry," Jake murmured hoarsely as he knelt in front of her. Ignoring the pain, he reached for her. His breath went shallow when Amanda came willingly into his arms. Her whimper of gratitude made his heart stop.

Jake angled his head, laying his battered cheek on her silky head. He held her close, stroked and soothed her, for what felt like hours. Eventually, her sobs eased. It took much, much longer for her tears to stop. Her shaking never did.

"J-Jake?"

He stroked her hair with his cheek, and murmured throatily, "Right here, princess." His gaze shifted to Tom Rafferty's body. A tremor ripped through him, and he tightened his hold on Amanda, as though he was trying to melt her body right into his own. If only he *could*.

Amanda was tempted to look into Jake's eyes, to discern what that husky timber in his voice meant, but she resisted. To do so would mean she would have to move, and Jake's warm, solid chest beneath

384

her cheek felt too good to surrender just yet, too comforting. The drumming of his heart was a steady, calming beat in her ear. "You won't l-leave me again. Will you?"

"I . . ." He knew what she was talking about. He didn't know precisely *how* he knew, he just did. Jake felt an unfamiliar stab of emotion in the region of his heart. It took a second for him to place it; it took even longer for him to admit it was guilt. "No, princess, I won't leave you."

"Y-you promise?"

"Yes." He stroked brisk paths up and down her arms, even as he angled his head and nuzzled her neck. Her hair smelled piny and fragrant. Her skin felt warm beneath his lips. Perfect. Holding her in his arms felt . . . ah, God, so damn perfect! Good and right and wonderful. How was he ever going to leave this woman? How was he ever going to let her go?

The answer came out of nowhere; it hit him like a rock-solid punch to the gut. He couldn't leave her. Not now. Not ever. Sometime during the last few weeks, this white woman had cut through the wall he'd erected around himself. Her easy smile and prissy ways had chiseled away his resistance, burrowed under his skin, snuck into his bloodstream. Somewhere along the line this woman had become an important part of him. Losing her now would be like losing a limb. No, that was wrong. An arm or leg he could live without. He could *not* live without Amanda Lennox.

A soft, muffled sob snatched Amanda's attention. She stiffened, and her head came up. For a split second, she wasn't sure what, or who, had made the noise. And then she remembered.

Roger. Dear Lord, with everything that had happened, she'd forgotten about the boy.

Swallowing a stab of guilt, she glanced up at Jake.

His jaw was tight, his gaze intense as he returned her stare. She wondered briefly what he was thinking. What had put that desperate glint in his eyes?

The moan came again, and the sound robbed Amanda of the chance to ask. "Roger," she whispered, and pushed against his chest. "Please, Jake, I have to go to him."

Jake's arms tightened around her. If Amanda had seen any emotion in his eyes a second ago, it was gone now. His gaze was narrow, unreadable. The muscle in his cheek jerked as he hauled her up against him once more. "The brat can wait."

"No, he can't. I . . . God, he must be terrified."

"So are you."

"I'm fine." Her chin hiked up a determined notch. Only her moist, trembling lower lip betrayed the lie. Something flashed in Jake's eyes, something that made Amanda remember all the other lies she'd ever told him, as well as her promise to never lie to him again. Sighing shakily, she amended, "I'm a little shaken up, but I'll be fine."

"Bullshit. Lady, you're shaking like a leaf."

"For God's sake, what do you expect? I'm in shock. I've never . . . k-killed a man before."

"Yeah, tell me something I don't already know. As far as I'm concerned, that's all the more reason you should stay put. I'll tend to the kid."

"No."

"Why the hell not?"

Why not, indeed? Jake was right, she *was* shaking like a leaf. Inside as well as out. But that was beside the point. "Roger is *my* responsibility. I insist you let me go to him."

Amanda struggled to pull away from Jake. She'd put barely an inch between them when she felt his palm against the side of her head. He muttered something—one of the curses he was so fond of, no doubt—and tugged her head down to his chest.

"You're beginning to annoy me again, Mr. Chandler."

"Jesus, lady, what the hell is with you? You just killed a man for me. You don't get much more intimate with a guy than that! Now shut up and sit still. You aren't going anywhere."

Amanda continued to squirm. "I want to go to Roger."

"I didn't ask what you wanted, princess."

"I'm telling you anyway. In fact, I'm demanding it. Now *let me go!*"

"No. Your knees are still too weak. You stand up now, you're just going to topple over again."

Amanda's tone was haughty and very, very proper. "I will not."

"Will too."

"Not."

"Too!"

"Liar."

That did it! Amanda reached out and curled her fingers around Jake's forearms, intending to forcibly remove herself from his no longer welcome embrace. "For crying out loud, they're *my* knees. Surely *I* would know whether or not—"

Jake sucked in a sharp breath. The world spun dizzily around him. A wave of agony bolted all the way up to his shoulder. From wrist to elbow, his arm felt like it was on fire. He couldn't suppress the gasp that hissed through his teeth.

Amanda paled and snatched her hand away. It was too late. The set of Jake's jaw said the damage was done. She fought a surge of nausea when she felt the warm stickiness of his blood coating her palms. "Oh, God. Jake, I'm so sorry. Does it," she cleared her throat, forcing herself to continue, "hurt badly?"

"Hell no, I was gasping in pleasure," he growled, pushing the words through tightly clenched teeth. *"Of course it hurts!"* He hadn't meant to shout at her, and

387

the second he saw Amanda's injured expression, he wished he hadn't. It took effort, but he softened his tone. "Take care of the kid while I tend this."

"If you want I could — ?"

The inky brow he slanted at her said that no, Jake did not want her tending him. For some reason that wounded her. Amanda ducked her head so he couldn't see the sheen of tears in her eyes, and clambered from his lap. "Excuse me," she murmured with rigid politeness, even as she hurried away.

Through slitted eyes he watched her hesitate as she passed Tom Rafferty's lifeless body, watched her stiffen then continue on. He almost, *almost* called her back. He wasn't sure what stopped him, excect maybe the instinctive knowledge that she needed time to digest what had happened. Come to think of it, so did he. Truthfully, he wasn't sure a dozen lifetimes would be enough time to come to terms with what Amanda Lennox had done.

Amanda Lennox had killed for him. A prissy white woman had put a bullet through a man's back — through a *white man's* back — to save the life of a half-breed. Did she have any idea of the danger she'd put herself in? Did she know what the law would do if word of what she'd done — and for *whom* — ever got out? Did she care? No, probably not. But she *should*.

Shaking his head, Jake plowed the fingers of his right hand through his hair and sighed. He glanced at Amanda, watched as she sawed through Roger's ropes with the knife. Surprisingly, when the boy was free, she clasped him tightly to her chest. Even more surprising, Roger hugged her back with equal ferocity.

Jake's gaze narrowed, and his attention dipped to the long, creamy taper of her throat. His blood ran cold when he pictured a roughly knotted hangman's noose draping her regal collarbone, a place where, by all rights, the finest diamonds and pearls money could buy should rest.

Though he tried to shake it free, the image lingered for a long, long time.

Chapter Twenty-three

The light of campfire flickered, breaking the night's darkness in a ring of muted orange light. An owl hooted in the distance. A chilly breeze stirred the ceiling of leaves.

Jake saw and heard none of it. Sitting with his back propped against a boulder, he studied the soft, deerskin toe of one of his moccasins as though it held untold mysteries. But . . . Jesus, he didn't see that either. What he *did* see—much too clearly, even though he wasn't looking—was Amanda Lennox.

She was sitting on the other side of the fire, huddled from chin to toe beneath a threadbare blanket. *His* blanket. The firelight touched off reddish highlights in the hair wisping around her face. Her cheeks looked whiter than normal. Her gaze was huge, haunted and intense, piercing the distance that separated them.

The distance wasn't really so much. So why, Jake wondered, did it feel like it stretched on for miles?

Amanda had been great with the brat, Jake could find no fault with her there. While he'd buried Tom and Henry Rafferty, he'd heard her crooning to Roger. The kid had sobbed on her shoulder. Amanda hadn't complained, she'd soothed. Jake had found himself wishing she would hold him in her arms like that and help ease some of his own torment. Unfortunately, being in Amanda Lennox's arms was what had *caused* his torment in the first place, so he figured that probably wouldn't work.

It wasn't until after Roger had fallen asleep that Amanda had fallen apart, in her own way; quietly, with dignity. She'd retreated to the other side of the campfire with a cup of coffee she'd yet to take one sip of—Jake knew, since his gaze had rarely left her mouth—and she hadn't spoken a word.

Neither had he.

And that, Jake thought, was the worst part. This brooding silence that crackled with a tension that seemed louder than thunder somehow. The silence made the distance between them seem greater. In the past they'd made love, they'd fought . . . but rarely had Amanda ever been this goddamn silent. He had been, many times, but never her. It was . . . *annoying*. Grating. It shouldn't be, but it was.

Gritting his teeth, Jake yanked the small leather pouch out of his shirt pocket and, ignoring the pain to his injured arm, rolled himself a smoke. His gaze was still on Amanda; his fingers performed the chore by a mixture of memory and habit. He stuck the cigarette into one corner of his mouth and lit it, squinting against the brightness of the flame as well as the sting of smoke in his eyes. His lungs burned with the first, deep inhalation; it was a familiar, welcome distraction from festering thoughts.

"Amanda—"

"Jake—"

Their words tripped over each other. Both snapped their mouths shut and exchanged nervous glances for the other to continue. Neither did.

Jake exhaled through his teeth, puffing a stream of grey smoke into the air. He rested his head back against the rock and closed his eyes.

Amanda bent her legs and tucked her knees beneath her chin. She smoothed the blanket primly over her shins and gazed at the snapping flames of the campfire. "You know we're going to have to talk about this eventually," she said, her voice soft, as though she was speaking to herself as much as to him.

"Yeah, I expect we will. Eventually."

Her gaze lifted, trailing slowly up Jake's body. Past firm calves and thighs, past lean hips and taut stomach, past broad shoulders and bruised copper throat. His eyes were still closed. Even at this distance she could see the thick, sooty lashes flicker against the sculpted curve of his cheek.

The muted light cast his straight hair an appealing shade of blue-black. The red bandanna he'd knotted around his forehead to hold the strands back from his face looked unusually bright. The flickering shadows defined the hollows beneath his cheeks, made the already hard line of his jaw look granite-hard.

"Why do you do that?" she asked. They were the first words that came to mind, and Amanda said them only to break the tension that was threatening to drive her loony.

His brows lifted, but he didn't open his eyes. Instead, he put the cigarette to his mouth, leisurely puffed until the tip glowed hot and red, then released the smoke in a long, slow hiss. "Do what?"

"Wear your hair so long? Wear a bandanna like a headband?" Her gaze dipped to the sheath at his belt. "Carry knives instead of a gun like normal men do?"

"Are you saying I'm not normal, princess?"

Amanda squirmed and thought that maybe the silence, tense as it was, would have been better after all. Less condemning. Of course, it was too late now. "No, Jake. I'm saying you aren't like . . . well, like other men."

"*White* men, you mean."

She bristled. "I didn't say that."

"You didn't have to." This time when Jake lifted the cigarette to his lips, he didn't draw on it. Instead, he pinched it between his index finger and thumb and frowned. His arm throbbed a protest when he flicked it away. His eyes opened, and he watched the glowing tip arch through the night. It sizzled out on the snow-dusted grass outside the circle of firelight. "Lady, when the hell are you going to get it through that stubborn-as-all-hell head of yours that *I'm not white*. Wishing my skin was lighter won't change the fact that it isn't."

"And wishing won't make my skin any redder," she countered tightly. "Have you ever thought of that, Jake?"

Her response—or maybe it was the firmness of her tone—seemed to take him by surprise. The force of his gaze snapped to her, making Amanda fidget. She saw his eyes narrow, saw the way he raked her face and neck and hands—every inch of white skin he could find—in a way that seemed almost condemning.

His voice was hard, edgy. "I've never wanted to change the color of your skin, Amanda."

"Never?" she asked, surprised.

"No."

"I'm sorry, I must have misunderstood. Maybe it isn't the color of my skin you'd like to change. Maybe it's the color of *yours*."

Jake leaned forward, sitting up to pillow one elbow atop his rock-hard thigh. The muscle jerking his cheek, combined with his tight expression, said she'd hit a nerve.

"I'm not ashamed of the color of my skin," he growled, and leaned forward still more.

"Aren't you?"

"No," he hissed, his eyes narrowing to angry grey slits. "I'm proud of it. Damn proud."

"Ah, yes, I can see that," she countered with a sarcasm that surprised even herself. She raked his flannel shirt and tight denim pants—*white man's* clothes—with a telling glance. The furious color in Jake's cheeks said her meaning was not missed. "You know, from the start you've told me all white people, even without knowing you, automatically label you a savage." She sighed and shook her head. "This may sound like a stupid question, but . . . hasn't it ever occurred to you that *you go out of your way* to give them that impression? You—"

"Shut up," Jake snapped, and pushed to his feet. He looked edgy, as though he was fighting the urge to stalk the distance between them and wrap his fingers around her throat—anything to get her to stop talking. "You don't know what the hell you're talking about, lady, so just shut the hell up!"

If her nerves hadn't already been raw, Amanda might have taken his grittily uttered advice and kept her peace. But her nerves *were* raw, and the things she was saying now were things she'd thought—but lacked the courage to actually *say*—at least a hundred times since she'd met this man.

Their time together was running short. It wouldn't be long before they reached Pony. The clerk had said a day, maybe two. Now that Roger was with them, they wouldn't have the freedom to talk that they'd once had—and had rarely used.

Did she want to look back on these last few days with Jake with regret? Did she want to constantly be reminded of all the things she should have said, but hadn't?

Amanda glanced up his sinewy length, their combative gazes locked. "It bothers you to hear the truth, doesn't it, Jake?"

"Not half as much as it's going to bother *you* when I plant my fist down your throat, Amanda."

A sliver of cowardice curled down her spine, but

she was surprised by how little effort it took to shove the emotion away. Perhaps it was having killed two men earlier that made the threat of being roughed up a bit lack its sting? Shrugging, she rested her chin atop her knees and averted her gaze to the fire. "You won't hurt me."

"You sound awful sure of that."

Though his tone was antagonistic, as though he *wanted* for her to fight with him, Amanda refused to oblige. She kept her voice dignified, controlled. "I am."

Prissy. *That* was the tone of voice Jake heard, the one that scratched down his spine like fingernails on slate. But, unfortunately, that was secondary—because what *really* grated on him was knowing that she was right. He wouldn't hurt her, couldn't even if he'd wanted to. And he didn't really want to.

"I'm going for a walk," he snapped, and spun on his heel. He'd no more stepped into the shadows where the warmth of the fire didn't reach when Amanda's voice rang out behind him, stopping him cold.

"Run all you want, but sooner or later you're going to have to stop and face the truth."

"And what, exactly, is the truth, Amanda?"

"That you're never going to be all white, no matter how much you may want to be."

"Dammit, woman, I don't want to be white!"

Amanda's voice lowered. "And you call *me* a liar!"

Well, that comment had Jake retracing his steps in record time. He didn't stop near the boulder, but instead stalked past it, his cat-silent steps angrily rounding the campfire. He stopped only when the toe of his moccasin threatened to make contact with her outer thigh. Hands planted solidly on hips, he stood glowering down at the top of her golden head. "I don't lie, Miss Lennox. Ever."

"You just did."

"Yeah? Then that's something I must have picked up along the way. I had a damn good teacher. *You.*" He reached down and banded his fingers around her upper arms, dragging her to her feet. He barely noticed the pain that shot through his arm as he hauled her up roughly against his chest. The feel of her breath whooshing from her lungs wasn't as satisfying as it should have been, but Jake was too confused to notice.

A question had been circling around them for the last four hours. He hadn't asked it. And, whether or not she saw it glinting in his eyes every time he looked at her, she hadn't answered it. Now, feeling her body crushed against him, Jake surrendered to an overpowering need to know.

"Why?" he asked roughly as he lowered his head so their noses almost touched. He caught a glimpse of his own reflection in her eyes. He hated the face staring back at him—*his* face. It was unrecognizable; a ruthless, furious savage hell-bent on tormenting a poor, quivering little white lady. Jesus, he'd sunk pretty damn low these days!

"Why what?" Amanda countered breathlessly. She couldn't help the shaky quality of her voice, of her body. Being this close to Jake did that to her. It weakened what little resolve she'd ever had. The feel of his hands on her, of his breath scorching her upturned face, flooded her with memories . . . and initiated a fire in her blood that she'd learned weeks ago she was powerless to douse.

"Why'd you do it, princess? Dammit, *why?*"

She could have asked, "Do what?" but it would only have stalled an answer, not avoided it. Amanda knew what the question was, just like she knew it had been only a matter of time before one of them came right out and asked it. Should she tell him the truth, even knowing she'd risk opening herself up to a world of pain that far outstripped anything she'd felt in the past? On the other hand, could she lie to him—again?

Yes, she realized suddenly, she could lie to him if forced. But she wouldn't. If she did, she wouldn't respect herself for it. And Jake would hate her. Because it would be yet another in a very long list of little "white" lies.

The fingers banding her arms tightened. He turned and maneuvered her backward, until the gritty trunk of a pine tree was biting into her back. And Jake Chandler's hardness was molding into her front.

They met thigh to thigh. Hip to hip. Soft, feminine curves to lean male hardness. She felt the breaths sawing in and out of his lungs. Their ragged rhythm matched her own.

"Tell me, Amanda. Why? I . . . dammit, I need to know."

Not half as much as she needed to say it, Amanda realized abruptly. Her hands came up, splaying his chest. Her fingers curled inward; she gripped his worn flannel shirt in tight, trembling fists.

Her gaze was trained on the inky hair that fell over his shoulder, on the braid and the small feather that rested against his chest. Slowly, her attention lifted, scanning his neck and noting the bruises Tom Rafferty's hands had left behind.

She met Jake's gaze unflinchingly, she wasn't sure how, and was reminded of the first time she'd ever seen him. Those silver-grey eyes of his had had the power to shake her world even then. Now, they had the power to break her in two with just one glance.

"Why, Amanda?"

Her gaze lowered, locking onto the tight line of his mouth. She released the breath she only now realized she'd been holding. Her lungs burned when she dragged in another. So did the tips of her breasts. Every breath she drew put her into sizzling contact with the solid planes of Jake's chest. "I . . ."

"Say it," he growled. Was it by intent or accident that his hips moved, crushing her against the tree? And did it matter? No. Either way, her response was the same . . . breathless, hot, nerve-shattering sensation. "Tell me, damn you! Why the hell did you—?"

"Because he was going to kill you!" The high, panicky, and sharp voice, that echoed in Amanda's ears was barely recognizable as her own. The enormity of what she'd just said, what she'd almost admitted, hit her like a slap. Her reaction was three times more devastating. She'd been shaking before, mostly on the inside. Now, her entire body began quivering with a force that stunned her. Her knees felt weak, watery. If not for the tree—and Jake—she would have collapsed.

Amanda would always wonder where she found the courage to continue speaking. It didn't matter that her voice came out as a hoarse whisper; one she could barely hear herself. The bands of muscles she cushioned beneath her fingertips rippled when she spoke, telling her that while Jake might have to strain to hear her, he was absorbing every word. "He was going to kill you, Jake. I couldn't let that happen. It would have . . ."

"What?" he asked, his voice low and raspy, filled with an emotion that it took supreme effort to keep out of his eyes and his expression. He stared down at her, stared *into* her, as though willpower alone could drag the words from her creamy white throat. "What would it have done?"

"It would have killed me," she admitted softly, and her chin lowered, her voice weakened. "A part of me would have shriveled up and died right along with you."

Jake's pause was long and tense, filled with the crackling of the campfire and the give and take of two equally ragged breaths. "Because you love me?"

His gritty tone made the words more a raw statement of fact than a question.

Amanda answered him anyway. She *had* to. "Yes, because I love you."

"Son of a bitch."

The response, uttered through gritted teeth, surprised her. It wasn't what she'd expected, wasn't at all what she'd wanted to hear. But then, what *had* she expected? That Jake would say he loved her, too? That he couldn't live without her? That he'd do whatever it took to keep her by his side. There was no denying that was what she wanted to hear . . . just as there was no denying that Jacob Blackhawk Chandler wasn't the type of man to say such a thing. Not to a white woman. Not ever.

He leaned closer and rested his forehead against hers. Both were beaded with nervous perspiration. Jake's eyes were pinched tightly shut, as though there were emotions swimming in his gaze that he didn't want Amanda to see and that he was having the devil's own time controlling.

"What's between us . . ." he said finally, hoarsely, "it won't work, you know. It can't. They won't let it."

"They? Meaning other white people?" A drop of anger warmed Amanda's blood. She focused on it as though it was a chunk of driftwood and she was drowning. In a way, she was. Only not in water. She was drowning in the ache of rejection. Again. "What people — no, what *white* people — think of you is very important to you, isn't it, Jake?"

"Yes." The pained way he said it told her this was not only the first time he'd made such an admission to another person, it was also the first time he'd confessed this to himself. His body tightened beneath her hands, humming with furious confusion. Amanda had a feeling Jake had surprised even himself. He surprised them both when he added huskily, "You don't know what it's been like for me, lady. You have no idea, couldn't even begin to understand . . ."

"Then explain it to me, Jake." Her fingers un-curled from around his shirt. She wasn't aware of when her hands traveled up his chest, over his shoulders. She was, however, excruciatingly aware of when her fingertips grazed, then traced, the puckered scar on the back of his neck. "*Make* me understand."

"No."

"But—?"

"No." His hand came out of nowhere, his fingers manacling her wrist, yanking her hand away. He moved back far enough to settle her arm between them and then he pressed in on her again. His body molded into hers; the fit was perfect. The feel of his hard, muscled length pressing her back against the equally firm tree hit Amanda like a wave of white heat. "Leave it alone, princess. I put that part of my life behind me years ago."

She could feel him pulling away from her. Not physically, but mentally. She let him go, because she had no choice. He needed time to deal with every-thing that had happened, with what they'd both just confessed. She was smart enough to acknowledge that she needed time too. Oh, not to deal with having killed Tom and Henry Rafferty—she was shocked to realize how quickly she'd come to terms with that. She'd done what had to be done at the time. One of them had been about to kill her, the other had been about to kill Jake. She'd stopped them. It was that simple.

No, what she needed time for was to come to terms with the fact that her confession had been hu-miliatingly one-sided. She'd given Jake a chance to tell her how he felt. He hadn't taken it. He hadn't admitted feelings for her, and she was starting to be-lieve the reason was because he didn't have any. The idea was devastating, yet the sooner she faced up to it the better off she'd be. Jake Chandler did not love her. And he never would.

"How much longer before we reach Pony?" she asked softly, breathlessly. It was either change the subject, or cry. The latter she refused to do. She didn't want Jake to see how badly he'd hurt her. Her pride couldn't take a blow like that; it had sustained one too many as it was.

Jake lifted his head and looked at her oddly. While his gaze registered surprise at the swift change of topic, he didn't argue it. If anything, he looked relieved. "Another day if it doesn't snow again," he answered cautiously. "Why?"

"I think you know."

You'll get your cousin back if it kills me. And I'll get . . .

What? What will you get, Jake?

My money. Every last cent of it . . . the sooner we get the brat back, the sooner I can be rid of you.

The remembered words hung in the air, thicker than the charred scent of wood surrounding them. The brat was back. In two days, Jake would be rid of her. Forever. Did the idea please him? There was no way to tell. His expression was as tight and as unreadable as ever.

With a growl, Jake pushed away from Amanda and spun on his heel. She tried not to notice the sudden chill that blasted over her in all the places his body had warmed her. Tried not to, but did. The question was, did Jake? If he made the observation, it didn't affect him enough to stop him from leaving.

"I'm going to take that walk," he grumbled over his shoulder, his long, silent steps never breaking stride.

Amanda watched him meld with the shadowy trees—the white bandage wrapped around his arm stood out in stark contrast. Her gaze blurred with unshed tears, and a lump of emotion wedged in her throat, clogging his name there. She didn't realize

401

she'd taken a step to follow him until she felt the support of the tree behind her melt away.

Given the chance, *would* she have swallowed her pride — bitter tasting though it was — and chased after Jake? The question would forever remain unanswered. She'd taken no more than a step when Roger tossed fitfully in his sleep and called out her name.

Amanda felt a weight of responsibility settle over her like a lead blanket. Though her gaze wavered between the boy and the spot where she'd watched Jake disappear, there was never a question in her mind as to what she had to do.

She'd been hired to take care of Roger. No matter that her life was falling apart. No matter that her insides felt ripped and shredded. She wasn't being paid to indulge in self-pity, she was being paid to get Roger to Pony. She hadn't done a very good job so far, but her job was still days from being over.

As she turned her steps to the child huddled beneath her blanket, Amanda realized that she needed to see this job through to its end much more than she'd originally thought she would. Not for the money — though she needed that too — but to help heal her battered self-respect. She'd rarely finished anything she'd started in her life, but this time she would. She needed to prove to herself that she could do it, and . . .

Oh, who was she kidding? She needed to prove it to *Jake,* no one else. He thought her a silly Bostonian princess — hadn't he said it often enough? She needed to prove that she wasn't . . . not anymore, thanks to the time she'd spent with him.

Since it was inevitable they would part company — he'd made *that* painfully clear — Amanda wanted to sever the ties between them completely and cleanly, in the way they'd originally agreed upon. She would get Roger to Pony, and she would collect her hard-earned salary from Edward Bannister. Then, she would pay Jake the money she owed him. Immediately and in full. Only in that way could she prove to them both what she doubted Jake even now believed. That, when she set her mind to it, Amanda Lennox *was* a woman of her word.

Chapter Twenty-four

"Stop it, princess. You look fine."

"I look awful."

"No, Miss Lennox, you don't," Roger said. "Honest. You look fine. Besides, I think my father is going to be looking at me more than you anyway."

The trio had reined in their horses at the very outskirts of Pony. Amanda, positioned between Jake and Roger, barely glanced at the small but busy mining town. If she'd had time to think about it, that would have told her something; it would have told her that boardwalks, false-fronted stores, and numerous tawdry saloons were becoming all-too familiar sights.

She cast a quick glance at Roger and was again stunned by how much the boy had changed. Bad dreams had kept him awake most of the last two nights, but he was easily comforted by Amanda's soothing touch and voice. More often than not, he clung to her until he found his way back to sleep.

By day he'd been sullen and introspective; not only wasn't he as quick to ridicule, but he was also not quick to talk at all. He rarely spoke of his time in captivity, and he *never* mentioned the Raffertys. When he talked at all, it was to voice his eagerness to be reunited with his father.

There were physical changes in the boy as well, the primary one being that he was noticeably thinner. The baby fat that had once rounded his cheeks and stomach was gone; his weeks with the Raffertys had melted it away. His arms and legs, hidden in the laughably large folds of Jake Chandler's clothes, now looked gangly and awkward.

Roger's rumpled attire reminded Amanda of her own. She sighed, and a scowl puckered her brow when she glanced down. The yellow muslin dress wasn't as bright as it had been when she'd bought it. The sun had faded the color from daffodil to watery butter. The fabric itself was wrinkled from having been crammed into her saddlebag.

Roger, she noticed with a touch of sarcasm, wasn't the only one who'd shed a few pounds. Last night she'd convinced Jake to return her corset. After weeks of freedom, the contraption felt tight and confining. Lord, she could barely breathe! She hadn't had to work the laces very tightly, however, and her bodice still felt loose, telling her that she had lost weight as well.

Her gaze had settled on her wrinkled muslin lap. She realized it only when a big copper hand inserted itself into her view and settled heavily atop her thigh. The imprint of those thick, familiar fingers burned through the cloth, branding like hot iron into her skin. A shiver rippled down Amanda's spine, reminding her to the second of how long it had been since Jake had touched her. Too long, the sizzling jolt of sensation that shot through her said. A surge of desire clawed at her, and that bizarre emptiness reasserted itself. Both left her feeling breathless and shaken.

"You look fine, Amanda," Jake repeated gruffly.

"I do? Really?"

"Uh-huh. All cool and refined and . . . princesslike." Untouchable, was the word Jake added to himself, because it fit her better. She looked poised, regal, cold as ice. Dignified. Ladylike. *White*.

Jake's hand reluctantly left her thigh. Like his gaze, his fingers strayed to the golden bun she'd knotted at her nape. He stroked the tight twist of hair; it felt like spun silk under his fingertip. His gut kicked, and it was all he could do not to tug the knot free and bury his hands up to the wrists in all that flowing, fragrant softness. He wanted to nuzzle his face in her hair, to suck into his body the sweet, sweet scent that clung to every sunlit strand.

He didn't do it, of course. It had taken her so much time to pin the thick, heavy tresses up, and she'd probably have a fit if he pulled it all down now. But the urge was there, and it was damn strong. When it came right down to it, he preferred the thick gold braid she usually wore; it made her look more human, more accessible, less prissy and refined.

Pain shimmied up his arm when Jake pulled his hand back. His calloused fingertips brushed that sensitive spot behind her ear. He saw her shiver, and knew she wasn't as unaffected by his touch as she wanted him to believe.

"I um suppose we should find Edward Bannister now," Amanda said, and the saddle creaked beneath her when she fidgeted. She chided herself for being silly; she felt nervous as a cat, but it couldn't be helped. Jake's touch did that to her. One glance, one touch—no matter how innocent—went through her like lightning. She couldn't think of a time when it hadn't. She didn't *want* to think of a time when it hadn't. But she was going to have to. Soon now, whether she liked it or not.

"You that anxious to get your money, princess?" Jake asked softly, so Roger wouldn't overhear.

What? What will you get, Jake?

My money. Every last cent of it. The sooner we get that brat back, the sooner I can be rid of you.

Amanda sucked in a sharp breath. "No, what I am is anxious to pay you."

His eyes narrowed, yet even through the shadows cast by the wide brim of his hat she saw his gaze sparkle dangerously.

"For services rendered, Miss Lennox?"

The way his gaze fed hungrily on her lips told Amanda that finding Roger was *not* the service Jake was referring to. Her cheeks paled, then flooded with color. Before she realized what she was doing, her hand lifted. Her open palm arched toward his cheek.

Jake's smokey gaze flashed with knowledge. He knew what Amanda was going to do before she knew it herself. He had plenty of time to deflect the blow if he wanted to. He didn't.

The slap was harsh and stinging—to them both.

Jake's head whipped back with the force of it. He turned back toward her almost immediately, and Amanda blanched to see the red imprint of her hand outlined against his deep copper skin. The muscle there ticked erratically. His jaw was tight and hard.

She made to snatch her stinging hand back, but Jake didn't give her time. His arm throbbed as, lightning quick, he grabbed her. His fingers banded around her slender wrist in a grip just shy of painful.

"I owed you that one, princess. But *only* that one," he growled, his gaze burned into her.

Amanda's breath caught when she remembered that first night. The fire. Jake's body molding into her back as he taught her how to whirl a stick in just the right way to start a spark. And then she thought of the match that he'd had all along, the way he'd tricked her. *Remind me to slap you tomorrow.* Oh yes, she remembered it, all of it. Dear God, how could she ever *forget?*

The fingers around her wrist tightened. "Don't ever slap me again, lady. Like you've said often, and I've always agreed, I'm like no . . . *gentleman* you've ever met. Next time, I *will* slap you back. Hard enough to make your prissy little head spin."

He released her so abruptly that Amanda had to grab the saddle pommel to keep from falling off the horse. She opened her mouth to apologize, plain and simple. For a split second she'd forgotten that nothing was plain and simple when it came to Jacob Blackhawk

Chandler. Not only did he complicate seemingly everything, but he also gave her no chance to utter a sound.

"I'll check around, see where Bannister's at. Sooner we get this over with, the better," Jake said over his shoulder as he jerked the reins and started guiding the white toward Pony's only street. "Wait here."

A few minutes slipped tensely past before Roger glanced over at Amanda. "He will come back, won't he?"

Amanda shrugged. She was trying to fight the feeling of desolation — and failing miserably. "Does it matter?"

Roger shrugged, and turned his gaze back to the swinging door of the false-fronted saloon they'd both seen Jake disappear inside of. "I guess not. Well, Miss Lennox, it seems the next logical question would be, do we wait for him?"

As it had for the past two days, Roger's oddly mature tone surprised Amanda. Except for the timbre, there was no similarity between this voice and the whiny, petulant one that she was used to having taunt her. She answered him question for question. "Do you want to wait for him?"

"Not really, but . . . well, to be honest, there's something about that man that scares me. I don't trust him, yet I don't *dis*trust him, either. Does that make sense, Miss Lennox?"

"Yes. I feel the same way."

Roger sat forward, eyeing her quizzically. "Do you think he'd be mad if he came back and found us gone?"

"Very." And a mad Jacob Blackhawk Chandler wasn't a man Amanda ever wanted to see again. Once had been more than enough, thank you. She shivered, remembering his icy hatred that night in his sister's cabin, the piercing glares that had looked right through her, his rough-to-the-point-of-violent touch.

Roger squirmed. While he was riding better these days, and seemed to have gotten over his unnatural fear of horses, Amanda couldn't help noticing how uncomfortable he was to be astride one. Surprisingly, he hadn't voiced a single complaint about it. Perhaps he'd sensed it would do no good? After all, horses were the only way to get to Pony.

"Do *you* want to wait for him, Miss Lennox?" Roger's tone said he would if she insisted, but that he'd rather not. Amanda knew that being this close and not being able to go on must be eating at him. He seemed every bit as impatient to put this god-awful journey behind him as she was.

"I don't see what harm scouting around for your father would do," she said finally. "And if we find him . . ." she shrugged, "well, I don't see what harm that would do, either." Except maybe to make Jake think she planned to collect her money without him seeing, and run off without paying him. His mistrust of her was strong enough to fuel such a conclusion, but she wouldn't let that stop her. Amanda knew she had no intention of leaving Pony until she'd paid Jake in full, and that was what really counted.

In the end, it took surprisingly little time to find out which house Edward Bannister lived in. Amanda simply stopped the first miner she passed and asked. He'd eyed her warily, but he told her what she wanted to know. And once he had, she realized she should have guessed on her own. What other house *would* Edward Bannister live in, except the biggest and best?

As she and Roger made their way toward the sprawling ornate structure, Amanda found herself wondering why Jake hadn't found out the information himself and returned by now. She was still wondering about that as she slipped from her saddle and tethered her mare to the porch railing.

The front door was flung wide open. It crashed against the outer wall of the house with a resounding slam.

The sunny day cast the porch—and the man standing in the open doorway—in shadows. Amanda didn't need to see all of the tall, thin man to know he was Edward Bannister. The resemblance between him and Roger was stunning; Roger had inherited the Bannister curls, the haughty tilt of chin, and the light blue eyes. Then, of course, there was the way Roger bounded up the stairs and catapulted himself into the man's arms. And the way the man in turn crouched down to wrap the boy in a tight hug.

"Over," Amanda whispered beneath her breath as she watched father and son embrace. "It's finally over."

Her thoughts turned to Jake. And, just as automatically, she felt the claw of desperation in her belly. Her smile faded as, once again, the emptiness and desolation closed over her like a cloying, oppressive blanket.

She took a little comfort in knowing that all wasn't completely over with Jake. She still had to pay him the money she owed him — after she'd collected it, of course. The thought brought her only a moderate surge of relief. It wasn't over with Jake yet, but it might as well be. He'd be out of her life soon enough, and once he was, she would be free to . . .

What? What would she be free to do? God, she didn't know anymore! Her original plan had been to get to the property her father had left her, but she'd lost sight of that goal long ago. It reasserted itself now, but weakly. Of course, she would still go to Washington — she had nowhere else to go — yet the thrill of achieving what she'd set out to do wasn't as fulfilling as she'd expected it to be.

Or was it the achievement that was lacking? Maybe not. Maybe what was lacking was her life. It was a life that now stretched out endlessly in front of her like the stark, lonely prairies she'd crossed. A life without Jake Chandler in it. Yes, Amanda thought, stark was an apt description, because —

"Miss Lennox, I presume?"

"I what? Oh, yes." Startled, Amanda glanced up into pale blue eyes set in a thin, sharp face. It took her a second to realize Edward Bannister had extended his hand, and another second for her to take it. His fingers felt cool and thin as they clasped hers.

Amanda tried not to compare his hand to a big, strong copper one of recent memory, but she couldn't help it. Comparisons were inevitable. It seemed like Edward Bannister, that *any* man, was going to fall short in her mind when compared to Jacob Blackhawk Chandler. Because in her mind, there simply *was* no comparison.

"Please, Miss Lennox, come inside," Edward nodded over his shoulder to the open doorway through which Roger had already disappeared. "It's almost lunchtime. The least I can do is feed you before you set out again."

"And pay me, Mr. Bannister," Amanda added, with an impudence that would have appalled Miss Henry. Odd, but the thought of appalling Miss Henry had Amanda fighting a smile. Jake Chandler's corrupting influence had no doubt done that to her. "Don't forget that."

Apparently Amanda wasn't the only one surprised by her boldness. Edward Bannister looked shocked, too. His pale blue eyes widened slightly, and she saw an uncompromising hardness in his expression that she'd missed before. But then he smiled, and the tension that had sparked the air was abruptly smoothed away. "Yes, of course, your money. I haven't forgotten, Miss Lennox. I'll get it as soon as we're inside. *Then* you can decide whether or not to stay for dinner. How does that sound?"

"It sounds wonderful," Amanda said, because it really did. The thought of any food besides jerky, beans, and canned peaches was superb—any food, she reassessed with a shiver, except snake. And the thought of sitting in a real chair, and dining at real table with a linen tablecloth and silverware was very appealing. Now, if she could also wheedle a long, hot bath out of the man, she really would think she'd died and gone to heaven!

411

Years of training made her automatically curl her fingers around the crook of Edward Bannister's elbow. Sending the man a radiant smile, Amanda allowed herself to be guided into the cool shadows of the house.

Jake glared down at the glass of bourbon in disgust. There had been a time when he'd been a drinker, but that time was years ago. He hadn't touched the hard stuff in a long, long while.

Until he'd met Amanda Lennox.

Now, for the second time in less than a week, he was sitting in a saloon, trying to get drunk. Because of Amanda. Everything he did and thought these days was because of her.

Yup, just one prissy white lady, Jake thought derisively. That's all it took to shove Jacob Blackhawk Chandler back in front of a bottle. Christ! He'd been so sure he would only take up drinking again if something catastrophic happened. Apparently he'd been wrong.

Then again . . .

His wounded arm stung as, with a scowl, he swirled the potent-smelling liquor around, watching as it coated the smudged sides of the glass. A shard of sunlight streamed in through the saloon's dirt-streaked window. The light hit the glass in his hand and split into a rainbow of color—one of which reminded him of Amanda Lennox's eyes, another of her hair.

The image that sprang to mind prompted Jake to down his drink in one fiery swallow. It was his third. The bourbon didn't cut as it passed his throat, but slid down nice and easy. He waved for the barkeep to refill his glass. The fat man did so reluctantly, but promptly. Jake wondered if the good service was in no small way prompted by the knife he'd set atop the chipped walnut bar before he'd even taken a seat.

In a flash, Jake remembered the barkeep's beady eyes, the way they had rounded when they'd fixed on the knife. The man's cheeks had reddened, and Jake could almost hear every word about "not serving his kind" scamper right out of the big man's mind. While the knife had kept Jake's glass full, his savage scowl had kept the other men in the saloon at a safe distance. They may not want him here — hell, he could feel their resentful glares crawling all over his back — but Jake had made damn sure they had no say about it. He needed a drink too badly.

No, what he *really* needed, badly, was to get the hell away from Amanda Lennox. The woman touched him, disturbed him in ways no other woman of *any* goddamn color ever had or ever would. Maybe with some time, some distance . . .

Nah, probably not. Jake figured he had about as much chance of forgetting his prissy white princess as he had of being crowned King of England tomorrow. While he could leave her — and he would, damn soon! — that didn't change the fact that he'd never be able to forget her. A part of her would always be inside of him. He had an uneasy feeling that an even bigger part of him would be left behind. With her. Always.

His scowl darkened. How long had he been in the saloon? A half hour? An hour? He didn't know. The ruckus of his thoughts had made him lose all track of time. Had Amanda waited for him like he'd told her to? And if she hadn't . . . ?

Jake reached into the inside pocket of his vest for a couple of coins. What he found instead was the white linen handkerchief he'd forgotten he'd put there. He tried to ignore the way the cloth seared into his fingertips. With a sigh, he reached past it and retrieved a couple of coins, which he tossed onto the bar. He then picked up his knife and shoved it back into place. The sheath slapped his outer thigh as he stalked toward the saloon's double doors.

He'd no more swung one of the doors open when Jake felt something else. Something as familiar as it was unwelcome.

Every eye in the place was on him. He knew it without looking, could feel the stares boring into his rigidly held back. Their gazes felt like crawly things on his skin. Some of the gazes were hostile, others were cautious, others merely curious.

Not a single one was friendly.

Jake was used to attracting attention wherever he went. It had ceased to bother him years ago. So why they hell was it bothering him now?

While he tried to overlook his resentment as he pushed through the doors and stepped onto the sunlit boardwalk, Jake knew damn well where his discomfort stemmed from. Amanda Lennox had planted a seed in his mind, and without his permission — Jesus, without his *knowledge!* — the blossom had flourished.

From the start you've told me that all white people, even without knowing you, automatically label you a savage. Hasn't it ever occurred to you that you go out of your way to give them that impression?

Did he? No, of course not. At least, he didn't do it consciously. It was just that . . . well, it was hard for a man to walk in two different worlds. One, the Indian's world, he'd decided long ago he didn't belong in; the other, the white man's world, had made that decision for him. Amanda didn't know anything about that. She may *think* she did, but she didn't, couldn't. Not really.

But was she right?

Jake narrowed his eyes against the glare of sunlight as he picked out the white, tethered to a post in front of the saloon. Compared to the other horses tied there, the one without the saddle looked out of place. It attracted attention. So did the knife at his belt, the moccasins on his feet.

Unconsciously, he fingered the strand of long black hair that fell forward on his shoulder. He felt the thin braid graze his wrist, felt the tickle of the small brown feather against his skin. He hadn't tied the bandanna around his forehead today, but he might as well have.

414

He could see by the looks he was getting that he appeared every bit the ruthless savage these white people had him pegged for.

Was she right?

Jake gritted his teeth and stalked toward his horse. And he thought that . . . yes, Goddammit to hell and back, Amanda was right! So what? It didn't change a thing!

Except maybe the way he looked at himself. The problem was, Jake had always taken great pains to never look at himself too hard or too often — and he was doing both now. Damn. Maybe this realization changed a hell of a lot more than he'd thought.

Distance, he thought as he untethered the white and vaulted lithely onto its back. Yes, distance. All he needed was some time away from Amanda Lennox and everything would be fine. His sense of perspective would come back. He'd start to look at himself in the same light he always had. He'd . . .

Oh, who the hell was he trying to fool? Himself? If so, it wasn't working. He wasn't stupid, and he wasn't drunk. He knew damn well that nothing, *nothing,* would ever be the same again. Everything had changed the second that prissy Bostonian princess had waded into his life — or, more accurately, the day he'd waded into hers. Damn, but she'd turned his world inside out!

Jake guided his horse in the direction he'd left Amanda and the kid. He knew before he'd reached the spot that they were gone. He wasn't surprised. It wasn't as though she'd ever done a thing he'd told her to. Right from the start, she'd opposed him. He would be lying if he said that wasn't one of the first things that had attracted him to her, the spunk he sensed beneath the cowardice, the passion beneath the ice.

It didn't take a lot of brain power to know where they'd gone. He'd learned the whereabouts of Edward Bannister's house his first two minutes in the saloon. Bannister was the richest miner in Pony. His residence was hardly a secret.

With a reluctant sigh, Jake turned his mount around and picked his way toward the house that sprawled out over what looked like the entire north end of town. The closer he came to it, the more uncomfortable Jake felt. That the house was an eyesore—so out of place it was laughable—didn't seem to matter. That a man had the wealth to build such an eyesore in the first place *did*. Compared to the rickety, clapboard buildings lining Main Street, that house was a mansion!

The hell of it was, it was too damn easy for Jake to imagine a woman like Amanda Lennox gliding through those spacious, expensively furnished rooms. He groaned and thought he could almost hear a silk hem rustling around her shapely legs as she walked, could almost smell exotic bath oils—the names of which he couldn't even pronounce—clinging to her forbidden white skin.

Oh, yeah, she belonged in a house like that, all right. She'd been born to it. She deserved to wear the kind of clothes a man like Edward Bannister could give her, to live in the kind luxury only a man as wealthy as Bannister could afford to keep her in. She deserved the best and . . .

Hell, Jacob Blackhawk Chandler certainly wasn't that!

"Again, Mr. Bannister, I thank you," Amanda said, and held out her hand to the man.

Edward smiled congenially and, bending slightly pressed her knuckles to his lips. His mouth felt warm and moist. Too warm and moist, Amanda thought as another mouth came to mind—a mouth that was hot and searing, a mouth that could make her blood fire when it grazed much more intimate parts of her than the back of her hands.

"Are you sure you won't reconsider staying?"

416

Edward said as he straightened. He didn't release her hand, but kept it clasped firmly, almost possessively, in his own. "Just for a few days?"

Amanda didn't pull away, it would be impolite, but she thought about it. Not for the first time that afternoon did she wonder about how easily she'd slipped back into rigid manners. Oh, how false the facade felt!

She inclined her head and smiled. "While I appreciate the offer, I've business to attend to in Pony." She thought of the money tucked away in her saddlebag, of how surprised Jake was going to be when she actually did pay him. "And, of course, I'd like to get settled in Washington before winter sets in."

"Ah, Washington. Such a lovely place," Edward replied casually. Amanda held her smile—through sheer force of will—though she was gritting her teeth. These pleasantries were straining her frayed nerves. "I visit Seattle once or twice a year on business. You wouldn't mind if I paid you a call the next time I'm in the area, would you, Miss Lennox?"

If it meant having to exchange small talk with him for any length of time, then Amanda thought that, yes, she would definitely mind a visit from this man. Of course, she couldn't tell Edward Bannister that. It would be rude. Instead, as inconspicuously as possible, she slipped her hand free and said sweetly, "That would be lovely. I'll look forward to it. Now, if you'll excuse me, I must . . . What? What is it?"

Amanda frowned and glanced over her shoulder to see what had brought that sudden, tight expression to Edward Bannister's face. What she saw was Jake Chandler tethering his horse to the post next to hers. Her heart gave an unsteady leap, and a genuine smile started to curl over her lips . . . until she noticed the sudden, coiled tension in the man standing beside her.

"What the hell do you think you're doing?" Edward snarled, his hands waving like he was trying to shoo away a pesky bee. "Get that horse off my land. You're kind isn't welcome h—"

"Mr. Bannister!" Amanda gasped. Her gaze shifted to Jake. The muscle in his cheek jerked angrily, and the dangerous glint in the gaze he narrowed on Edward Bannister made her catch her breath. Was this the sort of thing Jake faced all the time? The semi-tolerant way he was reacting told her it was. "Mr. Bannister, please, you don't understand. This man is—"

"A filthy half-breed," Edward sneered, though he took the time to pat Amanda's hand reassuringly. "I can see that, Miss Lennox. And I understand only too well." His nostrils flared as he pierced Jake with a disgusted glare. "I understand they have reservations for . . . his kind, and I understand that *he* should be on one instead of being allowed to roam free and accost decent people like us."

The temptation to slap Edward Bannister's face was strong and it took some effort for Amanda not to surrender to it. Her conscience insisted that she try once more to make Edward understand exactly who Jake was. Surely once he knew . . . ? "Jake hasn't accosted us, Mr. Bannister. For that matter, he—"

The intensity of having Edward Bannister's cold blue eyes stab into her wilted the words on Amanda's throat.

"Jake? Did you call him *Jake?* Miss Lennox, are you saying you *know* this . . . this . . . ?"

Amanda's spine stiffened, and her chin tipped haughtily as she pierced Edward Bannister with a regal glare. "Man," she supplied frostily. "And yes, I know him. He's—"

"How well?" Edward snapped angrily. "How *well* do you know this breed? Do you know him *intimately?*"

It wasn't the question that stunned Amanda speechless, so much as the contemptuous way Edward Bannister sneered it. That, and the vicious way he reached for her. His finger had no sooner bitten painfully into her upper arms than Amanda heard a foot slam onto the bottom step of the porch, hard enough to make the wood groan and threaten to splinter.

"Not a good idea, Bannister," Jake growled, and took another step up — just as loudly.

Amanda thought Jake must indeed be furious to have made *that* much noise. Edward Bannister must have realized the same thing, for she felt and saw a shiver ripple through his thin body. While his grip on her arms loosened, it didn't drop away.

"Don't do what?" Edward growled, his glare still fastened on Amanda. "I'll do anything I have to to find out what this . . . this . . . *lady* has been doing in front of my son! This is my house, my land. I can do any damn thing I please, and no half-breed is going to stop me!"

"Wanna bet?" Jake's voice was as sharp and as deadly as the blade of the knife he unsheathed from his belt. "One thing you can't do, Bannister, not here or anywhere else, is hurt the lady. I forbid it."

Edward Bannister was nothing if not cocky — both his wealth and his social position in Pony assured that. That was the only way Amanda could explain the fact that the man did not at that point turn fully around to face Jake. Amanda, on the other hand, didn't have to turn at all to see him. Jake appeared directly behind Bannister's narrow shoulder. His icy glare, she noticed, was as much for her as it was for the man holding her.

The long, curved blade of the knife glinted in the sunlight as Jake pressed just the tip against the nape of Bannister's neck. "I'll warn you only once. And you can thank the lady for that, because it's one more warning than I usually give."

"I'm not afraid of you, breed. Go ahead, cut me. We both know that if you touch one hair on my head, the residents of this town will string you up just as fast as they can find a rope strong enough to hold you."

"I'll keep it in mind." Jake's pause was short, succulent. "But I won't let it stop me."

Something about the emotionless way he said it

must have finally gotten through to Bannister. He let Amanda go so quickly that she staggered back a few steps. One of the squared porch posts slammed into her back when she stumbled against it. The bite of pain was the least of her worries. She still had to get around Edward Bannister to reach the stairs.

Amanda glanced at Jake, and he nodded briskly. Resheathing the knife, he grabbed a fistful of Edward Bannister's collar and hauled him roughly out of the way, giving Amanda more than enough room to pass. She did so quickly and without hesitation.

She didn't realize she was shaking until she started to descend the stairs. She had to hold tightly to the railing to keep from falling, her knees felt that unsubstantial. How was she going to climb onto the mare in this condition? She'd find the strength somehow — she'd do whatever it took to get away from Edward Bannister's hateful insinuations and insults.

Amanda knew the second Jake descended the stairs, though he made no sound and she wasn't looking. She didn't have to be. Her back prickled with awareness, even as it warmed to his body heat. His earthy scent wafted over her, calming her a bit. She knew exactly when he came to stand behind her, knew when he raised his hand, and when his big copper palm hesitated a mere inch from her shoulder. She also knew when that hand dropped to his side, as well as when and he swaggered to the white and vaulted atop it. The moment was etched in time; it was the exact second her heart stopped beating and her soul shattered into a thousand irretrievable slivers.

Fury. Had she ever felt so much of it, so intensely, as she did right now when she glared up at Edward Bannister? It coursed through her in hot waves; for once she didn't fight it. Anger made her reckless, and Amanda didn't fight that either. "Just so you know, Mr. Bannister," she said in her coolest, haughtiest tone, "what I was trying to tell you before — what you refused to hear — is that this *man* saved your son's life.

If it wasn't for him, Roger might be dead right now."

Bannister paled considerably, but Amanda had to give him credit for holding his ground — if for nothing else. Neither his physical stance nor his mental one budged an inch. "I'm sure if Roger had known he'd be indebted to a half-breed for saving his life, he would have done what any good Bannister would do . . . he would have died with dignity."

Amanda was still reeling from that parting shot when the man spun on his heel and stormed into his house. The door slammed behind him loud enough to make the sparkling glass panes in the windows rattle.

"Think you understand a bit better now, princess?" Jake asked harshly. "I told you it wouldn't work out with us. Now you know why."

Amanda could feel Jake's gaze on her as she scrambled off the horse, but she was too furious to give a damn. "Why of all the — !"

"Leave Bannister alone, princess. It doesn't concern you."

"I will not leave him alone. And I resent you thinking I should. Whether you like it or not, Jake Chandler, this entire incident most certainly *does* concern me!" With jerky motions she unstrapped the heavy saddlebag and tossed it onto the ground. Unmindful of the dirt she was grinding into the only decent dress she now owned, Amanda knelt in front of the saddlebag and tore open the flap. With jerky movements, she upended the leather satchel and scattered the contents around her. She sneered when she found what she was looking for — and lots of it, too!

Her fingers were still trembling; she had to count the money four times before she could be sure she had the right amount. Standing on watery knees, she walked around the mare, stopping only when she was close to Jake. She could have touched him if she'd wanted to. She didn't. It was bad enough he was so near she could feel every masculine inch of him invade

421

her.

"Here." With a toss of her head, she glanced up at him.

He met her glare with one insolently cocked brow. "What?"

"Here!" Both of her hands were curled around fistfuls of money. She lifted them, and slammed her fists simultaneously into Jake's rock-hard gut. If his *whooof* of surprise was anything to go by, she had done an admirable job of catching him off guard. Good. She wanted him off guard. She wanted his arrogant head *reeling;* the same way hers had been ever since she'd first set eyes on him. "Your money, Mr. Chandler. That *is* what you came here for, isn't it?"

Yes, it was. And since they both obviously knew it, Jake saw no reason to deny it. He *was,* however, shocked that he hadn't had to hunt Amanda down and wheedle it out of her. That, he'd been prepared for, expecting even. One of the many things he *wasn't* prepared for was the way Amanda let go of the money at the first touch of his fingers grazing hers.

Jake's wounded arm screamed a protest as he caught most of the bills, but not all. A few stray ones fluttered to the ground or were caught by the chilly afternoon breeze. He didn't see them. His gaze was riveted on Amanda — would the lady never cease to surprise him? He watched her stomp back to her saddlebag. Again, she knelt, and again she yanked money out of the shadowy interior. But only one handful this time.

Jake frowned. "Now what the hell are you doing?"

Was Jake laughing at her? Amanda's gaze snapped to him, but she didn't see even a hint of a grin. She'd smelled liquor on his breath, so maybe he was drunk; that would explain it. One thing was for certain, his tone had been riddled with amusement. That served only to rile her all the more. "Watch and find out!"

She slammed up the porch stairs, then hammered on the door with her free fist. It was opened too quickly for Edward Bannister to have been doing anything but standing on the other side, watching through the shield of curtains and glass.

"Now what?" he snapped, his gaze volleying between her and Jake. "I thought you'd left."

"I'm going," Amanda said tightly. "Believe me, I don't want to be here a second longer than I have to. Unfortunately, I forgot one minor detail."

"Which is?"

Amanda cast him her sweetest smile and, with more force than was necessary, punched her money-ladened fist smack into the center of Edward Bannister's bony chest. The man's breath poured from his lungs; the sound was more satisfying than anything Amanda could remember having heard in ages!

Bannister staggered backward from the blow, his expression half surprise, half pain. Since he hadn't realized Amanda had anything in her hand, he made no move to grab the money. Pity. The second her fingers uncurled, crinkled bills showered the porch floor. "What the—?"

"It's money, Mr. Bannister. *Your* money, to be precise. I've decided I don't want it."

Bannister's gaze rounded on the bills that were scattered over his shoes, over the whitewashed planks, everywhere. His mouth worked, but nothing came out. Obviously he'd never had anyone throw money in his face before. Especially if that money was originally his. It gave Amanda a sense of supreme satisfaction to know she was the first.

"A-are you crazy?" Bannister stammered. He bent and automatically started gathering up the bills before the breeze could toss them to who knows where.

"Yes, I must be," Amanda said in a tone that would have done any tea social justice—calm, cool, collected . . . *furious*. "I'm crazy to have taken a job where my employer was a prejudiced bastard like yourself. Lord knows *what* I was thinking."

Jake grinned. He knew damn well what *he* was

thinking: that his prissy little white princess had lost her cotton pickin' mind! He didn't say that, though. He couldn't. For the first time in his life, a woman had left him speechless.

He found his voice fast enough when Amanda spun on her heel and stalked toward the mare. Her face was flushed with fury, her green eyes sparkling with contempt. Her jaw was set in a hard, determined line that said . . . Jesus, she really *was* going to leave all that money behind! "Amanda . . ."

"Oh, shut the hell up, Jake," she snapped irritably. "I know what I'm doing."

"I doubt that, princess. I really do." Jake brought himself up short, a scowl furrowing his brow. Had Amanda just cussed? *Amanda?*

"Is that so? Well, this may come as a surprise to you, but I don't really give a damn *what* you think of me. Not anymore."

She swung up onto the mare, but didn't leave. Not yet. There was still one more tiny matter to take care of.

Her attention shifted to Jake, and she pierced him with a furious glare. "You're right. I should have listened when you said it wouldn't work out between us." Oh, but she liked the way Jake squirmed when she said that! And that red tinge to his copper cheeks was a heady sight. "But," she added tightly, leaning toward him, "not for the reasons you seem to think. You see, whether you believe it or not, Jake, it never mattered to me what color your skin is. White, red, black, green, I never gave a damn. I look at the man *inside* the skin. And when I look at you, I see only half a man. Sorry, but that isn't enough for me. *You* aren't man enough for me, Jacob Blackhawk Chandler!"

It was the bourbon. Obviously it had affected Jake more than he'd thought, to the point where he was hearing things. Amanda couldn't possibly have just said . . . . ? Yup, the victorious glare she sent him before sinking her heels into the mare's flanks said his hearing wasn't faulty.

Dammit, he'd just been royally insulted. The spunky little bitch! "Where the hell do you think you're going? Amanda? *Amanda!*"

"Washington, Mr. Chandler," she called back over her shoulder, her voice quickly receding. "Where I was going before I met you. Where I'll live perfectly happily *without* you." Under her breath, Amanda added, "And I will. If it kills me, Goddammit, I swear I will!"

It wasn't until Jake made a grab for the reins that he realized he still had the money fisted haphazardly in his hands. Dammit! Well, maybe *Amanda* was stupid enough to fling her portion back in Edward Bannister's face, but Jake was more practical. This was more money than he'd made in his entire life, and he had plans for it! He'd earned it and . . . by God, he intended to *keep it*.

Jake stuffed the greenbacks into his saddlebag, then spun the white around. Leaning low over the horse's neck, he growled a command in its ear to go. Quickly. Now.

The people milling about Main Street had the good sense to scatter. It was either that, or be run down.

Chapter Twenty-five

Amanda knelt on the hard, lumpy ground. Her smile was wide and proud. Every time she saw the first spark catch on a pile of dried grass and twigs she felt a heady surge of victory. Leaning forward, she blew on the first fragile teardrop of flame. Her smile broadened when it caught and quickly spread.

In no time the air was thick with the scent of burning wood, and Amanda was being warmed by the heat of a roaring fire. A sigh of contentment whispered past her lips as she sat back on her heels. Still grinning, she tucked the oversized box of matches into her saddlebag.

After a brief, almost guilty hesitation, she removed a can of peaches and a can opener from the leather bag. Stifling a yawn, she propped her back against the gritty trunk of a nearby pine and pried open the tin can.

There was a time when she would have turned her nose up at such a paltry meal. But not anymore. This was a delicacy! After days of eating nothing but jerky and beans, the peaches smelled sweet and syrupy and tempting beyond reason. Her stomach grumbled in anticipation.

She ate slowly, savoring each bit, letting the sweet, fruity taste linger on her tongue until it had almost disappeared before licking her lips and taking another bite. In no time she was scraping the bottom of the can, then shamelessly tilting her head back to drain every delicious drop of syrup.

Gone. Lowering the can to her lap, she sighed. This was her last can of peaches, and she wouldn't be getting more any time soon. Even if she came across a town that sold them, she didn't have enough money to buy them.

On second thought, she didn't have the money to buy *anything*. What little she'd had had gone into buying enough supplies to get her to Washington. Jerky and beans and an extra wool blanket had seemed like important purchases . . . at the time. Yet right now Amanda would trade them all for just one more can of peaches!

Not for the first time did she wish she hadn't acted so rashly. Throwing Edward Bannister's money back in his face wasn't the smartest thing she'd ever done in her life, though it had seemed a grand idea at the time. Now that Amanda was flat broke, the rebellious act had lost a lot of its appeal.

If she'd kept the money, she could have afforded to buy more peaches. She could also have bought a ticket on a stage instead of having to make the journey to Seattle alone, by horse. If she'd kept the money . . .

She wouldn't have respected herself, plain and simple. That was the *only* reason she'd thrown Edward Bannister's money back at him. Well, all right, maybe there was *one* more reason, but she didn't want to think about that. In fact, she'd gone out of her way to keep her mind clear of *those* traitorous thoughts for the last five days. She wasn't about to start thinking about them—about *him*—now.

The money. She would think about the money—or lack thereof—because anything was safer than thinking about . . .

Jake.

The name arrowed through her and stabbed straight through her heart. A bolt of pain cut through her, hot and sharp and jarring. In five days, the intensity hadn't lessened a bit. If anything, the empty ache inside of her had grown; it was more acute, more consuming than ever.

Five days, Amanda thought as she sat back heavily, breathlessly against the tree. Was that all the time that had elapsed? Just five days? It felt like a year—the longest, loneliest year of her life!

She didn't realize she was trembling until she felt her fingertips vibrate against the empty tin can. Even with the fire blazing, she felt cold. Icy chills washed through her from the inside out.

And empty. She felt so frightfully empty. She—

"The can, princess. You forgot to bury the can."

A shaky smile tugged at Amanda's lips as she glanced down at the can. She remembered Jake telling her to bury waste so that animals wouldn't be drawn to the scent during the night. Normally, she did. Tonight she'd been so tired and confused and lonely that she'd almost forgotten to . . .

Her smile evaporated. The hairs at her nape prickled, and the skin there heated as though it had been scorched by an invisible flame. Awareness shot down her spine.

She stiffened, instantly alert. The snap of a twig brought her to her feet. She fumbled inside the pocket of her skirt, her trembling fingers searching frantically for the pistol she was rarely without. Though her narrowed gaze scanned the ring of firelight, she saw nothing out of the ordinary.

Scowling, Amanda wondered if perhaps she wasn't losing her mind. These last few months had been traumatic, to say the least . . . it was possible. Maybe the voice she thought she'd heard—*Jake's voice?*—was a figment of her imagination. A product of wishful thinking?

"It *sounded* real," Amanda muttered under her breath, "but obviously it wasn't."

She waited a few more minutes—gun in hand, her body tense and alert—but heard nothing unusual. While she scanned the clearing a couple of dozen times, she saw nothing unusual either.

While her heartbeat steadied itself, her breathing remained harsh and erratic. She was no longer tired. The surge of adrenaline that fright had dumped into her bloodstream served to burn away fatigue. Right now she felt restless and . . . dirty.

She hadn't taken a bath last night because she hadn't camped near water. Tonight, she could hear the gurgle of the narrow creek where she'd tethered her mare a mere one hundred feet away. The crisp, cool water beckoned.

Five minutes later, after a thorough search, Amanda had assured herself that she was indeed alone. Five minutes after that, she was sponging herself off in the icy mountain creek.

The cold water made her gasp, and made goosebumps prickle on her arms and legs. Amanda didn't care. Being clean felt too wonderful, too rare. She quickly lathered and rinsed twice, then washed her hair, scrubbing viciously with her fingertips until her scalp tingled and the thick golden mass felt squeaky clean.

It wasn't until Amanda had toweled her hair semi-dry, and was in the process of heading up the bank wearing her only clean chemise—and clutching her clean, damp clothes to her chest for warmth—that she felt another prick of awareness at her nape.

Her shiver had nothing to do with the cold. It had everything to do with the shadowy line of trees her attention fixed upon. A twig snapped, and she blinked hard when she saw one of the shadows separate itself from the others. It was wide, that shadow, and shaped like a man. Her breath caught when the shadow took a step forward.

Jake, she thought, then instantly dismissed the idea. If Jake was going to come after her, he would have done it days ago. Besides, there was something about this shape—she wasn't sure exactly what—that didn't look quite right. Something that told her this man was not Jake Chandler.

Amanda dropped the pile of freshly washed clothes, barely noticing when they scattered over the ground at her feet. This time, she found the pistol in record time. She coaxed the hammer back with her thumb; the metallic sound of revolving chambers was loud and grating.

Did the intruder see how badly she was shaking? Could he hear the wild pounding of her heart, the ragged give and take of her breathing? Despite the brisk air and her recent bath, Amanda felt a bead of perspiration trickle between her breasts.

"You can come out now," she called, and was surprised that her voice gave away none of her anxiety. "The show's over."

A sense of deja vu tingled down Amanda's spine when she heard grass crunch beneath boot heels, and saw the shadow take another step forward.

A sliver of moonlight glinted off raven black hair. A pair of light-colored eyes burned out of the shadows, burned into her. It might have been her imagination, but she could have sworn she heard a husky chuckle blend with the normal night noises. And then all she could hear was the clatter of her heart, and the voice that shot out of the darkness; the tone husky, thick . . . oh, so wonderfully familiar!

"Pity. That was one *hell* of a show, princess."

Amanda fumbled the gun. It fell onto the pile of damp clothes with a muffled *thump*. She didn't notice. Couldn't. Her concentration was fixed on the way that voice wrapped around her like a scrap of sun-warmed velvet. "Jake?"

"Uh-huh. Expecting someone else?"

"No. No, of course not. I-I wasn't expecting *you*."

"I can see that." That, and a hell of a lot more than Jake thought his sanity could bear to see right now. For example, he could see the pale white chemise; the garment fell from her shoulders to her ankles in inviting white folds that looked like a splash of vibrant color against the night. And—he swallowed hard—beneath the nearly transparent linen he could see the dusky rose tips of her . . .

"What are you doing here, Jake?"

Her voice jarred his attention back to her face. Good thing, too! He'd been half a second away from stalking the space between them and hauling the woman roughly into his arms, whether she wanted to be there or not. That wasn't a good idea. Not yet, anyway. He was clinging to the shadows for a reason, wanting to give her only one shock at a time.

"Jake?" Amanda asked when he said nothing, but continued to stand there staring at her. Even through space and darkness, she could see the veiled hunger in his eyes. Well, all right, maybe she couldn't *see* it exactly, but she could *feel* it. Just as she could feel her own molten response. The irony of it was, Jake wasn't even all that close to her. He certainly wasn't as close as she would have liked for him to be!

"What am I doing here?" Jake repeated the question flatly and took another step forward, but not enough to reveal himself to her. "Why, I'm taking you up on your challenge, lady. It's about time you learned that you can't bruise a man's ego the way you bruised mine, then expect to turn and walk away from him. Maybe the pansies you knew back East would put up with that . . . but I won't."

His words were huskily spoken, filled with a raw, sensuous promise. They rolled over Amanda in a

431

wave of acute, sexual heat, reminding her of how very long it had been since he'd held her, touched her, loved her. If the time came, could she deny him? Deny herself? "So, you've come to prove you're man enough for me? Is that it?"

"Yeah, something like that." His gaze glinted out of the darkness, raking her from head to toe. He missed nothing. Not the way the moonlight glinted off her long, damp hair, not the way the thin chemise hid so little of her charms. Nothing. "Come here, Amanda."

Amanda sucked in a sharp breath. She wanted to—*Lord, how she wanted to!*—but she couldn't. Her pride wouldn't let her. She'd told Jake once that she loved him, and she still hadn't gotten over the humiliation of his silence. She simply could not open herself up to that sort of pain again. It hurt too much.

"Dammit, Amanda, come here!"

"No!" She shook her head and forced herself to take a step backward. It wasn't easy. Despite the cold night air, every nerve in her body was on fire with his nearness, with the promise of his touch. Ignoring the needs of her body in favor of the needs of her mind was the hardest thing she'd ever done.

"Don't make me hunt you down, princess."

Amanda knew he was losing what little patience he'd had with her. Still, she took another step back. Her body tensed, preparing to run fast and far if it came to that. "I don't want you to touch me, Jake. I don't ever want you to touch me again."

"Why? I thought you liked it when I put my hands on you."

"You thought wrong." And he did. Because she didn't like it . . . she loved it. However, she wasn't about to tell him that. Her shredded dignity wouldn't allow it.

His voice lowered a dangerous pitch. "Careful, princess. You keep pushing me, and I'll be more than happy to come over there and prove just how big a liar you are."

Oh, that hurt! It had been weeks since she'd lied to him, and he knew it! "Why you conceited, no-good, miserable . . . *bastard!* How dare you—?"

"Shut up, Amanda." Jake took a step toward her. Another. "I didn't come here to fight with you."

"No? Then what *did* you come for?"

"This," he growled, and as soon as he was within reach, he grabbed her.

Amanda didn't realize how close he was until she felt his fingers manacle her upper arms. With a flick of his wrist, Jake hauled her up hard against his chest. The air rushed from her mouth . . . and was swallowed up by his.

With a growl, his lips crashed down on hers. The kiss was long, hard, raw. Hungry and demanding. Amanda didn't want to flower open for him, Jake could feel her reluctance, but in the end she did. Nor did he want to need to taste her so damn badly, but he did.

His tongue stroked her, plundered and mated with hers until he felt her fingers, fisting his shirt, loosen, open, and caress. He caught her whimper with his mouth, and a shudder racked his body when he felt her melt into him.

He'd meant to claim her. To make her physically admit how much she'd missed him in the time they'd been apart—every bit as much as he'd missed her. He'd proved it to them both. But, as always, it simply wasn't enough. He needed more from her. So much more! He needed, *craved,* everything that it was in her to give. That was why he'd followed her, why he was here now.

Amanda Lennox, body and soul. *That* was what he wanted . . . what he intended to get. No matter what it took.

Jake felt her knees buckle, and he held her all the

closer. His mouth continued to devour hers as he lowered them both to the bed of hard ground and pine needles. The flowery smell of her soap mingled with her natural scent; both invaded his nostrils, invaded his *blood*, and made the fire roaring through his veins ignite to a feverish degree.

"Surrender," he panted against her kiss-swollen lips. He felt her breath rush over his face in hot, rhythmic waves as his knee tried, and failed, to nudge her legs apart.

"Don't." Her body stiffened beneath him. "Don't do this to me again."

"Please, princess. I . . . God, I need you. I *have* to have you." The words cost him. Jake decided it was a price he would have paid ten times over if it meant having this woman — *his* woman, dammit! — writhing beneath him again, and again, and again.

Amanda shook her head, as much in denial as to shake free the hot, moist mouth that was suckling the side of her neck. She couldn't let this happen again. She wouldn't be able to stand it if Jake loved her now, then turned his back on her in the morning. It would kill her. "No you don't. You need my body, Jake. You don't need me."

The taste of her salty-sweet skin created such a pleasure-pain inside of him that Jake didn't immediately hear her. When the words finally sank in, it was akin to being hit in the head with a rock. He stiffened, lifting himself to glare down at her. Her eyes looked huge, confused, shimmering with unshed tears. It cut Jake up inside to return her gaze. His voice was hoarse and ragged. "I need you, Amanda. More than I've ever needed any woman, anything, in my life, I need you."

He needed her, yes. But did he *love* her? And could she bear to ask him, only to find out that he didn't? "But I thought you said — ?"

"I know what I said, dammit! I — "

434

The words broke off abruptly when her hands strayed to his shoulders. The tip of her index finger traced the jagged scar on the back of his neck. She felt a shiver run through him. And then she felt . . .

Frowning, Amanda opened her hands and plowed her fingers through his thick hair. She froze, and her frown deepened. In the dim light, she would have sworn he'd pulled his hair back with a strip of leather, the way she'd seem him do often before. Yet . . .

Dear God, what had Jake done to his hair?

"Jake?" she asked softly, breathlessly.

He hesitated, and Amanda felt the heat of his sigh on her cheek and neck. "Well? What do you think?"

"I . . . I'm not sure," she said hesitantly. "It's too dark to see."

"Good. I got a little carried away and it—er—came out a little shorter than I'd planned."

Amanda's head reeled. "My God, you really did, didn't you? You really *did* cut it?"

"Yes."

She swallowed hard, only to find that a lump of emotion had lodged in her throat. With effort, she worked her voice around it. "Why?"

"Don't you know?"

"I want you to tell me."

His head dipped, his lips grazed hers. It was a feathery touch. The quiver of his lips against hers told Amanda just how much self-control it took for Jake to keep it that way.

"For you, princess," he admitted softly, huskily. Jake saw a tear slip from the corner of her eye, a crystal bead glistening in the soft, silver moonlight. Leaning forward, he sipped the salty drop away with his mouth and tongue. "I did it for you."

"But—"

"Shhh. I don't want to talk. I've waited too long to have you again, princess, and I . . . Jesus, I can't wait anymore."

This time when his lips claimed hers, there was nothing soft about it. Nor was there anything soft about Amanda's response.

Jake groaned and pressed her back against the cool, sweet grass. In a heartbeat he'd spread his weight atop her. He loved the way her body accepted his hardness, the way her legs wrapped around him when he nuzzled his hips between her thighs.

She was hungry for him. He could feel it in the way she arched beneath him, in the way her fingers dug into his back as though trying to tear the shirt from his body. He was hungry for her. Ravenous. He'd dreamed of this for days—for long, sleepless nights. In his fantasies, their lovemaking had been slow and easy and so goddamn good.

But that was fantasy.

This—having his woman hot and willing in his arms—was a reality almost too good to live through. Having his blood coursing through his veins, pounding in his head, drilling through his body, was more real than anything Jake had ever known and . . .

His good intentions shattered. He couldn't go slow. He wanted, *needed,* her too badly.

He stripped off their clothes with a speed that left them both breathless, then settled himself against her. For a long, torturous moment he was content merely to feel her beneath him, against him. Content to lick a hot, wet path down her throat, and savor the salty, forbidden taste of her on his tongue. Content to draw in deep breaths that were filled with the sweet, sweet scent that was uniquely Amanda Lennox.

But only for a moment. Because Jake's body had other ideas, other demands, and they were too sharp and strong and primitive to deny or ignore.

He lowered his weight atop her, curling one arm beneath and around her, holding her close as he arched forward. He claimed her in one, sure thrust.

She moaned and arched up to meet him. Her legs tightened around his hips as though she never planned to let him go. Jesus, the way he felt right now, Jake prayed to God she never would!

Home, he thought as he buried his face in her hair. *Home.*

Their lovemaking was wild, untamed. Hungry kisses merged with passionate caresses to drive their senses over the brink. The climax built quickly, quickly. It crashed over them in breathtaking waves of sensation, swift and jarring and acute.

If it ended too soon, neither complained . . .

Because the second time they took each other slowly, and with nerve-shattering ease.

The first light of morning tinged the cloud-dotted sky in fluffy, pale pink streaks that looked like they'd been swirled there by an artist's brush. That was the first thing Amanda saw when she opened her eyes. The beauty of daybreak paled in comparison to her second sight, that of Jake Chandler's ruggedly handsome face. His normally harsh features were sleep-softened and relaxed. Attractive. Heart-stoppingly so.

Smiling contentedly, Amanda stifled a yawn and lifted herself up on an elbow. Jake's arm flexed, but he didn't wake up. Though his possessive grip on her hip gradually loosened, it didn't fall away.

Amanda liked that. She liked waking up enfolded in Jake's embrace, in the same way she'd liked sleeping curled in his arms, her cheeks resting against his hard, warm chest. Her dreams had been filled with the lulling beat of his heart . . . and with memories of their lovemaking. Oh, yes, she did like this. All of it. Maybe more than she had a right to.

At some time during the night, Jake had carried her back to camp. Her body glowed when she remembered how he'd laid her down on the bedroll and

437

covered her with a blanket. Her blood sizzled when she remembered how he'd promptly joined her beneath it. And what they'd done. All night. Again and again and again.

Amanda felt her cheeks flame. Searching for any distraction from hot, steamy memories, she let her gaze, as well as her hand rake gently through Jake's hair.

The inky strands felt feather-soft as they sifted through her fingers; lighter from lack of length, but just as sleek, just as silky. His hair wasn't as short as he'd led her to believe. The back was just long enough to scrape the collar of a shirt—but, of course, since he wasn't wearing one, that was only a guess on her part, one she wasn't anxious to prove out. The front had been trimmed more severely. It now swept back from his face in an appealing way that accentuated and defined the high mold of his cheeks and the chiseled hollows beneath.

"Oh, Jake," Amanda sighed as she fingered into place a short, inky lock that had wisped over his brow. Why? Why had he done this for her? Why couldn't he say the words? Or didn't he feel the emotion behind them?

Her caress slackened. Her fingertips grazed his temple, and she cupped his warm, smooth cheek before her hand dropped onto his shoulder. She felt the dormant bands of muscle beneath her open palm. The puckered scar on the back of his neck, no longer hidden by a curtain of thick black hair, seared her fingertips.

Amanda stiffened and started to pull away, only to find her wrist abruptly ensnared by rough copper fingers. His grip wasn't painful, but it was tight, insistent. Her gaze lifted, and she found herself a willing captive of hot, molten silver.

"It's in the past, where it belongs," he said, his voice still low and gritty from sleep. "Let it go."

438

"Can you, Jake? Can *you* let it go?"

"Yes. With your help."

Only a declaration of love would have sounded sweeter to Amanda's ears. A trickle of hope warmed her blood. *With your help*. Surely those weren't the words of a man ready to saddle his horse and ride out. Were they? "Jake, I—"

"Amanda—"

A sudden, tense pause crackled between them. Amanda was the first to break it. "I should see to breakfast," she said quickly as, gathering the top blanket around her, she pushed shakily to her feet. Jake, she noticed from the corner of her eye, made no move to toss the other blanket over himself. Instead, he lay unabashedly naked, his hard-muscled body molded to the ground beneath him as though he were one with it. Wasn't he cold? If so, he didn't show it.

"You're making breakfast?" he muttered, and levered himself up on one elbow. The beginnings of a sarcastic grin tugged at one corner of his mouth, even as his gaze raked her. "I didn't know princesses could cook."

"We royals are just full of surprises," Amanda quipped. With a toss of her head, she walked toward her saddlebag. From over her shoulder she added, "Don't expect anything fancy. Jerky and beans is about the extent of what I can do. I'd offer you some peaches, but . . ."

She'd knelt down beside the saddlebag and thrown open the flap, rummaging inside by feel alone. Her voice faded when she felt the cold side of a tin can graze her fingertips. Frowning, she pulled it free. Amanda had to read the label three times before she trusted herself to turn only her glare on Jake. "You've been following me!"

His expression was as readable as a rock. That in itself was condemning as hell. "What makes you think so?"

She gestured to him with the can. "Peaches," she said triumphantly, as though that explained everything.

"I know what it is. I can read labels, princess."

"No, no, obviously you don't understand. I ate my last can of peaches last night."

"Yeah? So?"

"*So* . . . where did this can come from?"

"Your saddlebag?"

"Don't get fresh with me. This wasn't in there last night, Jake. I know. I would have eaten it if it had been."

Jake cleared his throat, shrugged, and glanced away. "Maybe you didn't see it."

"Maybe. Or maybe *you* put it there."

This time the grin that curled over his lips was full and steeped in secretive humor. His eyes twinkled devilishly. "Now why would I do that, princess?"

Amanda's breath caught. Lord, when he smiled . . . !

She lost her train of thought, remembering it only when her fingers instinctively flexed around the can. "You *have* been following me, haven't you?" She didn't wait for an answer; the broadening of his grin told her all she needed to know. "For how long? And . . . why?"

Jake sighed, and pushed to his feet. With every step that brought him closer, Amanda's heartbeat grew weaker. Her palms were suddenly moist. Drawing breath into her burning lungs took more concentration than she wanted to spare. Her gaze was fixed on Jake. The way the morning light kissed his body—*all* of his body—made him look sleek and powerful and . . . beautiful. There was no other word to describe him.

He stopped beside her, crouching until they were on eye-level. His calloused thumb scraped the delicate line of her jaw. As though he couldn't resist, he leaned forward and brushed his lips over hers. The contact was brief but jarring. To them both.

"Amanda, honey," he said finally, his tone serious and controlled—even though his gaze continued to sparkle with . . . what? "Did you know you're in Wyoming? You have been for about a day and a half now."

"I . . . *what?*" she squeaked, then blinked hard and frowned. Wyoming? Not Idaho? But how could that be?

"Yup. See, the way I figure it, at the rate you're traveling you should hit Mexico in a couple of months."

"Mexico? But I don't want to go to Mexico!"

Jake started to laugh, but swallowed the impulse back, thinking correctly that it wouldn't be appreciated. He cleared his throat, gave himself a second to compose his sudden humor, and said, "I know, princess. That's why I'm here."

This was getting confusing. "You're here because I'm in Wyoming, even though I want to go to Washington," she muttered beneath her breath, shaking her head. "That makes no sense, Jake. And what on earth does any of it have to do with peaches?"

His hand opened, holding the soft underside of her chin, drifting over the long, smooth taper of her throat. The pulse nestled in the base leapt erratically against his palm. "Yes, I put the peaches in your saddlebag. And yes, I added the extra slices of jerky that you may or may not have noticed yesterday. And yes, the two extra cans of beans the day before that. And . . ." he shook his head and sighed. "Amanda, you don't really think you can stoke a fire before you go to bed and still have it blazing when you wake up the next morning, do you?"

Her eyes widened. "You did that?"

"That . . . and more." He chuckled softly. "A

441

couple days back I tried to head you off, steer you West . . . but you're a stubborn little piece of royalty. Cute, but stubborn. You just stuck that prissy nose of yours up in the air, went around the pile of logs I'd set up, and headed due south."

It wasn't funny. Amanda *knew* it wasn't funny. Jake had been following her, watching her all this time and hadn't had the decency to show himself. She should be insulted. She should be furious! She wasn't. How could she be angry when she had Jake Chandler's husky laughter curling like warm honey down her spine, and his steely gaze heating her blood?

She reached up and cupped the back of his hand with her palm. Their gazes met; hers wide, his narrow, both intense and searching. "Why, Jake? Why would you do all that for me?"

"Because I'm anxious to get to Washington," he replied huskily. "Because I want to know what it's like to make love to my woman in a real bed."

Amanda's stomach fluttered. "M-make love?"

"That's what I said."

"Yes, but is that what you *meant?*"

"Yes. It isn't just 'sex' with you, lady. It never has been. Damned if I know . . ." Jake gritted his teeth and pushed abruptly to his feet. The curses he let loose were long and vibrant. "See? See what you've done to me? Jesus, now you've got *me* lying!"

With an aggravated sigh, he plowed his fingers through his hair, and grimaced. It felt short, light . . . unfamiliar. He wondered how long was it going to take to adjust to this new, shorter length? How long before he adjusted to the boots that he'd bought in the last town he'd passed through; boots that pinched the hell out of his feet. And the shiny new Smith & Wesson hanging off a holster whose leather was so new it squeeked; a gun he really wasn't good at using. And the saddle that sat in a shady spot beneath a tree; a saddle he still hadn't had the heart to put on the white.

How long was it going to take for him to adjust to all of that? Jake didn't know, but however long it took, he'd do it, work at it. Hard. For Amanda. And speaking of Amanda . . .

He glanced down at her. "I *do* know why it's so good with you. Do you want me to tell you, princess? Are you ready to hear it?"

"More than ready," Amanda replied, and braced herself. She was scared to death to hear what he was going to say, yet she also knew she'd go crazy if she didn't listen.

With a gentleness Jake didn't know he possessed, he drew her to her feet. Neither noticed when the blanket fell from her slackened fingers, and puddled on the ground around their feet. Both were excruciatingly aware of when he pulled her against him, molding her soft white curves to his solid copper body.

Home, Jake thought as he held her against him. Cradled in her arms was the sweetest place he had ever, *would ever,* know.

He angled his head, and rubbed the golden silk of her hair with his cheek. His breaths sounded deep, strained; the heat of them washing over her felt wonderful, inflaming.

"I love you, Amanda Lennox," he whispered softly, raggedly. "Jesus, I love you so much it scares the hell out of me!"

Amanda absorbed the words, let them slide through her in a wave of pleasure that made her shake. When Jake pulled her closer, she nuzzled against him without question. She wrapped her arms around his back, holding him close, as though trying to melt right into him and become a part of him— the way he was already a part of her.

"Er, princess?"

"Hmmm . . .?"

443

"This is the first time I've ever done this, so maybe I'm wrong, but I think you're supposed to say you love me, too."

Amanda smiled, and hugged him all the closer. "I do. I do, I do, *I do!* You know that. You—"

He inched back and, cupping her cheeks in his hands, stared into her eyes. "Tell me, Amanda. You said the words once, and I turned you away because I thought I had to. I won't turn you away now. Never again. Please, I need to hear you say it."

She sucked in a sharp breath, held it for only a beat, then, on its release, poured out the words that were in her heart. "You are my life, Jacob Blackhawk Chandler and I . . . Oh, God, I love you so much it hurts sometimes."

His sooty lashes swept down, and she watched his expression tighten in an acute pleasure-pain that seemed to radiate from his body to hers. She shivered, and a tear slipped free when she reached up and smoothed a palm over his brow, his cheek, his jaw. It fascinated her, the way her small white hand looked against a backdrop of burnished copper.

Her gaze lifted, locking with intense silver. There was no need to speak her thoughts aloud; Amanda could tell by the look in Jake's eyes that he knew exactly what she was thinking.

"I won't lie to you, princess. I won't tell you it'll be easy for us, because it won't be," he said, even as he turned his head, and his lips grazed her open palm. "Never forget those men in Junction, because there will be more of them. Dozens of them. There are going to be times when you'll to wish to hell you'd never met me. Are you sure you—?"

"Yes, Jake! A thousand times yes!"

His gaze darkened with pleasure. "Good. Because I don't think I can let you go, princess. I might have tried, for a while, but . . . dammit, I'm just not that trong."

"I'm glad. Because when it comes to you, neither am I. I don't want you to let me go, Jake. Not now. Not ever. Just hold me. Please."

He did. He held her and kissed her, loved and cherished her. He leaned into her, and held her so close to him that their heartbeats meshed. She moaned and clung to him as he lowered them both to the ground.

"Washington, Jake," Amanda sighed as he trailed hot, moist kisses down her throat. Lower, then lower still. "I . . . thought you wanted to get there quickly."

"We'll set out tomorrow. After we make a little detour."

"A detour?"

"I . . ." He hesitated, his warm lips poised over her collarbone. She felt the heat of his sigh seep into her skin. "I want to stop and see Little Bear and Gail. If that's all right with you."

She hesitated, stiffening slightly. "Are you sure?"

"Yes, princess. It's long past time I saw my nephews, don't you think?"

"No, Jake. What I think is that it's time you and your sister put the past behind you. Where it belongs."

She felt him pull in a shaky breath, felt him nod. "Yes, Amanda, that too. I owe Gail an apology, I know that now. The question is, will she accept it?"

"I think she will. I think—"

"Shhh, don't think, princess. *Feel.*" He pressed his open mouth against her upper chest. She felt his warm breaths mist over her skin, heat her blood.

She sighed. He groaned. Both lost their train of thought.

Jake shifted, working his way downward. Finding a rosy nipple, he suckled it into his mouth, quickly easing it into a firm, aching peak. Amanda arched against him, into him, her airy sighs of surrender wafting over his head, burning into his skin, into his blood. Ah, yes. She was a part of him. The very best part. The part he couldn't, *wouldn't*, live without.

Jake lifted his head, and looked down into her passion-darkened eyes. "Today, I want to make love to my woman until she *knows* she's mine. Always."

Smiling, she wrapped her arms around Jake's neck and drew his mouth to hers. "She knows," Amanda whispered against his lips. "But I don't think she'll mind you showing her again . . ."

"And again," Jake finished the thought for her, his voice husky and sweet and so filled with promise that it brought fresh tears to her eyes.

"And again," she sighed breathlessly.

His tongue sipped the moisture from her cheek, even as their bodies arched together, eager to quench the fire they'd lit inside each other.

It was a fire that would take at least a lifetime to put out.

THE BEST IN HISTORICAL ROMANCES

ME-KEPT PROMISES (2422, $3.95)

Constance O'Day Flannery

an O'Mara froze when he saw his wife Christina standing before him. She had vanished and the news had been written about all of the papers—he had even been charged with her murder! ut now he had living proof of his innocence, and Sean was not out to let her get away. No matter that the woman was claiming be someone named Kristine; she still caused his blood to boil.

ASSION'S PRISONER (2573, $3.95)

Casey Stewart

hen Cassandra Lansing put on men's clothing and entered the awlings saloon she didn't expect to lose anything—in fact she as sure that she would win back her prized horse Rapscallion at her grandfather lost in a card game. She almost got a smug tisfaction at the thought of fooling the gamblers into believing at she was a man. But once she caught a glimpse of the virile sh Rawlings, Cassandra wanted to be the woman in his emace!

NGEL HEART (2426, $3.95)

Victoria Thompson

ver since Angelica's father died, Harlan Snyder had been aning to get his hands on her ranch, the Diamond R. And now, st when she had an important government contract to fulfill, e couldn't find a single cowhand to hire—all because of Snyr's threats. It was only a matter of time before the legendary unfighter Kid Collins turned up on her doorstep, badly ounded. Angelica assessed his firmly muscled physique and ared into his startling blue eyes. Beneath all that blood and dirt was the handsomest man she had ever seen, and the one pern who could help beat Snyder at his own game.

FEEL THE FIRE IN CAROL FINCH'S ROMANCES!

BELOVED BETRAYAL (2346, $3.95)

Sabrina Spencer donned a gray wig and veiled hat before blackmailing rugged Ridge Tanner into guiding her to Fort Canby. But the costume soon became her prison—the beauty had fallen head over heels in love!

LOVE'S HIDDEN TREASURE (2980, $4.50)

Shandra d'Evereux felt her heart throb beneath the stolen map she'd hidden in her bodice when Nolan Elliot swept her out onto the veranda. It was hard to concentrate on her mission with that wily rogue around!

MONTANA MOONFIRE (3263, $4.95)

Just as debutante Victoria Flemming-Cassidy was about to marry an oh-so-suitable mate, the towering preacher, Dru Sullivan flung her over his shoulder and headed West! Suddenly, Tori realized she had been given the best present for a bride: a night of passion with a real man!

THUNDER'S TENDER TOUCH (2809, $4.50)

Refined Piper Malone needed bounty-hunter, Vince Logan to recover her swindled inheritance. She thought she could coolly dismiss him after he did the job, but she never counted on the hot flood of desire she felt whenever he was near!

Available wherever paperbacks are sold, or order direct from the Publisher. Send cover price plus 50¢ per copy for mailing and handling to Zebra Books, Dept. 3617, 475 Park Avenue South, New York, N.Y. 10016. Residents of New York, New Jersey and Pennsylvania must include sales tax. DO NOT SEND CASH.